BR
B.G.

SO-BNJ-939

114   A.J.S.

Winter Is Past

RUTH AXTELL MORREN

Winter Is Past

Steeple
Hill®

Published by Steeple Hill Books™

STEEPLE HILL BOOKS

Steeple
Hill®

ISBN 0-7394-3929-4

WINTER IS PAST

Copyright © 2003 by Ruth Axtell

I wish to dedicate this story to:

Yeshua ha Mashiach,
who taught me that little becomes much
in the master's hand;

To the Rebeccas I have known,
who went home early to be with Him;

And to Rick,
who has given me the opportunity to
study the male psyche up close over the years.

FOREWORD

When a cousin of mine began investigating the
possibilities of Jewish ancestry in our family's
Colombian/Venezuelan roots, I suddenly became
interested in the Sephardic branch of Judaism.
Soon I was fascinated with the story of the
expulsion of the Sephardic Jews from Spain in
1492.

In Spain, under the Inquisition, thousands of Jews
were forced to convert to Catholicism. However,
many of them continued to practice their religion
clandestinely. When they were expelled from Spain
and eventually migrated to Holland, the Middle
East, England and the New World, they were more
accustomed, perhaps, than Ashkenazi and other
non-Sephardic Jews, to leading a "double life"
between outward Christianity and inner Judaism.

During the early nineteenth century, when
Winter Is Past takes place, Jews living in England
were gaining greater acceptance in mainstream
Christian society, though the old prejudices were
still thriving. I've used this background in telling
the story of Methodist nurse Althea Breton and
her employer, Simon Aguilar, a Jew by birth who
has for political reasons become a member of the
Church of England. When Althea meets Simon for
the first time, she faces her own ugly prejudices
against Jews. At first afraid and unsure of what to
expect from this "foreign man," Althea realizes that
she has believed half-truths, not God's true word
regarding the Jewish people. Soon, through her
faith and newly gained knowledge of Simon and
his family, Althea comes to see that Jews, much

like Christians, are people of faith, family and love. Sadly, it took somewhat longer for England to officially acknowledge this.

The most famous story of an English *converso* is Benjamin Disraeli (1804–1881). He was a Sephardic Jew whose family migrated to England from Italy. Although his career in Parliament didn't begin until about a decade after Simon's, Disraeli, too, received baptism as an adolescent, attended a private school run by an independent minister and was elected to Parliament. Back then, only baptized members of Britain's official state church could receive higher education, wed legally or hold public office. Luckily, in 1858, a law was passed making it legal for Jews to be admitted as members of Parliament, paving the way for Disraeli as England's first and only Jewish prime minister.

For further reading on Sephardic Jewry, I highly recommend *The Cross and the Pear Tree: A Sephardic Journey* by Victor Perera.

Chapter One

❧

London, 1817

"So you're the miracle worker."

Althea stared back at the man addressing her across the wide mahogany desk, his eyes deep and dark and mocking. They held mystery and an ancestry centuries old. The small, wire-rimmed oval spectacles did nothing to diminish the force of the hooded brown irises fringed by thick lashes and framed by heavy, black brows.

"Lady Althea Pembroke," he stated when she remained silent, the mockery edging his tone soft as the feathery quill he brushed against his fingertips.

"I am Althea Breton," she answered the dark-haired man. When he continued looking at her from behind his desk, the sound of the feather against his skin magnified in the still room, she added, "Lord Skylar requested me to come."

"Yes, he spoke to me of you." The tone revealed nothing beyond the words. "But I believe he spoke to me of *Lady* Althea Pembroke. You are his sister, are you not?"

She removed her gaze from his, realizing the answer was not

a simple one. Why had Tertius compelled her into this interview, she asked herself for the hundredth time.

She took a deep breath, reining in her frustration like a woman gathering her skirts against the wind. "I am sorry for the confusion," she managed to say at last. "I am Lord Skylar's *half* sister. Perhaps my brother did not have a chance to explain to you."

He made a gesture of impatience with ink-stained fingers. They were long and pale, illuminated in the circle of light cast by the Argand lamp. "Well, Lady Althea—Miss Breton—whatever name you choose to go by, the important thing is, do you know anything of nursing? Your brother seems to think so."

Irritated by the insinuation she was operating under an alias, she compressed her lips to avoid any ill-advised reply. He didn't bother to await her answer, but looked back down at the papers he'd been studying when she'd been bidden to come in. So now she must speak to the crown of dark, disheveled curls, she thought, annoyed at his obvious inattention. It hadn't been her idea to come here, she wanted to tell him! She was here only as a favor to her brother, who'd practically begged her to hear his friend out. Now she was made to feel as if she were groveling for a position, when that was the last thing she was in need of. The last thing she desired. She was quite fine where she was, she wanted to clarify to those unruly locks.

As she looked at the bowed head and observed the rapid movements of the long, slim fingers, something inside her stirred, remembering her brother's stories. Had this man truly been unmercifully tormented at Eton by his fellow students, all because he was a Jew?

The word still gave her a shudder of revulsion as she pictured the greasy, black-garbed moneylenders in the East End. She tried to stifle it as she cleared her throat, deciding her best course was to get this uncomfortable interview over with. She spoke to the dark head. "If I can be of any help to your daughter, I would appreciate the opportunity to try." Her tone emerged sounding calm and collected.

When he did not answer immediately, she studied what she

could see of his features. They certainly belied the image she had had. The Honorable Simon Aguilar looked younger than she'd pictured a man of thirty-two with four years in the House of Commons. He'd been the youngest member of Parliament elected since Pitt the Younger, which proved his brilliance and wit, according to Tertius, qualities which her brother had first witnessed in the schoolboy at Eton.

Her gaze traveled farther. He wasn't handsome, more like arresting, she judged. His cheeks were clean-shaven, with only a shadow of beard against the pale skin; the nose not the hooked beak she expected, but high-bridged and chiseled; the lips a cushion of crimson accentuating the pallor of his skin. His physiognomy denoted a man of study, not a rapacious swindler of the poor. If the dim, book-lined shelves on either side of the room were any indication, he rarely saw the light of day.

He looked up, catching her observation. He waved a hand to a seat in front of the desk, as if just then noticing that she still stood in front of it like a servant awaiting orders. "Please, my lady, have a seat."

"*Miss* Breton," she corrected quietly but firmly, determined to get that established from the outset, as she took the chair indicated.

"Very well, *Miss* Breton. Could you be so kind as to explain to me why someone of your rank should want to lower herself to a position of nurse?"

Althea looked at him, aware it would not be easy to explain. He had removed his spectacles. The dark, hooded eyes stared back at her, their skepticism telling her beforehand that he would not easily accept whatever she told him. "Nursing ought to be seen as the honorable and noble profession it is."

His lips curved in a humorless smile. "Please spare me a eulogy on the glories of bathing a sick body and emptying its slop basin."

She colored and bit back a retort. Leaning forward and placing both her hands against the massive desk, her eyes sought an entry through the curtain of contempt and disbelief confronting her. "Mr. Aguilar, if you will permit me."

He raised a black eyebrow, looking like a falcon deciding the fate of its prey. She glanced down at her hands splayed against the polished wood, like a tiny sparrow's feet gripping the safety of a tree limb. She removed them and balled them in her lap, clearing her throat to give it more authority.

"My brother told me you were in need of a nurse for your child—a young girl, I believe." The words sounded clipped to her ears—she spoke in what the street urchins recognized as her "brooking no nonsense" tone.

At his curt nod, she continued. "I have some years' experience nursing the sick. I can assure you I am well able to care for your little girl."

"You hardly look old enough to have spent several years in the sickroom." He fingered his pen impatiently as he spoke, and she had the impression of hands never still.

"I am older than I look. My brother must have explained to you—"

He let the pen go and waved the same hand in the air. "Yes, yes, Sky filled me in on your impeccable qualifications. Lady of rank, renouncing all her worldly position and goods—including the honorific, I come to see—to become a Dissenter, live among the poor and tend to the sick. I hope they are grateful."

"I am not a Dissenter!" Realizing how sharp her voice sounded, she took a deep breath and began afresh. "*Methodist* is the correct term, if you must label me."

She felt her cheeks burn and was annoyed with Tertius for having divulged her personal history, then quickly understood her brother must have been trying to convince his friend of her qualities for the position—a position she was by no means convinced she should accept. She sat back and silently asked for grace to maintain her temper. Where was the fruit of patience she had cultivated for the past eight years?

"I only wish to help in any way I can," she added more gently.

It was Simon Aguilar's turn to take his gaze away first, using the moment to remove a handkerchief from his pocket to polish his spectacles. "Yes, well, there's not much anyone can do but make Rebecca as comfortable as possible and keep her entertained. Her original nurse left us last year when she chose the life of a baker's wife over that of nursemaid. I replaced her with a governess, who was with us up until about a month ago, when it grew too taxing for Rebecca to continue her lessons on a regular basis. That is not to say you can't teach her things or read to her when she wishes." He replaced his spectacles as he ended the summation.

Althea nodded, digesting the information, determined to keep her mind on the reason she was there. "What exactly is wrong with...Rebecca?"

He shrugged, toying instead with a brass seal on his desk. "The physicians each have a different opinion. But the truth is, none of them know." He scowled. "Some say a brain fever, others a blood poisoning or liver ailment. She gets sick very often and tires easily." Once again he fixed dark, brooding eyes on her. "The truth is, she is dying."

In the stillness Althea heard only the faint sound of a late-winter rain outside the windows behind the desk, the steady drone impervious to the plight of the individual lives being played out within. She watched her future employer's long, pale fingers realign the papers before him into a stack. She realized with a start that she was already calling him her employer.

No, Lord! she cried silently; she'd by no means accepted this as His path for her. Just as quickly, shame swept over her at her pettiness when a little girl's life was at stake.

"There's not a thing I or the best physicians in London—or you—can do about my daughter's condition, but make Rebecca as happy and comfortable as possible until then. Do you understand? Do you think you can manage that? You won't have an attack of the vapors the first time you face a crisis with her?"

Althea drew in a breath, her pity evaporating. If he'd seen half of what she'd seen in her six years in the East End, he would know it took more than an ailing child to overset her nerves. After a few seconds she answered dryly, "No, sir."

He dipped his pen into its inkstand. "I will pay you twelve pounds, fifteen shillings per quarter." His attention switched back to the stack before him. He made a notation on the margin of the topmost sheet. "Does that suffice?"

He looked up and she nodded, caught unawares. She hadn't even considered remuneration when her brother had asked—pleaded with—her to come here.

"I feel strange offering such pitiable wages to a peeress."

"I am *not* a peeress," she stated, exasperation edging her tone. "I have no hereditary title."

He looked back down, ignoring her comment. "One more thing. I am hiring you officially as 'governess' to Rebecca, although unofficially you will be her nurse. I suspended her lessons, as I said."

"But why the title of governess if I am to be her nurse?"

He replaced the pen in its stand. The long, almost bony, fingers pushed through the dark, thick curls, leaving them in more disarray than before. "Because, Miss Breton, as should be obvious to you, I would prefer my daughter not realize she is so sick as to need a nurse."

Althea bit her lip at her obtuseness.

He continued in a slightly more civil tone. "Besides, it is not the norm to have a young lady of noble birth working in one's household as a nurse. Governess would seem to excite less curiosity. It has a certain veneer of respectability to it. A nurse usually hails from the lowest dregs of society...at least, that has been my experience up until recently," he muttered, looking down at his papers once more.

He took up his pen, as something caught his eye on the page before him. He made another notation. Althea continued observing him, trying to reconcile his appearance and manner with the preconceptions she had of his people.

"What is it?"

She felt the blood rise in her cheeks, wishing for the first time in her life that she had more freckles to hide her heightened color. "N-nothing."

"You find me interesting to look at?"

"No...not at all."

"Does my Jewish heritage intrigue you?"

She started at his perception. After a few seconds she nodded.

"I expect your brother informed you of my conversion to the Church." His lips curled sardonically. "But I imagine you, as most, assume it was only skin deep—"

He rolled the pen between his fingers.

Her eyes were fixed on the motion.

"You are correct in your supposition that it was a conversion in name only. Indispensable, you understand, for my entry into Parliament."

He plucked at the dark sleeve of his jacket. "The marks of generations of Jewry cannot be so easily effaced, can they? Once a Jew, always a Jew—isn't that what you think?" She stared at him, disconcerted by the frank admission of the purely materialistic rationale for his conversion.

"Tell me, my curiosity is piqued, did I meet all of your expectations? What did you come here expecting to see? An old man hunched over in a moldering coat, counting out his coin? Fangs, perhaps? A gross deformity? After all, we are the Jesus killers, are we not?"

He didn't give her an opportunity to answer. "Well, Miss Breton, I can assure you, you shall be perfectly safe under my roof. I have managed to control the baser instincts of my race under this semblance of the gentleman you see before you." He leaned back in his chair, his dark gaze assessing her, making her feel as if she were the one at fault.

She found herself struggling to meet that gaze, which seemed to see beyond her pious garb and acts of mercy, to something deep within her of which even she was unaware. This was ridiculous, she told herself. She had nothing to reproach herself for; she had seen firsthand what those moneylenders had accomplished with their extortionary techniques.

Deciding she would merely ignore his words, just as he had so many of her own, she asked, "What precisely are you looking for in a nurse?"

He looked at her as if trying to explain something to an imbecile. "Miss Breton, I am frequently not at home. I need someone I can trust with my child. I need someone to take care of her as if she were her own. I realize that may be difficult for a childless woman, much less a hired one, to comprehend, but nevertheless that is what I require. That is what Rebecca needs." He sighed, raking a hand through his hair, a gesture Althea was coming to recognize as expressing his impatience with having to explain things to people of less astuteness or intelligence.

He gave her another assessing look. "I don't expect you to understand this. I only agreed to this interview because your brother spoke so glowingly of your abilities. Quite frankly, I must admit my doubt."

"I see," she said, bowing her head and looking down at her tightly clasped hands, their firmness belying her inner trembling. She did not know what she had expected from this interview, but certainly not the doubt, much less the downright hostility, in the man before her. All at once it occurred to her that she had come harboring those very same sentiments, yet had felt perfectly justified in holding them. The realization piqued her conscience. For a split second she experienced the clarity of God's spirit touching something within her. It was like a door opening upon an unused room, letting in a shaft of light. One could choose to shut the door, or allow it to open farther and flood the area. The latter way held an element of risk.

What had she expected from Mr. Aguilar? the still, small voice of the Spirit asked her. Gratitude for her condescending to leave her present position and come to his aid?

Her life was not her own. It hadn't been for the past eight years. Whether she came into this household as a nurse was not up to her, nor even up to Simon Aguilar, she thought, looking up at the man seated behind the desk.

All she needed to know was whether her Lord and Savior

Jesus was directing her to this household. Whether He was making her give up everything familiar, everything fulfilling—her very life's work—for a season—a season of unknown duration—to come and serve in this household was not the issue.

She met Simon Aguilar's gaze full on. "I can only say, give me a trial—whatever length you deem sufficient—a week, a fortnight—to satisfy yourself. I can only promise to do my best, by God's grace, to help your daughter Rebecca in any way I can."

Althea left, exhausted from the ordeal. She felt confused, deflated...downright terrified. How could the Lord possibly want her in the employ of one so irreverent and antagonistic of everything she believed in? She looked around at the neighborhood as she left the pale-blue stucco mansion on Green Street. Even the neighborhood contradicted all she'd given her life to in the past six years. Mayfair was as far from her present residence in Whitechapel as London from Bombay. She gave one last look down the street, taking in the black-painted, wrought-iron fences and neat tree-lined sidewalks as she mounted the coach. Before her ride was over, they would give way to the dirty, dilapidated buildings and muddy streets of the East End.

It took Simon a good quarter of an hour after Miss Breton's departure to return to editing his speech on the repeal of the Corn Laws. It wasn't every day the rank and file got the opportunity to address the ministers on the treasury bench, that coveted first row in the House of Commons. Backbenchers must stand awkwardly wedged between the tiered rows, clutching their notes but forbidden to read from them. Simon, gifted with oratory skills, relished the moment. After seven years in the House, he'd advanced from the top tier to the bench just behind the treasury bench, where Liverpool and all his cabinet lounged. He promised silently that he would make them sit up and pay attention.

But now the speech he had written in the wee hours of the previous night lay before him untouched as he thought about the woman he'd just interviewed. Simon twirled his quill between his fingertips more than once, his thoughts straying from the quotas and price fluctuations in imported and domestic wheat to the young lady who claimed to be a nurse.

Something more important than his career or the affordability of grain was at stake at the moment: his daughter's well-being.

Very few things took precedence over his political career and the affairs of state. In fact, they were the only things he was passionate about. Simon had come to the conclusion long ago that he was in essence a cold-hearted, calculating man. Although he would defend his family's honor to the grave, very few in that enormous tribe of Sephardic Jews known as the Aguilars truly engaged his heart.

He sometimes wondered if he even had a heart. The only proof to the contrary was his daughter. If anything showed he could still bleed it was Rebecca.

His fingers gripped the quill tightly until it broke. He would give anything to make her well.

He set down the mutilated pen and observed its ninety-degree bend. The question was, had he done right in agreeing to hire Miss Breton for a trial period? His glance strayed to the chair recently vacated by the lady in question. For indeed she was a lady, for all her Quakerish gown and renouncement of the honorific. Every well-modulated word, her very demeanor and bearing, spoke of good breeding. The kind of breeding his family had paid dearly for him to obtain.

Simon sighed, shoving aside the pen. He'd already been through three nurses—a fact he'd deliberately kept from Miss Breton.

At least she presented a more pleasing countenance than the other three, he admitted, recalling the slack-jawed, blank-eyed first nurse; the puckered mouth evidencing a lack of teeth and the greasy gray hair of the second; and the shifty-eyed, lipless third.

Miss Breton, by contrast, struck him as neat and self-possessed, in her gray woolen frock with its starched white collar.

Simon picked up a new pen from the inkstand and pulled out a fresh sheet of paper from a drawer. He dipped the pen in ink and wrote *Assets* on one side and *Liabilities* on the other, then drew a neat line between the two.

Underneath the column Assets, he wrote in lowercase the word *attractive*. He'd definitely list that as an asset, thinking it would be beneficial to Rebecca's well-being that she have a nice-looking nurse instead of an ill-looking one.

Simon went over Miss Breton's features in his mind's eye, from the head of frizzy, honey-hued curls that peeked through her plain gray bonnet to her small hands with their tapering finger-tips, which she gripped whenever she seemed to refrain from speaking out.

He'd liked her eyes. They were that indeterminate shade between gray, pale blue and sea green. But there was something very forthright in her gaze, giving him a sense that her yea would be yea and her nay, nay.

Not like the last nurse, who'd tried to make him feel better by lying about Rebecca's condition. Simon rubbed the back of his neck, still feeling the fury of discovering Rebecca with a fever he had not been told about.

He jotted down *honesty* under the Assets column, then blotted it carefully. After a few seconds, he added a question mark. He must still verify this quality. He would not be fooled a second time.

Yes, Miss Breton's countenance had been fair—good patrician features, which he'd expected of the sister of Tertius Pembroke, the fourth Earl of Skylar. His mind cataloged them: a straight, well-shaped nose, nice rosy lips, a firm chin and a high, pale forehead. She didn't look anything like Sky, however. She reminded him more of a country lass, the sprinkling of freckles across the bridge of her nose and the clear gaze evidence of sunshine and fresh air.

It was ironic considering she lived in one of the dirtiest parts of London.

He frowned again over the irregularity of her name. Breton? She had explained she was Sky's half sister. What did she mean by that? The old marquess had remarried? Simon wrote *Breton?* under Liabilities. He would question Sky about it the next time his friend was in town.

The main drawback to Miss Breton, he concluded, was her religion. A Methodist, she had called herself. He was familiar with the origins of Methodism in the last century under the Wesleys and Whitefield at Oxford. His lip curled in disdain; such a phenomenon would not have occurred at the Newtonian Cambridge, his own alma mater, the home of rationalism and mathematics.

The only trouble with religion, as Simon saw it, was that it was a way for the State to get its hands on hardworking people's money and place it in the hands of a few of its own class. One of the greatest fights he anticipated taking on someday in Parliament was attacking the entire body of law giving the Church the right to confiscate a tenth of every landowner's crop and cattle, in an ancient system of tithing.

The far more insidious evil of religion was the havoc it wreaked by the few who actually took it seriously. With them it was all or nothing, the result of which could be seen in the bloody wars and massacres over the continent in the last millennium, the brunt of which so often was felt by his own people.

Miss Breton, Simon could see clearly, fell into this latter category. He added to the Liabilities column: *religious fervor.* He underscored the word.

Lastly was the question of her nursing skills. They remained to be seen. He had only the word of Skylar—one of the few men he trusted—but still, Simon remained skeptical. He wrote *nursing skills* at the end of the columns, between the two, and added a question mark.

* * *

Althea awoke. She had been dreaming. She had been in the presence of Jesus! She knew it, recalled it vividly, still felt His presence all about her. She had no idea what time it was. Glancing toward the dormer window of her attic room, she saw no sign of light, but sensed it was earlier than her usual predawn time of rising.

She lay back against her pillow, trying to recapture the dream. Jesus had been talking to her; she remembered she'd been unburdening her heart to Him. He'd been revealing Scriptures to her. Her eyes had been opened, just as had those of the two disciples on the road to Emmaus. The Scriptures became so clear and simple when Jesus showed her. What else had He said? She closed her eyes, burying herself deeper in the pillow, not wanting to leave that place where she'd been, wanting to hear more from her Lord.

He'd told her to go to Mayfair, not to be afraid to leave her present life and enter the Aguilar household. He'd said very clearly that it would be her wilderness, but that in obedience she would yield much fruit, for that family belonged to Him.

The last thing she remembered was awaking with a Scripture verse impressed upon her mind. She felt wrapped in the Lord's love, confident that she could do all things in His strength.

Althea reached toward her bedside table and turned up the lamp. She saw it was just half-past three. In another hour, she would arise at her normal time. There was no sense in trying to get back to sleep. She had been waiting to hear from the Lord ever since she'd left Mr. Aguilar's residence. She'd spent the intervening days in fasting and prayer, seeking the Lord's direction. And now He had answered her. She had a keen sense of anticipation as she reached for her Bible. She wrapped herself in her shawl and sat against the pillow and bolster, the Bible against her knees.

She opened to the Book of Ephesians and rustled the pages to get to the second chapter. Her finger traveled down the page until it reached the fourteenth verse. That was the verse the Lord had given her.

"...who hath made us both one, and hath broken down the middle wall of partition between us."

Althea continued reading until she completed the chapter, then went back to the beginning and read the entire chapter through. Finally she sat back, her head lying against the pillow. There could be no doubt. The Lord was showing her that Jew and Gentile were considered one in His eyes, and that by His death and resurrection, He had created one new man out of both. She looked back down at the Scriptures, tracing the words with her fingertip as she reread them, feeling as if she were discovering them for the first time—and in a sense, she was:

"...to make in himself of twain one new man...that he might reconcile both unto God in one body by the cross, having slain the enmity thereby...through him we both have access by one Spirit unto the Father...ye are no more strangers and foreigners, but fellow citizens with the saints...built upon the foundation of the apostles and prophets, Jesus Christ himself being the chief cornerstone...unto an holy temple in the Lord...."

Paul was describing Jew and Gentile as a building fitly framed together as a temple of the Lord, as a habitation of His spirit. Althea sat still, stunned by the revelation. Her thoughts went to Simon Aguilar, a man cynical, impatient, arrogant, who clearly didn't listen to anyone he considered inferior, and whom, quite frankly, she didn't like.

Jesus loved this man and had died for him.

Chapter Two

✧

"Miss Althea, look at this!"

Althea laid aside her needlework and moved to the side of Rebecca's bed. The dark-haired, eight-year-old girl proudly held up a fan-like row of paper dolls she had cut out. "That's perfect, sweetie. Now you can draw their faces."

Rebecca got back to work happily, laying the dolls on the drawing board at her lap and taking up her pencil. Althea picked up the scraps of paper from the bed, thinking over the past fortnight. Simon Aguilar had agreed to hire her on the trial basis she had proposed. As soon as she had arranged her absence from the East End mission, she'd begun her residence in the four-story Mayfair mansion.

On the day she had arrived at the Green Street address, she had spoken only briefly to Mr. Aguilar. She had been too overwhelmed by her recent revelation to do more than nod at his brief instructions. She had had to fight the urge to look at him too closely. All she could think of were the verses she had read in the intervening days and the things the Lord had shown her. Had

Joseph, Jacob's son, perhaps looked like this man? Or David, the young shepherd boy chosen by God to build a kingdom?

He no longer had a mocking air, but one of hurry and distraction. He was on the verge of departure for a few days, he had told her. Anything she might need she could consult with Mrs. Coates, the housekeeper.

The only personal words they'd exchanged were at parting. Mr. Aguilar had given her his full attention then, restating his agreement to hire her for a trial period. He'd added, "I am only agreeing to entrust my daughter's care to you on the recommendation of your brother. He and I have known each other a long time." A slight smile played around his lips, the first evidence of humor he'd displayed that morning. Then he'd sobered once again. "I know I can trust his word. If he says you are fit to take care of Rebecca, I must believe him."

Before Althea had a chance to take encouragement or offense at the statement, he bowed over her gloved hand, then let it go and turned to Mrs. Coates. He gave her some last-minute instructions and told her that Althea was to be treated with the respect due to a member of the family. His mocking tone had returned for an instant as he quipped that the servants must henceforth watch their behavior as they had an "evangelical" in their midst.

That was the last Althea had seen of Mr. Aguilar.

"What do you think of this one?" Rebecca pushed her lap desk toward Althea. The first three dolls had smiling mouths and dots for eyes. Some had curls scrawled around their faces, others had what Althea took to be bonnets with ribbons tied beneath their chins. Rebecca's pencil pointed to the third one.

"She's very pretty. What's her name?"

"Althea," she answered promptly.

Althea smiled. "And which one is Rebecca?"

"I shall make her separately. I have to make her lying down."

Althea nodded, not knowing what to say.

They both turned at a knock on the door. A second later, Simon poked his head in.

"*Abba!* You're home!" Paper dolls forgotten, Rebecca held out her arms to her father. He entered with a smile and was at her bedside in a few strides. Father and daughter embraced.

Althea stood, feeling her heart beginning to pound as she wondered what life would be like now that Rebecca's father was back in residence. She had no immediate need for concern, as the master of the house had eyes for no one but his daughter. Althea took advantage of his distraction, taking the paper scraps off the bed but leaving the girl's handiwork for her father to see.

As she picked up her needlework and looked about the room, Mr. Aguilar still had not turned towards her. She heard Rebecca's happy chatter. "Did you just get back? Was it a long trip? What did you do?"

"Yes, I just arrived, and came immediately up to see my favorite girl in all the world."

"What did you bring me?" she asked, feeling in his coat pockets.

He sat back, playing along with the game. When Rebecca pounced on the paper-wrapped parcel, Althea smiled at the scene before exiting through the door to the connecting sitting room.

She set down her things and looked at the watch pinned to her breast. Deciding it was nearing time to prepare Rebecca's supper tray, she headed down the stairs.

She would know soon enough whether she had passed the trial period or not.

Althea braced herself as she entered the servants' basement domain. She had noticed in the week she had been in residence that the servants did very little in their master's absence. As usual at this time, a half dozen were seated around the dining table, sipping ale and chatting. The butler was hidden behind the racing news. No one bothered to acknowledge Althea's presence. By now she knew better than to make overtures. She knew from the experience of living in one of the meanest neighborhoods of London that eventually she would make headway with them. But her priority at the present was her new patient.

She went into the pantry and took the tray set out for Rebecca. "Good afternoon," she said brightly to the young woman counting out cutlery. When the woman mumbled a reply, Althea turned to the other kitchen maid.

"Hello," she said with a smile at the young girl slicing bread for the servants' tea.

The girl looked down. "Hullo, miss."

Althea heaved up the tray. She pushed open the door with her back and made her slow way up the two flights of stairs, careful not to spill the hot stew or the cup of milk.

She set the tray on the floor before giving a light tap on the door. At Rebecca's high "Come in" and her father's deeper one, Althea opened the door, then stooped to retrieve the tray.

"Are you ready for some supper, Rebecca?" she asked with a smile, nodding a brief greeting to Simon. "Cook has made some hot stew for you, and there's a compote for afterwards."

Simon came immediately towards her to relieve her of the tray. "Where's Harry?" he asked in annoyance. "You shouldn't be carrying this up yourself."

"It's quite all right, I can manage," she replied, surprised at his attentiveness now that he had noticed her. Seeing that he did not let the tray go, she relinquished it and made her way toward Rebecca.

She helped the girl sit up against her pillows and smoothed the coverlet over her legs. "You may set it on her lap," she said as she tied a napkin around Rebecca's neck. She waited silently while the child said grace, then stepped back.

"Look what my *abba* brought me." She held up a little carved wooden pony, which Althea admired.

"Now, make sure you finish everything up. Show your papa what a good girl you are."

She turned to face Simon, who was looking at his daughter in bemusement. Was it the fact that he had heard her say the grace Althea had taught her? Then he turned his attention to her.

"Good evening, Miss Breton. You disappeared before I could say a proper hello to you."

His gentle tone surprised her, so different from his previous manner.

He looked weary. Althea realized he hadn't exaggerated when he told his daughter he had come straight home to her. His cravat looked wilted, his dark coat rumpled, and his hair in disarray, though she was beginning to believe that was its usual arrangement.

"Good evening, Mr. Aguilar," she replied. "Welcome home."

"Thank you. Have you found everything to your satisfaction?"

Finding she could not answer truthfully, she turned toward Rebecca. "Don't let your stew get cold."

Rebecca had been watching the two adults, obviously finding anything her father engaged in more fascinating than the bowl set before her. "It's too hot. See the steam."

"I see," replied Althea. "Well, don't let it sit too long."

"*Abba,* did you know when Miss Althea was little, she used to go down to the kitchen and help the cook with the pastry?"

"Is that so?"

"Yes, she'd make little tarts out of dough, then have a tea party with her dolls afterwards. Can you imagine that?"

"No, I cannot," he replied, bringing a chair to her bedside as Althea moved away.

Rebecca sighed. "I'd love to sit with Cook and steal little scraps of pastry to make tarts for my dolls."

"Perhaps that can be arranged. What do you say?"

Althea turned to him, realizing he was addressing her. She smiled at Rebecca. "Yes, I believe we could arrange something," she said as she tried to imagine the slovenly, barely civil cook taking such a request from her.

"Look what Miss Althea showed me how to do today." Rebecca spread open the row of paper dolls.

"How pretty."

"Thank you. This one's Althea, and this one is Bertha—that's my blue-eyed doll, you know—and this one's Emily—that's the rag doll I sleep with—and this one's...."

Althea shelved some of the picture books they had looked at

that day, not wanting to interrupt the child but concerned she should eat her food. Althea had made it a point to sit with her and try all kinds of things to get her to clean her plate.

"What did you do on your trip? Did you get the bad people who tried to kill the prince?"

Simon chuckled. "No. I didn't catch them." He tweaked his daughter's nose. "Remember, it's not my job to catch the criminals, but to make laws that perhaps will help all people live more peaceably. Now, I see a young lady who is doing everything but eating."

She smiled, arching her neck back against her pillows. "I can't eat. I always eat with Miss Althea."

Simon glanced at Althea's kneeling figure. "Is that so? Well, I have an idea. Have you dined yet, Miss Breton?"

She shook her head, taken unawares. "No, sir."

"Well, then, that's it. We shall dine here with Rebecca and I shall tell you all about my trip—if you promise to finish up everything on your tray."

Before Althea could voice any objections, he rose and grabbed the bellpull.

When the maid appeared, Simon asked for a card table set up with two more supper trays. As these preparations were taking place, he excused himself to freshen up from his trip.

He removed his coat and handed it to his valet, who had been unpacking Simon's portmanteau.

"Feels good to be home, doesn't it?"

"That it does, sir," answered the manservant, holding out his arm for Simon's shirt and cravat.

"Thank you." Simon bent over the washstand and soaked a washcloth. He realized he was humming. What he'd told Ivan was true. For the first time in a long time it felt good to be home. His house had known nothing but illness and death for what seemed forever. As he scrubbed his torso and neck he analyzed what was different.

He pictured his daughter's cheerful demeanor, her enthusiastic chatter. She certainly was looking good. Simon had felt a welcoming warmth as soon as he'd entered her bedroom.

Perhaps Sky had been right in recommending his sister as Rebecca's nurse. Simon remembered how it had come about. He hadn't seen Sky in several years. They'd lost touch after university. As the second son, Sky hadn't had many prospects, and he'd been wild in those days. His father, the Marquess of Caulfield, had finally said he'd pay no more of the young man's gambling debts. Sky would have to make it on his own out in the Indies, managing one of the family's lesser estates.

Simon had run into Sky only a few weeks ago and found a wholly different man. Gone was the arrogant wastrel. In his place was a married man who radiated happiness and well-being. When he'd heard about Rebecca, he'd immediately launched into accolades of his younger sister, Althea. Told Simon she'd nursed him through a deadly tropical fever. Simon hadn't even known Sky possessed a sister, and thought once again they didn't look anything alike.

Taking a towel and rubbing his face, he contrasted the two— Skylar with his tall, lithe body, and lean, dark good looks, and Althea Breton, of middlish height and golden-haired. She gave the impression, he considered a moment, of a quiet, composed creature but with an inner fire. He'd lay odds that she'd bitten her tongue more than once during their interview at his deliberately provoking statements.

He still couldn't figure out why she should wish to be a lowly nurse when she was a daughter of Caulfield. As long as she made Rebecca happy, it really didn't matter, he supposed.

He took the clean shirt Ivan handed him and pulled it over his head, then turned to his man to deal with the complications of a cravat. He himself had no patience with their intricacies. Finally he shrugged into the coat held out for him.

"Take the evening off when you've finished here," he told the valet as he exited the room. "You deserve it after the journey we've had."

Winter Is Past

He returned just as a footman and maid were finishing laying the table. Althea prepared a chair for Rebecca, and Simon carried her over to it.

When the three sat down, Althea bowed her head. She heard Rebecca say, "Stop, we're going to say grace."

Miss Breton said a short grace, as Simon sat with his spoon lifted in midair in one hand, the other tapping a rhythm on the cloth. She flushed when she noticed his position, and lifted her own spoon.

"Isn't it funny how Miss Althea blesses the food before the meal, and Grandpapa blesses it before and after the meal, and we don't bless it at all?"

There was a silence as Miss Breton glanced toward him. He shrugged over his daughter's remark, saying, "We Jews are always looking for ways to ingratiate ourselves with God, I suppose."

Althea ignored the remark and turned to Rebecca. "You must eat some of your food. Your stew will be cold by now."

After taking a spoonful, Rebecca reminded her father, "Tell us about your trip."

He buttered a slice of bread before proceeding. "I went to some mills to see what I could discover about the people working there."

"What do they make in the mills?"

"Cloth." He fingered his napkin. "Something like this, although not quite. This is linen, but what comes out of the mills is mainly cotton. It comes from a plant. It has to be spun to make thread and the thread is then woven into pieces of cloth. People used to do this in their homes, but now they can do it much faster and make more in these large mills."

Althea made a silent motion to Rebecca to take another spoonful of stew. Instead the girl imitated her father and buttered some bread.

"Why can they make more in the mills?" she asked.

"Because they figured out how to use a thing called steam to make the weaving go much faster."

"But, *Abba,* why did you have to go to the mills, if the prince is here in London?"

Simon swallowed a spoonful of stew. "Because some people who were not very happy working in these mills tried to kill Prince George."

"Because he made them work in the mills?"

He considered her question seriously. "No. They worked in the mills in order to earn money to feed their families. But they have to work a long time and they receive only a little money afterwards. Sometimes it is not enough to feed their families. That's where we, the lawmakers, come in. Some of these workers expect the laws to be changed quickly so they can earn more money and be treated better at the mills." He fingered his napkin, trying to put things in the simplest terms. "Sometimes the laws don't change quickly enough to suit them, and some of the men become angry, but they don't know exactly who is to blame. They look to the Prince Regent as the head of their country. They don't understand why he can live in big palaces while their own children suffer cold and hunger."

"Will they do what they did to the king of France?" she asked in a whisper.

"No, no, it won't come to that here." His gaze strayed to Althea, noticing her attentiveness to the conversation. "England is a civilized nation." He turned back to his daughter. "And your father is working to change the laws, so the people won't become as angry as they did in France."

The next day, Althea entered the morning room promptly at half-past seven. Simon had requested her presence at breakfast. She had not yet entered this room since arriving, having taken her breakfast in the servants' dining room early each morning before Rebecca was up. A pale February sunshine filtered through the long windows at one side of the room.

"Good morning, Miss Breton."

Her employer was already seated at the breakfast table, *The Times* in front of him.

"Good morning, Mr. Aguilar." He stood as she entered the

room. "Please don't disturb yourself. I didn't expect to see you here so early."

"You'll usually find me here at this hour." He motioned to the footman. "What would you like—toast, eggs, tea, coffee? Harry will see to it."

"That's quite all right. I—I've been waiting on myself." She moved to the sideboard, asking the footman for the porridge. He indicated the silver dish, removing its cover. "Thank you, Harry," she said with a smile, comparing his prompt actions to how he had ignored her below stairs.

When she sat down, she bowed her head and said a silent blessing. Then she reached for the creamer. She noticed Simon watching her. He went back to his paper with no comment. She took a spoonful of the tepid porridge.

"Rebecca has given you her stamp of approval, by the way," Simon told her from behind his paper.

She smiled, remembering the little girl's mature way of talking. "I'm glad."

"You're not offended?"

She looked at him in surprise as he laid the paper aside to take a sip of coffee. "Why should I be?"

"That a little child should have the yea or nay of your employment?"

"It must be trying to have a stranger come in to make one 'more comfortable.'"

"What do you think of my daughter?"

Althea smiled. "Rebecca is a beautiful child."

"What do you think of her condition?"

Althea looked down at her bowl. "She is weak, as you said. She seems very thin and has little appetite."

He nodded. "She has lost weight in the past two months. Has her condition remained the same during my absence?"

"Yes. She wakes up frequently in the night, but then goes back to sleep. She sometimes complains of pain. It doesn't seem to be in one particular area, but throughout her body. I have given her the laudanum you left with me. She usually naps in the afternoons, and I try to keep her entertained in the intervening hours. I think it's good that she keep her mind on other things."

"I agree."

"She is very imaginative. I find her precocious for her age, and I think she needs to keep her mind busy with wholesome thoughts." Althea swallowed before venturing, "She enjoyed your explanation last night. I think it gave her lots to ponder."

"You didn't find it too frightening for a child?"

"It's difficult to say. She seems so old for her years, sometimes. But I think it helps her bear your absences better if she understands they are for the good of the country."

"I don't know how much good they will do. People seem more polarized than ever at this point. I have seen more riots and acts of arson in the past year than you'd care to imagine. With each one, Parliament merely takes away individual liberties and orders more executions and deportations. Hundreds are languishing in prison while the gentry is terrified of a revolution."

Althea understood what he was talking about since she herself had lived among the laboring class and was witness to their growing discontent and misery. Many of the people they received at the mission exhibited the effects of the drudgery and dangers of factory life: drunkenness, thievery, maimed and orphaned children.

Simon soon returned to his paper. Althea took the time to study him as she hadn't had the leisure to do since that first interview with him. How her outlook had altered since that day. Gone was the fear and revulsion, replaced almost with awe as she observed one of God's chosen.

At that moment he looked up at her. She flushed, once again subject to that ironic gaze.

"Yes? Was there something you wished to ask me?" he said.

She took a deep breath, knowing that since she'd entered his employ there was indeed something she must ask him. "Yes." She cleared her throat, realizing it wouldn't be easy. "I wanted to beg your pardon."

She had his full attention now. "Beg my pardon? What-ever for?"

She was loath to destroy the new, and she sensed fragile, rela-tionship with her employer since their supper the night before, but knew she couldn't continue without setting things straight. "At our first interview you said some things concerning your...your race, implying I harbored certain notions about it." She was no longer looking at him, but at the linen cloth under her hand. She moved her cup and saucer slightly over its starched surface. "You said—accused me—of expecting to meet someone deformed, avaricious..." Her voice trailed off in embarrassment as she re-membered how true his suppositions had been.

His voice cut into her thoughts. "Didn't you?"

She glanced up at his face. He hadn't moved. His paper lay on the table before him, his slim fingers holding each edge, his face expressionless, giving her no hint to what he was thinking.

She felt the color creeping up her cheeks. "At one time, yes, I harbored certain misconceptions of your race." Her voice came out barely above a whisper, ashamed of what it confessed.

"Well?" The ironic tone was back. "Is that what you wanted to tell me? Does residing in my household confirm your opinions?"

"I wanted to apologize." When he said nothing but continued to look at her, his eyes narrowed through his spectacles, she swal-lowed and continued. "It is true, I had no good conception of your people. But I can assure you, I no longer harbor any such preju-dices."

"To what do I owe this turnabout? Must I feel a paternal pride that my daughter in a mere week has managed to shatter the as-sumptions of a lifetime?"

For the first time, she glimpsed the pain behind the mockery and realized it was just as much self-directed. She hesitated only briefly before replying. "I have been recently reminded most strenuously that my Lord and Savior Jesus was a Jew."

He cocked an eyebrow. "Indeed? And who brought that startling fact to your attention?"

"He Himself."

He made no reply, but spent a few moments folding the newspaper. When it was back to its original shape, he addressed her. "I found Rebecca in such cheerful spirits yesterday evening, and looking remarkably well, I might add, that I was prepared to thank you and tell you to dispense with any further trial period. I do thank you." He held a hand up when she made to speak. "I will be honest with you, Miss Breton. I have already gone through three nurses. It is not my intention to scare you off before you've scarcely begun, but I must tell you I had little faith in finding the type of woman to fill my requirements—and those of my daughter. I have seen nothing but slovenliness, incompetence and the worst ignorance thus far. I do not wish to add *unbalanced* to the list."

The two sat looking at each other for a few seconds as the implications of what he was saying sank in. Althea let out a slow breath, not having expected to be seen as mentally unfit to take care of a child. "I understand." When he said nothing, she added softly, "Perhaps you should continue with the probationary period until you are satisfied with my sanity."

He rose. "We shall see. As I said, I was very pleased with Rebecca's condition upon my return." At the doorway, he turned. "I shall be in the library all morning. I will stop by Rebecca's room around one and spend some time with her before I go to the House. I normally don't return to dine, but if I manage to escape early, I come up to see Rebecca in the evenings."

She nodded, trying to take in what he was telling her.

"She enjoyed our dining arrangement last night. I shall talk to Cook about providing the same whenever I am home early. I wish you good day, Miss Breton."

Before she could reply, he was gone. She looked at his retreating figure with her mouth open. First he accused her of mental incompetence, then he made no commitment to her suggestion of continuing the trial period, and now he was suggesting they continue dining together!

Simon walked briskly down the hall to the library. He had much to do this morning before going to the afternoon session of the House. Parliament had recently reconvened and there were hours of debate to look forward to.

He entered his sanctum of books and papers and closed the heavy door behind him. Quiet. He looked down the length of the room with its large desk at one end and long windows over-looking the garden behind it. His refuge, the only place he felt truly safe.

All his security was held in this room. He glanced along the shelves stocked with calf-bound, gold-embossed books as some-one else might look upon a cavern filled with gold. Tomes and tomes, representing years of study, had made him what he was today. He sat down at the mahogany desk and contemplated the papers in front of him.

As much as he wanted to focus on them, his thoughts refused to be harnessed so easily. A woman's admission kept intruding. Of all the unheard-of absurdities, this had to beat them all.

Someone apologizing to him for the attitudes she held of his race—former attitudes, by her reckoning. He himself doubted anyone could let go of a lifetime of prejudices overnight.

Simon toyed with his quill pen, fingering its tip, which he no-ticed would need to be mended. He opened a desk drawer and removed a penknife. He busied himself with small tasks of this sort, all the while remembering Miss Breton's words. He could see it had cost her; she had not been comfortable uttering the words. He would almost hazard to say she had exhibited shame. But that was absurd. No one had ever been ashamed of hating a Jew.

What had brought this "apology" about, he wondered? He dismissed that ridiculous assertion of Jesus Christ. That would be the biggest irony of all: an apology in the name of the One who had been the greatest instigator of all the persecution his race had endured in the ensuing centuries? Simon's lips curled in disbelief.

Perhaps Rebecca had been responsible. Perhaps her childish innocence had won over Miss Breton to such a degree that she was forced to admit that Jews were human beings—of a sort?

Chapter Three

❦

After their last meeting, Althea hardly expected to see Simon again in the evenings for an early supper. In those days of upheaval around the country, parliamentary sessions often went on until midnight. She knew from Tertius, who was a member of the House of Lords, that members would leave the chambers to take their supper at a local restaurant or tavern, then return while speeches were still going on.

So she was surprised one evening when the footman came up and began setting up the card table in Rebecca's room.

"Your father says he shall be up presently to dine with you, miss."

Althea rose from the bed. "Why don't you set the table up in the sitting room?" she suggested to Harry.

"Oh, yes!" Rebecca clapped her hands. "I'm tired of being in this old bedroom."

"Very well, miss."

Simon entered Rebecca's room a short while later. "Good evening, ladies."

"Oh, *Abba,* you look so handsome!"

Althea looked at her employer, realizing the little girl spoke the truth. Although he was only of medium height and slim build, he presented a dashing figure in evening clothes. For once, every curl on his head was in place; his cravat was starched and brilliantly white. The dark jacket and knee breeches were impeccably cut. His spectacles only added to his elegant appearance. In one hand he balanced a parcel.

"Where are you going, *Abba?*"

"To the opera, after I've supped with my darling." He approached Rebecca, who sat in the armchair awaiting her papa's visit. He held out the parcel with a flourish. "For you, specially ordered from Gunter's…if you eat all your dinner."

"Ohh! Let me see." She quickly undid the string, and sucked in her breath at the sight of the luscious strawberry tart inside. "My favorite! May I have it now?"

He chuckled, taking the tart away from her. "After dinner."

He looked around for the table, and Althea quickly explained, "We decided to set up the table in the sitting room. So it would seem more like a real dining room," she added.

"Very good. Here, you take charge of dessert, while I bring Rebecca."

"I can walk. I'm feeling much stronger."

Althea watched Simon's face as he observed his daughter stand and walk toward him, a smile lighting her whole face. He held out an arm for her and escorted her to her seat at the table next door.

"Is this what it's like at a real dinner party, where the gentlemen escort the ladies into the dining room?" Rebecca asked as he pulled out her chair. She looked back at Althea, who stood in the doorway. "What about Miss Althea? Who is going to escort her?"

Simon made his way to the door. "I can do the job of two gentlemen this evening," he answered, offering Althea his arm. She laid her hand gingerly on it, and let him lead her to her place. After he held the chair out for her, he took his own seat.

"Speaking of dinner parties, I am going to give one of my own."

Rebecca's eyes widened. "A real dinner party? Right here in our own house? Oh, when? May I come?"

Simon smiled at his daughter, not replying to any of her questions right away, seeming to prefer to let her anticipation build. Althea was always amazed at the transformation in her employer when he smiled at his daughter. Although he was civil to Althea, the underlying tone of mockery never quite disappeared. But with Rebecca, he was charming, patient and kind. Althea caught herself contrasting his manner to her own father's, whose conduct had been characterized by a sort of offhand kindness, as if he had been afraid of demonstrating too much interest in his only daughter. Althea brought herself up short at the direction of her thoughts and quickly dismissed the mental comparisons.

The footman brought up their food, and they sat quietly as he served. Althea caught the slight grimace Simon made when he looked at his plate. After the footman exited, she asked, "What is it?"

He shrugged. "Nothing. Cook should know by now I'd prefer not to be served pork," he added in an undertone.

"You keep the dietary laws," she commented in surprise, having found very few signs of Jewry in his household.

"Apparently not," he answered dryly, taking up his fork, awaiting Althea to say the blessing, accustomed to it by now. "Old habits die hard. When you've had it instilled in you since birth that certain foods are unclean, it's hard to overcome such prejudices, no matter what the rational mind says."

She nodded in understanding, remembering how difficult it had been for her to break away from the rituals of the Church of England.

Rebecca knew by now that she would get no more information from her father until she had taken a few bites of food. As soon as she could, she swallowed down a mouthful and asked, "Are you going to Covent Garden tonight?"

"Yes, I have been invited to someone's box," he added with

drama. "We are going to see *The Marriage of Figaro*. The Prince Regent will be present."

Rebecca drew in her breath. "I wish I could be there. Is he as fat as his portraits? I don't think princes should be fat, do you, Miss Althea?"

"I think princes have a lot of food to eat, and find it hard to refuse it all," she replied with a look at Rebecca's plate.

"*Abba,* whose box are you going to sit in?"

"That of Baron and Lady Stanton-Lewis."

The names sounded familiar to Althea, echoes from a world she had briefly glimpsed though never felt a part of.

Rebecca repeated them. "They sound very grand. Do they live in a palace?"

"I daresay they have one or two in their possession."

Rebecca suddenly remembered something more important. "*Abba,* you said you were giving a dinner party. When?"

"Next week or so. I don't know precisely." He turned to Althea. "How long does one need to prepare for these things?"

Althea put down her fork, surprised at the question. She dug back in her memory to the days when she still lived at home. Simon's dark gaze was fixed on her, awaiting an answer. "I suppose it depends mainly on the number of guests invited."

He shrugged. "Oh, I don't know, perhaps twelve…sixteen."

She pursed her lips. "A week to a fortnight should suffice under normal circumstances."

"And what precisely are 'normal circumstances'?"

Again she hedged. "A normally running household—" How could she say a normally running household had a mistress? "You haven't entertained in some time?" she asked instead.

"No, not since Hannah—Rebecca's mother—died."

"Of course not. What I mean is, in order to prepare for a dinner party, a house usually undergoes a thorough housecleaning. A menu must be drawn up as well as a guest list, which requires a proper seating arrangement. Foods and wine must be ordered, flowers—"

Simon held up a hand. "Enough, Miss Breton. If you meant to scare me, you have succeeded perfectly. You make hosting a dinner party sound more complicated than passing a law through Commons." He drummed his fingers on the tablecloth, then just as suddenly stopped and focused his attention on her again. "I know what I shall do—I shall put you in charge."

Althea's fork dropped with a clatter this time. "I beg your pardon?"

He continued as if he hadn't heard her. "You can consult with Mrs. Coates, and together the two of you can oversee all the arrangements. You've had the experience growing up on a large estate. Mrs. Coates will be there to carry out your orders. There are enough servants, I trust, to do whatever housecleaning must be done in the interim. I shall fix the date for a fortnight from today, how is that? That should give you ample time to hire more servants if that is what is needed."

Althea could only stare at her employer. How had she got into this situation? A moment ago she had been eating a dry pork chop, and now she was expected to sit down with the housekeeper and plan a full-scale dinner party? She had not been a part of the fashionable world in eight years; she no longer knew who was who. And to work with Mrs. Coates—give her orders? She pictured the iron-faced housekeeper, or dour Giles, the butler, for that matter, taking her suggestions, much less "carrying out her orders." It was preposterous—no, downright impossible.

"Mr. Aguilar, I really couldn't possibly—"

"Oh, Miss Althea, say yes," begged Rebecca. "It will be so much fun."

"If you need someone to help you with Rebecca, we can have one of the maidservants help out for a few days."

"Say yes, Miss Althea, *please!*"

Meeting Simon's eye, Althea noted the ever-present trace of mockery, but this time it was laced with something else. Was it a challenge?

Sending a question and plea heavenward, Althea turned helpless eyes to her two dinner companions and swallowed. "Very well," she said barely above a whisper, asking the Lord for a miracle in the coming fortnight.

The matter settled to their satisfaction, Rebecca and Simon turned to other topics. "Miss Althea has promised to bring me downstairs to the yellow salon tomorrow."

Mr. Aguilar looked at Althea, one black eyebrow raised. "Indeed? What do the two of you have planned?"

"Miss Althea has promised to play the pianoforte for me. Then we shall look out at the garden. She has spotted a few snowdrops peeking out—isn't that right, Miss Althea?"

As Rebecca chattered away to her father, Althea was too distracted to remind her to eat her food. Her own throat had tightened so that not even a swallow of water would go down.

A dinner party in Mayfair in a fortnight... the event had all the allure of a cholera epidemic in the East End.

Althea's faint hope that Simon had forgotten his impulsive request of the previous evening proved in vain. The next afternoon she was summoned to the library.

Althea had not been in that room since the day she was interviewed there. Now, once again she stood before his desk, this time with a silent Mrs. Coates standing beside her.

"Here is a list of the guests I wish to be invited. Mrs. Coates, you will consult with Miss Breton and defer to her on all matters pertaining to this dinner party. Is that understood?"

"Yes, sir," answered the stout, gray-haired housekeeper, her hands folded in front of her.

"Miss Breton has mentioned something about a thorough housecleaning. Isn't that right?" He turned to Althea.

Althea cleared her throat, uncomfortable with the notion that she was the instigator of a major household upheaval. "That is correct, sir—at least of all the rooms that will entertain guests that evening."

"You will see to that immediately, then, Mrs. Coates?"

The housekeeper gave a short sniff, accompanied by a nod. "Very well, sir."

"That will be all. Keep me informed as things progress."

Feeling dismissed, Althea followed Mrs. Coates out of the room. In the hallway, she turned to the housekeeper. "Would you like to go over the guest list now? I have a few moments before I have to be with Rebecca."

Mrs. Coates, who had taken immediate possession of the scrawled sheet of paper, gave another sniff. "I can perfectly well see to it." She turned and walked off toward her sitting room, muttering "...Methodite do-gooder...."

So, that was the cause of the servants' unfriendliness, Althea thought. She stood for a few seconds before ascending the stairs to Rebecca's room.

"May we go down now?" Rebecca sat in her chair, just the way Althea had left her when she'd been summoned into the library.

"Yes, we shall go down forthwith. Do you feel up to walking if you take my arm?"

"Oh, yes!" Rebecca stood promptly.

Althea offered her arm and the two walked toward the door. The girl managed the stairs slowly, but once in the yellow salon, she was chatting away happily. Althea pointed out the signs of spring in the otherwise drab garden.

"See there, those little green shoots pointing through the dirt?"

"Yes, yes, I see them. What are they going to be?"

"Crocus. There! There are some coming through that patch of grass where the snow has melted. Now, look over there. Do you see the white flowers?"

Rebecca pressed her face to the glass doors. "Yes. Ohh, what are those?"

"Snowdrops. The very first sign of spring."

"They are so pretty. So tiny against the black dirt."

Althea straightened. "Are you ready for some music now?"

"Yes."

"Then, let us get you comfortably settled and tucked in."

Althea led her to a brocaded armchair and turned it so the girl could either watch her at the pianoforte or continue gazing out the window.

On her way to the instrument, Althea paused at the fireplace. Upon the mantel stood a brass candelabra. She ran her fingers over it curiously. "How unusual." She counted the holders. "Nine," she commented, turning to Rebecca.

"That's for Hanukkah," the girl said promptly.

"Hanukkah? What's that?"

"A holiday in December. Each night for eight nights we light a new candle and wait until it burns down completely." After a moment, she added, "We don't celebrate Christmas."

"I see. What is Hanukkah in celebration of?"

"It's about the Jewish people winning a battle. Papa knows the story better. We didn't light them this December. I was ill."

Althea nodded, then walked over to the pianoforte. She sat down, wondering what to play. She played a few scales to get her fingers warmed up. The sheet music in front of her was a hymn of worship written by Charles Wesley. She played the first few bars, then continued, enjoying the uplifting sounds. The second time she played it through she began singing the words. She finished that one and began to play and sing another she had been practicing: *"Come, my soul, thou must be waking/Now is breaking/O'er the earth another day: Come to Him who made this splendor..."*

She turned toward Rebecca with a smile. "Would you like to hear any more?"

"Oh, yes, please. Those are such cheerful songs."

Althea played a few more hymns, then glanced at the girl. Her eyes were closed and her dark head leaned against the back of the chair. Althea rose from the instrument.

She stood gazing down at Rebecca. The child looked fragile and wan against the bright, brocaded pattern of the upholstery. Her burgundy hair ribbon slipped across a pale cheek like a rivulet of blood. Her thin hands lay over the blanket, the veins blue bumps upon the snowy skin.

"I'm not asleep, Miss Althea." Her lips curved in a smile and she opened her eyes. "I was just listening to the music." After a pause, she continued, "It was all about God, wasn't it?"

"Yes, it was."

Rebecca looked toward the garden. "Do you believe in God?"

"Yes, dear."

The little girl gave Althea a straightforward look. "*Abba* doesn't."

"How do you know?"

"I've heard him say God is an outdated notion and no rational mind can accept Bible stories as anything but myths."

Althea considered the parroted words, shocked despite herself. "Do you believe in God, Rebecca?"

Rebecca tilted her head back against the chair. "I don't know."

Hiding her concern, Althea eased herself onto the arm of the chair and touched the top of Rebecca's head. "Why is that?"

Rebecca turned her eyes up to her. "I've never seen Him. I've never heard Him. Who is to say He is really there?"

Althea nodded. "You are absolutely right. If you have never felt His presence, you cannot say for certain He is."

Rebecca studied her. "You have felt His presence, haven't you?"

"Yes, dear," she answered with a smile, her hand stroking Rebecca's hair.

"What does that mean, 'feel His presence'?"

Althea pursed her lips, considering how best to reply. "I'll show you." Gently, she placed both her hands against the sides of Rebecca's head and turned it away from her, toward the garden. Then she removed her hands completely from Rebecca. "You can't see me, can you?"

Rebecca shook her head.

"You can't feel me touching you anywhere, can you?"

Again she shook her head.

"Now I shall stop speaking and you won't be able to hear me. Let's do that, shall we?"

Rebecca nodded her head.

Althea waited silently a little while, not moving. As the silence stretched out, she forgot Mrs. Coates's earlier scorn, the impossible task Simon had assigned her, and the myriad distractions that had clouded her real purpose in this household. As God's peace descended upon her, she gazed out the windows at the black outline of espaliered trees against the brick wall enclosing the garden. The ground was a patchwork of snow and brown grass between the gravel paths.

"Miss Althea?"

"How do you know I'm still here?"

Rebecca turned toward her a face radiant with discovery. "I can feel your presence, can't I?"

Althea smiled at her.

"Let's do it again!" Rebecca cried happily, turning her gaze back toward the garden.

"Very well. But this time, don't turn around until I tell you to."

Rebecca nodded happily.

They played the game several times, at Rebecca's insistence. The final time Althea quietly slipped outside the room and stood just beyond the doorway. After a while, she heard Rebecca's "Miss Althea? Miss Althea? Are you there? Where are you?"

Althea immediately stepped over the threshold. "Here I am. What did you feel that time?" she asked as she walked back to Rebecca's chair.

"I felt alone." The child's deep-set eyes, so much like her father's, stared up at her in wonder. "I started wondering whether you were still there. The room felt empty. I waited a little longer, but then I couldn't help calling out."

Althea knelt in front of her, taking both her hands in her own. "Sometimes we can't feel the Lord's presence, just as you experienced now. But once you *have* felt His presence, you'll know even then that He's still with you. Just as I was right nearby, just outside the door, God is always with you, even when you can't feel His presence. He promises us, 'I shall never leave you nor forsake you.'"

"How can I come to feel His presence the way I did yours?"

Althea rubbed the back of the girl's hands with her thumbs.

"You invite Him into your heart. And you believe in your heart that He will come in."

"Can I do it right now?"

Althea smiled. "Right now."

The little girl bowed her head and said a simple prayer beginning with "Dear God." Althea was unsure whether to tell her about Jesus, not knowing how the girl's father would feel about her evangelizing his daughter. Althea remained silent for the moment, knowing the Lord would guide her in that direction when the time was right.

For the present, she knew God heard the girl's prayer and would answer it.

A few days later Althea entered the house, the heavy front door shutting behind her with a *bang* on a gust of wind. She had had to bend her face downward during her walk, but the air had invigorated her. Surely if March were coming in like a lion, there was a good possibility it would go out like a lamb, she consoled herself as she wiped her boots against the mat in the quiet hall. She looked up startled at the sound of a throat clearing.

The housekeeper stood with her hands folded in front of her. She looked like a plump, curved urn, round on top and bottom, cinched in at the waist by her apron ties. Tight curls framed a face prematurely wrinkled, as if a sculpture's knife had slipped, leaving deep lines along her cheeks.

"Oh, pardon me, Mrs. Coates. I didn't see you standing there. May I help you with anything?"

"Yes, miss, if you please."

Althea wondered at the subdued tone. "Let me just hang up my damp things and I shall be right with you."

She joined the housekeeper in her sitting room.

"Would you like a cup of tea?" the housekeeper asked stiffly, gesturing toward the pot on the table before her.

Amazed, Althea took a seat at the table. "That would be lovely. It's quite cold outside." She waited quietly as the housekeeper

poured the steaming liquid into a cup and covered the pot with
a cozy.

Mrs. Coates sat down opposite her. A stack of correspondence
lay on the small table between them. Noticing her glance, the
housekeeper said, "Them's the replies."

"The replies?"

"For the dinner he's giving."

Not liking the way she was referring to their employer, Althea
said, "The dinner Mr. Aguilar is hosting?"

"That's right. The replies've been comin' in. Most are accep-
tances." Mrs. Coates sighed, her ample bosom rising. She pushed
forward a sheet of paper. "I was working on seating arrangements
when you walked in."

"I see. How are they coming?" she asked, looking at the blank
sheet of paper.

Mrs. Coates fingered the corner of the paper. "Not so well. You
see, he—that is, Mr. Aguilar—hasn't been too clear about how
he wants it. Only thing he told me was to seat him by—" she shuffled among the correspondence until she came to the right one
"—Lady Stanton-Lewis." She pushed the reply toward Althea.

Althea took the folded vellum. A hint of a floral fragrance
drifted to her nostrils as she unfolded the creamy sheet. Lord
Griffith and Lady Eugenia Stanton-Lewis accepted the invitation
to dinner at the residence of the Honorable Simon Aguilar on the
evening of the twelfth of March. Althea remembered the names
Simon had mentioned the evening he was going to the opera.

She made a greater effort to recall them from her days in London society. She remembered the name was a good one, but that
was all that came to mind. "Very well," she said, "let us put her
on Mr. Aguilar's right—unless, of course, we find someone who
outranks her. We shall need to look at all the other replies to see
where her husband ranks. Do you know if Mr. Aguilar has a copy
of the *Peerage* in his library?"

"I wouldn't know. It's been many years since there's been any
entertaining under this roof." Mrs. Coates sat back in her chair

and took a sip of tea. "Before the missus died, they did some entertaining, but it was mostly amongst their own kind. There's never been what you'd call 'society' here. I don't think they'd know much of such things."

Althea noted the disdain in her tone but said nothing. She took a swallow of tea, then pushed away from the table. "I think I shall just look in the library and see if he doesn't have a copy. That will help us in these arrangements."

"Very well, miss."

Althea entered the quiet library. No one went in there on the days when Simon was at the House. She closed the door softly behind her, trying to decide where to begin. On the two occasions she had crossed this threshold, her mind had been too preoccupied with the coming interviews with her employer to take in her surroundings to any significant degree. Now she could enjoy the peace and comfort of this room. It reminded her of her father's library on his country estate in Hertfordshire.

She walked slowly into the long vast room, breathing in the scent of book leather and paper, over which lingered the acrid tinge of a spent fire in an unswept grate. Walls of bookshelves on two sides accentuated the length of the room. Stacks of books and paintings along the walls waited to be shelved or hung, as if in the years since the original order of the room had been established, more books, paintings and *objets d'art* had been accumulated but no time or interest found to place them properly.

Rich carpets covered the floors, muffling her footsteps as she ventured farther into the room. Heavy velvet curtains framed the wall of casement windows at the far end of the room.

Midway the length of the room stood a fireplace with a sculpted marble front. Gilt-framed oil paintings, one above another, hung around the fireplace from ceiling to wainscoting. The walls beneath were a rich red. A welcoming group of brass-studded leather chairs and a small, upholstered sofa faced the fireplace. Althea touched a leather armrest, remembering the hours she had spent as a girl curled up in just such a chair, safe from all eyes.

She rubbed her fingers together, noticing how grimy they had become. She examined the rest of the furniture more closely, noticing the film of dust over every surface. Brushing the dust off her hands, she decided that was a problem to be tackled at another time.

The rest of the room was given over to floor-to-ceiling bookshelves made of dark oak. She began examining the bookshelves, looking for a classification system. She found histories; biographies; works in Latin, Greek and Hebrew, which made her wish she could spend a few hours in that section; another section devoted to novels, including many of the newest; stacks and stacks of old issues of *The Times* and *The Observer* as well as the newer more radical publications like Cobbett's *Political Register.* There were countless political and philosophical tomes. Althea also came upon a stack of pamphlets containing Simon's name. Curious, she riffled through these, reading the various titles he had authored: factory reform, parliamentary reform, arguments in favor of a minimum wage, abolition of the tithe. The topics sounded altogether radical for a member of the Tory party. She placed them back in a neat stack.

Althea ran her fingers one last, lingering time over the spines of the books. The wisdom of humanity contained in a roomful of shelves, she mused, craning her neck upward. Solomon had written, "Wisdom is the principal thing; therefore get wisdom...." But he had also begun the book of Proverbs with the preface "...the fear of the Lord is the beginning of knowledge."

Althea considered all the knowledge Simon had extracted from these centuries of human understanding and knowledge. But one thing he lacked, she thought, paraphrasing Jesus's words to the rich young man: the fear of the Lord, and without that, all the rest of the wisdom was in vain.

She finally spied copies of both Debrett's *Peerage* and *Baronetage.* They were placed in an area with some copies of *The Morning Post, The Court Guide* and *The Royalist,* a periodical known for its scandals and *on dits.* Clearly, Mrs. Coates's opinion that Simon knew nothing of society was ill-formed, Althea thought as she picked up one of the two volumes on family names and genealogies.

The rest of the afternoon was spent with Mrs. Coates, pairing off ladies and gentlemen for the dinner party, deciding who would escort whom into the dining room and where they would be seated.

"Oh, dear, Mrs. Coates, there is a surplus of gentlemen," Althea said, looking at the invitations laid out in two groupings.

"Don't suppose he knows many society ladies. As I said, he's lived a very quiet life 'til recently, mostly working in Parliament and visitin' his family. He's brought gentlemen 'round now and then for a bite to eat and game of whist." She eyed the scented note. "Never known him to entertain a female, leastways not here in his home."

"Well, we shall just have to do the best we can with what we have. Perhaps some replies will still come in."

As she located the family names in the books, she remembered more and more of the details from her two London Seasons. In the end there were only a few she didn't know what to do with. She supposed they might be colleagues of Simon's.

"I think we have done all we can this afternoon. You shall just have to consult Mr. Aguilar about these remaining names. You can show him our chart and he can pencil them in where he deems appropriate." She considered. "Perhaps I shall mention to him the imbalance in the number of ladies and gentlemen."

"Oh, very good, miss." Mrs. Coates stood as soon as Althea did, her face troubled. "You don't think he'll mind that we moved Lady Stanton-Lewis, do you?"

"Don't trouble yourself about it. I'm sure he'll understand that we had no choice in the matter, with a duke outranking a baron. If he has any objections, tell him to see me about it. Now, have you had a chance to review the menu?"

"No, miss. But, if you have a moment, perhaps we could go down now and consult with Cook?"

"Let me see if Rebecca is awake. I shall join you in the kitchen momentarily."

"Yes, miss."

The two exited the sitting room together, with Althea heading up to see Rebecca. When she told her about the dinner party arrangements, Rebecca wanted to know the names of the guests who had accepted. Promising to tell her upon her return, as well as to describe the dishes to be served, Althea went back downstairs to review the menu.

Mrs. Bentwood, the cook, was showing Mrs. Coates the menu when Althea joined them. Although she had been talking with the housekeeper, the moment Althea entered she fell silent. Mrs. Coates handed Althea the list. Althea took it from her without a word and began reading: Clear Consommé, Salmon with Shrimp Sauce, Dover Sole, Chicken Fricassee, Giblet Pie, Roast Pheasant with Egg Sauce, Haunch of Venison, Peas, Potatoes, Cauliflower, Kidney Pudding, Preserves, Tongue with Red Currant Sauce, Lobster Bisque with Champagne, Pastry Basket, Fresh Fruit, Syllabub.

The menu sounded appropriate. Althea had watched her family's cook prepare many such menus in the cavernous kitchen at the estate where she spent her childhood. She had probably spent more time in their cook's company than with her own family. Althea knew well the army of kitchen maids needed to successfully prepare such an array of dishes. She looked up at the cook, thinking of the overcooked meats, cold potatoes and dry puddings that had been her fare since coming to this household.

"This is quite an ambitious menu. Mrs. Coates tells me the master has not entertained in quite some years. Will you need any extra help—"

Mrs. Bentwood pulled herself up to her full height, crossing her arms beneath her bosom. "I'll 'ave you know I've worked in the finest 'ouses of London. Many's the menu I've planned."

"Yes, of course. Has everything been ordered?"

"Hit's all being taken care of."

"Very well. The menu looks very good. I wish you the best success with it. Let me know if I may be of any help." She turned toward Mrs. Coates. "I will go up to Rebecca, if you should need me."

Chapter Four

❧

"Miss Althea, what did you do before you came here?"

Althea looked up from studying the puzzle pieces on the lap table between them. She had soon discovered that Rebecca quickly tired of whatever activity she found for them to do and preferred to spend her time chatting.

"I worked with children, many your age." She smiled across at the girl lying back against her voluminous pillows. "But none quite like you."

Rebecca smiled in return. "What did you do with them? The same as with me?"

Althea straightened, easing the muscles in her shoulders. "Not quite the same thing. You see, these children don't live as you do here. Many have no home."

Rebecca's dark eyes widened into pools of wonder. "They don't? Where do they live, then?"

"Wherever they can. Some find shelter in a doorway at night, or inside a crate. Some band together and live in an abandoned building. Some find a sort of protection with an adult. Unfortunately that protection comes at a price." She answered Rebecca's look of bewilderment. "The adult obliges them to work for them. It usually involves dishonest work, such as stealing."

"Stealing?"

Althea nodded. "Children are quicker than adults. They can be trained to steal someone's pocketbook or watch."

"Doesn't the person know it?"

"No. The children are so quick and light-handed, the victim doesn't feel a thing. 'Tis only later, when they reach for their purse to pay for something, or need to take a look at their watch to see the hour, that they realize these items are gone. By then the children are far away."

"What do the children do with the things they steal?"

"They have to give everything to their protector. That person sells everything to another person. One who doesn't care that the items are stolen."

Rebecca mulled over this information for a few minutes. "What do you do with the children, Miss Althea?"

Althea laid down the piece she had been trying to fit in the puzzle. "I work with a small group of people who want to help these children. We have a place we call a mission. It's a building where all people, not just children, can come if they need a home. We give food to those who haven't enough to eat. We provide schooling for the children who haven't any school to go to. We have a small infirmary for those who are sick and haven't anyone to care for them."

"Did you do all those things?"

Althea laughed. "No, not by myself. I do a little bit of everything. I work wherever I'm needed—sometimes in the school, sometimes in the kitchen, sometimes tending the sick. That's why your papa hired me to come here. He knew—or he was told—that I could nurse you when you weren't feeling well."

Rebecca digested this. "Why did you leave that place? Didn't the people need you anymore?"

Althea hesitated. "No. The people still need care. But there are others working there. I wasn't the only one." She picked up a puz-zle piece and tried it with another. It didn't fit. "I came to you be-cause I felt this is where I should be."

Rebecca looked at her as if not completely satisfied. "How did you know about me?"

"My brother told me. He and your father used to be very close friends when they were boys."

"Is that true? How did they meet?"

"At school. They were a little older than you, but they were both far from home and a bit lonely, I suspect. Anyway, from what my brother, Tertius, has told me, they became very good friends."

"Why haven't I ever met you, then?"

"Well, my brother went away for many years, so he and your father didn't see each other for a long, long time. It's just recently that they met again."

"And that's when *Abba* told you about me!"

"In a way. Your papa and my brother started talking of all the things that had happened to them while they were apart. Your papa told my brother all about you—how smart you were, how lovely, how—" As Althea searched for another adjective, Re-becca finished for her.

"How I had no mama?"

Althea closed her mouth and nodded at Rebecca. The little girl's tone did not sound sad, merely matter-of-fact. "He said he needed someone to look after you while he was at work."

Instead of pursuing the subject of her mother, Rebecca's mind went back to the children. "Didn't you mind leaving the children to come here?"

"It was difficult for me to leave the children." She smoothed the coverlet under her hand. "I love them and I know they still need me." She smiled at Rebecca's serious expression. "I could never have left them if I didn't know so certainly that the Lord wanted me to come here for a while, to be with you as long as you need me."

After a little consideration, Rebecca replied, "I'm sorry you had to leave the children, but I'm glad you're here."

"I'm glad I'm here, too. Why don't you help me find another piece in this puzzle? Look, I think this piece goes here." Althea handed the girl a piece and indicated the area where she'd been working. Rebecca tried the piece and after a few attempts, got it in.

"It's part of the lion's head!" The emerging scene showed a train of jungle animals marching through a forest of palm trees and other foreign-looking vegetation. After her initial excitement, Rebecca lost interest in the puzzle again.

"Have you always lived at this mission?"

Althea glanced at Rebecca, unsurprised at her continued questioning. She'd become accustomed to it in the time she'd spent with the girl and was beginning to understand that her active mind more than made up for the inactivity of her body.

"No, I've only lived there, let's see, almost six years."

"Where did you live before?"

"I grew up in a big house surrounded by lots of parks and forests," she said with a smile, picturing the estate in Hertfordshire.

"Is that where you helped Cook with the tarts?"

"Yes," she said, her smile deepening. "I think I spent more time in the kitchen than with the family. Except in summer, when I was outside every chance I got."

"Didn't you have a mama, either?"

Althea glanced at Rebecca, surprised by her perception. "No, my mama died, too, when I was very young. I was probably about the same age as you," she added, "just a babe, when I lost her. So, I don't remember her at all."

"I don't remember my mama, either. Who took care of you if you had no mama?"

"A nice lady and gentleman. They became my guardians. They were very good to me."

Rebecca considered for a moment. "Did they become your brother's guardians, too?"

Althea looked down at her hands, considering how to reply. "No. They were his real parents. I—I just came to consider him as my brother, since we grew up together." Better that than get into the complicated truth of the actual relationship. "I had another brother, too, but he just recently passed away."

"That's too bad," the girl said softly. "It must be nice to have brothers. I have lots of cousins but no brothers. Mama died too soon."

Althea was silent.

Rebecca soon brightened again as a new thought occurred to her. "Did this brother know my *abba*, too?"

Althea smiled. "I daresay not. I believe your papa and Tertius—that is, the younger of my brothers—were only together in school. I don't remember your papa ever visiting us over holiday." Now she wondered whether that had had anything to do with Simon's being Jewish.

Tertius had never spoken of Simon. Althea had not realized what close friends they were until Tertius had pleaded on his friend's behalf for his daughter.

She gave Rebecca's hand a squeeze, acknowledging how close she had come to turning down his appeal. "The important thing is that the Lord had us meet now."

That evening Simon glanced from his sleeping daughter's bed to the sitting room door. Seeing the light shining through the door Miss Breton always left ajar, he approached it and tapped softly.

Hearing her bid him enter, Simon pushed open the door. He found her sitting by the fire, reading by lamplight. "Good evening, Miss Breton. I don't wish to disturb you. I just wanted to ask you how Rebecca was today. I didn't have a chance to see her before I went to the House."

She marked her place in the black, leather-bound Bible. "Rebecca was fine." She smiled, adding, "She became quite animated when she found out about the dinner party. I had to describe all the dishes to be served and go over the guest list with her."

Simon smiled, feeling refreshed by her smile. "May I come in?"

"Certainly." She stood, but he waved her back. "Please, stay put. I shall only linger a moment." He sat in a chair before the fire and sighed, feeling ragged after hours of debate. "How are things coming with the arrangements?" he asked perfunctorily, not really interested at that moment in preparations for a dinner party. He wondered if he'd been mad to even contemplate such a thing. "Have you and Mrs. Coates had a chance to sit down together?"

She fingered the edges of the book in her lap. "Yes, we did. I think Mrs. Coates and Cook have things well under control. I believe all the replies have been received. There should be thirteen in attendance aside from yourself."

He was thankful he'd put her in charge; maybe it wouldn't be a complete fiasco. Why was it, when he could wield power from his bench in the House, he felt absolute terror at the thought of hosting those same men and their wives in his home for an evening?

Althea spoke again. "That is a good number for a dinner party, particularly if one hasn't entertained in a while. It is better to start small."

"Is that a small number?" he asked, doubts assailing him.

"No, not all. It is a good number, as I said, neither too small nor too large a party, so that you will be able to give your attention to each one of your guests." She added, "Mrs. Coates has drawn up the seating arrangements. She will be seeing you about one or two names that remain in question as to rank." She hesitated. "There is only one problem, as I see it."

He looked inquiringly at her, wondering what else he must worry about.

"The gentlemen outnumber the women. We are lacking two females to make the numbers even."

"Is that an unforgivable social blunder? I confess to having more male acquaintances than female. It comes from working in Parliament and not having had much time up to now to mingle in society."

She nodded. "That is understandable. There is one other thing. You had expressed to Mrs. Coates the desire to have Lady Stanton-Lewis seated at your right. Since the Duke and Duchess of Belmont have sent their acceptance, I felt obliged to give them prominence. We placed Lord and Lady Stanton-Lewis just below them. Does that meet with your approval?"

He waved a hand, his mind wearied with questions of social etiquette. It had been a momentary whim to ask to be seated beside Lady Eugenia. Now he couldn't care less. "Do whatever you deem appropriate. You are the expert on these matters." Realizing Althea was really doing him an enormous favor in undertaking this responsibility, he tried to show some interest in the topic. "Will I be in disgrace for the uneven numbers?"

"Only with the very proper hostesses."

He looked at her more closely, noting the humor in her eyes. He'd never shared a moment of humor with her. "Since I am probably not acquainted with them, I suppose I shall survive."

"And give many more dinner parties," she quipped.

He gave her a crooked smile, running a hand through his hair. "If my first proves not to be an unmitigated disaster."

"Oh, I'm certain it shan't be."

Her tone was oddly comforting. Simon stretched out his legs before the fire, thinking of his earlier meeting with the chief whip. "I don't know," he began. "If my standing with my colleagues is any indication, I'll be lucky if anyone shows up." After Simon's speech on the Corn Laws, the chief whip had taken him aside and given him a thorough dressing down, with warnings that came down directly from Liverpool himself, he intimated. If Simon didn't toe the party line, he might find himself back in the upper tier. He had succeeded in his party because of his gift for oratory, but if he used it against his own party, he could forget about a junior lordship.

Simon sat in silence, gazing at the fire, contemplating this dilemma.

As if reading his thoughts, Miss Breton's soft voice penetrated his hearing at last. "How...how are things in the House?"

He sighed deeply, giving her his attention once again. "Much debate and little real action. The Tories don't want things to change."

"But you...are you not a member of the Tory party yourself?"

"Oh, yes. The party in power," he added with irony. "It doesn't mean I agree with everything they stand for. I'm beginning to think I disagree with more and more each day." He removed his spectacles and rubbed the bridge of his nose. "Words, words and more words. I used to enjoy them. Now it seems as if all we do is bicker and call each other names. We're worse than a bunch of schoolboys at times. In the meantime, there are more men out of work each day, widows and children are going hungry, and those with work are rioting."

"Yes, it does seem things have grown worse since the end of the war," she agreed. "We all looked forward to peace with France, but since then, there are so many discharged soldiers and sailors. We see so many idle men around the mission, with nothing to do but drink."

He looked at her in surprise, not having expected to be able to discuss these things with a woman, much less his daughter's nurse. Yet, because of her work at the mission, he realized, she was probably the one who would best understand.

A whimper from the other room caused them both to turn. Miss Breton immediately arose, with Simon close behind her. She pushed aside the bed curtains and knelt by Rebecca's pillow, feeling her forehead. It was hot.

"Althy..." moaned the girl, her head turning from side to side, her eyes still closed. "Oh, Althy, my head hurts so. My whole body hurts...."

"There, there," she answered in soothing tones, smoothing the hair off her forehead. "Your papa's here."

Rebecca opened her eyes. "*Abba,* you came home."

"Yes, dear." Simon sat on the edge of the bed as Althea moved to the night table to measure out a dose of laudanum. Simon continued speaking in soft tones, stroking his daughter's forehead as

Althea had done, while she administered the medicine. The two of them stayed there until Rebecca finally fell asleep.

When they returned to the sitting room, too restless to sit again, Simon leaned against the back of his chair, his forearms against it, vaguely aware of Althea adding coal to the fire. The new chunks sizzled as they touched the red-hot ones beneath. He stood, staring at the glowing coals but not really seeing them.

Abruptly he looked at her as she brushed off her hands. "How often do you have to give her the laudanum?"

She met his dark gaze as she bit her underlip. At last she answered him softly, "Almost every night."

At least she was honest with him. He grimaced. "It's funny—since you came I've been sleeping through the nights, but it's not because my daughter has been getting any better. She merely has a better nurse."

Althea looked down at her hands.

"I would like to apologize for doubting your abilities, Miss Breton."

She raised her head. "No apology is necessary. I only wish I could do more...." Her eyes had an appeal in them.

"You've made Rebecca happy. That's all I can hope for."

She continued looking at him, and he waited, wondering if there was something else she had to tell him about Rebecca. He was right.

"Your daughter needs something else to make her happy."

"Name it, and I shall do all in my power to obtain it."

"It doesn't cost anything." She smoothed her skirt. "Your daughter needs to know about God." She clasped her small hands in front of her, her gaze resolute.

He just stared at her, not expecting that reply. A short, humorless laugh erupted from him as he rubbed his forehead with a hand. "Well, I have to admit, that is something I can't give her."

They fell silent. After a while, Althea said, "I would like your permission to read some Bible stories to Rebecca. I gather from my conversations with her that she receives no religious training, neither Jewish nor Christian. If you'd rather, I would just read to her from the Old Testament—"

He waved a hand, almost in relief at having this topic so easily solved. "Old, new, *Tanakh, HaBrit Hachadashah*—you have my permission to read her what you like. I was exposed to both as a lad, and you can see what little harm—or good—they did me."

"Thank you" was all she answered.

She seemed satisfied and resumed her seat. Simon didn't leave, but began to walk slowly about the room, one hand covering the other in a fist. He almost envied Miss Breton her faith. She had a cause she'd be willing to lose her job over, he'd wager. How clear and simple things must be for her.

He thought about her tenderness with his daughter just now in the other room. He wished he could do something for her to express his real gratitude. He finally stopped before her chair.

"I have been meaning to thank you for what you have done for Rebecca. She truly seems happier since you've been here."

She looked up at him with a smile, and he suddenly saw the resemblance to her brother. They both had a sort of radiance.

"It is I who should be thanking you for giving me the opportunity to come here," she said.

Simon didn't reply right away but stood, considering her. On impulse he said, "I would like you to attend the dinner party next week."

She opened her mouth in stupefaction. "Oh, no, sir! That is not at all necessary."

"I know it isn't. Still, I would like you in attendance."

"Please, sir, I...I would rather not...."

He peered at her more closely, not understanding her reaction. Fool that he was, he had thought she'd be pleased, even flattered. Why hadn't he recalled her own admission of her opinion of Jews? Annoyed at both himself and her, he said, "I don't want to argue with you about this, but I really must insist that you attend. You are Lord Skylar's sister, for goodness' sake. Yes, I know, I know, his *half* sister.

"Furthermore, you are a lady in your own right, whether you choose to go by a title or not. I cannot have you *not* attend. I couldn't face your brother ever again, for one thing, nor my own conscience, for that matter."

Panic was visible in her eyes. "Mr. Aguilar, *please* don't concern yourself with appearances. My brother will understand if I decline to attend a dinner party. He knows perfectly well why I am here in your employ. He would never expect you to—"

Simon waved his hand impatiently. "I didn't mean that the way it sounded! If I cared about appearances I would never have hired you in the first place." His tone softened, sensing her aversion had nothing to do with him, but with some kind of fear on her part. "I merely thought perhaps you would enjoy an evening in polite society. You spend all your time in a little girl's company. As much as I love my daughter, I know it must be draining to be in a sick child's company twenty-four hours a day."

Her voice was perfectly composed. "Thank you for your consideration, but believe me, it is completely unnecessary. I am perfectly content to sit here."

He gave her an amused look, determined to get to the bottom of her refusal. "Do you always decline any and all overtures into society? Is that part of the reason you shut yourself away in the East End?" He narrowed his eyes at her. "I know what you are— you are a reverse snob, are you not, running away from your own class?" He saw the dismay in her gray eyes and knew he had touched a nerve. "What are you afraid of? Possible contamination with sinners? You can't expect me to believe you prefer to sit here alone night after night, hiding behind that gray governess garb. Is that the prescribed color of the Methodists, by the way? Is it the badge that proclaims them sin-free?"

She stared at him, her cheeks pink, her lips pressed together.

So there was a weakness there somewhere in her religious armor, thought Simon in satisfaction. She didn't realize he was a master at finding a person's vulnerability and exploiting it. He'd had to do so to survive. This time, however, he felt no satisfaction. Instead, her discomfort touched something in him. Suddenly he felt protective of her.

He pulled at his cravat, uncomfortable with the notion. All he'd wanted to do was repay her in some way. He'd ended up delving into something deeper that common sense told him was better left buried.

"If you can't bring yourself to join the company for your amusement, you can always come to make yourself useful, pouring tea or something," he ended in annoyance. "Think of it as helping me out. After all, you yourself said I needed a pair of ladies to even up the numbers."

She said quietly, "Very well, I shall come to serve."

He let out a breath and rubbed his temples. "Miss Breton, you try my patience."

"I beg your pardon, sir. I thought that's what you wanted. I shall attend your dinner party. Was there something else you required?"

He met her guileless gray eyes, and his frustration dissipated. He said gently, "I didn't mean my invitation to sound like an order. Let me restate it. Please *honor* me with your presence. You have done so much for Rebecca already. I wished to express my gratitude to you in some small way, that is all."

Once again her face flooded with color, although this time not in anger. She seemed embarrassed. "You needn't feel obligated— I have done nothing extraordinary—"

"Please, Miss Breton, will you honor me with your presence— of your own free will?" The last words were said a bit awkwardly, as he was unused to entreating people. Then he smiled, wanting to tell her not to be afraid, he had faced a lot worse situations than a simple dinner party.

He could see the struggle in her features. Finally, she gave a small nod and looked away.

"Very well."

* * *

After he left, Althea stood by the fire thinking about what her employer had said. Simon's words had hit their mark, although he probably didn't realize just how accurately. Did she indeed hide behind her simple gray dresses and pious acts? Why did she feel physically sick at the mere thought of reentering the world she had known all her life? Why was she so afraid of it? She knew it no longer had any power over her. She knew the Lord had set her free of its hypocritical standards.

She thought she had turned her back on it, following a different road the Lord had opened up for her. Had she in fact merely been running away?

If so, her appearance at this dinner party would be her first act of facing down her long-dormant fears.

"'…And who knoweth whether thou art come to the kingdom for such a time as this?'" Althea made her voice speak the words solemnly and prophetically.

Rebecca took up her cue, responding in the queenly voice of Esther. "'Go, gather together all the Jews that are present in Shushan, and fast ye for me, and neither eat nor drink three days, night or day: I also and my maidens will fast likewise; and so will I go in unto the king, which is not according to the law: and if I perish, I perish.'" Rebecca caused her puppet queen's head to bow down on the last word, her fingers bringing the arms together against the queen's breast.

The two had worked together the previous day fashioning the puppets for a presentation of *Esther.*

"What wonderful words—'if I perish, I perish,'" sighed Rebecca, her own hand against her breast.

"It says here that on the third day Esther put on 'her royal apparel, and stood in the inner court of the king's house.' We must fashion a properly royal gown for her," Althea suggested.

"Oh, yes, a royal purple gown, velvet perhaps, with silk ribbons."

"That sounds suitable. I shall consult Mrs. Coates about scraps of material."

"Maybe you could cut up one of my old dresses."

"I shouldn't think we need go so far, but perhaps there are some ribbons you no longer use."

"Oh, I have heaps of things. Let's look in my cupboard."

"Very well." Althea moved to the dressing room adjoining the bedroom. Rebecca was correct. Dozens of dresses were hung up, little kid slippers and boots lined the bottom shelves. Cupboard drawers were piled to the top with petticoats and stockings.

"You could dress a whole neighborhood of children with these clothes," she said, thinking of all the ragged children in the mission's neighborhood.

Rebecca laughed. "Look at the green velvet dress. That used to be my favorite. When I was littler."

Althea pulled out the dress and brought it to Rebecca, who put it up to herself. "I used to wear this to go to my grandmama and grandpapa's. Now it is too short."

"It is very pretty. Has it been very long since you went to your grandparents'?"

"No. I went to visit right before you arrived. *Abba* usually takes me for the holy days and sometimes for Shabbat. Grandmama always has lots of food. Mostly they visit me here, though."

"Perhaps if you are feeling a little stronger, he can take you again soon."

Rebecca's eyes lit up. "And we could put on the puppet show for them!"

"Yes, that is an idea. You could write up some invitations, just as your papa has done for his dinner party." Althea put a finger to her mouth. "I wonder where we can find a puppet theater?"

"Perhaps in my old nursery. That's where I used to sleep, until I got ill then *Abba* decided to move me down here. This used to be his bedroom, you know. And Mama used to sleep where you are now sleeping. But that was long ago. I don't remember that time."

"I see." So she and her charge were occupying the master suite. She had wondered at the size and splendor of the rooms and the presence of dressing rooms.

She returned to the dressing room and brought back some ribbons and a dress that looked absurdly small. "There seem to be clothes in here that go back to when you were an infant. I wonder if someone would mind if we cut this one up for the puppets."

"Oh, I'm sure no one would mind. I shall ask *Abba* tonight."

"Who goes over your wardrobe?"

Rebecca shrugged. "I don't know. Mrs. Coates, but she hasn't looked at my clothes in ages. The governess didn't do anything about clothes."

Althea considered. "I know some children who haven't even one good outfit of clothes."

"Really? Are they the ones at the mission?"

Althea sat back down by Rebecca's bed. "Yes, and many more that live around it."

Althea continued telling her about the children at the mission as she drew up some patterns for the queen puppet's outfit. They had made her out of an old stocking stuffed for a head, sewed to a piece of cloth for body and arms.

"Tommy used to steal fruit from the market." She spoke as she cut and sewed. "One night, he decided to break into the mission. He must have heard there were all kinds of things in it—food and books, even toys. Well, I hadn't been able to sleep that night, and I had come downstairs because I was going to fix myself a cup of tea. I heard the sound of shattering glass."

"Were you frightened?" Rebecca's gaze was riveted to Althea's face.

"A little, perhaps. I had known someone eventually would try to break in. You see, the house is in a part of London where there are many poor people."

"Is it like Mayfair?"

Althea shook her head. "No, not on the outside, at least. The houses are old and haven't been kept up. Many are boarded up because all the windows have long been broken. At night people shut themselves up because they are afraid of those around them."

"Why do you live there? Is it because you are poor, too?"

"No, dear. I have great riches." She smiled. "Like Esther."

Rebecca's eyes widened. "Are you a queen?"

Althea laughed. "No, though sometimes I feel like a princess. My riches are invisible most of the time. But even though you cannot see them, they are more precious than all the gold in the world. And so, like Esther who knew God had sent her to help her people, I, too, want to share my riches with those who need them."

"What are your riches like?"

Althea pursed her lips. "They bring life, for one thing. They bring freedom from fear. They bring joy."

"How did you get these riches?"

"By believing in God's goodness." Althea hesitated. "By believing God looked down from Heaven and saw all the poor people—even some people who seem to be rich, even people who live in palaces—and felt compassion on them because they didn't have any of these true riches. So, He decided to give them of these riches. He decided to send the very best of Himself to them, and if they received Him, they would receive these true riches."

Rebecca pulled her coverlet up, excited by the story. "Did it work? Did the people believe?"

"Some did, but others didn't. Some became so angry they killed the gift God sent."

"Oh," breathed Rebecca. "Then what happened?"

"Well, that was many hundreds of years ago. Since then, God has asked those who believe to share the riches with others who haven't heard. It's gone on from there. God sent me to that part of London, for example, to show these children and the grown-up folks around them how much He loves them and wants them to have these riches."

"Why did you come here, then? Do people here need these riches, too?"

Althea smiled, touching Rebecca's cheek. "People everywhere need them. I know God sent me here to meet you and let you know He loves you."

Rebecca's thin hand came up to Althea's. "I'm glad He sent you." She lay quietly for a little while. "Do you think Papa knows about these riches?"

"I don't know, dear. Perhaps he doesn't think he needs them." She added after a moment, "Sometimes people are afraid to believe in God."

"Why would they be?"

"I think they believe God might ask them for something, and they are afraid to give it."

"My grandmama is afraid of God."

"Is she?"

Rebecca nodded then smiled. "She's always saying, 'God forbid' and 'The evil eye spare me.' She puts things around the house and on the doors to ward off the evil eye. I always imagine God's big eyeball staring at me from the ceiling, looking to see who might be doing something wrong."

"God's Word tells us to 'fear God,' but I think the meaning is a little different from the one your grandmama has taken."

"How do you mean?"

Althea pondered how best to explain it. "Think of how you feel about your papa. You love him?"

Rebecca nodded.

"And you know he loves you?"

A more vigorous nod.

"You respect him?"

"Oh, yes."

"You respect him because you love him, isn't that so, and not the other way around? You don't love him because you respect him."

Rebecca thought about it. "You mean, I respect him because of my love for him, and not that my love comes because I respect him?"

"Exactly. Now, do you fear your papa?"

Rebecca giggled. "No, I'm not afraid of him!"

"Have you ever seen him angry?"

Rebecca screwed up her face. "I don't remember. Oh, yes, once. I was little and I went down to the library and heard him talking to the footman. I had opened the door and could hear him. He was angry at the footman, but I don't know about what."

"Was he shouting at him?"

"No, he wasn't shouting, but I could tell by his voice that he wasn't being very nice to him."

Althea could imagine the cutting remarks. "Were you afraid of your father then?"

"I wasn't afraid of him for my sake but for the footman's. I remember thinking I would never want him to talk to me like that."

"So, in that sense you fear your father. You know he is capable of being angry, but you wouldn't want that anger turned toward you."

Rebecca nodded. "That's right. Is that how it is with God?"

"Yes. He is our Heavenly Father. Because we love Him, we don't want to anger Him. But it's not because we are afraid of Him. It is because we love Him so much."

"Oh," Rebecca breathed in wonder.

Althea plumped the girl's pillow and smoothed her coverlet. "Why don't you take a little nap? We can continue with our puppets later." At the girl's nod, Althea stepped away, picking up the scraps. She stood a moment, watching her charge. *Oh, Lord,* she prayed, *heal her, let her laugh and run and jump like those children at the mission.*

* * *

The following week passed quickly with puppets in the mornings and dinner party preparations in the afternoons. Althea dug up a puppet theater in the nursery and had it brought down to Rebecca's bedroom. One afternoon after luncheon, they put on a performance for Simon.

Mrs. Coates began to thaw towards Althea as she perceived Althea's knowledge in matters of etiquette. She yielded more and more of the preparations to Althea's management. Under Althea's gentle persuasion a thorough housecleaning was begun. Curtains and carpets that hadn't been moved in years were taken out and shaken, floors mopped and waxed, dust covers removed from unused rooms. With Mrs. Coates as an intermediary between herself and Cook, Althea made sure orders for food were placed in time for the event.

Althea knew a dinner party could make or break a host, and the quality of the table was crucial. She surmised from the talk of the servants that this was Simon's first foray into the world of entertaining. She imagined that with his star rising in Parliament it was important for him to mingle in society. Althea threw herself into the preparations, vowing to do her best to make the party a success.

She didn't know what to do about her own attendance, and the day was drawing near. She had no evening clothes, and decided finally to use her brown merino. She made sure it was clean and reserved for that evening. She had mentioned the dinner party to her brother on one of his quick visits during a trip to London. He didn't share her misgivings about attending, but rather applauded Simon for insisting upon it.

On the afternoon of the dinner party, Althea finally escaped for a walk in Hyde Park. It had been several afternoons since she had been able to spare the time. The raw March wind felt refreshing against her face. She walked briskly along the Serpentine for an hour, then made her way back home. The house was still when she entered. She noted with satisfaction the gleaming entrance and the smell of beeswax. A vase of fresh orchids had been placed on a side table. She removed her cloak and prepared to ascend the staircase. Then she hesitated, her cloak over her arm.

Bracing herself, telling herself she had nothing to fear, she decided to go down to the servants' quarters and check for herself that preparations were fully under way in the kitchen. Mrs. Coates had assured her that Cook had everything under control, but Althea hadn't yet seen for herself.

She pushed open the door, and a group of servants stopped what they were doing and turned to look at her. They were all grouped around the long table where they usually dined. Something didn't seem right. The only one sitting was Mrs. Bentwood, who wasn't so much sitting as slumped over the table.

"What is the matter?" Althea ventured farther into the servants' domain. "Is anything wrong with Cook?"

Giles coughed. "It seems she has fallen asleep."

"Asleep?" Althea reached the cook and leaned over her, touching her on the arm. Her head did not lie cushioned on her arms, but rested sideways on the table itself. Deep, rough breathing emanated from her nostrils. Her lips parted slightly and Althea received the full force of her breath at close range.

She knew that smell. "Why, she's inebriated!"

Chapter Five

Althea looked up in indignation at Giles, then at Mrs. Coates, then at each of the younger maidservants and footmen in turn. They all stared back at her, their looks scared.

"How long has she been this way?"

Again Giles coughed, his demeanor no longer dour. "It's hard to say, miss. She seemed all right this morning. She was making all her preparations. Then she served us some soup at noon. After that...well, I don't know...I don't remember seeing her much after that. I was down in the wine cellar for a while, then upstairs inspecting the rooms."

Althea turned to Mrs. Coates.

"He's right, miss. It was after lunch we lost track of 'er."

Althea looked at the serving girls.

One bobbed a quick curtsy. "I work with Mrs. Bentwood, miss." She motioned to another girl in a dingy gray apron. "Me and Martha. She's scullery maid."

"Weren't you assisting Cook with this evening's preparations?"

They both nodded their heads vigorously. "Oh, yes, miss. But she put us to work first, scrubbing the pots and dishes from our dinner, then told us to start on the vegetables." She motioned to the other end of the long table littered with vegetables and parings.

Again Giles gave a discreet cough. "If you please, miss."

Althea turned questioning eyes to him.

"I...that is...we all know Mrs. Bentwood likes to take a nip now and then. Oh, nothing more than that. She's never shirked on her work. But she's not opposed to a little swig in her tea."

"I see." Yes, the explanation of all those overcooked and frequently cold dinners became clear. "This is more than a little nip, however."

"Yes, indeed. You are most correct, miss. I found this in the cellar." Giles held up an empty bottle.

Althea took the bottle from him and brought it to her nostrils. She didn't need the smell of stale rum to tell her what it was. Many such a bottle lay strewn in the streets of the East End on a foggy dawn.

"Where did she get this?"

"We don't know, miss. She must have had her own supply. I keep the wine cellar keys with me at all times." Giles tapped the key ring at his waistcoat.

Althea put her hands on her hips and looked around. "There is nothing to be done about Mrs. Bentwood now. How are the preparations for the meal coming?"

"Oh, Miss Breton, there's not nearly enough done," said Mrs. Coates, ringing her hands. "Without Cook, none o' us knows enough about cooking to carry on."

Althea turned to the first kitchen maid. "Show me what she has done." The girl showed her around the room then took her into the kitchen and pantry. Althea found the cook's scrawled menu and a few written recipes she had left beside it.

Back at the dining table, she addressed the assembled servants. "It is now three o'clock. We have between four and five hours to prepare a dinner for the sixteen people who will assemble upstairs. It is not much time for a dinner of this many covers. I'm going to need the help and cooperation of each one of you." She looked at each face in turn. "Can I count on all of you?"

"But surely, miss, you can't... We can't prepare such a meal," protested a chorus of voices.

"We not only can, but will. Mr. Aguilar expects a dinner to be served by eight o'clock this evening." She gave them a smile of reassurance. "I believe enough preparations are under way. I have sufficient experience in a large kitchen to guide me somewhat. I'm relying on your collective know-how to do the rest.

"Now, if someone would be so good as to hand me an apron, we shall begin." Althea began to roll up her sleeves. "Oh, yes, thank you." She took the large apron the kitchen maid had brought her. "What is your name, please?"

"Daisy, miss."

"Very well, Daisy. You stick by me." She glanced at Giles, who was still looking at her, his mouth slack. "Giles, could you and Harry be so kind as to take Mrs. Bentwood to her room? Or perhaps to your sitting room down here, Mrs. Coates?"

"Yes, miss, right away." Apparently relieved at being dismissed from the coming activity of the kitchen, the butler quickly signaled to one of the footmen to help him.

"When you come back, we can go over your wine selections," she told him.

"Yes, miss."

"Now, the first thing is to get the roasts in the oven," Althea told the remaining staff. "Daisy and I will see to those. Let's see, there's the pheasant and venison, which thankfully have already been dressed. Now, Mrs. Coates, if you would be so good as to don an apron and oversee the vegetables at this table.

"Oh!" Althea slapped her forehead. "Rebecca! I forgot about Rebecca!"

"That's all right, miss." A young parlor maid spoke up shyly. "I can take her tray up and sit with her."

"Oh, would you? That would be wonderful. Tell her I'll be in to see her later. Perhaps you could read to her?"

The woman blushed and began twisting her hand in her apron. "I'd like to, miss, only...only I can't."

It took Althea a few seconds to catch her meaning. "You can't read—is that what you are trying to tell me?"

She nodded, her eyes downcast.

"Well, look at a picture book with her. Sometimes she feels like reading, and you can have her read to you. If not, you can make up the story as you go along, with the pictures. Do you think you can do that?" She gave her an encouraging smile.

The girl nodded, her eyes hopeful.

"Martha—" Althea turned to the scullery maid "—you start setting up a kettle to boil water for the lobster. I may dispense with the bisque and simply serve the meat on a bed of greens. All right, to work...."

Nearly five hours later Althea took her damp handkerchief from her pocket and wiped the perspiration from her forehead. Her dress clung to her body; the only thing keeping her from collapsing over the suffocating coal stove was the knowledge that the clock was ticking without mercy. Every second counted.

She kept her eye on the various pots simmering before her, all the while stirring the sauce in front of her. She had concocted what she could from the cook's receipes. Other dishes she had improvised from all her girlhood years spent in the kitchen with her own family's cook, who had been more of a mother to her than anyone. She also drew on her experience in recent years from her work at the mission's kitchen. She knew what feeding a multitude entailed.

"How does this look, miss?"

Althea glanced at the tray Martha held out to her. She had filled the pastry cups with the creamy fricassee. "Very good. We shall have to keep them warm until they are ready to be served. Place them here." She indicated a spot with the tip of her wooden spoon, then went back to stirring.

"Miss, we've finished cutting the fruit into the crystal bowl."

"Very good, keep the bowl on ice. How is the syllabub?"

"All set. We're also keeping it cold."

"Miss Breton." Mrs. Coates came up to her with a look of concern. "Shouldn't you be getting upstairs to dress? It's going on eight. The guests are all here."

Althea looked at the watch pinned to her dress. "Oh, so it is. Let me just put the shrimp into this sauce and check on the fish." She removed the sauce from the stove, then opened the oven door and looked at the flat white fillets baking in butter. She tested one. "Yes, these are ready."

While Mrs. Coates took the pan out of the oven, Althea pricked the pheasant with a long fork. She basted it and the venison one last time.

"Daisy, come here and stir the shrimp carefully into this sauce. Giles, you will be able to oversee carving the pheasant and venison?"

"Yes, miss." Giles was sharpening the long carving knife with a whetstone.

"How does the table look upstairs?"

"All is in order. Sixteen places, with their place cards."

"And the sideboard?"

"All is in place."

"The wines?"

"Uncorked."

Althea walked to each servant in turn and gave last-minute instructions.

"Oh, thank you, Mrs. Coates," she said, taking a glass of lemonade from her. "That tastes wonderful."

"Your cheeks look so flushed. That stove is awfully hot."

"Yes, it certainly is. I begin to see why Cook might take to drink."

"Oh, no, miss. She's a disgrace. We shall speak to her in the morning, you can be sure."

"How is she? Have you looked in on her?"

"Snoring like to wake the dead."

Althea drained her glass, then proceeded up to her room. As soon as she had closed the door, she began stripping off her clothes. They were drenched. As she was walking to her basin, a knock sounded on her door.

"Yes, who is it?"

"It's Dot, miss, the parlor maid."

Althea opened her door a crack then, when she saw it was the young woman who had sat with Rebecca, bade her enter. "How is Rebecca?"

The young woman smiled. "Oh, she's fine. Dropped off to sleep while I was still talking, poor lamb. We had a grand time imagining the dinner party tonight."

"I was going to stop in as soon as I took off these wet things."

"I heard you come in. Would you like me to help you dress?"

Althea was going to refuse help, then thought about how late she was. "Thank you. Please come in. I must hurry. I should have been down by half-past seven. Could you help me undo these buttons?"

"Certainly, miss." Dot came toward her. "Oh, miss, is this what you are going to wear? It's beautiful!"

"What?" Althea turned. "Oh—" She hadn't noticed the dress draped across her bed. "My, who put this here?" She moved to the bed and picked up the garment. It was a beautiful evening gown of jade-green gauze over a white silk underskirt. Matching green kid slippers sat on the floor beside the bed. Alongside the dress were laid underclothes, gloves, hair ribbons, even a soft white cashmere shawl. As she picked up the dress, a note fluttered to the ground. Dot immediately bent to retrieve it.

Althea took it from her and unfolded it.

Dearest Althy, I heard you were attending a fashionable dinner party. Please accept this dress with my compliments. I have grown much too large for it, and I know it will suit you admiringly. Enjoy it on my behalf, as my dinner party engagements are few and far between at this juncture!

It was signed *Gillian,* her sister-in-law. Althea smiled despite herself. How like Tertius's wife. She looked at the maid. "I must hurry. Let me wash. I can't wear this garment in my present state." She walked to the washstand and began sponging off her skin. The maid handed her the fresh underclothes and petticoats.

"Oh, we must hurry!" It was past eight. She hoped Simon had not missed her. The maid brushed out her hair then dressed it for her. Althea turned toward the door without even glancing in the mirror. Instead she turned to Dot. "How do I look?" she asked quickly, not sure if she wanted to hear the reply. She felt a little naked with her upper arms and throat exposed.

"You look beautiful." The maid hesitated. "Haven't you no jewels, miss?"

Althea's gloved hand went to her neck. "Does it look too bare?"

"It looks very pretty, miss, but isn't it usual to have a few jewels?"

Althea nodded. She went over to her dressing table and opened a box. "I'll wear these," she said, taking out the only jewelry she possessed, a strand of pearls.

Dot helped her with the clasp. "They're just the thing," she said in approval, giving her one last looking over.

"My father gave them to me at my coming out."

"They're beautiful."

"Well, I had better go down." She squared her shoulders, feeling as if she were about to face a firing squad.

She bolstered her courage with scripture, which she recited as she descended the stairs.

By the time Althea reached the double doors leading to the main salon, her heart felt as if it were pounding in her throat. She gave her hair a pat with both hands, having no idea what it looked like. "'Not my will, but Thine,'" she murmured under her breath, wanting to run as Elijah had when he fled from Queen Jezebel.

The first thing that greeted her when she opened the doors was the noise. After weeks in the quiet household, Althea was no longer used to crowds. A buzz of voices greeted her. The light from the chandeliers and wall sconces gave the room a bright glow. Several gentlemen stood about in groups, their dark-colored evening jackets contrasting with the brighter gowns of the ladies. Although her reasoning told her there were not more than fifteen or sixteen people in the room, certainly not more than twenty, her senses felt an assault of noise, heat and light.

Giles spotted her over the crowd of heads and came toward her. His gaunt, wrinkled face suddenly seemed the friendliest one in the world.

"Very good, miss, that you're here. Mr. Aguilar told me to inform him as soon as you arrived."

"Thank you, Giles." Already she felt at a disadvantage, hoping she had not held things up through her tardiness. She ventured a few more steps into the room, wishing there was a quiet corner where she could fade into the background. As her breathing steadied, she noticed one or two gentlemen turn to look at her. She kept walking without meeting anyone's eyes directly, but smiling in the general direction of everyone. Before she could reach a wall of the room, Simon came up to her.

"What kept you so long? Dinner's long overdue!" His tone was a sharp whisper as his dark eyes frowned at her behind their spectacles. Not waiting for her answer, he turned to Giles, giving him the signal to announce the meal.

The couples began pairing up. Althea had no idea what the gentleman she had assigned herself looked like, so she stood waiting. All she knew about him was that he worked with Simon as a clerk of some sort.

A young man approached her and gave a discreet cough. "Miss Breton?"

She gave him a smile. "Yes, Mr.——" Oh, no, she could not recall his name.

"Charles Covington, at your service," he said, offering her a black-sleeved arm.

"Thank you." She made her way with him to the end of the line as the party proceeded to the dining room. Althea realized Simon had only been waiting for her for the dinner to begin. No wonder he had been annoyed. She could only hope the extra time had given the kitchen staff down below a chance to see to any final preparations. Wondering how things would proceed, knowing she could no longer do anything to assist them, she entered the dining room with the feeling that everything was out of her hands now.

Had Daisy remembered to stir the sauces and keep them warm until the proper time? Would Mrs. Coates and the kitchen maids remember the correct order of the courses? Peering around the table, Althea tried to discern whether the hot plates had been lit. The table did look beautiful, she had to admit, as Mr. Covington tucked her into her chair. The plate glistened. The crystal sparkled. Fresh flowers added a touch of color against the white damask cloth and china.

She watched the footmen. Giles stood back, with a nod here and a nod there, directing them in bringing in the first cover. Althea removed her napkin and spread it upon her lap as the footmen ladled out the consommé. Bowing her head, she said a short prayer of thanks. Looking up, she realized that her companion was holding out a covered basket of rolls to her.

"Oh, thank you," she said, taking one automatically. The conversation drowned out the other noises while the guests were being served, but once the footmen finished their task, the volume descended as everyone brought his attention to the food before him.

Now was the moment of truth, thought Althea as she took a spoonful of soup. It tasted like absolutely nothing to her. She put down her spoon and glanced around the table trying to discover the reaction in the others. Everyone seemed to be enjoying the soup. She mentally went down the list Mrs. Coates and she had gone over a dozen times, able now to fit names to faces.

Simon sat at the head of the table, his face looking relaxed, she noted with relief, as he spoke to his immediate dinner companions. Althea's gaze drifted to his right, where she had been forced to usurp Lord Stanton-Lewis's place for that of the Duke of Belmont, the highest ranking of the dinner guests. Her grace, the duke's wife, sat on Simon's left.

On the duke's right sat Lady Stanton-Lewis. A flash of recognition went through Althea. She now distinctly recognized Lady Stanton-Lewis. Althea had been seventeen and eighteen, respectively, during her two London Seasons. Lady Stanton-Lewis had been only a few years older, recently married and becoming a leader in the fashionable world. The shy, young Althea had envied her wit and beauty in a world where those qualities were highly esteemed.

Despite the duke between them, Lady Stanton-Lewis and Simon seemed to be having a lively discussion at the head of the table. Something Simon said caused Lady Stanton-Lewis to answer in a laughing retort. The duke and duchess joined in the laughter.

Althea had no fear that Lady Stanton-Lewis would recognize her that evening. The last time Althea had appeared in London society was eight years ago. She didn't remember ever having Lady Stanton-Lewis address a word to her; she doubted Lady Stanton-Lewis had known who Althea was back then, unless someone had pointed out her family connections. The two had been worlds apart then—Althea one of the dozens of young ladies on the Marriage Mart—someone's ward, at that—while Lady Stanton-Lewis was a seasoned young matron. She had made a respectable if not brilliant marriage to a baron. Althea calculated Lady Stanton-Lewis had been in her mid-twenties then, so she must be just over thirty now.

Althea's gaze roved down the table. The rest of the guests were untitled, although most of noble lineage: a couple of notorious dandies, a cabinet member and his wife, a few other members of the House of Commons with their wives, a prominent poet and some lesser individuals. Althea sat near the end, between the young Mr. Covington and an older white-whiskered gentleman in uniform. Colonel Ballyworth, she remembered, was his name.

Just as their glances met, she saw his mouth move, but she couldn't hear his words above the clatter as the footmen began removing the soup bowls and all the dishes and silverware around and under them, whether used or not. She could only smile at him while waiting for the noise to subside again.

A new set of plates was set before the guests and the next cover brought in. Althea looked and saw with satisfaction that the two kinds of fish arrived with their accompanying sauces and vegetables. Thus far, everything was going according to schedule.

"I beg your pardon, Colonel Ballyworth," she said to the gentleman who had addressed her earlier. "I didn't hear what you said a moment ago."

"Quite all right, m'dear." He took a hearty bite of sole. "I was just inquiring if you weren't the Marquess of Caulfield's ward?"

She smiled in surprise. "Yes, I am. Do you know Lord Caulfield?"

"Oh, my, yes. Since we were boys. How is Caulfield? He doesn't come up to London much anymore, does he?"

"No. He prefers the quiet country life in Hertfordshire."

Colonel Ballyworth chuckled. "He must have changed a lot since I last saw him. He was one of the leading rakes in his day."

"He has…mellowed somewhat since then, I believe. Now that he is awaiting the arrival of his first grandchild, he doesn't like to be away from Pembroke Park."

"Oh, no, I should think not." Colonel Ballyworth took a forkful of potatoes before turning to her once again. "And how are you, m'dear? I recall you during your London Season."

Her eyes widened. "You do?"

He chuckled at her amazement. "Quiet little thing, you were. Didn't think anyone noticed you, did you."

"That was quite some time ago. I'm certainly flattered you remember me."

"Oh, I never forget a face. Can't always come up with the right name, but never forget a face. Must say you look much prettier now than you did then."

She blushed. "I—I thank you."

"Oh, I'm not saying that you weren't an attractive thing then. Excuse my saying so, but at my age, you earn the right to speak your mind, and I always like a pretty face. You were so pale and timid back then that I guess a body wouldn't notice you much, sitting at the back of the room. But, my dear, when you walked into the room tonight, I saw more than one gentleman stand at attention."

She said nothing, but her glance strayed back down the length of the table. Had her employer noticed that she wore something other than her "gray governess garb"? She doubted it, watching his absorption with his immediate dinner companions.

The colonel's voice cut into her thoughts. "Excuse my asking, but what's your connection to Aguilar?"

She did not hesitate. "I am nurse—or perhaps I should say governess—" she remembered her correct title "—to his young daughter, Rebecca."

"Nurse-governess, eh?" He turned back to his plate and took a last bite of fish. "My, that was excellent. Not every cook knows how to prepare sole. I must send her my compliments."

Althea restrained a smile.

"Nurse-governess, eh?" he repeated. "I heard his little girl was ailing. What a shame." He shook his head, then took a sip of wine. "So, you were forced to seek employment. Pity you never married. Didn't Caulfield settle anything on you? Never knew him to be niggardly."

She shook her head. "My decision to enter my present employment did not have to do with my financial state. Lord Caulfield has always been most generous to me."

He looked more puzzled than ever. "I can't understand why some young gent didn't grab you up then. What's got into them nowadays? No starch in 'em. It's all in their shirt points, I guess. Now, in my day—"

Althea laughed out loud. "Colonel Ballyworth, please, I'm sure the fault was not in the young gentlemen who were presented to me. As you pointed out, I was a quiet thing who preferred sitting in the background."

The colonel eyed her shrewdly from under his bushy brows. "You look happy enough tonight. Don't tell me you're one of those bluestocking types that despises men?"

She shook her head, restraining laughter. "Oh, no, not at all. Don't forget I grew up with two bro—with Lord Caulfield's two sons."

"Pity about the heir...riding accident and all." Colonel Ballyworth tut-tutted before taking another sip from his glass. "How's the younger one turning out? I've heard good things about him, steadier head on his shoulders than he used to have. No one ever thought he could step into his brother's shoes..." The colonel frowned, looking at the pale amber liquid in his glass. "Heard some rumor of his getting pious—probably just some gossip."

Althea smiled. "I fear it is no gossip. Lord Skylar is a devout Christian."

Ballyworth just shook his head and sat back to let the footman clear his plate.

He dug into his next course with gusto.

Althea pushed her food around with her fork. She felt no appetite, the events leading up to the dinner still too fresh in her mind. She wondered whether the meats were cooked to a turn or had sat in the oven too long.

If the colonel were any indication, the former was the case. After a few hearty mouthfuls of pheasant and preserves, he took a swallow of the deep red burgundy the footman had poured into a clean glass. "If Lord Caulfield is as generous as you say, what are you doing working as a governess?"

"I chose to come here because Mr. Aguilar's daughter needed me. My— That is, Lord Skylar told me about Mr. Aguilar's little girl. Lord Skylar and Mr. Aguilar were close friends at school."

Colonel Ballyworth clearly couldn't puzzle it all out. He renewed his attack on his meat for another few moments.

He sat back, once again allowing the footman to remove his plate and refill his glass. He took a large swallow of wine, then wiped his mouth with the white napkin at this throat. "Now, tell me, young lady, how the ward of Lord Caulfield should end up as a nurse-governess. I may be an old codger, but I didn't earn these medals by being dense. I know Caulfield would never see a ward of his forced to seek employment."

"You are correct. If his lordship had his way, I'd be there with him at Pembroke Park."

"So, why are you not?"

"I had a different call on my life."

"Call, huh?" he grunted. "What was that?"

"To minister to the sick and needy, the orphan and the widow." Before he could draw the wrong conclusions, she added, "Prior to coming here, I worked at a Methodist mission in Whitechapel. We run an orphanage, feed the hungry, teach the illiterate and preach the gospel of Jesus Christ."

Forgetting his food momentarily, he eyed her. "So, it is true about Lord Skylar getting religious. Has the whole family gone Methodist?"

She laughed. "No, sir. I am the only one, though Lord Skylar has been most generous in his support of the mission."

"What's that about Methodism?" Mrs. Ballyworth addressed her husband from across the table.

"I'm inquiring about a certain charitable work in the city."

"Not Methodist, I trust." The turbaned lady gave a shudder, setting her diamond earrings to shaking.

"As a matter of fact, it is a Methodist charity," answered Althea.

The woman looked at her sharply, as if noticing her for the first time. Althea could feel herself redden. She gave a quick glance toward the opposite end of the table, fearing her employer's displeasure. She did not want to be the recipient of sharp words from him a second time that evening.

She caught Simon's glance and looked quickly away, hoping Lady Stanton-Lewis would draw his attention as she had been doing throughout the dinner.

Meanwhile the colonel's wife had begun a litany against the Methodist movement, her voice growing louder and louder. "...blasphemous...uneducated...drawing away the ignorant masses from the true Church..." Her rouge paled before the blood rising in her cheeks.

Unperturbed by his wife, who seemed to be addressing herself to the company at large, the colonel turned back to Althea and asked quietly, "How do you come to be a Methodist?"

"I came to know the Lord at a Methodist meeting." She looked down at the edge of the table, trying to sum up the turning point in her life in a few simple words. "I had grown up in the Church of England but had found no solace there. It had no bearing upon my life." She met the colonel's sharp gray eyes. "In one night, I felt the power of God and His word, and my life has not been the same since."

"When did you have this experience?"

"Almost eight years ago."

"And you left Caulfield's household to come to this mission?"

"Not immediately." Now came the difficult part, since she did not want to criticize her family in any way. "I spent another year in our local parish church, but it became increasingly difficult. There was much suspicion and enmity towards the Methodists. I...I finally had to leave. I had an invitation to come to London. I lived with a Methodist pastor and his wife and studied under them. In time the Lord led us to the East End where we began to work with the people." She smiled. "We are not too far from one of Wesley's original chapels up in Spitalfields. But we are closer to the Docks, where we bring the message of the gospel." She fell silent again as the footmen cleared away the dishes and laid a fresh cover.

"I'll wager you've seen some need there."

She looked at him. "Yes."

"You say a lot with that one word."

"The people of the East End live with very little hope. The men fall into the clutches of the bottle and the moneylender. The women bear children out of wedlock and haven't the means to clothe or feed those children afterward. My heart breaks at the sight of so many hungry, barefoot urchins, losing their innocence before they're yet five or six.

"Although our work is only a drop in what seems like an ocean of poverty, we cannot stop. If we can save any life, we feel that the time and work has been well worth it."

"You say this mission is in Whitechapel?" He looked at her keenly. "I'd like to visit your mission sometime."

Althea turned to him eagerly. "Would you? That would be wonderful—"

Suddenly Mrs. Ballyworth's voice, which had been heard across the table all the while, rose considerably. "Young lady, I don't know what your name is, or how you come to be here, but I will not tolerate this heretical talk. I will not permit it in my presence."

The entire table fell silent.

Chapter Six

Althea looked at each face frozen in shock, staring at her. Finally her gaze came to rest on Simon. He glanced from Mrs. Ballyworth to her then calmly took a sip of his wine.

"That is unfortunate, Mrs. Ballyworth, as I hold with the free exchange of ideas. If I didn't I wouldn't be able to tolerate the atmosphere in the House of Commons."

Laughter greeted his remark, and the guests went back to their conversations. Althea caught Mrs. Ballyworth's disgruntled comment to her dinner companion.

"What would you expect from a Jew?"

"You must pardon Mrs. Ballyworth," the colonel said. "She has very decided views on things."

"Yes." She took a careful bite of cauliflower, realizing how closely her view of Jews had coincided with Mrs. Ballyworth's not too long ago.

The young gentleman on her other side, Mr. Covington, asked her a question about the mission, and Althea turned to him. Her glance crossed Simon's once again, and she saw him regard her over the rim of his glass. She wondered whether he would speak to her later about this unfortunate incident with Mrs. Ballyworth.

Dinner was over at long last, and the women rose to leave the men to their port. Althea followed them from the room.

When they entered the drawing room, Giles approached Althea to ask permission to bring up the tea. She nodded approval. She waited in the background, seeing that most of the ladies took seats around the fire. Beginning to feel the fatigue of a long and trying day, Althea hoped the next hour would pass quickly with the serving of the tea. She would make herself useful in that way, as Simon had suggested. She certainly did not expect any of these women to find her at all worthy of conversation, especially after that outbreak in the dining room.

Althea was ready when the footmen entered, followed by Giles. As Harry set the tea tray on the table before the fireplace, Althea approached.

Just as she reached the area, Lady Stanton-Lewis swept in front of her, cutting her off from the footmen.

"I shall do the honors," she informed the men with a gracious smile. She seated herself in the center of the sofa, arranging her skirts around her.

Althea was left with nothing to do but step back as gracefully as she could, hoping no one had noticed. Giles gave her a questioning look, having known by previous arrangement that she was to serve the tea. She gave a short shake of her head and a brief smile.

She found a chair by a window and sat down. All the women had found companions and were chatting comfortably. Lady Stanton-Lewis poured tea, handing the cups to the footmen, who in turn brought them to each guest. Althea wondered what she would do for the next hour. She knew the men would take at least a half hour over their port. She glanced at her watch. Eleven o'clock. How she longed for her bed. She adjusted the shawl around her shoulders, feeling the slight chill at that farther end of the room. Then she clasped her hands on her lap, prepared to sit it out.

"Excuse me, miss." Startled, she looked up to find Harry at her elbow, holding out a cup and saucer to her.

"Oh, thank you." Suddenly, stupidly, she had the urge to cry. She took the cup and saucer from him, the cup clattering ominously against the saucer. She gripped them both firmly in her hands and set them carefully in her lap. "Harry——"

He smiled attentively. "Yes, miss?"

"Please send my compliments down to the staff. Tell them...tell them I'm very proud of each and every one of them."

His smile widened. "We pulled it off, didn't we."

She nodded, returning his smile.

She took a sip of tea, welcoming its warmth. She glanced at the ormolu clock over the mantelpiece, comparing it to her own timepiece. They were the same. Only two minutes had passed since her previous glance. She took another sip of tea. She wished she'd brought her sewing. She had not wanted to be here tonight; she had known it would be bad, but not quite this bad. Not one of these women talked to her; they didn't even look at her. Like a battlement, they were seated around the tea table in a semicircle, giving the intruder no chance to penetrate their midst.

Was it because of her religion? Were they reacting as the servants had? Or was it worse? Did they remember her from her first entry into society, and now wondered what she was doing working as a governess? Whatever the reasons, she felt as out of place now as she had then.

Her gloved hands touched the gauzy overlay of her sister-in-law's evening dress. What had looked so attractive at the start of the evening now seemed ludicrous. Her vanity had gotten the better of her common sense. She should be sitting here in her gray— what had Mr. Aguilar called it?—governess garb. It would certainly fit her role among these women more appropriately. This dress took her back ages ago to her first London Season.

Her guardian had purchased for her an entire wardrobe for the occasion. The most expensive silks and velvets, a whole ensemble of morning gowns, riding outfits, tea gowns, evening dresses, with matching shoes and bonnets, shawls and capes, as if he were trying to make up for a decade of paternal neglect.

But it had all ended before it had ever begun. In one evening, her world had been turned topsy-turvy, as Lord Caulfield, her guardian up until then, revealed to her that in truth he was her father. All those years since her infancy, when she'd been raised as his ward, she had been his offspring, the result of an entanglement of his on the Continent.

When she had asked why he'd picked the moment of her coming out to reveal the truth, she had discovered that although his timing might leave something to be desired, his motives were good. He'd told her he wanted to encourage her at the start of her Season in London. To know that she was a true Caulfield and not some ignominious ward of obscure French parentage should give her cause to hold her head tall among the ton.

It had had the reverse effect upon Althea. In a world where family name reigned supreme, suddenly Althea's foggy if respectable origins were delineated with damning clarity. Who would welcome the illegitimate child of Lord Caulfield, when he himself was not ready to acknowledge the connection publicly? The marquess might be pardoned his indiscretion—a man of his station and wealth could pretty much get away with anything. But who was she? On her mother's side, she was nothing—no, worse than nothing—the daughter of a French opera singer, she discovered when she finally managed to extract the whole sordid tale from her father.

Thus, Althea's first Season had gone from high expectation to horrible nightmare, as she struggled to make herself as inconspicuous as possible. She had sat it out on the edges of ballrooms and drawing rooms, saying as little as possible, waiting for some gossip to discover her secret, feeling a fraud every time she was presented as Lord Caulfield's ward, but too scared to deny it, and too afraid that by one careless word or gesture she would betray her less than noble origins.

For two Seasons she had survived that way, saying little, remaining obscure and unnoticed. Much as tonight, she could have been part of the wallpaper for all the notice she had garnered.

Until this evening, she had left all that behind. Why had the Lord brought her back to this arena where she didn't belong?

Althea glanced at the women before her. Didn't she belong? The still small voice of God's spirit asked her. Weren't they all the same as she had been? Sinners in need of redemption? The women gathered in the drawing room were treated differently and treated others differently merely because of their birth and fortune. Hadn't the Lord given Althea a treasure infinitely more lasting and more precious—that of His everlasting salvation? She might be illegitimate, but hadn't the Lord purchased an eternal legitimacy for her?

Althea flinched from the bombardment of questions. She closed her eyes and repented of her old fears of not belonging. She could feel her Savior's love enveloping her as she bowed her head, and she felt ashamed for letting her past overwhelm her for an instant. It was dead and buried.

A moment later, strengthened and reassured, she began looking at the women. Each was involved in an animated conversation. Some took out needlework, others snapped open fans, all the while talking and sipping tea.

Each woman seemed to have found her niche with one or two others, chatting comfortably and naturally, embroidery hoops mere accoutrements to the more essential business of verbal communication. What could each one be saying? Althea was too removed to catch more than a word or two; mostly she watched their lips moving. She closed her eyes briefly, letting the ebb and flow of female voices wash over and around her, never stopping, but punctuated by the *clink* of silver spoons against china like the cries of far-off gulls over the never silent sea.

In the midst of this reverie she felt the voice of the Lord coming up from deep in her heart, telling her to pray for each of the ladies. Slowly she reopened her eyes, focusing on the first one to cross her line of vision. The woman was an attractive, dark-haired lady, no longer so young, perhaps in her forties, but well preserved and elegantly attired in a white satin brocaded with gold. Althea began praying for her, not knowing anything about her; she prayed that the Lord would make His Son real to her. As she prayed a deep sadness filled her, and she sensed that the Lord was showing her something about this woman. The woman was looking at her companion and nodding from time to time in agreement, nothing externally suggesting sadness, yet the feeling persisted in Althea. She continued praying, her silent prayer becoming more fervent, and she wished she were in the privacy of her room to pour out her heart to God.

When she sensed the prayer was over, Althea's gaze passed over the women again. This time the Lord's spirit prompted her to pray for a younger woman. This one had a livelier demeanor and was leading in the conversation. Here Althea began to sense fear. Again, nothing in her countenance demonstrated it, but Althea felt the Lord's spirit reveal it to her. She remembered seeing the lady's husband at the dinner table—a young, handsome man. Althea sensed in her spirit that the fear had something to do with him. Perhaps it was a fear of losing him, and little did she realize that the more she tried to engage him, the more he eluded her. Althea felt a deep compassion well up in her, and prayed for guidance for the woman.

Oh, Lord, may she find You, and know that secret place with You, where she feels the security of Your love; where she needn't fear growing old, losing her attraction to her husband; where she will grow more beautiful, more radiant in Your love, knowing Your grace, becoming like the virtuous woman, whose price is far above rubies, whose husband trusts in her, so that he shall have no need of spoil.

Althea continued praying for her until she felt God's peace. Then she moved on to another woman. She prayed for each of the seven women gathered there, each time receiving a brief glimpse of something hidden from the natural eye. She ended with Lady Stanton-Lewis presiding at the tea table. The woman looked as beautiful as when Althea had seen her for the first time, ten years ago. Golden, fashionably short curls framed her face, silver leaves set like a victor's crown above them. Her skin was flawless, all cream and rose, her dress emerald satin slashed with silver. The neckline plunged from her shoulders to the point of the gown's high waist. Outwardly she was a vision of perfection.

Yet when Althea began to pray for her, she sensed danger and evil. She didn't know whether it emanated from the woman or went against her, but she felt a warning.

Lord, whatever it is, please prevent it. Let whoever is involved realize the danger in time, and seek Your protection. Let them know You as refuge and fortress, trusting in You to deliver them from the snare of the fowler and from the noisome pestilence.

She continued praying, sensing in the woman fear as well. This woman, for all her position in society, feared losing it to a rival. Althea realized she was continually on the lookout for any new rival to her place in society, and every word she spoke, every event she attended, was carefully calculated to assure her continued place of prominence. Althea wondered how tonight's dinner played in those schemes. She remembered Simon's request that he be seated beside Lady Stanton-Lewis, the only preference he had shown toward any of the guests. Althea knew the woman's husband was of an old, moneyed, Tory family. Perhaps Simon was looking for his influence and backing?

She remembered Simon's laughing countenance as he talked with Lady Stanton-Lewis. She had never seen him in company before and noted the different comportment from that of the man who sat and listened to his daughter or read children's stories to her. Gone, too, was the man who spoke impatiently to those under him. Tonight she had glimpsed the society man, and perhaps the politician as well. The biting wit was still present, but tonight he was among his equals and betters, who laughed at his jests and gave as good as they got. Althea could

Winter Is Past

now understand what her brother had told her of Simon's rise in Parliament. According to Tertius, no one was ever asleep during Simon's speeches. Though he'd started out as a young, obscure member on the backbench, he'd quickly caught the attention of the prime minister and other cabinet ministers through his brilliant, witty addresses. He'd even garnered the favor of the Prince Regent, who'd begun inviting him to Carlton House.

Althea's gaze swept around the room again. She felt drained and invigorated at the same time. For a few moments she had been privileged to understand what lay behind the mask each exquisitely dressed lady wore. She felt humbled, too, by God's grace in giving her this understanding. Not one of these women was immune to pain or fear—or worse, she thought, her glance straying once again to Lady Stanton-Lewis.

Worst of all was the fact that each lady was hopelessly lost. The fact came to Althea in blinding clarity. Each person under Simon's roof that evening was fighting a losing battle against hell and not knowing it. The Lord was bidding her to pray in the silent watches of the night for their salvation.

Althea looked toward the double doors, startled from her thoughts by the sound of their opening. A few of the men walked in, laughing and talking. The women gave their attention to them immediately, putting down their work. Althea glanced at the clock and saw with astonishment that a full hour had passed.

Stifling a yawn, she rose as the rest of the gentlemen entered, deciding now was the best time to excuse herself. She would check on Rebecca, then retire for the evening.

She exited without being noticed and entered the corridor. She leaned against the closed doors a moment, still in awe of the experience she had just been through. She had never felt such an acute perception of individuals as she was praying for them. Sometimes in the stillness of night, the Lord would lay someone on her heart to pray for, but it had never been as real and immediate as had happened this evening.

Her senses were still reeling. It was as if the Lord had given her a deep and valuable lesson in forgetting herself and looking through His eyes. *"To be about the Father's business."*

She took a deep breath and made her way to the staircase, leaving the muffled sounds of laughter and voices behind her. A deep weariness engulfed her as she grasped the handrail and began her ascent. It came to her how much she had lived since she had opened her eyes that morning before the first light of dawn.

Suddenly Althea looked up at the sound of soft, rapid footsteps coming down from the landing. Simon hurried down, not seeing her, his eyes focused on the carpet. Althea watched him for a few seconds, as polished and debonair in his evening clothes as the most titled gentleman present.

Simon glanced up and saw Althea and immediately broke into a smile, feeling a sudden desire to share his success with someone.

"I just looked in on Rebecca," he added a bit sheepishly, embarrassed at being caught.

"Is she sleeping?" she asked softly.

Her presence, like her voice, always had a calming effect on him.

"Like an angel." He stood on the step above her, trying to contain the feeling of suppressed energy inside him. He felt as if he were grinning like the village idiot.

"That's good," she answered quietly. Simon kept looking at her, bringing his grin to a small smile he couldn't quite suppress. As he continued regarding her he noticed his drab little nurse was positively radiant herself.

"You are looking very pretty tonight," he found himself saying.

She flushed as if not expecting that. "Thank you."

"I'm not certain what it is." He continued studying her, his eyes narrowed, a finger to his lips. "Yes...I see...you are no longer in gray."

He paused, his gaze traveling down her long, pale throat, pearls glistening against it like orbs on a snowy landscape, on down to her lower than normal décolletage. She had on a very elegant gown indeed, equal to those of the other ladies present that evening.

"That is a very becoming shade," he added. "It transforms you, somehow. You should wear it more often."

Her pale skin flushed up delicately, suffusing her throat and cheeks, hiding the pale scattering of freckles across the bridge of her nose. He felt a spurt of pleasure, watching her feminine reaction, and realized she was not only a pious nurse, but a woman as well. Feeling magnanimous with his own victory, he decided to continue the compliments.

"There is something else."

She looked up at him, her hand going to her throat. "Yes?"

He eyed her hair. It was swept up but in a softer manner than the coronet she customarily wore. Curling tendrils escaped, forming a golden halo around her face. "Your hair. You've done something to it."

Her hand went to her hair. He smiled at the typically female response. "I— That is, is something amiss?"

He shook his head. "No. It is quite becoming. Softer, somehow."

"Oh." She looked away from him, settling her gaze somewhere around his cravat. "Thank you," she whispered.

Simon found himself not wanting to move. He discovered he enjoyed paying Miss Breton compliments. "How is everything with the ladies?"

Her eyes moved upward again and he realized how pretty they were. He had thought them gray, but now saw them a pale green with hints of blue. They were fringed by light brown lashes, which glowed golden in the candlelight.

"Everything is going very well," she answered.

"You're not going up already, are you? The entertainment is just beginning. Perhaps you could play a little for us."

He gave his most charming smile and he was surprised when he felt her sudden withdrawal.

"I...I'm sorry." She looked away from him. "I'm a little fatigued."

"Of course, how thoughtless of me." He moved aside immediately, suddenly tiring of the game. "Rest well."

She stepped past him and walked up a few steps.

Still he did not move. "Miss Breton?"

She turned to look at him standing below her. "Yes, Mr. Aguilar?"

"You were wrong about the size of this dinner party."

She frowned. "I don't understand."

"You said it was a good number, not too large and not too small, which would give me a chance to give my attention to each one of my guests."

"That is correct."

"I fear I didn't have time to greet you all evening, and now you are running away."

She made a motion with her hand. "Do not trouble yourself. I wasn't a guest. I was there to 'make myself useful,' don't you remember?" she added with a smile.

This time her smile was neither shy nor feminine, but one of comradeship. He found it oddly comforting, like a friendly hand held out over a dangerous course. He returned it. "As well you did." He looked at her standing there, probably unaware of how regal she looked. "Thank you for all your help. Thank you for attending."

"It was nothing. I'm glad the evening was a success for you." She bowed her head then turning, resumed her walk up the stairs.

Still he stood, watching her, until she moved from his view.

In the early morning hours Simon entered his daughter's room once again. The house was silent, the last guest having departed. Simon began untying his cravat, tired but satisfied. He gazed down at his daughter's sleeping form; a familiar feeling of helplessness engulfed him each time he looked at her like that. He strained his ears to hear her breathing, always afraid one of these nights it would stop altogether. But although he heard nothing, he finally distinguished the slight rise of her chest in the dim light.

He glanced toward the door to the sitting room. All was dark. Many a night, a light still showed through the cracks—but not tonight. Miss Breton must indeed have been tired. Simon moved to the curtained window. He stood looking down, his hand pushing aside the velvet draperies a fraction. Lamplight lit the quiet streets at intervals, yellow aureoles in the dark and foggy night. Only one coach rolled past. Most of the residents of Mayfair were abed. Far off, the watch called out the hour.

Simon replayed the evening in his mind. Everyone he had wanted had attended. It had been a good mix: lords and ladies, key political figures, and some literary types to round out the gathering.

For his first foray into the fashionable world, it had gone well. To invite the upper echelons of society and have them accept his invitation—he'd waited a long time for that. Who would have dreamed such a thing possible when he'd been a lad at public school, at the mercy and scorn of these same people and their ilk? Some of the men who now sat in the House of Lords had been the ones who had most tormented him in school, calling him an Ephraimite and concocting the cruelest jests at his expense.

But this evening had been the beginning of a new phase for Simon. After a decade of toiling, he was beginning to see the fruit of his labor. The fashionable world was beginning to hang on to his words and follow his lead. It was more than politics. It was being a leader in society, an originator of ideas.

He relished those moments of witty sallies and repartee at the dinner table. His brow clouded an instant as he remembered the only awkward moment in the evening, that slight scene at the other end of the table between Miss Breton and the colonel's wife. A stupid conversation about religion. Simon curled his lip in disgust. Wasn't it always the way? He hoped his remark had put things in their proper perspective. It would not do to have it noised abroad that he had a Methodist under his roof. That was clearly not fashionable.

He should have known when he'd insisted Miss Breton attend the dinner party that the topic of religion would come up. He'd thought her well-bred enough to avoid the topic. Perhaps it hadn't been her fault, he conceded, thinking about how quiet and unassuming she normally was. He knew Mrs. Ballyworth could be an outspoken harridan.

His thoughts turned to the shy, retiring Miss Breton. He thought of her reaction to his compliments that evening. So, the pious maiden had a feminine side, after all? He thought of the pleasure he'd taken in bringing it out. It had given him more pleasure than courting the greater ladies of society. He wondered why. Was it something of forbidden fruit?

Simon rubbed his cheek thoughtfully as he thought about a remark Lady Stanton-Lewis had made when he'd rejoined the ladies after dinner. Simon tried to recall what it was; he hadn't paid much attention at the time, his thoughts still on his encounter with Miss Breton on the stairway. Lady Stanton-Lewis had said something about the governess actually presuming to preside over the tea table and how she'd quickly put her in her place. He wondered now what had transpired. Had Lady Stanton-Lewis, too, noticed how attractive Miss Breton appeared and feared a rival? Lord knew, aside from Lady Eugenia—who was in a class by herself—none of the women this evening, with their overfed, bejeweled, pomaded appearances, could hold a candle to Miss Breton. There was a freshness, an understated elegance, in Rebecca's nurse. Tonight her manner and her bearing epitomized the lady.

For all her efforts to appear a woman of humble origins, she could not hide her aristocratic heritage. He shook his head, a smile playing about his lips. He was giving far too much thought and attention to a paid employee under his roof.

With an effort he turned to Lady Stanton-Lewis. Now there was an intriguing situation. The woman had taken a definite interest in him at the last social events he'd attended. He thought back. It had begun at the Summerstons' ball, where his hostess had introduced him to her. He remembered how entertaining she'd been, employing the kind of wit he appreciated—ridicule. She seemed to know something about everyone, most of it not complimentary. He had been quite amused by her conversation at the kind of gathering he usually found tiresome, though a necessary evil in his political rise.

Lady Stanton-Lewis was quite knowledgeable about the inner workings of government, and seemed on a first-name basis with various members of the House present that evening. She'd amazed and flattered Simon with her awareness of his record on the backbench. He knew her salons were important events, and he coveted an invitation from her. Only the powerful elite were invited, both Tory and Whig.

Ever since the ball she'd singled him out, and he knew it was only a matter of time, if he played his cards right, before he would be admitted to her salon. He noticed how his invitations had increased since meeting her and wondered idly whether she had anything to do with it. He wouldn't be at all surprised. He knew how these things worked.

He had no illusions about himself as attracting the eye of hostesses. He did not possess any vanity about his own personal assets. He was neither a dandy nor a person who had ever known how to woo the ladies. Married young in a union arranged by his parents, as was the custom for them, he was almost as quickly widowed, and had spent the intervening years struggling to learn the ins and outs of government. He'd had no time for the opposite sex, until now....

Despite his family's fortune and his own rising position in government, he knew the stigma of his name as well as the taint associated with his family's fortune in trade and banking. But a connection with people like the Stanton-Lewises could prove a powerful asset indeed.

Besides, he hadn't been involved with a woman since Hannah passed away. Eight years. Eight long, lonely years. He usually didn't let himself think about it, driving himself instead to succeed in his career. Work had engulfed him during those years, for if he did nothing else, he was determined to be acknowledged for his mind. They might despise his heritage, his looks, his family name, his fortune, but they would come to admire his mind.

The only relief he'd permitted himself in those eight years was Rebecca. The only bright spot. The apple of his eye. And now she was being taken away from him. He glanced toward his daughter's sleeping form, then turned his eyes toward the dark, overcast sky, his hand twisting the curtain in a sudden surge of helpless rage. If there was a God, as Miss Breton seemed convinced of, he was a mean-spirited, vengeful one whom Simon had no interest in knowing, but whom he would fight with everything that was in him.

Chapter Seven

❧

The next morning Simon looked carefully at Althea over the edge of his newspaper when she entered the dining room promptly at half-past seven. Their glances met as soon as she stepped over the threshold. She smiled at him.

"Good morning."

Her smile seemed bright and genuine. There were no discernible signs of fatigue from the previous night's entertainment, or any shyness over his compliments.

"Good morning." He went back to the article he had been reading as she moved toward the sideboard. The words about the foreign secretary's announcement concerning the Holy Alliance and its next congress were mere black ink marks on paper as his ears caught the sound of silver against china, and the soft murmurs between Miss Breton and Harry the footman.

When she at last sat down, Simon looked over his newspaper again, and then stopped in annoyance at the bowed head saying grace over the bowl of porridge. Did she never eat anything but porridge? As she straightened and reached for the teapot, he cleared his throat. Again he was interrupted, this time by Harry, who sprang to take the teapot from her.

Simon frowned, watching Harry's attentiveness to his nurse. Miss Breton smiled up at the footman, again murmuring her thanks. Since when had Harry become so quick on his feet?

Finally Miss Breton's attention was free. He waited as she took a sip of tea. "How did you enjoy the dinner party?"

She smiled, looking beyond him. "Quite well, thank you."

He narrowed his eyes at her, unable to detect any dissembling in her look. Her smile seemed fresh, almost dreamy, as if she too were savoring a success over the previous night. He thought once again about the remark made by Lady Stanton-Lewis, and it intrigued him enough to pursue it.

"The ladies treated you well?" he asked, this time putting his newspaper down enough to take a sip of coffee.

Her glance met his, but it was a straightforward look. "The ladies treated me as well as could be expected." Then she took a generous spoonful of porridge.

"Meaning?" His cup clinked against its saucer.

She glanced at her spoon and laid it carefully at the edge of her bowl before replying. "As befitting ladies of their station, they cut me dead."

He took this in, realizing if he hadn't before, the power Lady Stanton-Lewis wielded. "Every one?"

She nodded. "Every one."

"Even Lizzy Appleby?" He mentioned the wife of a colleague who seemed mild-mannered and eager to please.

"Even Lizzy Appleby." Althea tilted her head to one side. "I fear they little understood how to treat me."

"What do you mean?"

She looked back down at her bowl, toying with her spoon. "I occupy that nebulous position of governess—neither quality nor servant. Hence, my presence must needs be ignored." She glanced at him, a smile playing about her mouth. "In truth, I cannot say I blame them. A woman of dubious noble birth, a professed

Methodist, employed as a governess in an unmarried gentleman's establishment—" She coughed, her cheeks reddening. "A Jew at that."

They looked at each other for a few seconds, Althea's eyes registering shock at her own remark, when suddenly Simon began to laugh. A second later, she joined him.

When their laughter subsided, he remembered something else she had said in describing herself. "What did you mean by 'dubious noble birth'?"

She looked at him in surprise. "Didn't my brother tell you?"

He shook his head. "Tell me what?"

She smiled. "I was under the impression he had to tell you everything about me in order for you to agree to hire me."

He smiled at the recollection. "Was I so very difficult about it?"

She shook her head. "You had good reason."

"So what was Sky supposed to tell me? Is there some blemish in your family's history that no one is supposed to know about and yet somehow everyone does?"

She looked at him steadily. "Not in my family's history. In mine. I am Lord Caulfield's illegitimate daughter."

Simon didn't know what to say. He looked at Harry, who was standing like a stick but had no doubt heard every word. He wanted to laugh at the irony; here, he'd been likening Miss Breton to his ideal of a lady and she was no more than Caulfield's by-blow.

He met Althea's direct gaze once again. "I believe we could debate whose situation is the more tawdry—a nobleman's illegitimate daughter or a moneylender Jew's son."

She put her chin in her hand and considered. "It does present an interesting question."

Once again Simon felt curiously warmed by that comradely remark. He sat back and looked at her in sympathy. "We're even, then, for the present. I'm terribly sorry about the evening. It must have been dreadful for you. And here I was congratulating myself earlier for insisting you attend. I thought you were having a grand time."

Her eyes widened in surprise.

"Oh, come now, Miss Breton. Earlier in the evening you were holding court at the far end of the table. You had Colonel Bally-worth and young Covington positively rapt. At one point I thought the whole table would erupt in controversy."

She had the grace to blush at that and look down. "That wasn't about me. The Lord merely gave me an opening to talk about the mission, and I used it. Believe me—"

He waved away her excuses. "Yes, yes, I know. You did nothing. Their attention had nothing to do with a charming young lady telling them some heartrending stories about the plight of the poor in our city."

She frowned at him, her color high. "Are you saying I attempted to prey upon their sympathy? If you think I was exaggerating in any way, I challenge you to go down there and see for yourself—"

"Miss Breton, calm yourself. I meant no such thing. I trust your word implicitly. I applaud you wholeheartedly if you manage to get some of them to loosen their purse strings. Anyway, that's not what we were talking about. I truly apologize for any discomfort I caused you in obliging you to attend the dinner. The fault is mine." He regarded her silently for a moment, realizing how flattered old Ballyworth must have felt, having this young lady's attention through dinner. With her color high and those wisps of curls framing her face and those ingenuous eyes looking at a man with disconcerting directness, there was more to Miss Breton than he had first supposed. He noticed he was staring when she broke the connection and looked back down at her bowl.

He tried to get back to his paper, but found it difficult to let go of the previous night's event. Finally he put down the paper and pushed aside the remains of his toast. "How did you cope, by the way, with the ladies' insufferable behavior?"

She glanced up in surprise as if she had already put the whole thing behind her. For some reason, that annoyed Simon. Once again, a dreamy smile appeared on her face, which only increased Simon's irritation.

"Don't be sorry—the evening wasn't wasted."

"You're being too generous, Miss Breton. Lady Stanton-Lewis mentioned something in passing that set me to wondering. But what you've told me sounds much worse than she implied."

Althea raised an eyebrow. "I'm surprised Lady Stanton-Lewis noticed my situation. She gave no indication of it."

Simon smiled in understanding. "I am not surprised. I find Lady Eugenia Stanton-Lewis a typical specimen of polite society—a product of her environment, if you would." He considered a moment, hesitating before continuing. "Now you, on the other hand, are not typical at all. That is why I'm curious how you managed."

"It wasn't so bad. Well, at first, a little, I must confess." She smiled. "More than a little...more than I care to admit."

He looked at her keenly, knowing exactly what it meant to be ignored in a roomful of people. He didn't know which was worse—to be ignored or ridiculed.

She was toying once again with her spoon. The two were silent a moment, each focused on personal thoughts. Simon finally spoke, "What did you mean—the evening wasn't 'wasted'?"

Althea smiled again, her gaze wandering back to the window. "I was feeling quite uncomfortable, when the Lord led me to pray for each of those ladies." She cleared her throat as if hesitating. "He...enabled me to really look at each one as I prayed, and suddenly I began to see things I normally would not have." She looked at Simon, as if wanting him to understand something inexplicable. "It was the most extraordinary thing. It was as if I knew each one—truly knew them, had experienced their tears, their sorrows, when they're all alone and no one is watching. Suddenly I could see past the fancy evening gowns and jewels." Her gaze reached out to Simon. "I could feel the Savior's love for them, how much He wants to embrace them if...if they would only permit Him."

Her heartfelt words ended in a whisper. The room was silent.

Simon glanced at Harry, whose attention was fixed on Althea. Finally she gave a deep sigh, as if coming back to the present, and smiled.

"Before I knew it, an hour had elapsed, the gentlemen were coming in, and I could gracefully retire."

Simon shoved himself to his feet. "Very touching." He managed to keep his tone dry, but his heart was pounding. "I must be off. I thank you for the interesting narrative." Before she could reply, he was walking to the door.

And he didn't know the half of it, thought Althea as she watched him depart the dining room. She tried not to feel hurt at his abrupt departure. For a few moments it had seemed that she'd broken past his usual irreverent view of the world. They had shared a moment of understanding and then, at her mention of the Lord, it was as if she had dashed a bucket of cold water on him and he'd remembered himself. As Althea finished her bowl of porridge, she tried to tell herself that he wasn't rejecting her, but her Savior. Her Savior had endured much more rejection than that when they'd spit in His face and nailed the stakes through His hands. Althea rose, dismissing the moment of self-pity.

Yes, there was much more to the story than she'd told Simon, she reminded herself, remembering all the moments leading up to the dinner party. He didn't realize how close he had come to having no dinner to serve. Althea straightened her shoulders, knowing she must face the kitchen staff—and principally the cook—that morning.

Harry sprang to open the door for her. "Thank you, Harry." His attentiveness hadn't gone unnoticed by her. "How are things downstairs this morning?"

"Fine, thank you, miss." He cleared his throat. "All 'cept Cook, that is."

She nodded. "That is to be expected. I shall be down presently, as soon as I finish with Rebecca's toilette."

An hour later, Althea stood before the kitchen door, wondering what she would find that day.

It was not what she had expected. She stopped short at the

crowd that awaited her. All the servants were present, some sitting, some standing. All stood when she entered.

Giles stepped forward and bowed. "Good morning, Miss Breton."

She started at his polite tone, then looked around at each one in surprise.

"Miss Breton," Giles continued, "on behalf of all the staff, I would like to express our appreciation of your efforts yesterday afternoon. We don't know how we would have managed without you. We are all deeply grateful." Again he bowed. Before she could reply, all the servants had swarmed around her, each one expressing his or her thanks.

"Oh, miss, we didn't think 'twas possible—"

"If you 'adn't a come in just then—"

"'Ow did you hever learn to cook like that—we wouldn'ta believed hit if we 'adn't seen hit with our own eyes!"

"All the guests sent compliments down to the kitchen—"

Althea just stood there, too stunned to do anything else. She felt her eyes fill up as she glanced into each excited face and thanked the Lord for what He had done. In one evening He had accomplished what she hadn't been able to in a month. *They shall all come to know You,* she vowed, as she nodded into their smiling faces.

"Mr. Aguilar sent 'is compliments to Cook for such han excellent meal! 'Is very words! Han excellent meal!"

At the mention of Cook, all eyes turned to the woman in question. Up to then Althea had wondered where she was. Now she saw her, slumped at the dining room table, her head cradled in her arms. The room fell silent.

"May I speak to her?" she asked Giles.

"Mrs. Coates and I have reprimanded her severely this morning. She knows if she ever so much as takes a drop again, she will be dismissed on the spot, without references. You have leave to speak to her if you think it will do any good." His tone suggested Cook was beyond redemption.

The cook meanwhile had lifted her head enough to glare at them. Althea sucked in her breath at the sight of her red, puffy face and the resentment in her eyes.

Althea approached her. "Why don't you come up to my sitting room, Mrs. Bentwood, so we can talk privately?"

The cook continued glaring at her. Althea just waited calmly, meeting her gaze. Finally Mrs. Bentwood looked down and began to heave herself out of her chair. Knowing how awful she must be feeling, Althea gave her a hand. When they reached the upper floor, Althea changed her mind and led Mrs. Bentwood directly into her bedroom and bid her lie on her bed.

She could sense the tension in Cook's body, but gently and firmly, as she had had to do many times at the mission, Althea got her to lie on the bed, then took a coverlet and spread it across her legs.

She turned to her dressing table and soaked a handkerchief in vinegar water. As she laid it on Mrs. Bentwood's forehead, the cook tried to protest, bringing an arm up to remove it.

"There, Mrs. Bentwood, don't fret," she said in a soft tone, all the while keeping the cool handkerchief against the other woman's skin. "You just lie still a while. Rebecca's occupied right now and I have a few moments."

When the handkerchief was warm, Althea replaced it with a fresh, cool one and brought a chair up to sit near the bed. "It must be difficult for you. I got an inkling of it last night," Althea said with a soft chuckle. "I thought I would expire over that hot stove."

"Oh, miss, they don't know wot hit's like." Mrs. Bentwood turned her head to look at Althea, her hand grabbing at Althea's wrist. Her red-rimmed eyes were filled with tears. "Day in, day out, bent over that stove. Hit's enough to suffocate a body."

"Yes, I can imagine. In the summer it must be an inferno."

"Oh, awful, miss. Not a bit o' air. There are days I think I'll pass out."

Althea flipped over the handkerchief. "What happened yesterday?"

The cook started to cry. Althea sat quietly as Mrs. Bentwood tried to talk through the sobs. When they subsided, Althea asked, "So you hadn't cooked a dinner party menu in some time?"

Cook sniffled, and Althea pressed a clean handkerchief into her hand. "No, miss. Hit'd bin ages, 'fore I ever come 'ere, even. Oh, I used to be a fine cook." She sniffled again. "A fine cook. I worked at some o' the best addresses in Mayfair. You ask them." She gave a firm nod. "Started out as scullery maid at No.7 Grosvenor Square, then moved up to kitchen maid, then an assistant cook. Then when the opportunity come to be full cook a few blocks away, I jumped at the chance. We 'ad dinner parties every week there. The best families, they didn't stint on those menus. But then the master died and the missus stopped entertainin'. When she decided to move to the country, I couldn't habide the thought o' leavin' London. When they advertised for a cook 'ere, I come on."

"This place 'as been me doom." Her voice dropped and her sniffles resumed. "I shouldna' never come 'ere. Lost hall me skills."

"What was so wrong about coming here?" Althea asked curiously.

Cook sniffed in disdain. "Oh, hit just weren't quality, not wot I were used ta. They didn't know the first thing about hentertainin', for one thing, and even if they 'ad, oo'd a come? They weren't nobody."

"But Mr. Aguilar is a gentleman, and I'm sure his wife must have been a lady," Althea persisted.

"Gentleman! 'Is manners might seem so, but heveryone knows 'e's nothin' but a Jew! Don't tell me they change just a 'cause they change their clothes and shave off their beards."

"Oh, Mrs. Bentwood, shame on you! Mr. Aguilar has been nothing but a gentleman since I've been under this roof."

Mrs. Bentwood turned her head away. "Has I said, 'is manners might seem it, but 'is kind are foreigners, no matter wot they do to 'ide it."

"So, you weren't happy since you came here?"

"Oh, I could manage, I suppose, but hit weren't the same as I was used to. No parties, no society. They were just a young couple, newly wed. The wife was barely eighteen."

"What was she like?" Althea couldn't help asking.

Mrs. Bentwood's voice softened. "Oh, she was all right, I suppose. Pretty little thing. Let me do pretty much wot I pleased in the kitchen. She spent most o' 'er time visitin' with 'er family. So, I got used to preparing simple meals. She died so soon after they was married. Felt kinda sorry for 'im." She gave a sigh. "Since then, the master's lived a bachelor's life, dines out more'n 'e does in, I 'ardly 'ave to do hany fancy cooking for upstairs. Mainly hit's cookin' for us below stairs, and Rebecca, o' course, but she 'ardly eats, poor mite. And now looks like she'll share 'er poor mama's fate. Cursed lot, those people 'ave."

"Hush, Mrs. Bentwood. Rebecca will not die."

The cook looked at her, removing the handkerchief from her forehead. "'Ow do you know she won't die?"

"Because Jesus came to 'heal the sick and set the captives free.'"

Mrs. Bentwood's eyes narrowed in suspicion. "'Eard you were one o' those Methodites. Don't you be tryin' nothin' with me."

"Do you go to church, Mrs. Bentwood?"

The cook turned away. "'Aven't been in years."

"Why not?"

She shrugged. "Why should I? Thar sits all the quality, Sunday hafter Sunday, in their fine coats and furs, an' we servants huddled in the back, slavin' for 'em. There was nothin' in church for us. I got more comfort from the bottle."

She stopped talking. Althea waited quietly a moment before resuming the conversation. "When did you start drinking?"

"When me Charlie died. Oh, not a lot, not right away. But I found hif I 'ad a nip hor two when I went to bed at night, it 'elped me to sleep. Then on my day off I stopped goin' to church and 'ad no family to visit, so I started drinkin' a little then. I don't do it very often, I swear!" Again she took Althea's wrist in her hand, her eyes imploring her. "You can ask Giles, or Mrs. Coates. Yesterday was the first time. I suddenly realized wot I was expected to do! I couldn't cook that kind o' meal! I 'adn't done that in so long. So I thought I'd take me a glass just to settle me nerves, and then I 'ad another. I don't remember anything more after that."

The two women looked at one another a long time. Finally Althea said, "Mrs. Bentwood, do you want to be free, really free of all the loneliness and fear?"

A few days later, Althea and Rebecca were writing out invitations to their puppet show, when Simon stopped in.

"Oh, *Abba,* you are right in time to receive your invitation."

Simon approached his daughter, who was sitting in a chair by the window of her bedroom. "Let me see."

He opened the card she handed him.

You are formally invited to a special presentation of *Esther, Queen of Persia and Medea* to be presented on 25 March, at 4 o'clock at No. 10 Green Street by the Upper Room Puppeteers. Rain or shine. R.S.V.P.

"Don't you like it, *Abba?*" Rebecca smiled up at him. "Grandpapa and Grandmama and all the aunts and uncles and cousins shall hear the story of Esther."

"So you shall be telling a heroic tale?"

She nodded. "How Queen Esther saved her people from death." She picked up the other invitations. "I have invited Grandmama and Grandpapa and Aunt Tirzah and Aunt Simcha and all the uncles and cousins. Do you think they will come?"

Simon rubbed her head. "I'm sure they shall. Who are the Upper Room Puppeteers?"

Rebecca gave a smile of satisfaction. "Oh, that is Althea and me. We call them the Upper Room Players, because I'm up here in the upper room! What do you think about that?"

"Very reasonable."

"We want to hold the show downstairs in the sitting room,

however. You must see the costumes Althea is making for the puppets. She cut up some old dresses of mine...."

At the mention of her name, Simon turned to look for Althea. He found her stripping Rebecca's bed. "We have housemaids to do that."

Althea didn't pause in her movements. "Oh, that's quite all right. I consider this right in the line of a nurse's duties."

He observed her for a moment, then said, "I can't figure you out—why someone with your upbringing would lower herself to do menial work."

Althea smiled. "I would reply but for fear my words would only sound trite in your ears."

"No, I promise to accept as sincere what you tell me."

She looked for skepticism in his face, but found only curiosity. "Very well." She finished tucking in the sheets and turned to take the coverlet off the chair. She faced him, her arms full. "For love." She smiled, expecting mockery.

Instead he gave a slight shake of his head. "I don't think such love exists."

He turned his attention back to his daughter.

"It's a pity your show will come after Purim."

Rebecca's eyes widened. "That's Esther's feast, isn't it?"

He nodded. "How would you like to go to Grandmama's for the Shabbat meal tomorrow afternoon?"

Rebecca clapped her hands. "Oh, yes! That means tonight she lights the candles, doesn't she? Oh, can't we go tonight, too? Please!"

Simon laughed and squatted down by his daughter's chair. "Not tonight. It's too late for you to be out. I want you good and strong for tomorrow. It will be a long day." He turned back to Althea. "Please be ready to accompany Rebecca tomorrow. We shall leave at noon."

Althea straightened from the bed. "You want me at your family's gathering?"

His tone was curt. "Rebecca might need you."

"Oh, yes, Althea, you must come! We have so much fun at Grandmama's. You'll meet all my family. There shall be singing and dancing afterward."

Althea found it hard to imagine what it would be like in a Jewish household on their Sabbath. She knew so little of them. They were always pictured in caricature in anything she had ever read about them. There was an old synagogue near the mission, and those who attended kept to themselves, scurrying in and out of it as if afraid of attracting notice.

Simon stood and went towards the bellpull, rubbing his hands. "Good, that is settled, then. Let's have some supper."

Chapter Eight

The following noon, Althea descended the Aguilar coach across town in Bloomsbury Square, in front of an imposing white stucco mansion. Although many of the residences were just as grand as in Mayfair, this quarter was not considered fashionable, being known as an area for those whose fortunes had been made in trade.

One of Simon's brothers arrived just as they were entering. He came in with his wife and children, creating quite a crowd at the entrance and giving Althea a chance to observe without being given more than a passing notice as Rebecca's nurse. She recognized Simon's mother and his two sisters from times when they had visited Rebecca. Everyone embraced, and she heard many *shaloms* and *shalom aleichems,* as well as other phrases in a foreign tongue.

Just as Althea turned from handing her hat and cloak to a maidservant, Simon beckoned her.

"Mother, you have already met Rebecca's nurse, Miss Althea Breton." He motioned Althea forward.

Suddenly she found herself the object of a dozen eyes.

"Althea, you haven't yet had the pleasure of meeting my father. Father, Miss Breton." He presented her before an elegantly dressed gentleman, stockier than Simon, with iron-gray hair and dark, piercing eyes. "Leon Aguilar," Simon told her. Immediately she was being introduced to Simon's three brothers, Daniel, David and Nathan, all resembling the elder Aguilar in some fashion.

Dozens of children were running around, and the women were all talking together as if they had not seen each other in months.

"I'll present you to the patriarch, my grandfather," whispered Simon, leading her by the elbow to the drawing room, to a frail-looking elderly man with a beard who was seated as if he had been placed there out of harm's way. As Simon made the introductions, his grandfather smoothed his beard, regarding her.

"You are Rebecca's nurse?"

"Yes, sir," she replied as she rose from her curtsy.

He patted her hand. "You take good care of her." With that he looked away from her, addressing someone in a fast string that sounded to Althea's ears like Italian.

The rest of the company was assembling in the spacious, well-appointed room. Simon found her a seat before rejoining his brothers. Althea looked around the room in wonder. If not for the strange language and more boisterous behavior of the company present, Althea would have said she was in a fashionable drawing room of any upper-class English household. The room was tastefully furnished in the latest fashion, pale green walls and white wainscoting, delicate white friezes and marble busts in curved niches, and elaborate drape festoons above the long windows overlooking the square below.

The women seated around her chattered in a mix of English and the foreign language. Just as at the dinner party, they ignored Althea, but she expected it here, realizing she was no more than Rebecca's nurse to them. She sat quietly, watching Rebecca. But Rebecca forgot her, being too taken up with her cousins. Laughing and shrieking could be heard from their corner of the room.

Althea smiled, thanking God that Rebecca seemed to be getting stronger and could enjoy a day with healthy children her own age.

They were soon called in to dinner. There wasn't the formality of the English dinner party. Here mothers gathered up their children and, like hens, directed them toward the dining room. The men followed leisurely behind them, more interested in their conversation than in the enticing smells emanating from the table.

Althea followed last of all, smiling at two of the children that had stayed to play with their toys on the floor. She extended a hand. "Come along, I think there is a wonderful dessert for the children who come to the table."

The two boys looked up at that and scrambled to their feet. Disdaining to take her hand, they hurried ahead of her. She smiled and continued behind the rest. Most of the family was seated, while a few mothers were still tying napkins around their children's necks.

Simon's mother was just coming around to the end of the table when she spotted Althea. She stopped short at the sight of her. Althea smiled, wondering what was wrong when the woman didn't smile back but looked almost frightened. Instead of addressing her, Mrs. Aguilar called sharply to Simon.

He was still standing by a chair conversing with one of his brothers when he looked up. When he saw Althea in front of his mother, he quickly came over.

"What is it, Mother?"

"Es una ajena?"

"If you mean, is she a Gentile, yes, Mother, Miss Breton is *ajena.*"

She said something else rapidly in that strange tongue.

"Don't trouble yourself. I'll take the consequences. Remember I'm an apostate already, with enough sins to burn in hell for all eternity." He smiled at Althea as he spoke the words. "This is merely a small blotch on my already tarnished soul." As he spoke he propelled his mother to her chair and seated her. "If it will make you feel any better, I will put an extra offering in the poor box next Shabbat."

He came back for Althea. "Come, let's find you a place."

Shaken by his words and his mother's fearful look, Althea hung back. "It's quite all right, Mr. Aguilar. I can eat elsewhere—in the kitchen—if they'd prefer. I don't mind."

His pressure increased on her arm as he led her forward just as he had his mother. "Nonsense, you are here for Rebecca's sake." He glanced around looking for his daughter, and seeing her smiling face between two cousins, he led Althea to them. "Come, Isaac—" he spoke to a boy beside Rebecca "—allow Miss Breton your place and you move down there."

The boy obeyed his uncle at once, looking curiously at Althea. She was thankful that most of the company, too involved in their own conversations, hadn't noticed anything.

Although the food had a foreign quality to it, Althea enjoyed it very much. The central dish was a one-pot stew rich with meat, vegetables and white beans. The food tasted spicier than she was accustomed to, with the flavors of garlic and lemon and allspice permeating it. There was also more rice and olives and other things she considered exotic. She found the braided loaf of bread deliciously moist. At the end of the meal they were served lots of fresh fruit, which Althea marveled at in winter. A thick, sweet coffee and almond marzipan followed.

The men dominated the conversation, but everyone spoke, the women amongst themselves or to their children. Althea slowly sorted out the members of Simon's family: his two oldest brothers, with their wives and children, were seated toward the head of the table next to the father, as befitted their position of prominence. The grandfather sat next to Simon's father, eating little. Every once in a while Simon's father would look at his plate and chide him about eating. "What are you doing, *Abba?* Are you going to eat us out of house and home? What, is the food not good enough for you? I got these figs all the way from the Holy Land and you turn your nose up at them?"

She noticed that Simon's father conversed mainly in English, as did his brothers, while the women spoke in the strange tongue. She wondered whether it was due to the men's being involved in the business world. Despite their fashionable attire, all of the men wore dark skullcaps, which gave them a foreign appearance. Even Simon had donned one. Gone was the English gentleman, member of the House of Commons and the Church of England. Amidst this dark-haired, gesticulating family group, the small round cap flattening the top of his curls, Simon could have been sitting in a Jerusalem synagogue.

Farther down the table sat Simon's married sister with her husband and children, then his youngest sister, who was unmarried, although betrothed to the young man sitting next to her. Beside the older children sat a young man who looked very much like Simon, but who was rosy cheeked and laughing wholeheartedly with the children. He had none of Simon's cynicism in his features. It was Nathan, Simon's youngest brother, who was only eighteen. She imagined Simon must have looked like him when her brother, Tertius, had known him.

There were several others at the table. Simon had warned her on the way over not to be surprised at the number of people. In addition to one's family, it was traditional at the Sabbath meal to invite any impoverished family or members of the synagogue, the children's tutors, students of the Torah far from their own homes, and any other needy people. Looking at the long table, Althea was reminded of the noisy meals at the mission in Whitechapel.

In a brief lull, she heard Simon's oldest brother, Daniel, say, "I heard you gave a speech in the House this week. If I hadn't known who was telling me, I would scarcely have believed it."

"Why is that?" answered Simon, looking steadily at his brother as if knowing what was coming.

"Wanting to reinstate the Elizabethan labor laws that we managed to repeal during the war? You want the courts to fix a worker's minimum wage? What will you ask next—that we guarantee them holidays and pay them when they stay home?"

Simon looked into the glass he was holding. "You cannot expect men, women and children to work efficiently at the starvation wages some of them are earning now."

David, the banker and second eldest brother, added, "And you cannot expect men to invest capital into new enterprises if they are not going to receive back an adequate return on their investment."

Simon countered immediately. "If an owner wants to see his mills burned to the ground and more looting and rioting, he will continue his greedy way of wringing out the last shilling he's invested. The Spa Fields Riots we saw in December were no isolated incident—"

David's voice rose. "We will not permit a revolution in this country. Your talk, Simon, is dangerously Jacobin. You're in Parliament to safeguard our interests, not to work against us."

Althea saw Simon's face darken at that remark. Before he could answer, his father entered the discussion. "If we pander to the ignorant mass of workers, we'll soon be making no money at all. Now is the time to advance. Everyone is clamoring for capital, and thanks to the gains we made during the war years, we are among the few who can offer it. You cannot undercut what we have taken a decade to build—"

"I'm not undercutting anything." Simon raised his voice to be heard over the others. "If Parliament doesn't act soon, this country will be on the verge of another civil war, except this time it will not be about religion, it will be between those on the brink of starvation demanding their due from the moneyed classes. If you don't want a Reign of Terror as we saw across the Channel—"

"Oh, come," said Daniel, who oversaw the family's various commercial enterprises, "the English would never behave like the French."

"There is a powerful sentiment building up against the Regent," Simon said more quietly. "I know, I've heard the clamor of the loom worker, the weaver, the miner. Don't you hear the Jeremy Benthams and Will Cobbetts stirring them up?" Suddenly he turned to Althea, gesturing toward her with his glass. "Ask Miss

Breton, who runs a charity in the East End. She sees the results of our indifference to the laborer. What are the products our factories produce besides cloth and machinery? Tell them, Miss Breton."

Suddenly Althea had the attention of all those present. She looked around at the eyes fixed on her, the women staring blankly and the men in utter disbelief. Was it because she was a woman, or a Gentile? she wondered. She met Simon's gaze, for once not mocking or challenging, but strangely encouraging. He gave a slight nod, probably only seen by her.

She cleared her throat. "Since the growth of the mills, we have seen more and more people leave the land and come to the towns and cities seeking work. There is inadequate housing for them. Mothers and their small children spend hours crowded over dusty looms in dim light and inadequate ventilation. There are terrible accidents sometimes. But that is not the worst of it. What is happening since the end of the war is that as orders have fallen off, workers are dismissed without a thought to their well-being, and they have nowhere to go. They used to live off the land and hold a variety of jobs. Now, when there is no job at the mill, the man and his family starve." She saw she had her audience captive now, and she leaned forward, looking directly into their eyes, knowing these were the people who could effect change. "Many children end up on the street. This is no exaggeration. At our mission we manage to feed all those who come to us, but I know it's only a fraction of all the poor in London. If you go farther, our cities to the north abound in mills—Birmingham, Manchester, York...."

As she fell silent, feeling her heart pounding at what she'd had the temerity to say, her gaze fell upon Simon's father at the head of the table. Leon Aguilar gave her a withering look before turning to Simon and addressing him exclusively.

"In my day a woman thought only of marrying and providing her husband with children."

Althea's face burned and she dared not look at anyone. She

kept her face bent over her coffee cup. The verse came to her: "There is neither Jew nor Greek, there is neither bond nor free, there is neither male nor female: for ye are all one in Christ Jesus."

Simon and his father continued their discussion, and she only managed to catch the tail end of his father's remark.

"...I paid enough to get you a seat in Parliament. It would seem the least we can expect is that you defend the interests of business and stop befriending the factory worker."

Althea's eyes lifted as she looked quickly across to Simon. She could see the anger and shame at the remark, but just as quickly he parried his father's thrust.

"If it weren't for those like me who are working to repeal the Corn Laws and do away with some of the tariffs, you wouldn't be able to operate at all."

All the brothers and the father laughed at that. As she watched Simon's laughter joining the others, Althea was reminded of what Tertius had told her about the torment Simon had endured during his schooldays. Bloody but never bowed. She knew the debates in Parliament were by no means friendly, and she wondered if he enjoyed the swordplay with words. She shuddered inwardly, unable to imagine enduring it daily.

At the end of the meal Althea saw a different side to Simon's father. He stood over the table, the fringe of his prayer shawl visible beneath his coat, and closed with a blessing. He didn't shut his eyes to recite the prayer, and at one point his gaze crossed hers. As his deep voice intoned the words in Hebrew, Althea could imagine Moses or Jacob speaking such a blessing over the people.

After the meal, the family gathered once again in the drawing room. Whereas the men had dominated the dinner conversation, the women gained in prominence after dinner as those with musical ability began to sing. Although she didn't understand the words, Althea was captivated by the haunting melodies. Nathan played a mandolin to accompany his sisters.

* * *

"They're singing in a form of Spanish called Ladino." Simon spoke quietly into Althea's ear as he took a seat beside her.

She nodded her head, keeping her gaze on Simon's two sisters and the elder girls singing together.

"These are traditional Sabbath melodies which have been sung for centuries."

"Is that the language they were speaking earlier?" she whispered back.

"Yes."

"Your family still speaks this form of Spanish, even after so many years out of Spain?" she inquired.

"Yes, it's a form of Spanish, mixed with Hebrew. My generation and the next—" he nodded towards his nieces and nephews "—barely speak it, though we understand it well enough."

The tone of the songs changed. "It sounds like Gypsy music."

"It's from the same part of the world. Andalusia, or as we say in Ladino, *Sepharad*."

She nodded in comprehension. "Hence Sephardic?"

"Yes. For us it simply means 'Spain.' You'll find a reference to Sepharad in *Obadiah*."

He was amused at the look of surprise she cast him. "I thought you didn't read the Bible."

"Oh, I've read my share. I had the traditional scholarly upbringing for a male Jew until I was thirteen. Every family must have its scholar, you see." His glance strayed to Nathan. "Now perhaps the mantle will pass to my younger brother's shoulders."

"How so? I should think your present profession involves quite some scholarship...I mean, all those pamphlets you've published."

He could see her hesitation at the last remark. "You know about those?"

She looked down at her hands. "I—I was looking for something in the library one day and came across them. I'm sorry."

"It's quite all right. Feel free to look for anything you might need in the library." He gave a rueful smile. "Unfortunately, as you heard over dinner, my writing does not find favor in this household. The only true scholarship for the Jew is to spend his life pouring over the Torah. My life as a Torah scholar reached its zenith when I received my Bar Mitzvah at thirteen. A few short years later I was sprinkled at the baptismal font at St. Michael's."

"Why ever were you baptized?" she asked curiously.

He regarded her through his oval spectacles. "I was the sacrificial lamb, you might say. Haven't you gathered from my father that he desires to wield power in both worlds? A Jew has no rights in the Gentile world. Our only dominance comes through money. Filthy mammon, didn't your Jesus call it?

"Well, money certainly has its advantages," he continued, his gaze straying to the singers, "but it also has its limitations. The English pride themselves on regarding family name and Church higher than money. They refuse to admit that money is the driving force behind the two.

"My father, in his wisdom, looked around to see how he could improve his family's lot in this land they had adopted a few generations back. It wasn't enough that he'd doubled his father's wealth. He wanted entry into the more rarified spheres of influence. So, he looked at his prime resources—his four sons." He gazed at Althea sardonically. "What is one among so many? He could spare one to the Gentile world, even though that would mean that in the eyes of the Jewish world the son would be declared dead."

"How could your father contemplate doing such a thing?" she whispered.

"The Sepharad has a long history of playing a double game. We learned to feign conversion in medieval Spain, yet continue to practice our religion in secret. Do you find that distasteful?"

She looked down again so he could not read her expression. He wondered why he was telling her the most shameful things about his heritage. Why not regale her with stories of the great scientists, philosophers and sages the Sephardic people had produced?

"The consequences must have been dire for someone to deny his faith," she said quietly.

"It was either baptism or death at the hands of the good Spanish friars. There were hundreds of thousands of these 'conversions.' Many of our kin rose high—it is even said one of the popes was of Marrano stock.

"In time, to make sure our conversions were genuine, the Catholic Church instituted the Inquisition. Of course, it was no coincidence that the Marranos held great wealth, and once they were exposed, the state had a right to all their properties. Convenient, wasn't it?

"It was a great sport for a churchgoer to come to an auto-da-fé—an 'act of faith'—and watch one of these counterfeit Christians burned at the stake after a confession had been extracted.

"Unfortunately, the Spanish Church found there were simply too many of us. They hit upon an easier method—simply expel us...after forcing us to leave behind our gold and silver and jewels, naturally."

Simon smiled at the look of growing horror in Althea's eyes. "So you see, we are used to surviving. It should, therefore, not surprise you that my father knows how to play the game.

"His only dilemma was, which son could serve as a Marrano here in England, where there are no auto-da-fés, but where few doors are open to the Jew?" Simon nodded toward his eldest brother. "Well, not Daniel there, the firstborn. As you could perhaps gather from our dinner conversation, he will step into my father's shoes. Already he manages most of the factories we have accumulated during the war years. And what about David there? He doesn't have enough imagination and flair to enter the world of politics. He does have a mind brilliant in finances, so my father put him in charge of our growing banking concerns. Besides, both of my elder brothers are Jewish to their very core, appearances notwithstanding. They easily rub shoulders with their Gentile equals in the world of commerce and finance, but in their private lives, you see for yourself, they are most at home in their ancient culture.

"Then came the third born, myself." He inclined his head. "A skeptic almost as soon as I could read the Scriptures, and with a wit and irreverence that was the bane of my Hebrew tutor, but which my father soon found a way to exploit. I was the one chosen to receive baptism and catechism in order to grant me entrance to the finest schools of Britain.

"First Eton, then Cambridge, the place where statesmen are formed. Then to find me a borough where I could be guaranteed election. You've heard of the 'rotten boroughs'?"

Althea nodded. "They are the areas where there are very few votes needed to become elected to Parliament, are they not?"

"Do you know I sit for a borough in Surrey which comprises only one vote?" At her amazement, he repeated, "A total of six houses, and only one vote."

"Only one person was responsible for electing you to Parliament?"

"That is correct. And how difficult do you think it would be to buy one vote? You heard my father over dinner—he bought my seat in the House, and now he expects his return."

"You mean someone agreed to vote for you for a price?"

"You think they would vote for a Jew—albeit a Christianized one at that? But who is fooled by a skin-deep conversion? My father, the banker, found his price—the man, as a well-respected member of the landed gentry, was up to his neck in debt, and in danger of losing the property that had been in his family's hands since the days of Charles the First." Simon smiled thinly. "All it took to pay off his debts was his vote. One tiny vote."

He watched Althea digesting the world of politics and money, while he tried to fathom why he was exposing himself to her. It really was quite sordid when boiled down. "Have I shocked you, Miss Breton?"

"You have, indeed. I was aware of the rotten boroughs, but not—not—"

"Not face-to-face in all their rottenness, is that it?"

She looked at him as if at a loss to respond.

At that moment, the singing ended, and Simon's grandfather was handed a large thick book. He opened it and began to read in that foreign tongue.

"He is reading from the *Me'am Lo'ez.*"

"It's not the Bible?"

"You might say it's our Bible, that of the Sephardic people. It's written in fifteen volumes," Simon explained. "It's an accumulation of legends, histories and wisdom of the ages. You must get Grandfather to tell you our own family's history sometime. Do you know he still has the key to the family's old house in Toledo?"

Althea's eyes widened. "How many years ago did your family leave?"

"This year we celebrate our three hundred and twenty-fifth year of exile from Spain. We left the same year good Columbus sailed for the Americas. The last boatload of Jews was forced to leave the port of Cádiz in the year 1492."

"Where did your family sail?"

"Not many countries would accept our detestable race in those days. Some went to the Levant, quite a few started a colony in Salonika, which began to thrive. My own ancestors chose Holland. We lived there peacefully for more than a century until Oliver Cromwell once again allowed Jews to settle in the British Isles. Then a great-great-grandfather decided things might be more favorable in the city of London—and here we are, the ancient family of the Aguilars. Not a pretty story, is it."

As Althea turned her attention to his grandfather's mellifluous voice, her expression as fascinated as if she understood every word, Simon felt a curious release.

Despite having regaled her with his family's greed and ambition, he felt no scorn from her. Instead, there was a bond of understanding.

* * *

That night Althea went to sleep with much on her mind. Rebecca went to bed tired but happy, talking of her cousins and her puppet show.

Around midnight Althea was awakened from a dream about leaving Spain in a big ship, while the cries of a little girl left on land reached her on the deck. She awoke to realize it was Rebecca crying.

Through the haze of a deep sleep, Althea pushed aside her warm covers and faced the cold air. Reaching for her wrapper and shawl and pushing her feet into her slippers, she gradually became fully awake. She stumbled toward the doorway, her heart constricted as always by the girl's cries.

Seconds later she was by Rebecca's bedside, turning up her lamp. She smoothed the girl's hair from her forehead.

"Althea, I feel so much pain. My belly hurts." Rebecca doubled over.

"Maybe the food was too rich. Let me go down and make you some tea."

"No! Don't go away. Don't leave me alone." Rebecca began to cry and reached for Althea's hand.

"I won't leave you. Here, let me rub your belly." Softly Althea began to croon in her ear as she rubbed her hand against the little girl's stomach.

After a few minutes of tranquility, Rebecca doubled over again. "Oh, it hurts."

Althea retrieved the chamber pot and held it by the bed. "You'll feel better if everything comes out."

The girl continued to whimper in pain, Althea patting her back as she held her over the pot. Finally she heaved and threw up her dinner. Althea brought a wet washcloth and glass of water to her and helped her erase all the traces. "Now, let me dispose of this, and get you some chamomile for a cup of tea. I shall be right back."

"I don't want to be alone."

Althea was in a dilemma. "Do you want me to call your papa?"

"Oh, yes, please call *Abba*."

Althea stirred up the embers and added some coal. Then she filled up the teakettle she kept on the hob. "There," she said, brushing off her hands, "I'll leave that heating while I go down a minute."

"Is *Abba* coming?"

"Yes, let me just get him."

Althea went out into the corridor, realizing she was not sure which room was Simon's. She looked at the door directly across the hall, deciding he would most likely be as close to his daughter as possible. She rapped lightly on the door. A second later she tried again, this time a little harder.

"Yes? What is it?" came the muffled reply.

"It is I, Althea, Mr. Aguilar. It's Rebecca—"

Simon was already opening the door. "What is it, what's wrong with her?" His hair was tousled, his eyes sleep-filled as he tied the belt to his dressing gown.

"I'm so sorry to disturb you. Rebecca had an upset stomach. She's better now, I believe, but wants you. I need to go downstairs to get her some tea."

"Of course," he said as he rubbed the sleep from his face. "I'll stay with her. You go down."

When she returned, she found Simon had parted the curtains on the far side of the bed and now sat on its edge, singing softly to his daughter. It sounded like one of the haunting melodies his sisters had sung earlier in the evening.

Althea went about making the tea. When she finally turned toward the bed with a tray in her hands, she could see that Rebecca had fallen asleep. "I don't think she'll be needing this," Althea whispered as she placed the tray on the bedside table. "I fixed you a mug, as well. I didn't mean to get you up from your bed."

"As long as you drink the other cup," he said, taking the cup from her.

Althea sat on the chair beside Rebecca's bed. The two sipped in silence.

"You said she threw up her meal?"

"Yes. Maybe she had too much excitement this afternoon."

"Undoubtedly. She is no longer accustomed to her boisterous cousins."

"But she was enjoying herself so much." After a moment, Althea added, "At least we didn't have to give her more laudanum. She seemed to feel better right away. I'm sorry I woke you—it was just that she didn't want to be left alone."

"Call me whenever she needs me."

The two were silent after that. Althea mused that many were the sickbeds she'd sat at over the past few years, but she'd never quite imagined the scene she found herself in at the present. A little girl, her wealthy Jewish father, in an area of London she never imagined she'd live in again.

She swallowed a sip of tea, then held the hot mug in her lap, wrapped in both hands. "I woke from a dream that I was leaving Cádiz on that last ship in 1492. A little girl's cries turned out to be Rebecca's."

Simon chuckled. "My stories made an impression on you. Did they dispel or merely confirm your opinion of my people?"

She shook her head in the dark. "I knew little about your people, and I admit what little I knew was mostly hearsay. Well, not quite all. I have met some Jewish moneylenders firsthand in Whitechapel, and their conduct is not flattering to your race."

"I can well imagine." He took a sip of tea. "I hope you understand that their predominance in the moneylending field has little to do with choice. They have been denied entry into most professions in Christian Europe since the Middle Ages."

"I begin to better understand that. I also know there is greed and avarice in every culture. It is not limited to the few Jews I have seen in the East End."

Rebecca mumbled, and Althea leaned forward. But the girl resumed her quiet sleep.

This time Simon broke the stillness. "Now that I have given you an outline of my family's history, as well as my own infamous journey into Parliament, why don't you give me a little of Miss Breton's history? Why she is here, nursing a sick child, instead of being in the thick of a London Season."

His question paralleled her own train of thought of a moment ago. She smiled in the dim light.

Before she could formulate a reply, he said, "Your brother didn't speak of your past, he only spoke your marvels. I received the impression you'd practically resurrected him from the dead."

"The Lord brought my brother back from near death. When he returned from the West Indies, he had a recurring fever. It nearly killed him."

"He said you were the only one able to nurse him back."

She smiled slightly. "The Lord sent me to him." She paused. "I—I had been estranged from my family for some years on account of my faith. But I felt a tugging to go to him, felt that he needed me at that time. It turned out that he was very ill." She took a careful sip of her tea. "The Lord led Tertius out of the darkness into the light. His healing was an added blessing."

Simon made no comment. After a moment he brought the conversation back to his original question. "So, why aren't you enjoying the London Season instead of sitting here in obscurity, little better than a low-paid menial servant?"

She looked down into her tea. "I have had my share of London Seasons."

"Oh? You don't look old enough to have already reached a point of satiety with all that society offers."

"I am twenty-six, long past the age of London Seasons."

"Then, why are you not enjoying the role of young matron among the ton?"

"As your father said, married and producing an heir?"

"I apologize for my father's ill-timed and ill-judged remark. Women have a narrowly defined position in our culture."

"As they do in fashionable society. In any case, you don't have to apologize for your father. He merely spoke his mind."

"As I will mine—why *aren't* you married with an heir or two?

Though I still maintain you are not so old as to be completely on the shelf."

"Oh, quite on the shelf by society's standards." She rubbed the rim of her cup with her fingertip, wondering whether to proceed. Something about the night and the hour gave her the courage to speak. "Well, to be perfectly honest, I had only one offer during my two London Seasons."

"Oh, come, Miss Breton, that I don't believe. I know how these things work. Marriage is arranged by title and portion, both of which you had. It is not so very different among my people. My marriage was arranged from the time I underwent my Bar Mitzvah."

"You were promised to your wife when you were thirteen?" she asked in wonder.

"Oh, yes. My father and Hannah's father saw it as a mutually profitable alliance. Her family was in iron and steel, ours in cotton mills and finance. We were in the middle of the war. We quadrupled our fortune between orders for armaments and uniforms for soldiers and loans to the Crown."

"I see." Although she knew well how marriages were arranged, it sounded so cold-blooded, pairing a wedding with a war.

"So you can't convince me you had only one offer, Miss Breton. I know your world doesn't operate so very differently from mine. And that is aside from the obvious considerations—an attractive, personable young lady of good birth."

Attractive, personable—was that how he saw her? "You are correct when you say our worlds are not so very different. Where you miscalculate is the part about my good birth. You forget I was Lord Caulfield's illegitimate daughter."

"But Tertius made it very clear you are his sister. If your father brought you up in his home, he must have acknowledged you fully."

"No." She hesitated, looking down at her mug. If his entry into Parliament was ignoble, it was no less so than her own history.

"You see, when I was brought to live in the marquess's household at the age of two, I was acknowledged only as Lord Caulfield's ward. No one, except Lord Caulfield himself, knew my origins. To Lady Caulfield and her two sons, Edmund, the eldest, and Tertius, and to the vast troop of servants and retainers at Pembroke Park, I was Lord Caulfield's ward. I grew up believing I was the orphan child of his good friends across the Channel who had died in the Terror of 'Ninety-three."

"And what was the truth?"

"What I have told you." She took a sip of the now lukewarm tea. "I was the result of Lord Caulfield's indiscretion with a chorus member of the French opera."

"Ah!"

She smiled at his shadowy figure across the bed. "You see?"

He nodded. "A lot has been explained to me now."

Feeling vaguely annoyed by his knowing tone, she asked, "Such as?"

"Why a noblewoman with London society open to her would renounce it all to live among the lower classes of London."

"What makes you think that would be the reason?"

"Knowing that you were merely the illegitimate offspring of a lord, no matter how exalted his title, might make you feel unworthy of the full honors due his lineage."

"Don't assume too much, Mr. Aguilar," she said quietly, shaken to the core at how clearly he'd discerned her original feelings, though he was incorrect in his conclusions. "I could do the same from my vantage."

"Fire away, Miss Breton. I have a thick skin."

She considered. "Perhaps you place too high a value on reaching that rarified milieu of 10,000 families which comprise the Fashionable World merely because it is something that has been denied you."

"Up until now."

"Up until now," she agreed. "Just be aware that the mere fact that the door seems to be opening does not make it worthwhile.

The apostle Paul tells us that although all things are lawful to us, not all things are expedient."

"I take your warning into due consideration, Miss Breton." He placed his mug down on the night table. "However, this evening I find your history much more intriguing than my own. When did you become Lady Althea, as your brother refers to you?"

"My—" She cleared her throat. "My father revealed my true background to me, and acknowledged his relationship to me, just before I entered my first Season. But he didn't make it publicly known at that time. Lady Caulfield was alive then, and none of us wanted to cause her any pain, least of all myself. Although we had never been close, she had never treated me unkindly. I never knew how much of the truth she knew or suspected—I suppose she had made some conjectures over my parentage, but she never let on what she knew.

"After her death, my father insisted on acknowledging me publicly. He wanted to bestow his name upon me and accord me all that he felt was due me."

"But you have not accepted the title of 'Lady,' nor the full benefits falling to the only daughter of the Marquess of Caulfield?" His tone reflected his incredulity.

"I have the full benefits, if you mean I have my father's love and affection." She didn't mention that it had taken many years to receive those. "As for his fortune, I use my share to help alleviate the needs of the poor at the mission. And going by 'Lady Althea' would do me little good, and perhaps some harm, in the neighborhood where I've been called to work."

She fell silent, wondering what he thought of her now that he knew her background, wondering still more what he would say if he knew the whole story of her disgraceful second Season.

Chapter Nine

❦

Sunday morning Althea awakened tired but with a sense of purpose as she went down to the kitchen. She found Cook and her two kitchen maids and scullery maid already waiting for her at the dining table.

"Good morning." She smiled at them as she laid her black Bible on the table. "Will anyone be joining us?"

"Good morning, miss. No, miss, no one else is joining us. Mrs. Coates is visiting with 'er relatives. Mr. Giles went out early. The footmen are around but they say they don't want no part with Methodism, beggin' your pardon."

"That's quite all right." She sat down and opened her Bible. "Before we continue, let me explain something. The reason we are gathered here has nothing to do with Methodism. We are here to hear and study the word of God. You are all free to attend the church of your choice, but as I noticed you didn't go to church—" Althea turned to Mrs. Bentwood "—I invited you as well as anyone else who would care to, to join me in studying the Scriptures on Sunday morning.

"Shall we begin?" She smiled at each one in turn. They all nodded their heads. "Now, I realize some of you cannot read, but
don't let that deter you from hearing our Lord's word. I shall ask
Mr. Aguilar's permission to begin teaching you the alphabet, and
I'm sure you'll be reading in no time. For the present, just listen
as I read. Let us all turn to the Book of Saint John."

In the afternoon Althea knocked on Simon's library door with
the express intention of obtaining such permission, as well as to
speak to him about a few other household items that had been
on her mind. When she found no one in, she didn't know whether
to be relieved or disappointed. She wasn't quite sure how she
would face her employer this morning after her candidness of the
night before. She had told him things she had not discussed with
anyone but her brother and her pastor, and that not for many
years.

Giving herself a mental shake, Althea put on her things to go out
for her walk. There was a hint of spring in the March air as she made
her way to Hyde Park. She walked down Park Lane, bypassing the
most traveled areas where people went to see and be seen. She
wandered toward the open meadows, where sheep had been let
out to graze after their winter confinement. She could imagine
their sense of freedom in those vast pastures after a winter in their
stables. When she allowed herself to compare her present restricted
life to the one she had lived prior to taking on this nursing assignment, she could easily experience a sense of frustration, of asking,
"Why, Lord?" or "How long?" She knew it was at times like these
that she must most trust and obey and have patience.

She walked briskly, her head bowed against the wind, humming into her muffler, taking pleasure in the physical exertions of
walking and breathing deeply. She slowed her pace as her body
warmed. She began contemplating her bucolic surroundings far
from the city noises and to voice her thanksgiving in song.

When she was ready to turn homeward, she spotted a lone
rider. As he drew closer, she thought he resembled Simon. She

knew Parliament was not in session that afternoon. What should she do? Wait until he drew nearer? Or choose another direction?

She was being silly. She did want to talk to him. Why did she feel shy after her confessions the evening before? She braced herself to face the encounter.

"Good afternoon, Miss Breton." Simon reined in his horse and tipped the curly brim of his beaver hat to her.

She looked up at him, and he was struck with how beautiful she looked. Her cheeks were flushed, her hair wind-tossed about her bonnet. Even her gray pelisse couldn't detract from the health and well-being she radiated. He realized he no longer thought of her as a gray governess; since the dinner party he'd begun thinking of her as a golden girl. Her hair was a deep burnished shade of gold, somewhere between blond and brown. He caught himself wondering what it would look like loose; he imagined a mass of curls, for wherever a strand managed to escape its tight coronet, it caught the light in a dazzle of gold.

"Good afternoon, Mr. Aguilar," she replied, her gaze sliding away from his as soon as she'd uttered the words.

She looked as if she might resume her walk. Before she could do so, he dismounted and came toward her, keeping a loose hold on the reins. "I trust you were able to get some rest last night?" he asked in a solicitous tone.

"Yes, thank you," she replied breathlessly.

"You have walked a long way."

"No— Yes. I—I was just on my way back. Rebecca will soon be waking."

"Yes." He continued looking at her, remembering their late-evening conversation. "No more dreams of exile?"

Her high color spread over her entire face. "No, no dreams at all."

Was it possible she was embarrassed over the things she had told him? They were certainly no worse than his own revelations.

To put her at ease, he looked away from her to the tree-dotted landscape beyond.

"Rebecca was tired today," he commented.

"Yes, she's napping now."

He glanced back at her. "I've sent for her physician. He'll be coming by tomorrow morning."

"I see."

He sensed disapproval and frowned. Dr. Roseberry was one of Harley Street's finest—if one went by his fees and the recommendations of the hypochondriac matrons of Mayfair.

"He doesn't do her much good," he conceded, "but for what it's worth, I thought he should take a look at her."

"Yes, certainly."

She seemed on the verge of adding something, so when she remained silent, he pressed her. "Is there something else I should be doing? You are the one closest to Rebecca. If there is anything I have neglected, please tell me at once."

She hesitated so long, her gray eyes fixed intently on him, that he knew she wanted to speak yet struggled to do so.

"What is it?" he asked quietly, having come to trust her judgment implicitly concerning his daughter.

Finally, she just shook her head and looked away. "No. It was nothing. You are doing all you can."

Simon would have insisted but stopped himself. It struck him with a certainty that she would have said something in a religious vein. Well, he'd already given her permission to see to his daughter's spiritual needs. He would give her no encouragement to minister to *his*. He turned to his horse and stroked its nose.

"Mr. Aguilar?"

He could hear the hesitant yet determined voice. "Yes?"

"I wanted to ask you...a few...things."

Intrigued, Simon turned his full attention back to her. "Yes?" he prodded her when she didn't answer right away.

The wind continued to tousle her hair beneath the bonnet.

She cleared her throat. "That is, I meant to ask you earlier, but you were not in your library. Perhaps this is not the time—"

"It is as good a time as any. I am meeting someone presently—" He took a look up and down the avenue, but not seeing the person he expected, he turned back to her. "Fire away, Miss Breton."

She looked disconcerted. "It's...yes, well...three matters, actually." She cleared her throat again, a sound he was beginning to notice hid her nervousness when she was determined to pursue a course that daunted her. "The first, ahem...is that I've begun a...a...Bible study in the kitchen...this morning, as a matter of fact." She hurried on. "You see, I noticed that most of the servants don't attend any kind of church service, and I thought I would make myself available to any who wished to study the Scriptures with me. I...I should have asked your permission beforehand, and I wish to apologize, but if I could—"

Was that all that had her so bothered? He waved a gloved hand. "It is your and the servants' day off. You have no need of my permission with whatever you engage in in your free time. If that is the way all of you choose to spend your morning, I have no objection. What else?"

He hid his smile at her look, which showed she'd not expected such a quick dismissal of the topic she'd found so difficult.

"Oh, thank you, sir. That is most kind of you."

He smiled openly this time, realizing it gave him pleasure to please her.

"The other matter—or the second matter, that is—is the state of some of the serving maids."

He quirked a dark eyebrow upward. "Their state?"

"I mean to say the state of their education is what concerns me."

"Their education? What are they lacking in order to perform their jobs?"

"Literacy."

"Literacy?" What was she talking about? "Does this hinder them in carrying out their duties?"

"Well, yes, as a matter of fact. The fact that they do not know how to read can be injurious. For example, the other night—"

She stopped in mid-sentence as if regretting what she would have said. Betraying some behavior of the servants?

"At any rate, I was busy with something and I needed Dot— that is, one of your parlor maids—to sit with Rebecca for a few hours, and she was not able to read to her."

"Well, now, I don't imagine that caused a great upheaval in the running of the household," he drawled.

"No." Althea smiled. "Rebecca ended up reading to her. But that is not the point. The point is that a young woman of Dot's capacity ought to be able to read."

"Yes, well, be that as it may, what did you have in mind, Miss Breton?" He glanced back down the path, knowing he should soon be seeing the one with whom he had a rendezvous.

She hurried on as if conscious that he was pressed for time.

"I would like permission to begin instruction in reading to those servants who wish to avail themselves in their free time— and my free time, I might add. I won't take any time away from what Rebecca needs—"

He scrutinized her through his spectacles. Was she planning on crusading through his entire household? "Very well, Miss Breton. You wish to reform my household in the spiritual and educational realms. I will concede what I did when I first hired you. A trial basis—isn't that what you proposed then?"

She nodded vigorously as if afraid he might go back on his word.

"Very well. Undertake another trial period, shall we say a month, in which you implement these improvements in the well-being of my servants?" Frankly, he doubted she would see much improvement in a month's time. As for her finding the time, he thought she was being optimistic to think she could sandwich a general literacy campaign between her nursing duties. Rebecca had been remarkably well throughout Miss Breton's sojourn. If she should take a turn for the worse, he didn't want to think what that would entail.

He moved away from her and remounted his horse. "If we see

you are making progress for their betterment, and it doesn't interfere with your duties to Rebecca, as you say, then you may carry on with them. Agreed?"

She expelled a breath. "Agreed, Mr. Aguilar, and thank you. Thank you very much."

"Don't thank me. You haven't proved yourself yet. Though I have no doubt that you will, as you did with your first trial. Now, was there anything else, Miss Breton?"

He didn't expect anything but another expression of gratitude.

But she took another breath and continued. "The final thing has to do with the kitchen. Could you please authorize someone to come in and improve the ventilation over the cookstove?"

He stared at her in utter bewilderment.

She hurried on. "It is stifling to work down there. Cook's health is in danger. I've seen many kitchens where they have improved the ventilation by the placement of a small window leading to the street. I could recommend a carpenter or mason—"

He held up a hand to stop her litany. "Please, Miss Breton, I don't need a sermon." He tapped his riding crop against his leg, as she stood still, biting her underlip, looking strangely appealing. He looked down the path again, seeing a rider at last, off in the distance. The sight brought him back to his reasons for being out in the park today.

He turned his attention back to Miss Breton, suddenly amused at the temerity of all her suggestions in the space of a few minutes. "Very well, Miss Breton, see to whatever it is you need. If it means an improvement in the food Cook sends upstairs, I support the improvement in full measure. Although I must say she rose to the occasion the night of the dinner party."

She smiled widely at that. "Thank you, sir, I shall tell Mrs. Coates and Giles about your decision."

He raised an eyebrow. "My decision? Somehow I feel as if I had very little to do with it. Now, is that all you wished to request?"

He knew his mockery was unmistakable, but she ignored it. "*Thank you*, sir! Yes, that is all for the moment."

"I am glad to hear it, Miss Breton." He touched a hand once more to his brim. "In that case, I must bid you farewell. I am meeting Lady Eugenia, whom I see riding toward me at this very moment."

"You are riding with Lady Stanton-Lewis?"

Simon turned at the sound of dismay in Miss Breton's voice. She was watching the rider approach.

"Yes," he replied, looking down at the nurse, a trace of defiance in his tone. Why did he feel as if he was doing something wrong and must justify it? "I am beginning my apprenticeship in that heretofore forbidden world of society we discussed last night." He added, "Wish me luck."

"I don't believe in luck anymore," she answered quietly.

"What is it you believe in, then?"

"That 'the steps of a righteous man are ordered by the Lord.'"

He looked at her for a moment longer. "So be it. Pray for me, then." Again he gave her a mocking salute.

Althea watched him ride toward Lady Stanton-Lewis. Her heart was troubled. Yes, she would pray for him.

"Now, you copy these letters for me." Althea pushed the slates toward the two kitchen maids. She watched them for a few seconds. Martha's tongue stuck outward as she struggled to form the alphabet letters on the slate.

"Look, Miss Althea, how do you like my tarts?" Rebecca clamored for Althea's attention, pointing to the tart tray. In front of her lay the remains of rolled-out pastry dough.

"Quite nice, dea'," said Mrs. Bentwood, approaching the table with a saucepan and wooden spoon. She set them down on a pot holder upon the scarred wooden table. "Now we shall spoon some o' this mincemeat into each one."

Rebecca's face brightened as she reached for the spoon.

"Now, mind you don't burn yeself," cautioned Cook, handing her a pewter spoon. "Use this 'ere smaller spoon, and dip it in like this. Not too full, now." She demonstrated with a couple of the tart shells.

"Let me try, Cook." Rebecca leaned forward, eager to take the spoon.

Mrs. Bentwood straightened, relinquishing the spoon at last. She watched the girl fill the first couple of cups. "Yes, that's right. No, not too much, mind, you don't want it to spill over. Put a mite more in that one, or the pastry might scorch. That's a good girl." She looked over at Althea and winked. "She might make a cook yet, what do you say?"

Althea smiled. "Yes, indeed."

Rebecca turned wide eyes to Althea. "Will they be ready for our tea party?"

"Oh, I imagine they shouldn't take too long in the oven. Isn't that right, Mrs. Bentwood?"

"That's right, miss. Then a little while to cool, then we'll 'ave Dot take 'em up to you just in time for tea, eh?"

At that moment the door to the servants' dining room swung open. They all stared openmouthed at Simon, who strolled in as if he entered the servants' quarters every day. He looked around and smiled when he spotted Rebecca.

"There's my missing daughter!"

"*Abba,* were you looking for me?"

He came over to the table and straddled a chair. "I went up to my daughter's room and no one was about. I went into the sitting room, and not a soul there. I went looking in the yellow salon to see if she might be listening to Miss Breton playing her pianoforte—" he glanced at Althea "—but there was not a note of music to be heard." He tapped his temple with his forefinger. "Then I got to thinking, and recalled something Miss Breton had told me."

Rebecca giggled, enjoying his roundabout tale. "What did Miss Althea tell you?"

His gaze lingered on Althea, and she could feel her color rising.

"She said something about teaching some maidservants to read," he said, and looked at the two maids, who began to giggle and look down at their work. Then, hearing the hammering, he glanced toward the open doorway to the kitchen. "I also recalled something about carpentry work."

"How did you know I would be with Miss Althea down here in the kitchen?"

He looked at her sagely. "I said to myself, if I am any judge of Miss Breton, she will begin her improvements immediately. And that means I shall find her down in the kitchen supervising her new tasks. Wouldn't it follow that she would take my daughter along with her—" he gave the tarts a significant look "—especially considering my daughter's wish to try her hand at baking?"

Rebecca clapped her hands. "You remembered! My *abba* is the cleverest man in the kingdom—isn't he, Miss Althea?"

Althea could only smile. "It certainly looks that way, doesn't it."

Simon touched his daughter's nose. "Now, I have something to consult the two of you about, if you can set aside your tasks for a few minutes."

Rebecca promptly put down her spoon. "What is it, *Abba?*"

He smiled. "Something you'd like, I think. Do you know next week is the Passover week?"

"Is it? Will we go to Grandpapa and Grandmama's for the Seder dinner?"

"Something better."

Her eyes widened. "What?"

"All the family is going to spend the holiday at Uncle Daniel's country house." He turned to Althea. "My brother has a place by the seashore at Ramsgate. The family regularly gathers there in the summer."

She smiled. "How lovely."

He gave his attention back to Rebecca. "We shall go a little earlier this year, but since it has been fair weather, I think we'll manage fine. What do you think?"

"It sounds delightful. Doesn't it, Miss Althea? Oh, you shall love it. It is right by the sea."

"I thought this would give Miss Breton a chance to have a little holiday of her own," he interjected gently, laying a hand on Rebecca's arm.

"But, *Abba*—"

"When you hear the reason, you shall be very glad to let Miss Breton have her holiday."

Althea waited, wondering what he would say. What would she do with her time? Would she go back to the mission? That is what she had longed for since she arrived. And now? Had she grown so attached to her young charge that suddenly the thought of being left behind gave her a feeling of being abandoned? Had she become so involved with her new household that she felt a disinclination to return to her old life? These thoughts unsettled her to the point that she didn't listen to what Simon was telling his daughter.

"So you see, Rebecca, Miss Breton is needed with her brother and his wife right now. But she'll be back here soon enough."

"My brother? What is it?"

Simon addressed her. "I had a visit from Tertius today while you were out for your walk. He asked me to spare you for a fortnight. His wife is expecting any day now."

She put a hand to her cheek. "Of course! How is Gillian? Why didn't he wait—"

"He was rushed, and wanted to get back as quickly as possible. He daren't leave his wife for even a day. Besides, he was afraid you wouldn't ask me to relieve you of your duties for a fortnight, so he came directly to me.

"I told him it was perfectly all right. We have this holiday coming up. Since Rebecca is doing so well at the present, I decided to risk traveling with her. We will make the journey in easy stages. This will give you the opportunity to be with your family, as well, during your own Easter holiday. I imagine you would want to be with them."

"Yes," she finally managed to say. Had she become so engrossed in the Aguilar family to the neglect of her own? "That is most kind of you."

Just at that moment one of the workers popped his head into the dining room. "Come have a look, miss?"

Althea stood immediately. "This is Mr. Aguilar, the master of the house. Perhaps he should be the one?"

The man touched a hand to his cap. "Certainly. Sir?"

Simon rose. "Let us see what is being done to my kitchen."

They all admired the new frame window nestled between the freshly mortared stones set high in the wall beside the stove.

"Well, I must return to my own work," said Simon. He turned to Althea as the others began moving back to their tasks. "Your brother said he would be by to collect you on Friday evening. Is that sufficient time for you?"

She nodded, reminded again of the holiday plans.

"We've had another terrible massacre," he told her in an undertone.

Her hand went to her throat. "Oh, no! Here in London?"

"No. Just outside Manchester." He removed his spectacles and pinched the bridge of his nose. "It was to be a peaceable march. Weavers from Manchester organized a pilgrimage to London to present their petitions before the Regent. They didn't get very far."

She searched his face. "What happened?"

"Local troops fired on them just outside Manchester in Stockport. Poor, unarmed marchers," he said in disgust.

"Oh, dear!" she breathed, closing her eyes.

"Yes, it wasn't a pleasant sight, by the reports I've received. A group of wretched, half-starved workers thinking to walk all the way to London. They've arrested several individuals. I imagine they'll transport most, if they don't execute them."

She looked at him, feeling the pain of their families. She forgot her own situation as she thought of the people she worked with at the mission, whose plight was so similar to those Manchester workers. How could she have not wanted to go back?

"You will be busy, I imagine, in the wake of this news?" she asked finally.

"Yes. Something must be done to make the Tories see that reform is no longer a matter of debate." He replaced his oval spectacles, his tone turning brisk. "If I don't see you before Tertius comes for you, I wish you a pleasant journey and holiday."

She realized he was saying goodbye. "Thank you." Why did she feel so forlorn at the thought of not seeing him and Rebecca for a fortnight? "I wish you each a blessed holiday as well. I—" she hesitated "—I shall pray for you both."

He gave a ghost of a smile. "Thank you."

To her surprise his tone held no irony or contempt, merely resignation. Before she knew what he was doing he reached up. With his finger, he rubbed her cheek. She put up her hand. "Wha—"

"Flour. Is baking among your many abilities, Miss Breton?"

"I am called on to do many things at the mission," she said breathlessly, still feeling his touch.

He nodded. "I am beginning to see that." He stepped away. "Good day, Miss Breton."

Chapter Ten

Althea looked down at the sleeping baby nestled in her arms. She touched the back of her forefinger gently across its feathery-soft cheek. Everything perfectly formed in miniature, each little eyebrow, the dark-lashed crescents of its closed eyes, the tiny nose, the little bow of red lips, down to the plump, dimpled chin barely visible above the knitted blanket swaddling it.

Her heart overflowed with love for the girl-child just born to her brother and his wife. Little Judith was truly a miracle baby. Althea looked across the room at Tertius and Gillian sitting on a settee. He was reading and she was knitting little booties. Every once in a while Tertius would stretch out his hand to Gillian and touch her. She would respond by putting down her needles and covering his hand with hers. The connection only lasted a few seconds, but Althea knew they were communicating more deeply than words. It hadn't always been so.

Little more than a year ago, when Althea had come to nurse her brother and meet her sister-in-law for the first time, Gillian had been full of hatred toward her husband, a hatred borne of hurt. Tertius had been on the brink of death. Nothing short of the miraculous could have restored his health and healed the breach between him and his wife.

The little girl in Althea's arms was living proof of that miraculous power. Althea repeated her thanks to the Lord, a prayer of thanksgiving that had been ever-present on her lips since she had come to Pembroke Park for the Easter holidays.

Little Judith moved her lips in sleep, and Althea shifted her position slightly. What a little thing, she thought, once again marveling at the miracle of birth. Althea had assisted at the birth, which had taken place a few days after her arrival. She was grateful now to Simon for arranging her time off.

The two weeks in the company of her brother and sister-in-law, as well as of her father, had also done Althea a world of good. She realized how much she had missed being part of a family, instead of an outsider.

She looked up when she heard her father enter the sitting room.

"How was your walk?" asked Tertius, putting down his book.

"Excellent. I feel hale and hearty," Lord Caulfield affirmed, pounding his chest. "It's not everyone my age that can still walk a couple of miles around a parkland and not feel winded."

"That's right, Papa, I think you are fitter than I," Gillian added with a laugh.

"Well, you can be forgiven anything, my dear." Her father-in-law came over to her and gave her a quick tweak on the cheek. "You've given me new life with the birth of my first grandchild."

Gillian put her hand in her father-in-law's. "Glad to oblige. I hope Judith will be the first of many."

"I should hope so, I should hope so," he muttered, walking over to where Althea sat, "especially as my only other hope lies in my confirmed spinster of a daughter here."

"Hello, Father." She gave her father a shy smile, knowing the sight of her with a baby only reminded him more vividly of her unorthodox way of life. She was sorry she could not please him in this seemingly simple matter of marriage and children, but there it was. The Lord had another path for her, and she would not look back.

She glanced once more at her brother and his wife. Although being in their company for a fortnight, witnessing their domestic bliss, reaffirmed her belief in God's faithfulness, she had also had moments of fighting the temptation to make comparisons between her life and theirs. She knew her life was as it should be, and that she was where the Lord wanted her to be.

"Here now, don't go hogging the baby." Her father's gruff voice broke into her thoughts, and she relinquished the precious bundle into his arms.

"How's my sweet little Judith? There, no need to be alarmed," he reassured her when she began to stir. "It's only Grandpa, come to see his favorite little granddaughter in the whole entire world...."

Althea smiled, watching her father bring his face up close to his granddaughter's. She was glad he finally had a little girl to lavish his attentions upon. While she had been growing up as his ward, he had never dared overdo any signs of affection. As a result she had always longed for more than the occasional careless pat on the back and "carry on" attitude.

Althea rose. "I must go upstairs before dinner and finish my packing."

"Oh, Althea, I wish you didn't have to go back so soon." Gillian began her familiar wail at the mention of Althea's departure.

"Now, you know we've been all through this," she replied.

Tertius grasped Gillian's hand. "Don't give my sister a hard time, you little termagant. Isn't it enough you have my father and me enslaved?" The loving look in his eyes belied the words. Gillian just laughed at him and accepted the kiss he planted on her hand.

"All right, all right, I shall excuse you. But who will save me from my overbearing husband when you are gone, I ask you that?"

"I am here, my dear," answered Lord Caulfield.

Althea left them laughing together.

Upstairs in the quiet of her old bedroom, she confronted the packing she had begun earlier in the day. She would be taking back more than she'd brought, since Gillian had insisted on giving her several dresses she could no longer wear, vowing that her maidenly slimness was gone forever, replaced by a new matronly figure that demanded a whole new wardrobe.

Althea had obliged, knowing she would never wear half the gowns, but knowing as well that she could find many women to give them away to. All the time she was packing, thoughts of her return to the Aguilar household hovered at the edge of her mind. Like the evening fog rising from the Thames waiting to engulf the city's buildings at the least change in wind or temperature, Althea's thoughts sought any unguarded area.

Only with difficulty had she held them at bay throughout the fortnight, keeping busy and standing firm against their invasion. Now she worked with single-minded focus, separating, folding and placing garments in her trunk, inspecting all drawers and cupboards for stray items, taking a last look under the bed, into the dressing room....

With a room swept clean of all personal belongings except those few things she would still be needing that night and the next morning, Althea stood, her hands on her waist, looking absently around. It was still too early to dress for dinner, but too late to do much else. It was the traditional time to lie down, but that was the last thing Althea felt recommendable for her state of mind.

She wandered to the window, looking over the parkland surrounding the hall. Everything was turning green, a soft delicate green overtaking the brown of field and forest like the downy fuzz on a baby's head. Pembroke Park was one of the loveliest places on earth, she thought, her gaze roaming over the hills and trees in the distance. Despite the absence of a father and mother during her girlhood years in the large, brick Tudor mansion, Althea had grown to recognize that she had had a wonderful childhood in many ways. Kindhearted servants had supplied a father and mother's warmth, and she had had a freedom to explore hill and dale around her.

Her guardian had provided her with a good education once she had come of age to be sent away to a young ladies' academy. It was one of the few things he could give his daughter what he could never manifest in public. No one would fault a guardian in providing his ward with an education.

Here and there daffodils offered bright splashes of yellow around the parkland. Althea watched a squirrel sprint from one hedge to another in the formal gardens. The peaceful vista only soothed Althea momentarily, before her thoughts turned with the certainty of a compass point back to London.

With a sigh, she let them overtake her. She was tired of standing guard against them. She thought first of Rebecca. She had missed the little girl more than she would have imagined possible for a child she had known barely two months. She had wondered many times how the girl was doing among all her boisterous cousins. Althea chided herself for her worry, knowing her father would watch over her. She knew, too, her heavenly Father was watching over Rebecca, as Althea kept Rebecca in her prayers.

The one she'd desperately avoided thinking of now came to mind. As the day approached to return to Simon's residence, Althea's agitation increased. Ever since the afternoon he had touched her cheek, she could no longer deny to herself her growing awareness of him as a man. *Awareness* was as far as she would venture in defining her sentiments. Simon's touch had only brought to the surface what had been growing for several weeks, so gradually she hadn't even noticed it. When this awareness of her employer as more than just the father of her charge had begun, Althea wasn't quite sure.

In the past fortnight, she felt she'd worn out the carpet praying to the Lord to take her feelings away. She didn't understand them. She hadn't even liked Simon when she'd first met him and she still didn't like many things about him.

When had her respect and admiration for him grown to outweigh her response to his imperfections? She admired his work in Parliament. His qualities as a father were above reproach. Indeed, she had never seen the kind of patience and devotion in a father as he exhibited toward Rebecca. She suspected her feelings were borne from this very thing, observing him almost daily in his interaction with his daughter. Not only was he so different from the way her own father had been, but compared to the fathers she had occasion to observe in the East End, Simon was exemplary. Althea was accustomed to seeing men abandoning their offspring at birth, or if they did raise them, it was with the liberal use of the rod. How many children were not led astray by their fathers' example of drinking, brawling and whoring?

And she could certainly not fault Simon as an employer. Although perhaps a bit distant, he treated all his servants fairly. She had never heard a complaint of anyone not receiving his wages on time. He had treated her with extreme fairness, even going so far as conceding all her requests. She recalled with deep gratitude how he had allowed her to teach the servants and, most of all, to teach his own daughter.

But for all his good qualities, there were the other things. She could see an intellectual arrogance and worldly ambition in him that she feared would lead to a disappointment. She thought of the proverb, "Pride goeth before destruction, and an haughty spirit before a fall." She prayed that it shouldn't be so with Simon, but she feared for him nonetheless.

Most of all she knew she could never give her heart to a man who had no reverence for God. She could not avoid the same conclusion she'd arrived at throughout the past fortnight. She must keep away from Simon Aguilar as much as possible. She was there to serve his daughter. She would do her utmost to help her, but she must remove herself from all but the most necessary contact with the girl's father.

Althea turned from the window praying once again that God would grant her the grace to see her assignment in the Aguilar household successfully through to its conclusion. She could see no clear way ahead; she felt as if she were in the middle of one vast desert. Her beginnings were already obscured; there was no turning back; her destination was equally out of sight. There was no help for it but to keep putting one foot in front of the other, trusting that the Lord would see her through, even if she didn't understand it all at the time.

Simon came into the library and put his finger to his lips. "She's coming," he whispered dramatically to his daughter, who sat in a leather armchair by the fire, her legs swinging in anticipation.

She leaned forward, her eyes sparkling, her hands grasping the arms of the chair. "Oh, I can't wait!"

"Her brother's coach has just driven up. Giles knows what to do. Now quiet!" He came to sit in another chair.

Tea had been set out on a round table before the fire. They could hear only a few sounds through the thick door.

Before Althea reached the front door, Giles had opened it for her. "Welcome home, miss."

"Hello, Giles." She gave him a surprised smile. *Home,* she thought in bemusement. No, it wasn't home, but it was nice to feel a sense of welcome at her return. "How is everyone? Rebecca? Have they returned?"

"Oh, yes, miss, everyone's back. We are all fine here," he answered. "Harry, help the coachman with Miss Breton's baggage."

"Hello, Miss Breton." Harry sprang forward at Giles's words to take her portmanteau from her.

"Hello, Harry, how are you?" she asked, untying her bonnet ribbons.

"Right as rain, miss."

"Let me take your things, miss," said Giles. "I am instructed to tell you to freshen up, then to come down to the library at your earliest convenience."

"Oh?" What strange instructions. It sounded like a summons. Was she to be dismissed? Was that the Lord's answer to her prayers? "Is something wrong?"

Giles put on his most unrevealing expression. "I couldn't tell you, miss."

"No, of course not." She took a look around her, seeing only closed doors. The smell, however, brought a sense of recognition—and welcome. Each house had its own distinct smell, and she noticed she had come to know this one's. It was not unpleasant, not like the smells of cooked food, stale beer, and human and animal waste present in most of the streets and stairwells near the mission. Nor was it the centuries-old smell of brick and mortar of Pembroke Park.

Althea breathed in the smell of this house, noting its familiarity. This house was a mixture of old, settled wood with decades of beeswax rubbed into it, leather-bound books and paper and dust that had sat for a long time. She gave a faint shake of her head. Would she still recall this scent years from now when she was a graying spinster living in the East End?

"Well, I shall go up, then," she said, removing her gloves but still hesitating.

"Very good, miss." Giles turned to direct Harry and the coachman.

Seeing there was nothing left for her to do, she started up the wide stairs. She knocked, then peered into Rebecca's room, but it was empty. No sign of anyone—the bed made, all the dolls and books in a neat row on the shelf. Althea tried to silence any worry or disappointment. The little girl she'd thought about so much and prayed about so fervently was nowhere to be seen. Could she have stayed on with her relatives? Had she grown worse? Had Simon decided she should live with her grandparents now, and was he going to inform Althea that her services were no longer required?

Althea caught herself in the mirror. She looked pale and frightened, making the freckles scattered across the bridge of her nose stand out in relief. This was ridiculous. If she was to be dismissed, she had better find out about it sooner rather than later. She marched through the sitting room into her own room. Her luggage had already been deposited on the floor.

She removed her pelisse, then rolled up the sleeves of her dress. She poured some water into her basin and bent over it to wash

her face and hands. Patting them dry with a towel she felt somewhat better. She rebuttoned her sleeves, then unpinned her hair.
She quickly hunted for her hairbrush in her reticule, and gave her
scalp a stiff brushing, as if doing so would rid her of some of the
nonsense filling her head.

Having re-pinned her coronet, she gave herself one quick look
in the glass, smoothing her skirts and readjusting the kerchief
around her neck. It would have to do for the coming interview.
She was wearing one of Gillian's castoffs, a dark blue wool set off
by the white kerchief. With a final pat to her hair, Althea turned
away from the glass.

The house was completely silent when she descended. She
knocked outside the library door, feeling as if she'd gone back in
time and was once more awaiting the interview with her brother's
school friend. How could a mere fortnight away from Simon
Aguilar put her in such a state of anxiety?

"Come in." The deep muffled voice came through the thick
wood.

Simon looked toward Rebecca's sparkling eyes. This time it
was she who held her finger to her lips. He gestured silently with
his hand for her to follow him. He took a seat at his desk and had
her crouch behind it, out of sight.

"Come in."

Althea opened the door and entered. Closing the door behind
her, she stood at the entry, making no move to go farther. She
spotted Simon at the other end of the room.

"You're back," he said in a serious tone.

"Yes, sir. You asked to see me?"

"Yes, come in. Don't just stand there."

He watched with amusement as she started at his tone then
drew her shoulders back and marched toward him.

"Mr. Aguilar, where is—?"

Before she could finish the sentence, Simon gave a nudge to
his daughter—and up she jumped.

"Surprise!" she shouted to Althea, as Simon stood and added, "Welcome home."

She approached the desk, looking from one to another, her hand at her throat, her mouth agape. For a moment he thought she was about to faint. He quickly went around the desk and took her arm. "Look what we've prepared for you." He propelled her toward the table laid for tea before the fire. The pleasant fragrance of Althea's hair reached his nostrils, and he realized he'd rarely stood this close to her, or touched her. Seeing she still looked pale, he led her to the couch by the fire.

"We wanted to welcome you with a tea party. Doesn't it look cozy?" Rebecca smiled at Althea, taking her hand.

"Oh, yes, dear, it does look cozy, indeed." Her voice still sounded faint to Simon.

"It's just tea, not a banquet," he teased, trying to lighten her mood. He hadn't realized how much he'd missed her face and her voice until he'd seen her standing there at the door. His daughter had clamored for some kind of welcoming celebration and he'd acquiesced. How glad he was he'd heeded her.

Rebecca looked at her coyly. "It was my idea to surprise you. Were you surprised?"

Althea laughed, and Simon thought he'd never heard such a clear, sweet laugh. It sounded like unmitigated joy. He wondered whether he'd ever in his life laughed like that.

"You certainly did surprise me. When I didn't see or hear anybody about, well, you can imagine the things that started going through my mind."

She met his gaze, and he realized how worried she must have been when they hadn't appeared.

"Did you think we were still at Ramsgate?" Rebecca asked delightedly.

Althea smiled and nodded. "Yes, I thought you'd be having too good a time and would not want to come back here," she replied with another laugh, taking both Rebecca's hands in her own.

For some reason Simon hadn't been able to take his eyes off

her since she'd entered the room. She was looking very fetching. The midnight blue transformed her gray eyes to blue and emphasized the gold of her hair and fairness of her complexion. He imagined it was how she must have looked during her London Seasons before she'd got it into her head that she must remove herself from society and hide herself in the slums of London. He approached the low rosewood table before the couch.

"Here, will you do the honors?" He held up the teapot.

Althea looked at him over the silver pot, and suddenly he knew she was thinking about the night of the dinner party and how Lady Eugenia had usurped her place. The intimacy of their present tea party hadn't occurred to him until that moment. What would the grand lady say if she could see the private tableau now? He realized he didn't really care. What she didn't see was no concern of hers.

Althea began to pour the tea. "Cream, sugar?" she asked him.

"Just a touch of sugar, please," he replied, taking a seat in a leather chair closest to the couch.

"Rebecca, could you take this to your father, please?" She watched his daughter bring him his tea. "You are looking so well. The sea air must have agreed with you."

Rebecca came back to her with a smile. "It did. I think God heard your prayers, Miss Althea. I feel lots better."

"I'm so thankful." She looked at the plateful of cake and tarts on the table. "These look delicious. Did you help make them?"

Rebecca nodded. "This afternoon."

Althea arranged a plate for Simon and handed it to his daughter.

"How was your stay in Hertfordshire?" Simon asked when they were all settled with their tea.

"Very pleasant, thank you," she answered, stirring her tea.

"How is the newborn?"

"Lovely, surrounded by doting parents and grandfather."

"What's her name?" Rebecca asked.

"Judith Elizabeth."

"That's pretty. When was she born?"

"Only three days after I arrived at Pembroke Park." Althea looked at Simon. "I must thank you for allowing me to go."

He shrugged, though he felt pleasure that he had been able to do something for her. It struck him suddenly that she wasn't a person who really needed anything. "I'm glad it all worked out. How is Tertius?"

Althea smiled. "Very happy. I don't think we shall see him in London anytime soon."

"No, I should imagine not."

"We have some big news, too, Miss Althea," piped up Rebecca from her chair.

"Yes?" She put her cup down, her smile fading.

"Auntie Tirzah is getting married next month. We are all invited to the wedding."

"You remember my youngest sister?" Simon asked.

"Oh, yes. She sang beautifully. The young gentleman with her at your family's house—that was her intended, was it not?"

"Yes, Solomon Cardoso. Nice chap."

"Yes, he seemed so," she said quietly.

"He'll be my uncle when they're married," Rebecca explained.

"He will, indeed. Your Uncle Solomon."

"Where is the wedding to be held, in Ramsgate?" she asked, directing her question to Rebecca.

Simon replied for his daughter. "Oh, no. It will be here in town. My sister has invited you."

"She has?" She looked surprised, her hand going again to her chest. "That was nice of her."

Simon frowned at her tone, which merely sounded perfunctory. He had expected her to be pleased. Did she feel uncomfortable with his family?

"Miss Althea, we want to take you to Ramsgate with us the next time we go. We had such a lovely time by the seashore. *Abba* promised me if I'm as good as I am now in May, we shall all go. Would you like to come with us?"

She seemed at a loss for words. "Let us wait until then, shall we?" She looked down, taking a sip of tea, as if afraid of saying more.

"I'm so glad you're back, Miss Althea. I've been missing you so."

"Have you? I've missed you, too. What have you been doing with your time?"

Simon continued to watch Althea as Rebecca chattered away. He was glad his daughter had formed a bond of affection with her nurse. It was important that she have a mother figure to look up to. It was true she had lots of family, and they visited her frequently, but it was not the same as having someone under her roof, there for her all the time. He was grateful to Tertius for having recommended his sister. Simon watched Althea push a wayward curl away from her forehead. She was a woman who cared deeply about those entrusted to her.

He could never live up to her ideals, but that was not to say he could not admire them from a distance.

"I'm starting a book," Simon said, when his daughter had turned her attention to her tart. He didn't know why he was telling her. For reasons he didn't care to analyze, he wanted her to know.

Althea turned her eyes on him, a look of expectancy in their gray-blue depths. "You are? Tell me about it."

He shrugged, suddenly embarrassed. "Oh, the usual, the need for parliamentary reform."

"That's wonderful! I'm sure it will get people to understand."

"I shall be working on it over the next several months. I thought I'd tell you so if you see me closeted in this library for hours on end, you'll understand why."

"I'm sure it will be a very valuable work."

Simon rose, suddenly uncomfortable with the coziness of the arrangement. The three of them could be a family sitting around the fire drinking tea like this. "Well, I must go and change. I shall be dining out this evening. I leave you in good hands, Rebecca."

"Oh, *Abba*, can't you stay?" Rebecca pouted. "Are you going to visit the baron again?"

"Yes, how do you know that?"

Her eyes twinkled, her disappointment forgotten. "I saw the invitation on the front table."

"Invitations to Lady Stanton-Lewis's salon have become quite coveted. All the most sought-after artists, poets and politicians gather there." He found himself addressing Althea more than his daughter, and that irritated him. It was almost as if he were offering her explanations, yet he had reached his majority long ago.

Chapter Eleven

❧

Late that evening Althea sat reading her Bible in her sitting room. It was growing late, but she was almost too tired to move. The fire was warm and snug. She felt a deliciously drowsy feeling steal over her. Her bedroom would be cold. She shouldn't have stayed up so long after a full day of travel.

She had thought she would be in bed by nine, but it had taken a while to settle Rebecca. The girl had been too excited by Althea's return and had wanted to tell her everything about her stay at the seashore. She had also wanted to hear more details about Althea's time at her brother's and had not been satisfied until Althea filled her in at length.

Althea sat back against the chair, contemplating the glowing coals. It had been a good day, all in all. There had been nothing to dread. Her first fright at not seeing Rebecca had been ridiculously unfounded. She could smile now at her worries. Rebecca had told her how it had been her idea to plan the surprise welcome.

Everything had gone well with Simon, as well. She was glad

about his writing. He seemed rested from his holiday at the seashore. She was concerned about his continued friendship with Lady Stanton-Lewis, but there was little she could do about it. He was a grown man who ought to know what he was about. At least she knew where his affections lay, and she would bury any personal feelings she'd harbored, even the recollection of them. They would be as deeply obliterated as if they were under that pile of red coals before her.

By the time she had said her last good-night to Rebecca, Althea had felt the need to sit down with her Bible. Only God's word could settle her, bringing peace and quietness to her soul. For the past few hours she had been reading and meditating in turn over the Word. The peace had come, as she had known it would, and now she felt she would sleep like a baby.

She started at a knock on her sitting room door, which as usual she had left ajar to Rebecca's room.

"Hello. Did I startle you? Were you asleep?" Simon pushed open the door and peered in.

She took a deep breath, shaking herself fully awake. "No, not at all, though if you had come a few minutes later, you might have found me so."

He smiled, entering the rest of the way. "I thought you'd have retired long before now, but I saw the light still burning."

"Yes, I thought I would have, too. I must have slept more than I realized in the coach today."

"How was your journey?"

"It was fine."

"May I sit down?"

"Yes, of course." She would tell him about Rebecca and then bid him good-night.

He stretched his legs in front of the fire. "This feels good. It's still quite cold outside, for all that spring is here."

"Yes." He had on evening clothes, but he looked slightly disheveled, like a gentleman who has come from making all the social rounds. "The London parks looked beautiful as I rode by today, with all the narcissus in bloom," she said in an attempt at polite conversation.

He didn't answer right away. Althea fingered her Bible, wondering whether to continue reading. Perhaps he was just relaxing a little before turning in for the night and didn't want a chattering female beside him. He had probably just come from hours of stimulating conversation at the salon.

As if reading her mind, he spoke up. "People from all over the Continent come to the Stanton-Lewis house to look at the collection of books and folios, and here you sit night after night with the same book. Tell me, Miss Breton, don't you get tired of reading the same words? How many times have you read them by now? Ten, twenty?"

She smiled slightly. "I've lost track."

"You remind me of a great-uncle of mine. He spent his whole life pouring over the Talmud. Didn't do him much good. I heard from those who were at his bedside at the end that he was as terrified of the fires of Gehenna as any reprobate."

She touched the book in her lap. "Blessed assurance doesn't come from reading mere words on paper. It comes from having the spirit of God on the inside. He's the one who breathes life into these Scriptures."

"So, why didn't my uncle have the spirit on the inside?"

Instead of answering, she took her Bible and opened it to the Book of John. She began reading from the first verse, "'In the beginning was the Word, and the Word was with God, and the Word was God....'"

She kept reading through to the tenth verse. "'He was in the world, and the world was made by him, and the world knew him not.'" As she read the eleventh verse, she glanced toward Simon. "'He came unto his own, and his own received him not.'"

"You are saying the Messiah came to His people, and we didn't realize it."

"I'm not saying it. This book is."

"A matter of opinion, some would have it."

"It is a matter of studying the Scriptures with 'the eyes of your understanding enlightened,' as the apostle Paul describes." When he didn't say anything, she hastened on. "Believe me, I never would have read about Christ as the Jewish Messiah in the Scriptures if God's spirit had not revealed it to me through the Old Testament prophecies. Before that time, I thought the Bible was just for Christians. I believed Christ came to save the Gentiles. I believed the Jews were guilty of murdering our Savior, not that He had anything to do with *their* salvation."

She placed her hands flat on the open pages in front of her and leaned forward. "When Tertius first asked me to come here, I was horrified. My first reaction was to refuse outright. I simply could not conceive of coming into the household of a Jew.

"You were perfectly right when you accused me of picturing you as some greedy, ambitious moneylender." Althea waited to see his reaction before continuing her tale. "My brother had to practically beg me to come to that interview with you. The only thing Tertius and I could agree upon was that I would seek the Lord's counsel." She permitted herself a slight smile. "Believe me, though I set myself to seek the Lord's will in prayer, my mind was pretty well made up in one way, and it would take a divine act to get me to change my views of the Scriptures."

"I assume you received such an act, since you are here."

She nodded. "It didn't take the Lord long to point out my error." She smiled. "Perhaps the urgency of your situation moved Him to show me in a matter of days." She looked down at her hands, knowing she was coming to the critical part. "I had been praying for only a few days, when...I had a dream." She was afraid of looking at him, afraid she would only read disbelief or mockery. She sneaked a glance, but saw he was listening to her intently. "Jesus appeared to me in the dream. He told me to come here. He also told me to go back to the Scriptures. He even gave me one particular verse." She riffled the thin pages, afraid of losing Simon's attention if she stopped talking for even a second.

She arrived at the second chapter of the Book of Ephesians.

Her fingers ran down the page until they reached the fourteenth verse. She kept her forefinger on the Scripture and looked up. Simon's attention was still upon her. "I woke up with Ephesians 2:14 clearly in my mind."

Although she could have quoted it to him by heart by then, she preferred reading it to him. "'For He is our peace, who hath made both one, and hath broken down the middle wall of parti- tion between us.'" She emphasized the parts she wanted him to understand. She risked a glance at his face to see if he had. "Don't you see he is talking about both Jew and Gentile? I went back and read and reread the entire chapter. It's Paul, a Jew, a Phar- isee of Pharisees, writing to the new converts—Gentiles—at Ephesus. He's explaining how Jesus has come to reconcile the two of us. Listen." She ran her finger farther down: "'...to make in him- self of twain one new man...that he might reconcile both unto God in one body by the cross....'

"One new man! Jew and Gentile! In one instant, the Spirit of God opened my eyes to show me that your Messiah was also my Messiah. The promise of salvation, which had been given to the Jews through the Scriptures for centuries, had now been made available to the Gentiles.

"You can't understand how that revelation changed every- thing. It came to me only days before I arrived here, but I spent that time poring over the Old Testament, *your book,* looking up every Scripture I could find about salvation, about the Messiah, every prophecy, and I discovered for the first time that Jesus was your Messiah." She looked at him marveling. "I never knew that. We Gentiles only received Jesus because you had rejected Him. But many of your people didn't reject Him. The Christian Church was full of Jews at the beginning—it was made up of Jews." She laughed. "As you guessed, I had read the Bible, oh, perhaps dozens of times, and I had never seen that. It took the Spirit that God has planted on the inside of me to reveal it to me."

She fell silent, having nothing more to say. She could reason and argue, read more Scriptures, but if Simon could not understand what she had just told him, more would not convince him. The minutes spread out, and with it, Althea's hope began to diminish, hang onto it though she would; it slowly pulverized as completely as the spent coals on the grate, falling to form a pile of white ash.

Finally Simon brought his fingertips together in a pyramid. "If Jesus gave you this grand revelation, why did He take so long about it?"

She laughed again, almost in relief. "Don't you see? Sometimes God can't show us things until we're willing to be shown."

"How profound, Miss Breton. Unfortunately, to my ears it sounds too much as if you would have a person give up all modern learning and philosophy and turn back to something that was written centuries ago and caused more disagreement and wars than all other philosophies put together."

She slumped in defeat. He had listened to her so intently, she had believed for a moment that he was beginning to understand. But the veil still had not been lifted from his eyes.

"I know one thing, Mr. Aguilar, I will not be terrified on my deathbed as your uncle was. I will not question whether my life was lived in vain. And I will know where I am going."

One afternoon in late April before leaving for the House, Simon went in search of Althea. He hadn't seen but glimpses of her in days. Although Rebecca seemed fine, he still wanted to talk face-to-face with her nurse. He'd almost say Miss Breton was avoiding him. He missed their brief early morning chats at breakfast.

He finally located her by the muffled sound of music coming from the yellow salon. He opened the door silently and stood listening. He had never witnessed her playing. Rebecca was upstairs visiting with her grandmother.

Althea struck the last few notes of a hymn. As the last note died away, she must have sensed his presence, for she whirled around on the pianoforte bench.

"How long have you been there?"

"I didn't mean to startle you," he reassured her. She seemed more flustered than the discovery of his presence warranted.

"I thought you had already left for the day," she said in a more collected tone.

"I was on my way out, but remembered I needed to do something, so here I am. You play well," he added.

Her hand went to her throat. "Th-thank you."

He peered more closely at her. "I haven't seen much of you lately. Is everything well with you?"

She looked down at her lap, clasping her hands in it. "Yes, of course."

He wasn't satisfied. He tried another tack. "Rebecca is doing well, is she not?"

Althea nodded vigorously, still not looking at him directly. "Oh, yes."

"Perhaps we shall even see the day she no longer needs a nurse," he teased.

If he thought to disconcert her, he was disappointed. She looked at him, a glow in her eyes.

"Oh, I pray for that day! I know we shall see the time when she can join all her cousins in their boisterous games."

He considered the notion. "Well, I appreciate your prayers, for whatever they're worth. I know if there is a God, He would be a cruel God indeed if He didn't listen to your prayers, Miss Breton."

She gazed at him as if longing to tell him something. No doubt more about that Savior of hers. Simon switched topics before she had a chance.

"Speaking of Rebecca's cousins, I stopped by to remind you that Tirzah's wedding is next week. It will be held at the bridegroom's house, as is customary, but we will start out from my parents' house. I know the celebrations will go on until late into the evening, and I've got permission for you and Rebecca to stay the night at the bridegroom's. This way, you can put Rebecca to bed early, so she won't get overtired by all the excitement."

Althea nodded. "She talks of little else these days. The bride-groom's parents won't mind having us, will they?"

"No, not at all, it's all arranged." He fingered a button on his coat. "I will accompany you, of course, in the coach, but I shall return here in the evening, then come and collect both of you in the morning after breakfast. Is that satisfactory to you?"

"Yes, of course. Whatever is best for you."

"Good, it's settled, then." He turned to go. At the door he paused, turning back to her. He said without thinking, though he realized as he spoke that he must have been considering the no-tion for days, "Wear the green, will you?"

She looked puzzled. "The green?"

"You know—that dress you wore to the dinner party." He felt a warmth steal over his face, as he questioned why he cared about her apparel.

Her hand went back to her throat. "Oh—"

"You'll wear it, then?" Better she had no chance to think too much about it, or wonder why he was making such a request.

Giving her no opportunity to refuse, he nodded. "Good. I must be off. Until this evening."

He strode down the hallway, trying to focus on the coming de-bate in the House, yet feeling a sense of anticipation at seeing Miss Breton once again in an evening gown at a social event.

The day of the wedding dawned bright and warm. Althea didn't have time to worry overmuch about which dress she wore, since Rebecca awoke early and was clamoring for her attention in help-ing her dress. Without bothering to analyze the right or wrong of her motives, Althea quickly washed and donned her sister-in-law's green gauze along with the pearls her father had given her.

"You look beautiful, Althea," exclaimed Rebecca as soon as she saw her.

Althea remembered the girl had not seen her the night of the dinner party, and she hadn't worn the gown since then. "Let's get you dressed." She went into her wardrobe and took out the dress

Simon had ordered especially for this day. It was a beautiful pink frock with lots of lace and frills. Althea helped Rebecca don petticoats and dress before tying her sash. "Let's get your shoes on and let your papa know we're ready."

They drove past Mayfair and Soho toward Bloomsbury. The trees were fully green now, and lilacs were in blossom everywhere. Once at Simon's parents, there was an air of frenzy as the bride was readied for her short journey to the groom's residence. Althea clasped Rebecca's hand as they watched the bride come down the steps of her house accompanied by violinists and a drummer. All the company sang a song as she was helped into an open carriage. The musicians followed in a coach, with the rest of the party bringing up the rear. The groom's parents lived a few streets down. There the bride was met at the entrance by servants who served her and all those of her party with a cup of sorbet and rose water.

They were ushered into the spacious drawing room where the furniture had been cleared out with the exception of chairs arranged along the walls. In the center of the room stood a little platform with a canopy decorated with flowers.

Althea looked on in wonder during the ceremony, not understanding a word, since it was conducted in both Hebrew and Ladino. Bride and bridegroom stood under the canopy as they were joined in matrimony by the rabbi. Solomon, the young bridegroom, wore a white robe. She noticed the rabbi wore one as well, with the prayer shawl draped over his shoulders. All the men wore their skullcaps, and many prayer shawls were visible beneath their dark jackets. Toward the end, a glass was broken by the bridegroom's foot.

Immediately following the ceremony, creamy cakes were served to everyone. Between mouthfuls, Rebecca explained to her that seven blessings had been recited over the couple.

After the cake, the guests were invited to the dining room to partake of the wedding feast. Althea sat wedged between Rebecca and another guest as plate after plate of food was served.

Rebecca told her how the bridal couple had fasted until the ceremony.

Much of the food had a foreign quality to it, and much of the language was incomprehensible to Althea, but she didn't really mind. Rebecca kept her amused, and she was touched that on this occasion Rebecca seemed content to stick close to her.

Althea could barely see Simon, who was at the far end of the table, grouped with his male relatives. She noticed toast after toast being made to the newlyweds. As the afternoon waned, many of the guests drifted back to the drawing room where an orchestra was tuning up.

By this time Rebecca began to tire of sitting among the adults. "Will you mind if I leave you for a while, Miss Althea?"

Althea squeezed her hand. "Of course not. I'm enjoying watching everyone. Go on, have fun with your cousins."

Althea remained in the dining room a bit longer, sipping the deliciously dark coffee set before her. When the silent waiter kept refilling her cup, she finally had to cover it with her hand. She suspected the sweet, rich drink would prove potent in large quantities. As the dining room emptied, she rose with a company of women and followed them out. They made their way back to the drawing room.

A large group of guests were singing around the bridal pair. Many of the elderly guests sat at the periphery of the room on the gilded, straight-backed chairs set out. Althea found a seat among them. Soon the dancing began. Althea watched the first sets of dancers fall into formation. Even the music was different, faster and livelier than most of the minuets and country dances she had learned as a girl. She tapped her slipper to the tempo, enjoying the gusto of the men and women as they formed a ring around the dance floor.

"I'm so glad you could come to my wedding." Tirzah stood by her chair.

Althea smiled up at the dark-haired girl in greeting. "Thank you for having me. It was a beautiful ceremony."

Simon's sister looked beautiful in her white silk dress and lacy veil, dark curls framing her delicate features. She took the empty chair at Althea's side.

"May I?"

Althea made a gesture of welcome. "Please do."

She stretched out her legs, her satin slippers peeking out from her hem. "Ah, it feels good to sit a moment. Why is it they make the bride and groom stand so much at a wedding?" She laughed. After a moment, her eyes caught sight of Rebecca across the room. "It's so good to see my niece looking so well."

"Yes, indeed."

"*Nu,* how are you getting on with my brother?"

Althea averted her eyes immediately, wondering at the directness of the question. "Very well, thank you. Mr. Aguilar is a very fair employer."

"Employer? Oh, yes, of course. But really, Miss Breton, I hope he is not treating you as a mere employee. You've been a salvation to Rebecca. I can see she adores you. Believe me, she didn't warm to the other nurses. Not that they were there long enough. Simon is very protective of Rebecca. He didn't give any of them a second chance." She shuddered. "Not that I blame him. You should have seen some of them. They would have given me nightmares had I been Rebecca's age." She laughed. "But you're different. You've become special to Rebecca. I hope Simon has made you feel part of the family. I hope we have, too, here today."

Althea was touched by the young woman's attention. "Thank you, Miss Aguilar. That's most kind of you."

"Mrs. Cardoso, now," she corrected with a smile.

"Of course, I do beg your pardon, Mrs. Cardoso."

"Since I consider you part of the family, please call me Tirzah."

Althea impulsively reached out her hand to the other girl. "Of course, Tirzah. And please call me Althea."

"Althea. What a pretty name." After a moment, Tirzah commented, "Simon says you are the sister of one of his closest friends."

"Yes, they knew each other at Eton."

"I'm glad they were friends. I don't think Simon had too many friends there. If you'll pardon my saying so, it's not easy being a Jew—or convert—" she added with a dry laugh "—in your world, Althea."

"Nor a Methodist."

Tirzah gave her a startled look, then grinned. "Yes, Simon has mentioned that you are of a different sect—"

She tipped her head to one side, reminding Althea of Simon. "You are not what I expected."

"What were you expecting?"

"I couldn't fathom how a lady of quality could be accepting a post of nurse, until Simon explained that you were of a different religious persuasion. You feel that God has called you to serve in this capacity."

Althea asked the Holy Spirit to give her the right words. Then she began speaking, formulating the words slowly. "When you realize what the Son of God did on this earth, offering Himself up as a living sacrifice for our sins, to make atonement for us for once and for all, then it becomes easy to turn around and obey Him when He calls us to do something for Him. It is no longer a matter of good works—that is, of trying to feel right before God, or trying to gain one's entry into heaven by the weight of one's good deeds."

Althea looked at Tirzah, to see if she was understanding anything she was saying. The young woman was smiling politely. Althea continued. "It comes down to the realization that we have all sinned and come short of God's glory. Because of that, we are all in need of a Savior—one who stands in our place, receiving the condemnation and judgment we deserve—so that we might receive deliverance."

Althea felt Tirzah was regarding her as if not quite sure what to make of her. When the groom came over to reclaim her, Tirzah turned to him with a big smile.

"There you are, Solomon!" She rose immediately to meet him,

her hands held out. Before leaving with him, she turned back to Althea. "Well, it has been a most illuminating conversation with you, Miss Breton—I mean, Althea. I hope we can chat again sometime."

Althea prayed for the young bride as she watched her forging through the now crowded room with her new husband. A little while later a maid came up to Althea to ask her whether she would like to accompany Rebecca upstairs to help put her to bed. "Mr. Aguilar sent me to show you the way."

Althea glanced around the room but didn't see any sign of Simon. She rose and followed the maid to where Rebecca held hands with her cousins, trying to imitate the chain the dancers had formed. Amidst much protest she finally agreed to go with them. As they ascended the stairs, the noise of the music became a distant hum. The maid showed them to a small room two flights up, prepared for an overnight guest.

"I was told to ask your excuses for the daybed set up for you here," the maid told Althea. "We have so many guests staying, and Mr. Aguilar assured us it was all right—that Rebecca would want you close by."

"Yes, it is quite all right."

Rebecca chattered away all the while Althea helped her put on her nightgown and wash her face and clean her teeth. The two sat on the bed afterward, Althea brushing out Rebecca's thick dark curls.

Rebecca couldn't stop talking about the bride and groom. "Wasn't Aunt Tirzah beautiful? Her cheeks looked so rosy when she said her vows. And Solomon—he's now Uncle Solomon—he looked so dashing." She twirled a curl around her finger. "Miss Althea?"

"Hmm?" Althea brushed in downward strokes.

"What kind of husband shall I have?"

Althea put down the brush and began separating the hair into three thick strands. "Ask God to pick him out for you, and you'll know your future husband will be just right."

Rebecca craned her neck around to Althea. "Will He do that?"

Althea gently straightened the girl's head around again. "Yes. 'Are not two sparrows sold for a farthing? And one of them shall not fall on the ground without your Father. But the very hairs of your head are all numbered. Fear ye not therefore, ye are of more value than many sparrows.'" Althea tugged on the half-finished braid. "So, if God knows every one of these beautiful locks, He can certainly pick out a husband for you."

Rebecca giggled. "Althea? If God can do that for me, why hasn't He picked out a husband for you? Haven't you asked Him?"

Althea's fingers stopped their braiding. "Perhaps I haven't."

"Why not?"

Althea resumed braiding, then tied a ribbon at its end. She sighed, letting the braid go. "I don't know precisely. Perhaps I've been too busy to think about a husband. And when I was young enough, I didn't know God the way I do now."

She rose to clean out the hairbrush. When she returned to the bed, she smiled. "Besides, I already have a husband."

Rebecca stared at her wide-eyed. "You do?"

"The Bible says, 'For thy Maker is thine husband; the Lord of hosts is His name; and thy Redeemer the Holy One of Israel; The God of the whole earth shall he be called.'"

Rebecca listened rapt at the words. "How do you know so much of the Bible? Have you memorized it all?"

Althea laughed, drawing down the covers. "No. But I have spent years reading and studying it. And I've had some good teachers.

"Come on, in you go." When Rebecca crawled under the covers, Althea continued. "You know what that verse is talking about?"

Rebecca shook her head.

"It's talking about the nation of Israel, the Jewish people," she added.

"Oh. You mean *Abba* and Grandpapa and Grandmama, me...our family?"

"Yes. God is like a husband to his people. It says He shall be called the God of the whole earth. That means He's my husband, too."

Rebecca's face broke into a smile. "So you don't need to get married?"

"When you enter into that place with God, He fills you up, so He's everything to you—father, friend, brother, husband."

Rebecca sat gazing up at the ceiling, pondering this. "I should like to enter that place." She turned her head to glance at Althea. "And I should like to see God pick out a husband for you here on earth, too, since you haven't had time to ask Him for one for yourself."

Chapter Twelve

Simon stood outside the door that had been left ajar. He had been lifting his hand to knock when he overheard Rebecca's questions to Althea about marriage, and stopped, curious to hear her answers.

As the conversation took on a religious turn, he wondered whether it was right for Althea to instill her theology in his daughter, but just as quickly he admitted he had nothing better to offer her. He ran his uplifted hand through his hair in frustration. All he had were empty platitudes, nothing that could really help her in the face of death, if indeed she would have to face it.

He cleared his throat and gave a light knock.

"Come in!" came his daughter's voice.

He pushed open the door. Both females turned to him, his daughter bright-eyed and smiling, as he usually found her when she was talking with Althea. Althea half turned toward him, attractive in her pale green gown, her upswept hair golden in the lamplight.

"I came up to bid you good-night."

"Are you going to dance with Miss Althea?"

"I don't know." He considered the idea, distracted momentarily from his earlier, more sobering thoughts. "I suspect Miss Breton is more accustomed to grand ballrooms where dancing is very formal and elegant."

He turned to Althea, noticing she did not participate in the conversation. He watched her hang up his daughter's clothes.

"Were you not trained in the minuet and waltz?"

She replied with her back to him. "I haven't danced in years. Besides, I have probably danced more simple country dances, which are not nearly so formal as the minuet."

"You don't find the dances downstairs excessively primitive?"

She set Rebecca's slippers beside her bed. "I enjoyed watching the dancers. It put me in mind of the marriage of Cana."

"I'm afraid you may be disappointed by our poor example here, then. You will find no miracles at this one." He didn't know why he was always trying to provoke a response from her. Was it because he resented that he seemed to need these dialogues with her more than she did?

"Oh, I think our Lord was enjoying Himself just fine before He was ever asked to turn the water into wine."

Althea lowered Rebecca's lamp, and Simon held the door open for her, forcing her to accompany him out. He could smell her sweet fragrance as she passed by him. Soft, wispy tendrils curled around the nape of her neck. Simon caught himself thinking what it would feel like to kiss that part of her skin. The notion astounded him and he stopped momentarily, gripping the door handle.

He had to quicken his stride to catch up with her. Halfway down the hallway, he asked, "Doesn't your God allow dancing?"

She seemed to consider his question. "I think God enjoys seeing his children enjoying themselves."

"Then, why is it you haven't danced in so many years?"

"Perhaps I never enjoyed it much the few occasions I did dance."

"Perhaps you never had the right partner." Why did he continue this ridiculous topic of conversation? Was it because she was being so annoyingly serene in her replies to him tonight?

"Perhaps not. In recent years there's been so much else to do that I haven't even thought about dancing."

The woman beside him had done wonders for his daughter—shouldn't that be enough? Why was he trying so desperately to get her to betray her beliefs? Disgusted with himself, he excused himself when they reached the drawing room.

"Well, I shall leave you to enjoy the festivities as your Savior did. I don't believe He partook in any dancing either, did He?" He could have kicked himself when he saw that brief look of reproach in her eyes. Their conversations always seemed to end this way lately—when he managed to track her down, he thought sourly—in some sort of draw. "Can I get you some refreshment or anything?" he added lamely.

"No, thank you. I'm fine." She was the first to move away.

He watched her wend her way across the crowded room, looking for an empty seat. The least he could have done was find her one.

Thoroughly vexed with himself, he went over to where his younger brother stood with some other gentlemen.

"So, Nathan," he asked, slapping his brother on the back, "how is the apprenticeship?"

"Fine. I'll be glad when it's over, though." He smiled sheepishly. "I won't feel like quite such a slave. *Abba* has promised me a real position at the bank."

"Banking it will be, then? Not commerce?"

"Well, I did my best to convince him I was more a banker than a businessman. If I find—or if David finds," he added with a grin, "that I'm not suitable, they'll stick me in the factory under Daniel."

Simon returned the smile, knowing that of the two brothers, they would both prefer working under David, the banker. The industry giant, the eldest, ruled like his father, with an absolute authority.

"Sorry you didn't go into politics, as I did?" asked Simon.

"Would you take me under your wing?"

Simon fingered the knot of his cravat. "I never considered it. I didn't think you'd be interested. Would you be?"

"Well, I've been doing a lot of reading in history, on my own."
He hesitated, reddening. "It seems rather interesting, being able
to shape the course of nations and all."

Simon smiled at him. "That's it in a nutshell. Let me give it some
thought. It wouldn't be easy, you know." Neither spoke the obvious word—*conversion*—but he knew they were both thinking it.

Nathan gave another grin. "No."

"So, you'd have to think about it very carefully. Perhaps you
should try the route Father suggests for the first year or so, and
if you find you can't stand either finance or commerce, come talk
to me again."

Nathan nodded and turned his attention back to the dance
floor. Simon followed his gaze across the dancers.

"I feel sorry for your Miss Breton. She's not dancing, and yet
she looks as if she'd like to," his brother observed.

Simon spied Althea. She had managed to find a chair and now
sat primly, wedged among the elderly matrons who enjoyed
watching the younger people dancing. He observed her, wondering how his young brother knew so much. Althea's attention
was on the dancers, her gaze following their rapid movements, her
lips slightly parted, her chin moving up and down in time to the
music.

"She's not *my* Miss Breton" was all he said as he continued
watching her.

Something seized him, a bit of mischief—he didn't know. He
gave Nathan a sidelong glance. "Why don't you ask her to dance?"

He could see his younger brother's cheeks turn pink. "Me?"

"Yes, why not?"

"She—she wouldn't dance with me!"

Simon shrugged. "You don't know until you try." He moved
toward a group of men and gave his attention to them, leaving
his brother to take up the challenge or not.

Simon soon became involved in the conversation. When he
next turned around, his brother was gone. He glanced around and
found him standing in front of Althea's chair. Simon watched as
Nathan just stood in front of her, not saying anything until she

looked up at him. He watched his brother speak, noticed her puzzlement and request for him to repeat what he'd said. Nathan bent forward and tried again.

This time Simon saw comprehension dawn in her eyes, quickly followed by confusion as she put a hand to her breast, mouthing the word *Me?* He felt sorry for his brother, just standing there, probably thinking himself a fool. Just as Simon was beginning to regret having teased him, he watched Althea smile, shake her head, then stop as she studied his brother's face. Simon found himself holding his breath just as he imagined Nathan must have been doing as the seconds ticked by. Then he saw the decisive squaring of the shoulders he was beginning to recognize in Althea when she resolved on a course of action she considered a challenge. She gave a brief nod and stood, smoothing her skirts and giving a quick pat to her hair before allowing his brother to escort her onto the dance floor.

Simon continued watching as his brother taught Miss Breton the steps, saw rather than heard her laughter as she made mistakes. Their lighthearted laughter reminded him of that of two children. He felt something queer inside him. Before he could examine it, he found himself walking toward the two dancers.

Unable to stop himself, he cut in, pressing his brother's shoulder and saying, "Do you mind, Nathan?" Without giving him a chance to agree or disagree, Simon stepped into his brother's place among the dancers.

He watched Althea's confusion, then acceptance at the change of partners. "I haven't danced in years, either," he told her above the noise. His hands gripped hers; his arm went over and around her head several times as he twirled her around, their bodies coming together and separating in time to the music.

When the tune ended he was loath to let her hands go, so he took one and tucked it in the crook of his arm and led her off to the side. He freed her hand but continued holding it loosely in his own. It felt small. Her face was flushed, the tendrils of hair sticking to her forehead damply.

"Let me get you some refreshment. Stay here."

When he returned, he was more relieved than he could say to see she had obeyed his command. He handed her a cup of punch.

"Thank you," she said, taking it from him. Their gloved fingertips touched. "It tastes wonderful."

He watched her, thinking how soft her skin looked, wondering what it would feel like to rain kisses down her throat. His glance dipped lower to that shadowy valley between her breasts, just visible above the silky green material. Feeling his blood begin to stir, he shifted his gaze.

She was not looking at him, but holding the cup near her lips, her attention upon the dancers.

"I was watching you when Nathan approached you," he told her. "You didn't expect to be asked to dance, did you."

She shook her head, not meeting his eyes. She took another sip of punch.

"Why did you accept his invitation?"

She looked down at her glass. "I don't know. Perhaps I remembered all those times I had sat out dances during my coming out, wishing to be asked but feeling terrified lest I be discovered if some gentleman should ask me." She shrugged, meeting his eyes at last. "I saw that same fear in your brother's face, and suddenly he seemed so young. He had no reason to ask me to dance. He was just being polite. I'm not anything to anyone here tonight."

You are to me, thought Simon, and suddenly he felt very protective of her. She seemed infinitely precious. He caught himself the next second, amazed at this sentiment. A physical reaction he could explain away. But an emotional one? This woman was merely his daughter's nurse. She was someone who goaded him. He had been brought up to regard a woman as one charged with making a home for her husband, bearing his children and satisfying his physical needs. When had he begun to lean toward Miss Breton to fill his emotional needs? It was a terrifying thought, a situation that left him more vulnerable than he'd allowed himself to be since his school days.

"Come, let's continue dancing." Not permitting her a chance to refuse, or himself a chance to question his actions, he removed the glass from her hands and took her hand once more, to lead her back to the dance floor, just in time to join a forming set.

Althea no longer knew what time it was nor how many feet she had stepped on. She and Simon joined hands and skipped around the dance floor. His grasp was firm and sure. Patiently he taught her the steps, laughing with her when she stumbled, telling her she could tread on his feet all she wanted—he would invent a reason for his disability when he hobbled around the House tomorrow. Every time she tripped, his arms went round her, and for an instant, her body was flush with his, his arms enfolding her, so close to him she could breathe the scent of his starched cravat, feel the textures of his clothes against her bare arms, his chin resting on her hair.

After the surprise at finding herself in his arms, she had abandoned herself to the music, keeping her mind focused on the intricate dance steps, and refusing to think beyond that.

She had never seen this side of Simon—carefree, boyish, his laugh deep and rich.

When the music stopped, she said, "Enough. I don't think I can stand up for another one."

"You did very well, Miss Breton, for not having any Sephardic blood in your veins," he said with a smile, once again tucking her hand in his arm in a protective and possessive way and leading her off to the side. "Here, sit down." He indicated an empty chair. "Let me get you some more refreshment."

"Thank you," she said, breathless, "would you?"

She dared not examine too closely the feeling of well-being that had invaded her entire body. She felt warm and alive. She began to ask the Lord what it was all about. Was she wrong to be enjoying this moment with her employer? She watched the dancers; everyone seemed exuberant.

Before she knew it, Simon had returned and held out a glass

for her. She turned to him with a grateful smile. "Thank you. I'm glad to see you got some for yourself this time."

"How did you enjoy your first Jewish nuptials?"

"Very much."

"You must be tired."

She felt herself blushing, conscious of the way he was looking at her. She had never seen that look on his face. It was tender and humorous and like a silent communication.

"Yes, a little."

"I'll escort you up to your room as soon as you've finished your punch."

"Yes, all right." Was it disappointment she experienced? Nonsense. She must know when a carefree moment had ended and it was time to return to normal. She drained the last of her punch and looked at him.

"All ready?"

"Yes, quite." She stood.

He held her by the elbow this time and cleared a path for them through the thinning crowd. Once outside Rebecca's door, he said in a low tone, "I shall be by to collect you and Rebecca tomorrow morning. Sleep in. I won't come by too early."

"Thank you." With an effort she looked into his eyes, wondering what he would see in hers. "I hope you won't be too fatigued tomorrow."

"Not to worry, I'm used to late evenings." He chuckled, looking down at his feet. "I might have to put my feet on ice, though."

She laughed as she looked downward. When she raised her eyes once more, he was no longer looking at his feet but at her. He was giving her such a warm look, she was glad of the low lights in the corridor to hide the color she could feel stealing over her cheeks.

"Was your evening enjoyable?"

"Oh, yes, thank you. Thank you for teaching me all those dance steps." She was babbling, so she stopped and took a deep breath. "You are blessed to have such a wonderful family."

His grin was lopsided. "They are tolerable."

She frowned, remembering his younger brother. "You don't think your brother minded that you cut in?"

Simon smiled, shaking his head. "No. Don't worry about Nathan." Still he stood there, giving her that strange look, a half smile tugging at the corner of his lips, as if he knew something she didn't.

"Well, good night, then, Miss Breton. Pleasant dreams."

Her throat felt constricted. "Good night, Mr. Aguilar."

He took her hand and brought it up to his lips. She could feel the pressure of his lips against the back of her gloved hand. Her heart felt as if it had stopped. Her feet couldn't move. Time itself had ceased to move.

The chimes of a clock at the end of the hall shattered the illusion. Althea sucked in her breath. At the same moment she withdrew her hand, Simon let it go. She could no longer see his face. He gave her a last bow before moving quickly down the hallway.

Althea opened her door. She clicked it shut behind her, then stood with her back against it. Her heart, having ceased to function a few seconds ago, now pounded with deafening thuds. She brought her gloved hand to her face and pressed the part that Simon's lips had touched to her own lips. She breathed in the scent of him and gave a soft moan. *Oh, God, oh, God.*

Simon descended the stairs quickly, too restless to retire for the evening. What had got into him this evening to pay court to Miss Breton, of all women? He who'd prided himself on being in control of his actions in all areas of his life had allowed some impulse to rule him tonight.

"There you are, Simon—"

His father's voice cut into his thoughts. Simon stopped short in the hallway. Leon Aguilar had just exited the ballroom and stood waiting for his son.

"Good evening, Father." Of all his offspring, Simon was the only one who didn't address him as *Abba.* It had started at Eton, when Simon had begun shedding more and more of his ancestral customs and emulating the English boys around him.

"How's Rebecca?" Leon Aguilar's tone was gruff and abrupt. "Can she sleep through all the noise?"

"I think she's sleeping fine," Simon answered absently. He didn't want to lie to his father that he hadn't actually checked on his daughter. He realized that he had trusted Miss Breton to do so. Suddenly he did not want to tell his father he'd just escorted Miss Breton up to her room. That annoyed him even more, so he deliberately said, "I took Miss Breton up to her room. I'm sure she'll see how Rebecca is doing."

His father nodded, although Simon didn't like the look he was giving him, as if he saw past the words to something deeper.

"Come with me for a moment. I feel like a smoke."

His father didn't wait for him to reply but began leading the way to a quieter room. "Mr. Cardoso told me to use his study. It should be down here somewhere. Ah yes, here we are." He opened a door to a small, book-lined room whose main feature was a large desk and two armchairs facing it.

They seated themselves in the two chairs. Simon waited quietly while his father lit a cigar. At his offer of one, Simon shook his head. He'd learned to tolerate the smell, though he didn't like it. His aversion stemmed from his days at public school when a gang of upper-form boys had forced "the little Ephraimite" to smoke an entire cigar, coughing and retching, his eyes tearing, his lungs on fire, until he'd puked up all his dinner. The boys had found this uproariously funny. That's when they'd had the idea of "examining him" to see if he really was circumcised. They'd yanked down his pants, laughing at the evidence of his Jewry till they were in danger of wetting their pants, then they'd run away as soon as they heard Mr. Simmons, the evening floor watchman come along. They'd left Simon frantically pulling up his trousers, wiping his face clean, to meet the suspicious old man alone.

Simon shook off the memory, focusing on his father's words. "Nice wedding," grunted Mr. Aguilar between satisfied puffs.

"Yes, it's been quite a celebration."

"Tirzah will do well with Solomon. Solid sort of chap. The Cardosos are good people, too."

"Any business plans together?" Simon ventured, doubting his father would have turned all sentimental at this juncture.

"Oh, yes, but there's time for that. Let them enjoy the nuptials." He chuckled. "Even the Good Book says a man newly wed must keep away from the front lines of battle and enjoy that first month with his wife."

"Of course." Simon tapped the arms of the chair with his hands, wondering what his father wanted. He knew him well enough to be sure he never wasted words.

"You know it's been eight years since Hannah died."

"Yes." Were weddings supposed to remind every widower of his departed spouse?

His father looked at the tip of his cigar. "It's time you were thinking of remarrying."

Ah. Simon's tapping fingers slowed their rhythm. Now they were coming to it.

His father looked at him from under heavy brows. "Any prospects?"

Simon put his fingers together in a pyramid and looked over them at his father, keeping his tone neutral. "No."

"Oh, come, son. You are beginning to get a name for yourself in the world. I read about you in the papers. Don't tell me you haven't caught the attention of some wealthy lady."

Simon raised an eyebrow. "A Gentile?"

His father shrugged. "If she has the right name and connections, we needn't hold that against her necessarily. What is happening with the prime minister, by the way? Wasn't he considering you for one of the junior lords of the treasury?"

Simon rubbed his face, too tired for this type of conversation at such an hour. "He still is. Nothing's been decided yet."

His father took another puff, exhaling with evident pleasure. Simon took a breath through his mouth to escape the smell that was making him nauseated in the small, close room.

"Well, you mustn't keep a thing like this hanging too long. There are only three junior lords, and you don't know when another will open up. If you dawdle, someone can come along and snatch it from under your very nose."

"I'm well aware of that."

"That position is only one step away from a Cabinet position. And a salary of one thousand pounds a year is quite a jump from what you're getting now. You'd be reporting directly to the chief whip. You'd be moving from the backbench to the treasury bench, you'd be at the heart of the power."

"You're not telling me anything I don't know." It rankled Simon that his father was right. He was always right. When was he going to realize Simon knew the rules of the game very well and didn't have to be told them?

His father ignored his son's tone. After a few moments, he said, "Marriage to the right individual could help move things along. We must consider it from all angles—the right family name—perhaps even a title—a member of the Church, and—" he struck the ash off the tip of his cigar with one decisive tap against the ashtray "—any rumors of your Jewishness would be squelched."

Simon breathed outward. So that was it. His father thought his advancement was being held up because of doubts over the validity of his conversion.

He offered no comment. His father continued puffing in silence.

"Your name has been cropping up lately along with that of Lady Stanton-Lewis in the gossip sheets."

Simon's glance connected with his father's. "I've been to her salon a few times. Many unmarried gentlemen gather there."

"But none of their names have been linked to hers as yours has."

Simon shrugged, beginning to drum on the chair arms again. "I can't help what the gossipmongers say."

"They would say, Where there's smoke, there's fire."

When Simon didn't reply, his father continued. "It's never good business to pay too much attention to a married woman. You're single, young still, with an ambition to make it in politics, and for all your British polish, you're still a Jew. You need to guard your reputation more than most."

"I shall take your advice to heart." He knew his father spoke the truth, but the words chafed him. Perhaps because for his whole adult life he'd been doing nothing but guard his reputation.

His father continued to smoke. Simon waited, wondering if there would be anything more. If Lady Eugenia was all his father wanted to bring up, Simon could feel some measure of relief. Lately, he'd been raked over the coals every time his father read about what Simon had said in Parliament.

He might be playing with fire with Lady Eugenia, but Simon felt no real concern from that quarter. She was just seeking to be amused, as he himself was. To a man who had never gone after sheer amusement, it had a surprisingly liberating quality to it.

Simon's relief was short-lived, however. His fingers stopped their drumming at his father's next words.

"I noticed your dancing with what's-her-name—the nurse."

"Miss Breton?" he said carefully, watching his father's face.

"That's right. You two seemed to be having yourselves quite a time."

Simon shrugged, though he could feel the tingling at the back of his neck. His father seemed to have eyes everywhere. "I just felt sorry for her, sitting with all the old women. She's been good to Rebecca. It was nothing."

"Careful when you start feeling pity for a woman. She can get you ensnared before you know it."

Simon laughed, though he felt sick inside. Is that what it had been? Mere pity that could turn a man's insides on fire and make him behave like a fool? "Oh, come, Father, as you said, she is just Rebecca's nurse."

"That's right, and it would do you well not to forget it. She's an employee under your roof, under your protection. Two things your grandfather taught me, and they've stood me in good stead all these years. Leave married women alone, leave the hired help alone." His father turned to the desk and pushed the fat cigar against the ashtray. He stood, brushing off any ash from his shirt-front and waistcoat. He looked at Simon. "I have the names of some nice young debutantes making their appearance this Season. I'm going to ask my friend, Lord Woodsbury, to arrange for you to meet them at a few social events. You just let me know which one you favor, and we'll take it from there. All right?"

Simon stood so that he was eye level with his father, the acrid smell of the extinguished cigar insinuating itself into his nostrils. "As you wish, Father."

His father gave him a hearty pat on the back, leading him out of the smoke-filled room. "You won't regret it. We'll see you a prime minister before you're forty, eh?" He chuckled. "Let me find your mother. I think we'll be getting along home. It's getting late."

"Good night, Father."

Simon left his father and walked to the end of the mansion, looking for a quiet spot. He finally found an unused room, cool and dark. He stood by the window, looking out at the night sky, wondering why his father's announcement had left him so cold. He had had no qualms the last time his father had arranged a marriage for him. He'd barely known who his betrothed was, hadn't even exchanged any words with her when his father and Hannah's had arranged their betrothal. All he knew of her was that she was a pretty brunette who sat with her mother and sisters up above in the gallery of the synagogue faithfully every Sabbath and holiday service.

He remembered feeling only relief that she was pretty. The match, based purely on economics, could have yielded an ugly lump of a woman to be the one to warm his bed over the next few decades.

Hannah had been pretty enough and compliant enough with

the twenty-two-year-old lad who'd fumbled on that first night, but who'd eventually figured things out on subsequent attempts.

It hadn't turned out badly, either. Hannah had been a nice girl, a good wife in her short life. It hadn't been her fault that she wasn't around to warm his bed for very long.

Why did he now feel as if he were bound for the slaughter a second time—first handed over to the Gentile world in the realm of education and religion, in a gesture of political fealty—and now, sealed forever through matrimony? This final act would obliterate any hint of the Jew in him. It would also mark the final surrender of his identity. It was what he'd wanted, what he'd worked for, so why did he hesitate?

There was no denying the truth of what his father said. Was his posting to junior lord—which had been a certainty only a few months ago—delayed because of questions over his ancestry? Would marriage to a Gentile woman of high birth silence those qualms for good?

Or had his radical political views on certain issues so shaken the old-line Tories that they now regretted their prior willingness to promote him?

Simon put his two hands up against the window, feeling his well-ordered life beginning to unravel. The years of self-imposed discipline, of denying himself many worldly pleasures in order to succeed in his career, apparently were of little merit in the eyes of his colleagues. He clenched his fists against the cold glass, wanting to rail at those old men in the party who wielded the power through their names and fortunes. He wanted them to feel the sweat and sacrifice he'd expended to get where he was. Did it count for nothing?

After many moments of contemplating the situation from every angle, Simon lifted his head and peered through the dark glass. Very well, he'd marry his little Gentile heiress—one with a powerful enough name to give him the freedom to spit in the eye of all those Tories who controlled their party.

The decision, instead of giving him peace, only made him feel as if a noose were tightening about his neck. Miss Breton's words came back to him. *"One new man...."*

Could there ever be a place where Jew and Gentile could meet without either giving up who he was?

Chapter Thirteen

The next morning Simon did not come for Rebecca and Althea, sending instead his coach and groom. When they returned to the mansion on Green Street, they discovered Simon had gone away for "a few days," as Giles informed Althea.

Althea told herself it was for the best. The Lord would not suffer her to be tempted above what she was able to handle. She set herself to work, resuming her lessons with the kitchen maids, preparing the Bible studies and entertaining Rebecca. Taking advantage of the beautiful spring weather, she took Rebecca out for a drive in the coach every afternoon.

On the third day after Simon's departure, Rebecca complained of a sore throat at bedtime. By midnight she was thrashing in bed, her forehead burning to the touch.

Althea spent the remainder of the night applying cold compresses, praying and pacing. By dawn, she summoned the physician. Althea was livid with anger when he didn't arrive until several hours later, the typical society doctor who would do nothing to disturb himself. He felt Rebecca's pulse, took her temperature, bled her, administered a sleeping draft, and pronounced a fever and ague. He admonished Althea to watch her closely and call him if there should be any change.

By that afternoon, Althea called Mr. Russell, a young surgeon, who had recently started lending his services at the mission. She watched as he checked Rebecca. After a lengthy examination, he walked with Althea out to the hallway, rolling down his sleeves.

"How is she?"

He looked at her gravely. "You want the truth?"

Althea nodded.

"It doesn't look good. From all you've told me of her history, and what I see now, I fear it is more than just a case of a fever. She does have that, but it's the other that concerns me more. This infection will further weaken her.

"I've seen only one other case like hers, but I've been studying it. There isn't much known about it, except that it seems to attack a victim's defenses. It is somehow connected to the blood. Most victims die within a couple of months. I'm surprised at how long this little girl has lasted, and you say she's been quite well the past few weeks?"

"Yes, her family was beginning to hope...." Her voice trailed off.

"I don't want to extinguish your hope." He gave a slight smile. "I've seen more than one miracle in my profession, perhaps more since I have begun to work with you at the mission. Continue as you have been."

She knew he was referring to more than just her physical ministrations. With a heavy heart she accompanied him to the door.

"Thank you for coming all the way across town at my summons."

"Just obeying the Master's call." He smiled at her. "He is no respecter of persons. I'll check up on her in a few days if I don't hear from you sooner." He gave her one last look. "It won't be easy."

After he'd gone, Althea climbed wearily up the stairs. Where, oh where, was Simon? Why wasn't he there when she—when his daughter, she corrected herself—needed him?

After checking on Rebecca, Althea went into her own room. She didn't need the surgeon to tell her it was going to be a long, difficult battle. She took her Bible and went to the edge of her bed to kneel.

When she arose some time later she felt refreshed and ready to face the enemy. She went back to Rebecca's bedside. "'You shall not die, but live, and declare the works of the Lord,'" she said out loud to the sleeping form and to anyone else who might be within hearing range.

Afterward she went downstairs and explained the situation to Mrs. Coates and Giles.

"I'll help you nurse her," offered Mrs. Coates. "I can sit with her in the afternoons so you can get some sleep."

"We need to keep the other servants away from her as much as possible, since the fever might be contagious."

"Shall I send someone to inform Mr. Aguilar?"

Althea turned to Giles gratefully. "Oh, yes, please, would you?"

The next few days blurred one into another, as Althea sat her vigil by Rebecca's bedside, administering the sleeping drafts, trying to get liquid down her throat, sponging her hot body down, changing her sheets and night things while trying to disturb her as little as possible. Through it all she did battle of another sort.

"You shall not have her, Satan. You get your filthy hands off of her," she would say out loud in the stillness of the night. "The Lord is your shepherd, Rebecca, you shall not want...though you walk through the valley of the shadow of death, you will fear no evil, for He is with you; His rod and His staff they comfort you."

Lord, strengthen her, let Your life flow through her little body, she prayed, kneeling by Rebecca's bed. *Let Your healing virtue course through her veins. Oh, Lord, You healed my brother—You brought him back from the dead.... Let us see Your glory here!*

* * *

Althea started awake. Someone had touched her. She found herself kneeling on the floor at Rebecca's bed. She must have fallen asleep there praying. "Who—wha—?"

"Shh. It's all right. It is just I, Simon."

Althea pushed her hair away from her forehead. "What time is it?" She still felt disoriented.

"Just past two o'clock," he whispered in the dark. "I have just returned. How is she?"

Althea yawned and rubbed her stiff neck. She tried to rise, but too quickly. Her feet felt numb and she lost her balance. Simon grabbed her arms from behind to steady her.

How tempting to lean against his frame. But, no! Althea jerked forward, remembering the past week. She approached the bed, looking down at Rebecca. Her breathing sounded good. She touched the girl's forehead. "Oh!" She turned to Simon, forgetting all else. "God be praised! Her fever has broken. Feel! Feel how wet her forehead is!"

Simon stretched his hand out obediently. "Yes, it feels normal to the touch. Has it just broken?"

Althea nodded. *Oh, God! Oh, God! Thank you! Oh, thank you!* Suddenly she could contain her joy no longer. She didn't care who saw her. She knelt back down at the bed, buried her face in the covers and began to weep, praising God through her sobs.

"Oh, Lord, I thank you...Oh, Lord, how merciful art thou...merciful indeed...Oh, my God, you heard my prayers...." Her praises were whispers between sobs.

After a while she became aware of Simon beside her. He had knelt beside her and now put his hands on her two arms.

"There, there, Miss Breton. It's all right. She's all right. Calm yourself." Gently he turned her toward himself and embraced her, comforting her all the while with gentle murmurings.

"I came as soon as I received the message. You should have called me sooner," he whispered against her hair. "There, there, Miss Breton." His hands stroked her back in long, steady motions.

"Sh-she was so s-sick," she sobbed against his coat. "Maybe I shouldn't have taken her out those a-afternoons when you first went away. The weather was so warm, and Rebecca seemed so well. Sh-she's been so well—"

"I know, I know." His long even strokes against her back matched the soft rhythm of his words. "Don't reproach yourself."

She brought up her sleeve to wipe her nose and cheeks. "I called Dr. Roseberry immediately, but what he left her didn't do any good; her fever continued unabated. I finally called for another one—a surgeon who helps us at the mission—"

"That's quite all right. You did the right thing." When he noticed her sniffling and seeking to wipe her face, he removed one of his hands to extract his pocket-handkerchief. Gently he eased her face up to his and began wiping her cheeks and nose.

She took it from him and blew her nose. "I'm sorry. I'm making a mess of your shirtfront."

He chuckled, a low sound vibrating deep in his chest. "That's quite all right, Miss Breton. I'm quite travel-stained as it is. A few tears shall do my clothes no great harm."

She blew her nose one last time and dabbed at her eyes. "I'm not crying because I'm upset. It's only I'm...I'm so thankful. You don't know how sick she's been."

He replaced his other arm about her back. "I only wish I could have been here. I shouldn't have gone away. I traveled to Manchester."

Once again the soft rhythm of his voice against her hair, the safe embrace of his arms and the reassuring smell of him were soothing her. As her euphoria subsided, she gradually became aware of their position.

On her knees on the floor, embraced by her employer. Too close, much too close to him. If she but lifted her head a fraction, she would be inches from his lips.

Oh, God, help me, she cried inwardly. She knew in that moment she was powerless to move.

She sensed the quiet inner voice of the Holy Spirit telling her that the comfort she derived from Simon's embrace was illusory; this man was spiritually dead and rushing headlong to his doom if he wasn't awakened in time. If Althea succumbed to a moment of stolen pleasure, she would seal his doom.

She pressed the handkerchief to her mouth to stifle a moan. It cost her everything she had, but gently she began to break away.

As soon as Simon felt her pressure against him, he loosened his hold. He rubbed the back of his neck. God, what had he been doing? He'd gone away in an effort to regain a proper perspective—and what did he do the moment he stepped in the door, but rush to embrace his daughter's nurse? Where would it have led if Miss Breton hadn't displayed her customary restraint?

"I'm sorry," she whispered with a sniff, making an effort to stand. "Here I am keeping you on the floor, and you've just arrived. Please forgive me."

He had to get his senses under control. The feel of her body under his hands was like a life-giving elixir to his yearning soul. Those few moments of holding her warm softness fractured all the foundations he'd built up since boyhood. Had he succeeded in doing nothing in all those years but deny the clamors of a soul that longed to be loved? The emotional weakness his rational mind despised so much had never been obliterated, he could see now, but merely covered over with layer upon layer of self-denial.

This devastating discovery propelled him into immediate action. He took Miss Breton by the elbow and helped her up off the floor. "Here, sit down, Miss Breton. There is no need for you to keep apologizing. I should be at your knees thanking you for all you've done for Rebecca." As he spoke, he gently pushed her into the chair.

"Can I get you anything?" he asked, raking a hand through his hair. "A cup of tea?"

She shook her head violently, twisting the sodden handkerchief in her hands. "No, no, not a thing."

Simon moved to the other side of Rebecca's bed, wanting to increase the distance between the two of them. He no longer trusted himself. He pushed aside the curtain and bent over his daughter's sleeping form. Gently, he began to stroke her forehead. "She seems peaceful now. Her skin feels cool."

Althea sat mesmerized by the love and tenderness on his face as he looked down at Rebecca. He seemed to have forgotten her, and she was content to watch him unobserved. His face devoid of cynicism was beautiful, and she pictured one of God's angels, standing just so, a dark-haired cherub or archangel. In the dim lamplight, she drank in the planes and curves of his profile, the smooth expanse of pale forehead against the tousled black curls, the thick dark brows and inky lashes. He wasn't wearing his spectacles and his deep-set eyes glowed in the lamplight. The light outlined the high bridge of his nose and brought into relief the cushion of his crimson lips. The stubble of a beard shadowed his cheeks. Dark sideburns emerged from the unruly hair. How she wished she could take her fingers and bring some order to his curls.

Instead she crossed her arms more tightly against her belly, like a person huddled against the cold.

He looked across the bed at her. "Miss Breton, you must go to bed. You look exhausted and cold."

Suddenly aware of what she must look like, her plaited hair in disarray, her nightcap askew, her eyes red and swollen, she looked away from him. "I'll be all right. I can doze here."

"Nonsense, I'll sit the rest of the night with her."

She looked at him aghast. "You? You've just come from a journey. You're the one exhausted."

He took her by the arm and began urging her toward the sitting room door. "We can argue tomorrow about which one of us is the more exhausted. In the meantime, you get into your bed and sleep. I can make up my sleep in the morning." They had arrived at the door, and he took her chin in his fingertips and turned her toward him.

For a moment Simon thought he would kiss her. His reason told him he stood at a precipice. One small step forward—the distance between those parted lips and his—and he would be over the edge.

Behind him lay all he'd worked for and built since his boyhood:

his family's approbation, the respect and admiration he'd fought tooth and nail for in the House—including the prime minister's, and now the acceptance of London's ton.

He released her chin and rubbed his face in an attempt to physically restrain himself. When he spoke, he was light and teasing. "Something tells me even if you sat up all night with my daughter, you would still rise in the early morning and put in a full day's work, whereas I shall be perfectly easy sleeping until noon." He looked at her a few more seconds, through half-closed eyes. "Good night, Miss Breton. Pleasant dreams."

She said nothing, merely bowed her head and scurried into the dark room.

Rebecca remained very weak for several days, gradually regaining a little more consciousness each day. True to his word, Simon sat up with her every night. He also assigned the maids portions of each day to sit with her, so that "Miss Breton wouldn't sicken on them," for he found her far too pale—"even her freckles are disappearing," he teased. Rebecca giggled weakly, while Althea reddened at the thought that her freckles had not passed unnoticed by him.

One afternoon as she returned from a brisk walk, a habit she'd suspended during Rebecca's fever, she heard muffled laughter through the library door. Just as she began to untie her bonnet ribbons, the door opened and Lady Stanton-Lewis appeared.

"Now, Simon, I shall expect you there tomorrow evening. You can't get out of it just because half the company present are dead bores."

Simon made a remark Althea didn't catch. Feeling extraordinarily uncomfortable at the thought of meeting the two of them, Althea's eyes darted about for escape. Lady Stanton-Lewis tapped Simon against the arm with her fan. "How naughty of you." She gave a low, throaty laugh. "What would Griff say?"

The two began to walk toward her. Althea stood still, not knowing where to go. Lady Stanton-Lewis in her elegant lavender afternoon dress and hat stood almost as tall as Simon. Althea could not help marveling at the lady's ensemble; every accessory matched, from kid boots to ruffled parasol. Lady Stanton-Lewis pulled on a pair of lavender gloves.

Simon caught sight of Althea. "Ah, there you are, Miss Breton. I must say, you look refreshed from your walk."

"Good afternoon, Mr. Aguilar." She turned to Lady Stanton-Lewis, her lips feeling stiff. "Good afternoon, my lady."

The lady ignored her greeting. She gave a final tug to her gloves and turned to Simon. "Be a darling and accompany Winnie tonight to White's. I need you to keep an eye on him for me." She lowered her voice. "I depend on you."

Whether Althea's presence there inhibited him from saying something more tender or not, he only quipped, "Then, heaven help you."

Lady Stanton-Lewis laughed as he opened the door to escort her to her awaiting curricle.

Althea began her slow ascent up the stairs, suddenly feeling as if she were a hundred years old.

Late that evening Simon sat at cards with a group of men at White's. It was the first time he'd been admitted into the men's club.

It was thanks to Lord Stanton-Lewis that he'd gained entry. The baron was nowhere to be seen at the moment. The last time Simon had caught a glimpse of him, he'd been deep into a game of hazard. Simon had tossed the dice for a few rounds, but had soon found the winning and losing of vast sums of money on the throw of a pair of dice an incredible stupidity.

He'd finally settled on what he supposed was a rather tame hand of loo with a group of dandies of varying ages.

"It's been a frightful bore since Brummell fled for the Continent last year. London hasn't been the same since," commented one named Algernon with a yawn. He was a regular at Lady Stanton-Lewis's, although Simon hadn't quite figured out the attraction for her. To Simon's eye, the aged dandy had nothing to offer but an exaggerated opinion of himself.

"I suppose London became a bit unseasonable when his debts topped forty-thousand," Simon replied dryly.

"I heard he's holding court in some rooming house in Calais." Snickers of laughter greeted the remark of a Lord Islingworth, another perfumed and pomaded dandy, whose manicured fingers stretched lazily forward to take his cards.

"Only the best ton is permitted entry, by all accounts. One can't pass through Calais without presenting one's card," said a youngish fop going by the ridiculous name of Winnie. He was the one Lady Stanton-Lewis had asked Simon to look after. With good reason, he thought, seeing the pile of vouchers Winnie had already signed over to Islingworth. He turned his high, starched neck cloth toward Algernon. "Saw you at the Regent's grand fête at Carlton House last week. Sad crush there."

"Frightfully."

Algernon took up his cards. "Since he and Brummell had their falling-out, London has been in a sad decline."

"I say it's too many people being let into fashionable circles. These days you're as liable to run into a factory owner at Lady Richardson's as a peer of the realm," drawled Islingworth.

"You just have to know whose parties to attend. Some hostesses are still maintaining their ton."

"At least White's hasn't followed the general decline," sniffed Winnie. "Here the little black ball still rolls."

All but Simon smiled slyly. He eyed his cards, wondering what they thought of his presence there tonight.

"And there's always Almack's," added Winnie. "The patronesses haven't bowed to any outside pressures. They keep watch over the vouchers as assiduously as a reformed prostitute her virtue."

The others laughed. "Not even the Duke of Wellington was admitted when he arrived seven minutes too late for the dancing."

Algernon gave Simon a measured look from across the round table. "Heard you got a voucher."

Simon nodded. "For next week."

Islingworth narrowed his eyes at him. "Lady Castlereagh must have approved you."

"I guess she didn't blackball me," he answered. They all laughed at that.

"Mind you're not late," Winnie warned him with a chuckle, laying down his hand on the green baize cloth.

"And wear the right attire. Knee breeches or black tights—no trousers or pantaloons or you'll be turned away."

"Almack's isn't all it's cracked up to be," Islingworth remarked in a bored tone as he picked up the cards for the next trick. "Nothing but weak lemonade and lukewarm tea with a few dry biscuits to pass as refreshment, and strictly regulated dancing."

"At least they finally approved the waltz," put in Winnie.

"Long after the entire Continent was dancing it," said Islingworth disparagingly.

"But you must admit, the place does keep out the vulgar roturiers that seem to find their way into every other nook and cranny of society these days," said Winnie in defense of the venerable establishment.

"You won't find any rich bankers at Almack's," Algernon agreed.

The conversation turned to horses, then back to gaming. Finally it came to women. It seemed each one had either a ballet dancer or an opera girl tucked away somewhere. Simon thought about Althea's parentage and wondered whether it ever occurred to these men the far-reaching consequences of their actions. At least Althea had a father who had given her his name, but how many gentlemen would acknowledge an illegitimate offspring?

After another trick, Simon excused himself. He'd lost half the amount he'd allotted himself for playing and decided not to try to recoup his losses. He preferred losing twice the amount over enduring more of their conversation. He sauntered down to the billiard room and watched the play for a while, but soon found himself calling for his coach. There were several places he could stop in at the hour of ten. The opera and theater would just be over, with their crowds going out to supper or to various routs and balls.

But Simon instructed his coachman to take him home. Since his return a fortnight ago, he'd been out every night Parliament wasn't in session. And when the House adjourned early, he usually made his way to either Lady Eugenia's salon or to some party for which he'd received an invitation.

He would come home in time for his late-night watch with his daughter. He'd usually find Althea curled up, asleep on the armchair. As soon as he had roused her, she would scurry out of the room before he had a chance to so much as ask her how she was. He wondered at times whether she was fleeing him as much as he her.

He couldn't forget the feel of her in his arms that first night back, no matter how much he tried to dismiss it. But her warm body, the clean smell of her nightcap beneath his nostrils, the soft tendrils of hair escaping their braid, all continued to tease his memory. He hadn't forgotten his father's warning to him. It would do no good to let any sentimental feelings for Rebecca's nurse influence him at this time. So, he let her run away without trying to detain her.

In a careless moment, he had jokingly confided to Lady Eugenia his father's plans for his second marriage. To his surprise, she had been in wholehearted agreement, reviewing his father's candidates with him. Like a general planning a campaign, she'd listed the pros and cons of each one of the half-dozen debutantes deemed favorable, and finally settled on the top two choices. Simon had ironically thanked her for leaving him any choice in the selection at all.

She had laughed, saying, "You shall thank me afterward for helping you make the selection. Don't tell me you want the tedious task of courting each one of these silly little chits yourself, do you?"

He had to admit the prospect did not entertain him.

"I know you shall find these two candidates acceptable. They'll make you good little wives if you house and feed them properly. Buy them some nice trinkets, give them a generous line of credit at the mantua maker, and they'll give you no trouble at all."

"You make them sound like the perfect mistresses rather than wives."

"What is the difference? You want them to be available when you need them, yet to not interfere in your other activities."

Simon entered his silent house, depressed with his thoughts. Giles had left a lamp for him. Simon turned it up and proceeded to remove his wraps. He looked toward the library. It was a little past ten, still early enough to do some work. His book was not advancing very rapidly, since he'd been staying up most nights. His mornings, which used to be his most productive time, were now spent abed. He was becoming just like those fops he'd observed with contempt earlier in the evening.

Hardly, another voice told him. No matter how like them he dressed and talked, he would never succeed in hiding his origins. He knew they tolerated him at places like White's only because he was known for his originality and wit in the House and because of his favor with the prime minister. He'd even managed to amuse the Prince Regent the handful of times he'd been in his company.

Lady Eugenia's marked attention had no doubt also opened doors. She gave him an opportunity to display his wit, thanks to her salon. Because of his popularity there, other hostesses were coveting Simon's name.

Without any conscious decision, Simon began to climb the stairs and, reaching the top, directed his feet toward Rebecca's room. Since it was earlier than the time he usually appeared there, he gave a light knock. Althea's immediate reply told him that she was still awake.

"Good evening." He kept his hand upon the door handle, gauging her reaction to his appearance.

"Good evening." She looked up from her reading, displaying surprise at his presence.

Since she made no further comment, he felt obliged to explain. "I'm home a little earlier tonight and thought I'd see how things were going."

She sat up straighter and closed her Bible, leaving a finger in her place.

He advanced into the room and brought another chair over to the bed, hoping she would not leave right away as she had every other night.

"How is Rebecca?" he asked quickly, to keep Althea engaged.

"Sleeping quietly." She added, "She's still very weak and only drank a little broth this evening. I read to her some, but don't know how much she took in."

Simon touched his sleeping daughter's hand. It rested lightly on the coverlet. Her fingers were long and slim, the fingernails long ovals. He remembered the joy when she'd been born and he'd held her in his arms for the first time. She'd been a healthy, robust baby then, her vigor in sharp contrast to Hannah's weakness after the birth. Hannah had contracted a fever in those days following the birth and died.

But that real paternal love—fierce, tender, heartbreaking—hadn't occurred until Rebecca was a year-and-a-half-old toddler, reaching for him, her dark curls tousled, her ruffled white pinafore crumpled, calling out *"Abba"* as she wrapped chubby arms about his neck and planted warm, wet kisses on his cheek.

Rebecca had thrived despite her mother's absence. He'd been sure she'd live to be a hundred. Now her pallor and thinness reminded him again of Hannah in those last few days of her life.

He looked toward Althea, relieved she hadn't left yet. Suddenly he didn't want to be alone with his thoughts.

"Were you ever at Almack's during your London Seasons?" he asked abruptly.

She fingered the lace at her collar. "Yes, once or twice, with my father—my guardian then," she amended.

He quirked an eyebrow upward. "I thought it was extremely

difficult to get entry. Your father obtained a voucher for you despite your obscure origins?"

She smiled faintly in the lamplight. "Yes, it surprises me, too, now that I think of it. Back then, I accepted it since I knew my father—my guardian—was admired and respected by the patronesses. I'm sure it was only as a special favor to him that I was admitted."

He found himself vaguely irritated that she had with such apparent ease already gone and done at the tender age of seventeen what he'd had to wait until thirty-two to achieve. He loosened his starched neck cloth, marveling at the irony of it. It was laughable, actually: she'd been there and could barely remember the experience, and he'd wanted to gloat over his triumph.

"Why do you ask about Almack's?" Her soft voice intruded into his thoughts.

"I have a voucher for next Wednesday's dance."

"I see. Congratulations."

He rested his head against the back of his chair and stretched his legs out before him. "Do you know the significance of this?" He gave a dry bark of laughter. "A Jew in the hallowed halls of Almack's?" When she made no reply, he said, "Tonight I sat in White's for the first time."

She set her Bible on the bedside table and smoothed her skirts over her knees. "Are you happy with your achievements?"

"Do you know for how long I have had to watch my reputation most assiduously? Every word spoken, every place I went, every engagement I accepted, my mode of dress, everything down to the last detail—all carefully calculated to advance my career?" When she shook her head, he continued. "Now, for perhaps the first time in my life, I have a modicum of liberty to choose my friends and engagements. It's quite a heady feeling."

She merely looked down at her hands.

"It's funny," she said at last in a low tone, "your words remind me painfully of my own conduct during my only two London Seasons."

He raised his head towards her to hear her better. "Indeed? How is that?"

She was looking not at him but straight ahead at the wall, and did not answer immediately.

"I told you that my guardian did not reveal to me that he was in fact my real father until the eve of my coming up to London. In the space of an evening my entire world changed. I discovered I was the illegitimate offspring of a nobleman and a woman little more than a prostitute." She kept her eyes firmly fixed ahead of her as she pronounced the last word. "Everyone knows—at least in the circles that I grew up in—that women on the stage lead scandalous and immoral lives."

Simon realized as she continued to speak in a low monotone that her London Seasons might not be a matter of vague recollection but of painful memory.

She gave a strangled laugh. "You said once that I had run away to hide myself in the East End because of a sense of shame about my background." She looked across Rebecca's sleeping form and addressed him directly. "You were only partly right. I didn't hide in a mission—that came about much later. But I did feel vastly unworthy here among the quality, from the time my father first revealed the truth to me."

Simon waited patiently when she fell silent again. He could see it took great effort for her to speak. As the silence drew out, he wished he could beg her pardon, tell her he didn't need to know the painful facts—he knew how difficult it would be to have to stir up his own humiliating past—but he didn't say anything. He realized he needed to hear her story.

At last she gave a sigh that seemed to come from the depths of her. "So, although my coming out had all the trappings of respectability, I knew in fact that I was nothing but an impostor. I didn't deserve to enter the best houses of London. I had been brought up with the knowledge of my guardian's family name and fortune and had been taught to venerate his ancient lineage. And now, here I was, a blot on that crest.

"Do you know what my greatest fear was?"

She smiled sadly at him, and he felt as if she knew everything he had experienced that evening at White's. He shook his head.

"My greatest fear was that I should be discovered." She gave a half smile. "For someone who was shy and retiring to begin with, I became positively reclusive. At every great house, every ball, every rout, I hung back, looking for the darkest recess, trying to pass as unnoticed as possible. Just as you, I felt I had to watch every word and gesture. But mine was the fear I would reveal my sordid past by a mere look or movement. I was terrified they'd somehow see my mother's connection to me."

"What finally happened?"

She gestured with her hand and gave a choked laugh. "I was discovered, of course."

Simon waited, breathless.

She put a hand to her mouth as if it was still painful to admit. After a moment she resumed her tale. "There was a man during my second Season. I shan't call him a gentleman, because he wasn't, although he passed for one with his family name and fortune. He was old enough to have known my father when he was in France. He put two and two together. He behaved exactly as I was afraid people would when they knew. He thought I would be just like my mother."

Simon leaned forward, his body tensing.

After a moment, she continued. "The funny thing was, no one ever knew."

"Are you saying what I think you're saying?" he asked in a careful tone.

She nodded her head, looking back at the wall as if reliving the scene. "I was raped."

The stark words affected Simon more than tears or hysteria would have done.

He felt as if he had been punched in the gut. He covered his face with his hands, wanting to have the words unsaid.

"Have I shocked you, Mr. Aguilar?" The words were spoken softly across the bed.

He removed his hands and looked at her serene face. Knowing what effort it took to overcome the events in one's past, he could only stare at her. "What did your father do?" he asked after a moment.

"He never knew."

"He never—? God, woman, what do you mean? Didn't you ever tell him?" At the shaking of her head, rage filled him. "You know what Lord Caulfield would have done? Your brother? They would have called him out! The swine wouldn't have survived a day. He deserved nothing less. Why in heaven's name didn't you tell your father the truth?" he ended in frustration.

"I was too ashamed. The man made me feel so dirty. At first he had only tormented me with the secret of my birth. He seemed to derive some sort of...of pleasure from seeing my fear of discovery. Then he began pawing and groping me during dances—" She didn't continue. "I was able to escape him...and I tried never to find myself alone with him, but he was obstinate and clever. He managed to lure me into an empty library or some quiet nook and begin taking liberties with me, telling me he would keep my secret in exchange for my favors. It got so I was terrified to go out, dreading to see him, yet he seemed to haunt every place I went.

"Finally, that old, lecherous man wasn't satisfied with a stolen kiss here or there. He— Well, he did the unthinkable."

She gave a hollow laugh. "You remember I told you I had only one offer of marriage during my Season? Well, it was from a younger son, of a good family. His offer was a respectable one. My father urged me to accept it. My father was ready to draw up the betrothal papers—but how could I even consider it? I was not only a prostitute's daughter but soiled goods in my own right. I begged and pleaded with my father to take me from London. I told him I didn't wish to marry. I told him I'd do anything as long as he'd take me from London."

Simon could feel the blood pounding in his temples. He didn't want to know any more. He'd never dreamed he'd be hearing what he had heard from her lips. He had always imagined her a pure, untouched young woman who'd chosen not to marry because of her religious convictions.

But she, like him, had her past. How she had needed a defender in those treacherous waters of society. And she had had no one.

"Where was Tertius?" he asked curtly.

"He had gone to the West Indies by then. As a second son, there were not many opportunities open to him here. Father sent him there, hoping it would be the making of him."

"Yes, I remember now. And your older brother?"

"I couldn't tell him, any more than I could tell my father. I was too ashamed. I had never been close to my brothers. They were so much older than I, and when they were home, were aloof. I realized afterwards they must have suspected something about my birth, and it would have been natural to resent me for their mother's sake. I could not blame them."

Simon longed to cross the space that separated them and gather her in his arms. He wanted to erase all that, even the memory of it. But she spoke before he could put thought into action.

"That's when I left London for good. I retired to my family's country estate in Hertfordshire after that second Season, vowing to my father that I'd take care of him for always if only he didn't make me go back, or ever marry. Poor man, I think he believed I was suffering a broken heart over some suitor." She smiled. "He thinks that's why I've never married, that I'm still pining over some long lost love."

Simon wanted to tell her that not all men were dishonorable, but he stayed seated, his hands gripping the arms of his chair. If he loosed his hold, he was afraid of what might happen. That way lay only danger. He told himself that the best way to show her that not every man was like that blackguard was to prove it to her. As long as she was under his roof, she was under his protection, and he would do all in his power to see to it that no man ever hurt her in that way again.

Without thinking, he said gently, "Not all men are so despicable. It doesn't have to be awful...in marriage..." he ended awkwardly. What was he trying to tell her?

She didn't meet his eyes. Instead, she brushed off some imaginary particle from her skirt and said nothing. After a few minutes, she looked up with a smile, as if to put the past behind her. "The Lord didn't let me continue to live in fear for long. It was not long after I returned to Hertfordshire that I had an encounter with my Lord and Savior, and my life took a completely different turn. When I came to accept Jesus as my Savior, He set me free of fear.

"Your words tonight reminded me how I used to live in fear of what people would think of me," she finished.

He should have known the conversation would invariably lead to religion. Hadn't he known that when he'd come up here? What kind of a glutton for punishment was he? And where had her God been when she'd needed Him?

Chapter Fourteen

After Althea's revelations to him, Simon began to avoid her again, afraid more than ever of his growing attraction to her. Now compassion was added to admiration and need. Instead, he turned toward Lady Eugenia, haunting her salon almost every evening. When she invited him to call her Eugenie, he knew he had crossed an invisible line and entered into her most intimate circle.

Nothing inappropriate had yet been spoken by either, but every look and word was fraught with meaning.

Simon did not know what held him back from accepting the invitation in her eyes. He continued weighing every angle. He knew that he wouldn't be the first with her, nor did he delude himself that the lady's sentiments would be engaged. It would be a liaison of pure sensuality and mutual gratification.

But he also took his father's advice seriously and knew the most sensible thing to do was to fall in gracefully with the elder Aguilar's plans and wed some nice, respectable debutante.

Why, then, did he have this urge to cast all caution to the winds and let himself be led down this treacherous path of intrigue and vice? As the weeks went by, Simon often felt caught in a frenzy not entirely of his own making. Half his day and evening was spent in parliamentary debate, where he performed a balancing act between the rights of the workers and the interests of the owners and financiers, trying to satisfy both the demands of his conscience and the demands of his backers.

His evenings were a series of social engagements where he'd navigate a game more hazardous than any found at White's. Finally, when he'd had his fill, he'd go home to sit by his daughter's bedside. Every night he seemed to wage an internal battle—whether or not to seek Miss Breton out in her sitting room. More often than not, he'd lose, drawn to her for reasons he couldn't understand. He sometimes thought of her as his conscience, put there to torment him, and yet he couldn't escape his need to hear what she had to say. Perhaps it was because he sensed she would always tell him what she thought, without fear of his approval or disapproval.

They often talked politics or theology, and she was forever quoting to him from that Bible that should be in tatters by now from the amount of time she spent poring over it. Many were the times he'd deliberately put a hypothetical situation before her, which mirrored what he was in fact facing, and ask her mockingly what her God would say about it. Many were the evenings he would lose patience with her replies, realizing afterward that he was more angry at himself for caring what she thought. He realized, too, that she never gave him the answers he wanted to hear. Everyone else would understand and advise him in a logical, sensible way. Even his father would offer good common sense. Althea would quote some verse that made no sense in his world. Other times she would just promise to pray for him without giving him her opinion, and yet he had a sneaking suspicion he knew what she was thinking.

There was also something restful about her presence, no matter how much she might anger him at times. The more he paced and gestured with his hands, the more quietly she sat with that Bible on her lap.

One time she tried to explain the similarity between his family's religious rituals and those of the Church of England. According to her, both had become empty of real significance and become merely efforts to justify their adherents before God through their good works. She tried earnestly to make him see that no good work would ever be good enough to wipe away man's inherently sinful nature.

Her eyes lit up. "You gave us Moses, Abraham, Jacob, Joseph, all the great prophets. You gave the world Jesus!"

Simon stared at her, caught for a moment, not by her argument but by her genuine love for his people. He studied her. "You are the first Christian I've ever met who has had anything admiring to say about my race. Normally you come across as a little mouse, quiet and demure, always in your gray, but when you speak of your Jesus, you reveal a passion within you that nobody would suspect. Your eyes light up first, then your whole face. You become beautiful."

She made no reply, and the two continued to regard each other until he became aware of the danger. As if sensing the same, she cast her eyes downward.

"If you see any beauty in me, it is but Jesus in me. It is His beauty coming through."

"My wife, Hannah, was beautiful," he said absently, receiving for an instant an image of her fresh young beauty and childish ways. It had been a long time since he had been able to picture her.

"Was she?" Althea asked softly.

"Yes," he answered shortly, remembering for an instant how little he had had the privilege of enjoying a wife. He brought his attention back to the woman sitting before him. Suddenly he contrasted her with his young wife. Hannah had been a child-bride, still a little girl living more with her mother than with her new husband. Althea, on the other hand, was a fully mature woman, used to being on her own for many years. "You are nothing like her, you know."

She said nothing. He knew he should stop talking before the conversation became impossibly awkward. He sighed, raking a hand through his hair. Before giving them either a chance to say anything more, Simon wheeled about and went to stare out the window. He heard Althea leave the room, quietly shutting the door behind her.

Simon continued to spend his nights at Rebecca's bedside. He'd finally doze fitfully until dawn, when the maid Dot came up to relieve him. He then would retire to his own bed to sleep until noon. He would spend the early afternoon with Rebecca, making her laugh and doing everything to hide his fear at her growing weakness. She hadn't recovered her natural buoyancy since the fever.

Rebecca was visited regularly by the new surgeon, a serious, intense young fellow whom Simon formed an immediate antipathy toward. He told himself it was because he wasn't a doctor, not even an apothecary, but a crude surgeon, probably the son of a butcher. Simon eyed him sourly when he spoke to Althea, with whom he exhibited a friendship and respect. His conversations with Althea as she escorted him down the hall and stairs reminded Simon that Althea had had a life of her own before she'd come under his roof.

The surgeon told him frankly that the illness was following its natural progression; if anything it had delayed its inevitable end. The cases he had witnessed or read about succumbed in a matter of months, not to the illness so much as to other infections, which attacked the weakened body. He told him the only thing Simon could do to prolong Rebecca's life was keep her as isolated as possible so she wouldn't be exposed to any other illnesses. Her body was now too weak to resist any further battles.

Russell gave him a final sharp look and said only an act of God would change his daughter's fate.

Simon cursed and shut himself in his library. God must be laughing at him. Well, He wouldn't have the last laugh, he vowed.

So often of late he felt as if his life were caught in a piece of the factory machinery he spoke so eloquently about, but he was powerless to extricate himself from its never-ending, frenetic motion. If anything, he stepped up the rhythm, almost as an act of defiance.

Whenever he rose stiffly from his chair by Rebecca's bedside at dawn, he knew by then Althea was on her knees praying. He had gone to the door of her sitting room one morning and had heard the muffled sound of her voice.

He had lifted his hand to knock, but then dropped it again, realizing that she was praying to her God.

Althea almost dreaded seeing Simon. It seemed as if they could never enter into a meaningful conversation without Simon's lashing out at her faith. He couldn't understand how much it hurt her—not because of herself, but because she knew how much he was hurting himself by rejecting the only One who could save him.

When it was time for Simon to come up to Rebecca's room for his afternoon visit, Althea always found an excuse to go into the connecting sitting room or downstairs to the pianoforte. One afternoon as she sat reading in the sitting room, she heard him come in and speak to his daughter. A moment later, he knocked on her door and poked his head in.

"What are you doing there all by yourself? I promised Rebecca a treat. Please come in and partake with us."

Althea closed her book, flustered at his sudden cheerful tone.

He had brought them each a strawberry tart. He was helping Rebecca to sit up against her pillows. "I went out especially to get you this, so you had better eat it all up."

"It looks delicious, *Abba*. Thank you ever so much."

He spoke to his daughter about some of the parties he had attended. Althea could see the effort he made to keep her mind amused. He gently urged her every so often to take a bite. When she had at last eaten three-quarters of it, she pushed it away, saying she could absolutely eat no more.

Simon took her plate away from her to set it on the table. He stood for a moment by Althea's chair.

"They are trying the men involved in the Blanketeers march," he told her quietly, referring to those that had been arrested in the march from Manchester earlier in the spring.

"It doesn't look good for most of them," he said, answering the question in her eyes. "I think there will be at least half a dozen executions."

She put her hand to her mouth in a silent exclamation.

"Can nothing be done—from Parliament?"

"No one will listen to reason. They're all afraid of revolution and think by snuffing it out, it will disappear."

He looked at her ironically. "Can nothing be done by the religious community? I don't see the churches protesting. And those like your mission are too poor to have any voice."

"We don't need the world's wealth."

"Oh, come, Miss Breton, isn't that somewhat hypocritical? At least we Jews are not ashamed of our wealth. If offers us one of the few protections against the world."

"At least I have lived among the people I aim to help," she countered. "How can you champion the factory worker from Parliament, when you know so little about him, when your world is so removed from his?"

"I don't have to live among them to sympathize with their suffering," he answered dryly. "Unlike you, it doesn't mean I want to share it. I have enough of my own suffering," he added under his breath.

She bit her lip, ashamed of her accusations.

Over the next few days she puzzled over Simon's behavior. Everything she told him seemed only to exasperate him, and yet he continued seeking her out and bringing up controversy. He seemed to delight in provoking her, making it a point of telling her of his latest exploits in society, when he came in the evenings and found her reading or knitting by Rebecca's bed or in her sitting room. While he rarely mentioned

Lady Stanton-Lewis directly, she could sense her presence in every sentence.

These late-night conversations reminded Althea of Nicodemus, and she told Simon so one evening.

"Who was he?"

"I thought you knew all there was to know in the Bible."

"Nicodemus must have slipped my recollection," he said, stretching his legs out lazily before him as if in preparation for a good story.

"Well, Nicodemus was a very respected man in Judea, intelligent, well-versed in Scripture, a leader, wealthy...."

Simon smiled. "He sounds better and better. Go on with your tale."

"It is no tale. Anyway, despite everything he had, Nicodemus was drawn to the rabbi Jesus."

"Jesus styled himself as teacher of the Jews?"

"Oh, yes, that was one of his principal ministries, among prophet, preacher, miracle worker and redeemer of Israel."

"Yes, yes." He waved a hand impatiently. "So what did this Nicodemus see in Jesus?"

"He knew for one thing that Jesus must be a prophet. He knew only one sent by God could perform the miracles Jesus performed."

"So what happened?"

"Well, it was a tricky thing for an upstanding man, a leader in the Jewish community to go openly to this Jesus. So he visited him by night."

"Ah." He looked up at the ceiling, his fingers forming a pyramid. "So you see me as secretly seeking out this Jesus? I'm afraid I shall have to disappoint you, Miss Breton. I doubt I'll prove so apt a pupil as your friend Nicodemus."

"Perhaps you haven't so able a teacher."

"Oh, I find you able enough. Your pupil just isn't interested in the material."

Then, why do you keep coming back to hear? she silently asked in vexation.

* * *

One evening before Simon had come in, Althea sat knitting by Rebecca's bed.

"Miss Althea, I'm afraid to die." Rebecca's large brown eyes stared at her through the dim light.

Althea looked up, startled. "I thought you were asleep."

"What if I'm still alive when they bury me? Do they ever make a mistake?"

Althea immediately knelt by the girl. She clasped Rebecca's hand in hers and held it up to her cheek.

"Don't be frightened. We each have to face that moment when we depart this earth. God knew we would be afraid because we weren't certain what we would be going to. So, do you know what He did?"

Rebecca shook her head against the pillow, her dark eyes never leaving Althea's face.

Althea smoothed the girl's forehead with her other hand. "God sent His most special emissary to show us the way. Do you know what an emissary is?"

Again she shook her head.

"It's a messenger. God sent us His most trusted messenger, His most beloved one, so there could be no mistakes. He sent us His very own Son, a part of His very Self, to show us the way.

"And do you know what that messenger was supposed to tell us?" Rebecca shook her head. "He was supposed to tell us about eternal life. You see these bodies of ours?" She moved her hand clasped with Rebecca's closer to the girl's face. "They'll get old and worn. Yours feels a little weak right now, doesn't it? Sometimes it hurts?" Rebecca nodded. "Well, these bodies are like suits of clothes. Someday we are going to shed them for better ones.

"God's Son came down upon this earth and put on one of these suits of clothing so He could feel our pain and our weakness and our fear. He came among us so that He could tell us about our Heavenly Father's love for us. He knew we could never enter His Father's world on our own, because of our sin."

The girl was listening raptly.

"You see, every time we do something bad, we draw apart from God. He is holy, and I'm afraid these old, sinful garments of ours cannot stand to be in His presence. His presence is glorious.

"But, you know, God had a plan to overcome this situation. He sent His special emissary, His Son, Jesus, to make a way for us to Heaven. He asked His Son if He would come and take all our sin on Himself. He paid the price, so that we could come into the Father's presence, clean and whole. Jesus said if we would receive Him, He would make us a part of Himself, so that He could take us with Him into Heaven when our turn came to leave this earth."

"Am I a part of Jesus?"

"You can be if you receive Him as your Lord and Savior. Do you know what His name, Jesus, means?"

"No."

"It means 'God will save' in the language of your ancestors. They were awaiting this Savior for many, many generations before He appeared on earth. When Jesus came, He told the Jewish people, 'For God so loved the world, that he gave His only begotten Son, that whosoever believeth in him should not perish, but have everlasting life.'

"The world—that means you and me, Rebecca. He loved us so much that He sent His Son to die in our place so we might have everlasting life with Him. Do you understand?"

"I think so."

Althea waited for a few moments before speaking again. "Do you want to receive Jesus as your Lord and Savior?"

She nodded. "Yes, please."

"All right. Just pray after me. Dear Lord, I know I've sinned...."

Rebecca repeated the words of the short prayer after Althea. Afterwards she fell into a peaceful sleep. Althea stayed kneeling, praying and thanking God.

In the days following this prayer, Rebecca was eager to hear more about Jesus. Althea began reading to her directly from the gospels concerning the life and ministry of Jesus. Rebecca listened attentively, and would protest when Althea put the Bible down.

The next night, as if to steal her joy at Rebecca's conversion, Simon entered the room in a particularly belligerent mood. He reminded Althea of a little boy determined to get his way by sheer argument.

He began with the latest report of his social exploits. When she made no reply, but continued knitting a muffler, he said, "You of all people should applaud me if I am at last breaking free of the shackles of tradition and the hypocritical standards imposed by society. You're always preaching the 'freedom' to be had in true religion. Well, now I begin to go where I please, see whom I please, say what I please."

She said nothing but gave him that gentle look that seemed to irk him further.

"If Lady Stanton-Lewis amuses me, and I her, why shouldn't I spend time in her company?" he finally blurted out in irritation. "That's what all this is about, isn't it?"

When she still said nothing, he said, "Miss Breton has that disapproving look on her face. Go ahead, tell me what you are thinking."

"I'm thinking," she said over the clicking of her needles, "King Solomon wrote in one of the Proverbs that 'there is a way that seemeth right to a man, but the end thereof is death.'"

"So, I'm playing with fire, is that it? My father echoes those sentiments."

"Your father is perhaps wise in this area."

After a few moments, Althea continued. "Jesus talks about corruptible and incorruptible seed, the one leading to death, the other to eternal life."

"That sounds like something the good curate tried to drill into me in catechism classes. 'The wages of sin are death,' or some such nonsense to prepare me for water baptism." Simon paced the room. "You Christians are happiest when you're harping on sin." He stopped right in front of her chair and pointed a finger at her. "My theory is that it's all just an excuse for not living life— and for being bigoted and narrow-minded about others who might be taking advantage of the life God gave us!"

"That's what the world generally accuses us of," she countered quietly, "when they can't even begin to understand what living is really about. Jesus promised us life 'more abundantly' and believe me, He knew what that meant! He also warned us the world would not be able to understand."

"Life more abundantly!" he answered scornfully. He gestured impatiently toward Rebecca. "Is that what you call what my daughter is doing? Living!" He glared at her. "Oh, I know what you're going to say, I know I'm supposed to be some kind of prodigal. I deserve what I'm getting, but what about her? Does she deserve this?"

She didn't say anything, but there was anguish in her eyes as she longed to tell him that his daughter now had eternal life.

"Why doesn't your Jesus heal her for your sake? Don't think I don't know how much you pray for her! I've seen you kneeling nights in your little sitting room. I've heard your weeping. Why doesn't your precious Savior hear you? What more does He want of you? A pound of flesh?"

Althea's eyes were brimming with tears. He needed answers she couldn't give. Her silent tears angered him all the more.

"Go on, go to bed." When she didn't move, he said it more roughly. "Go! I need to be alone."

Hurriedly she gathered her things and left.

A few nights later Simon came home feeling inordinately weary of fighting. As he entered Rebecca's room, he felt an immediate peace. Althea was sitting in her usual place by the bed, knitting again.

"Good evening. How is she?" he asked, looking toward his daughter's ghostly form.

"Fine." Althea smiled. "She was quite lively this evening. We played a few games before she fell asleep."

He removed his spectacles, rubbing his eyes, too tired for the moment to move away from the door. Finally he walked toward his daughter, stepping in front of Althea. He stooped over Rebecca, touching her soft cheek. One dark braid lay across it. He pushed it gently out of the way.

Then he turned to Althea, who had risen, the ball of yarn in her hand. He found himself near enough to touch her. She stood, probably waiting for him to step back. He didn't oblige her. He just stood there, looking at her, caught by a sudden, overwhelming desire to hold her and be held by her. He needed something she had—wanted something... Unable to articulate even to himself what it was, he stood mute.

He had seen her as the comforter of his child. And lately he had come to see her also as perhaps the only thing that stood between himself and insanity, like a steady rock in the maelstrom of his life. He had fought with everything in him to avoid seeing her as a woman.

But he couldn't anymore.

His eyes traveled the length of her, comparing her freshness and honesty with the artifices of the society women he'd just come from; he observed the rise and fall of her breast, the heightened color of her cheeks, and with a certainty, he knew that she was just as aware as he of their position as man and woman.

He tugged at the knot of his cravat to keep himself from reaching for her and kissing her until he forgot everything else. The very thought filled his senses. The only thing that stopped him was the knowledge that if he took such a step, he would never recover. Every instinct, every fiber of his being, told him this woman was like no other he'd known.

He felt immobilized, his mind battling these thoughts, powerless to move either forward or back—all he could do was continue to study her in the low lamplight. Within the space of a few seconds he watched the questioning look in her gray eyes turn to worry and worry turn to acknowledgment. Time drew out, but still he didn't move. Without a conscious thought, he brought his hand up to her face and ran his fingers over the contours of it, like a person who knows he cannot have something and yet must nevertheless linger over it, even if it means enduring the agony of denial. He held his breath at the downy softness of her cheek.

"Do you know I once thought you weren't beautiful?" His voice emerged a ragged whisper.

At her imperceptible nod, he half smiled. "You did? What gave you that idea?"

"You." Her own voice was low, husky.

"Me? How?"

"The way you spoke of Rebecca's mother—how beautiful she was."

"Ah." He recollected the remark. "I'm sorry to have given you that impression. Hannah was a beautiful woman, it is true, but in saying that, I didn't mean to imply that you were any less so."

She looked down then at her yarn and knitting needles. "It doesn't matter. I don't expect you to find me beautiful."

He lifted her chin with a fingertip and touched her lips with his thumb, silencing her. "I only meant that the two of you were very different. She was dark, you are fair. She was a child, you are a woman." He continued looking at her, fascinated by her features. "You are beautiful, *Miss* Althea." He imitated his daughter's name for her, lingering over each syllable of her name, capturing its essence on his tongue and against his teeth.

"I've realized it for some time." As he spoke, his voice a low rumble in his throat, his finger moved as if of its own volition over her features. "Such a clear countenance. 'There is no guile' in Althea," he said, quoting Scriptures back to her. His forefinger caressed her cheek and temple and came to rest on her forehead. "She harbors only thoughts that are pure and true, nothing self-serving." He traced her cheek once again, his tone becoming rhythmic. "So rosy and soft, with those delightful freckles scattered about—" he touched the bridge of her nose "—giving her no end of vexation if her heightened color is any indication. But I wouldn't have even one removed...not a one." The pad of his thumb moved over her cheek, his fingers cupping her face. "Such soft skin, it gives no evidence of the tears spilled over it." His fingertip traced the imaginary path of a tear and continued down the curve of her cheek, feather light until it lay once again gently over the rise of her lips where it had begun its journey.

"Such wisdom from these lips, as her God gives her, to comfort a man's soul—if he would but let it." He continued stroking their crimson softness, expressing thoughts he hadn't until that moment even dared formulate to himself. "Do you know how often I have found myself of late with the desire to kiss them? I've found myself wondering whether you have hidden all your womanly feelings so deep beneath that prim exterior that you are no longer aware you even possess them."

He felt her breath against his finger, but she didn't move or speak, captivated as much by his words and touch, apparently, as he was by her nearness.

"But I've stopped myself from discovering the answer to those questions. Do you know why?"

He watched her shake her head slowly from side to side. "Because, my dear Miss Althea, I'm afraid the answers would be my undoing."

As her eyes widened, he smiled again. "Yes, indeed. You terrify me. I begin to have my answer to one question, at any rate," he continued. "I don't believe, my dear, sweet Althea, that you are immune to my touch."

He took her chin in his forefinger and thumb and watched her gaze drop to his lips. His tongue clicked against his teeth. "What am I going to do about you? I can't seem to get you out of my thoughts. You've insinuated yourself into my gut like some stubborn malady, giving me no peace."

Her gaze returned to his in alarm at those words and he curled his lip upward. "Those eyes, which look at me so sadly sometimes, and at others, flash anger at me, sometimes gray, sometimes green, at times even blue, but always true and honest in what they believe."

His smile disappeared as he acknowledged the longing in his being to hold this woman and feel her nearness. "Do you know why I cannot satisfy my hunger to kiss you?"

Again she shook her head mutely, as if incapable of speaking.

They stood for a moment longer, gazing into each other's eyes. For Simon it was a desire in him that he knew he would no longer be capable of containing if he didn't remove himself from the room very soon.

His legs could no longer obey even if his mind were capable of sending the command. Reason evaporated as Simon drew his hand around the nape of her neck and pulled her gently forward, at the same time leaning downward, knowing nothing but that in another instant he would be able to discover firsthand the answer to the question that had been burning for so long in his mind.

His lips hovered over hers an instant as he whispered, "This is why." The next second, their lips were touching, the sensation sending a thrilling shock down through his limbs. The softness of her barely parted lips was all that he had imagined and more.

One touch and he wanted to bury himself in her. But he held back, whispering her name, drawing her close with his two arms. "Don't be afraid, my dear Althea," he whispered as he nuzzled her lips and cheeks, then traveled down her neck, breathing in the scent of her. He wrapped his two hands around her head and brought her head upward. He opened his eyes, his lips playing over the surface of hers. Her head was thrown back, her eyes closed.

Was she recalling her terrifying experience? Was she comparing his touch to that other man's? Dreading that, Simon hesitated. His thumbs massaged her temples lightly. Feeling no resistance in her, he drew his face down to hers again, taking her lips once more in his. This time he deepened the kiss, nudging her lips apart.

His arms drew downwards, his hands caressing her back, pushing her towards him, needing to feel her against the length of him.

His body throbbed with pent-up need. He needed to stop— He mustn't—his brain told him, as his lips kept exploring the sweet depths of her mouth.

After an initial hesitation, he could feel Althea kissing him back. Finally her own hands came up and wrapped themselves around his neck. He hugged her closer, wanting to feel her very heartbeat.

After some time, he looked at her again. She opened her eyes at the same moment. He could see the dazed wonderment gradually turn back to reason. He knew, as each second ticked by, thoughts and fears over the consequences of their kiss began to destroy the enchantment. How he wanted to hold her closer and turn back time, but he knew it was impossible.

His voice came out thick and unnatural. "I knew once I tasted of you, I would never recover."

Althea began pushing away first. He sighed, expelling the air in one swift gust, and offered no resistance as she stepped back.

She touched a hand to her lips and closed her eyes an instant. "I'm sorry, I don't know what came over me," she whispered.

He reached out and touched her hand lightly. "Don't be sorry. That's as absurd as saying you're sorry Rebecca is ill."

She opened her eyes and met his gaze warily, confusion warring with self-reproach.

He removed his hand, and it almost hurt him physically to break the connection with her, but he knew the moment of madness was over. He shifted back and leaned against the bedside table. He smiled sadly, his gaze never leaving hers.

"You and I come from different worlds, Althea."

When she said nothing, he rubbed a hand over his jaw, wishing—wishing— "No matter how much I've tried to erase my past, it's there. It's who I am. A Jew. A Hebrew. An *Ephraimite*." He infused the word with all the British contempt he'd heard all the years of his life.

* * *

Althea swallowed, her heart breaking at the pain she knew he masked, or thought he'd conquered. There was only One who could take that pain away. What could she say to him? Cry out that she didn't care about his background? That she'd go anywhere with him? Face anything with him— Hadn't she already faced the loss of all things pertaining to her old life? But there was One whom she couldn't forsake, her Savior, and his, if Simon would only let Him into his heart.

As if reading her mind, Simon smiled again, the smile bittersweet this time. "But that wouldn't matter to Althea, would it? What does she care where I come from? No, what probably concerns her more is who I am now and where I'm headed. My place in Parliament and in society is of no import, is it? For after all, what does Althea care about worldly things? No, she would probably rejoice if I turned my back on everything I've struggled to attain over the last decade of my life."

His eyes narrowed, his tone assuming its habitual mockery. "You wouldn't like to reenter that world that treated you so cruelly, would you? You wouldn't want a husband who would be continuously in society. You couldn't abide the thought of mingling with the London ton and hosting countless dinner parties for them, could you?

"You'd prefer I forget Parliament, forget a brilliant career, give up all my dreams and live in obscurity, my life dedicated to some lost cause somewhere. Wouldn't that be more to your devout tastes? Wouldn't it, Miss Breton?" His scornful tone ended in one of frustration.

She shook her head in protest, still unable to speak a word.

"Until I take up this cross you're always harping on, giving up everything else, you won't be satisfied, will you? Always insisting this is about the same God of Abraham, Isaac and Jacob. It would make you happy, wouldn't it, if I 'converted'?" He made the word sound like a profanity. "Then we would all be one big happy family—Jew and Gentile."

She continued to shake her head at his accusations. Her cheeks felt hot. She took another step away from him and almost tripped over the chair behind her. She groped for its arm and stepped away even farther, needing to get away from him.

"You don't understand! You see so much, you care so much and yet you are still so—so blind!" Her voice, which had started as a pained whisper, rose. "You are right. I don't care about 'worldly' things if that means caring what the world thinks. I would go anywhere, face anything with you—be it a life of abject poverty or complete obscurity—or—or—" she sputtered trying to get the words out, hardly realizing what she was about to say "—or a life as the prime minister's wife. Whether it was scraping together our last farthings, or planning the most elaborate dinner parties to sit and smile and endure however many setdowns I must for the sake of your career, I would do it *gladly!* I would face both your family and mine!

"But I would do *none* of this if it meant forsaking my God, and *yours!* Not even for you, Simon." She ran towards the door, horrified at the enormity of what she'd done tonight.

At the door to the sitting room she stopped, her knuckles gripping the handle behind her. For a long moment, they both looked at each other, the expanse between them like an ocean.

Finally she turned and wrenched the door open, feeling her heart ripping in pain as she did so, and ignoring his final "Althea!" as she closed the door behind her.

That night Althea paced her room, her heart in turmoil. She never dreamed Simon could feel anything even remotely touching what she felt for him, but tonight the veil had been ripped aside, showing her a man of strong passions held in powerful check. For that she must be thankful, because she had realized tonight how weak she was. She herself had not dared acknowledge the depth of her own feelings for her employer.

But she could no longer deceive herself. She might have fooled herself over the past few weeks that theirs was but an intellectual parley. If anything, she'd felt nothing but impatience and mockery from him the more she'd held her ground.

But tonight he'd shocked her. She'd shocked herself. There had been nothing intellectual or rational about their encounter. His touch had paralyzed her, and she'd been astounded at the depth of her own passion. If he hadn't let her go, could she have gone? She didn't have the answer to that. She had only the evidence of her own response to him, her soul drinking in every soft word he spoke as her body yearned for his touch.

She realized her weeks of denying all such feelings, rather than diminishing them, had only served to intensify them. She fell upon her bed, crying for forgiveness for any secret thoughts she had harbored for Simon. She pleaded with God. *What would You have me do? Why do You want me here? Simon is no closer to accepting You than my father is!*

Your Word says not to be unequally yoked with unbelievers. I have kept Your command. I have kept myself apart. What would You have of me here? Your Word promises I will not be tempted above what I am able to bear.

The thought came to her of the apostle Peter when the Lord had given him the vision of all the unclean animals being lowered to him on a sheet, and commanded, Rise and eat.

You wanted to show Peter something, which he didn't understand immediately. What are You trying to show me in this household? I know You cannot wish me to give myself to Simon, not in his present spiritual condition, but what is it then that You would have me do! Show me, Lord, for I am weak, I am ignorant. I don't know what to do!

She fell asleep at last, in her clothes, her face tear-streaked, knowing nothing but that somehow the Lord would sustain her through this test.

Chapter Fifteen

❧

Althea needn't have concerned herself with things in the short run. When she rose the next morning, late and disoriented, Simon had left her a note by her breakfast plate. It was brief and to the point. Its short contents left her relieved, vexed and deeply hurt. In it, he apologized in the most formal tones for having expressed himself the evening before most inappropriately. He was deeply remorseful. He begged her to erase the incident completely from her memory, and she could be assured it would never occur again as long as she was in his employ.

He remained her obedient servant, *Simon Aguilar.*

She swallowed, felt the tears well up in her eyes, and wiped them away angrily. Her eyes were painfully tender; she thought she'd cried all the tears she could possibly produce. How horribly sentimental she was becoming of late. What had gotten into her?

She washed her face with cold water, then went up to Rebecca's room. Of course she was relieved with the tone and contents of the message. The Lord had made her a way of escape;

He had heard her pleas of the night before. She needn't be concerned over Simon's attentions anymore.

Her face flamed at the recollection of the things she'd said to him. She'd practically thrown herself at his feet and declared her love for him, telling him that she'd be willing to go with him anywhere.

The Lord's voice told her not to be ashamed of her love for Simon.

Love. The word came as a revelation. She whispered it to herself. All those pent-up feelings that had erupted the night before had been nothing more, nothing less, than love.

For so long she had shunned any hint of attraction to a man. That man so long ago in her past had insinuated she was nothing but the lecherous, wanton product of her mother's illicit liaison with her father. The shame when he'd exposed her origins in all their lurid details, quite different from her father's whitewashed version, had crippled her. When the man had violated her, Althea had reasoned in a horrible, twisted way that she deserved it.

Althea put her fist up to her mouth, remembering the horror when he'd lifted her skirts and thrust himself into her again and again on that sofa in some long-forgotten house in Mayfair, while people in the other rooms danced and ate and played cards.

Now she thought with wonder over her body's reaction to Simon the night before. She had felt no dread or fear when he'd touched her. He'd touched her so gently that when his lips had at last parted hers, she'd longed for the fusion of their two bodies. The revelation stunned her, and her mind went immediately to God's covenant of marriage: "...and they twain shall be one flesh."

For the first time in her life Althea began to question whether she had really allowed the Lord to set her completely free. Or had she refused all thoughts of marriage to any man, out of fear of the marital act?

Her mind began to wonder if it was love her mother had felt for her father. Had her mother experienced the desperate longing for her father that Althea was feeling for Simon?

Had her mother succumbed and fallen in sin out of love or lust? She would never know.

Althea turned from her silent meditations at the window, asking God for His grace in the coming days. She knew she must bury her love for Simon and fix her attention on Rebecca.

She renewed her prayers for Rebecca, declaring all the promises for healing and wholeness in God's word for those who believed. She knew that she herself could not leave Rebecca's side until she saw her well and whole again.

One afternoon Simon stopped on impulse at his parents' residence.

The house was quiet, with only a silent maid dusting and polishing. Simon found his mother in her sitting room doing needlework. She gazed in delighted surprise when he poked his head in the door.

Speaking to him in Ladino, she stood. "Simon! What a pleasant surprise! What are you doing here at this time of day?"

He kissed her on the cheek. "I had a meeting nearby and thought I would visit my mother. Do I need an appointment?" he teased.

She swatted him on the arm. "Don't talk such nonsense. Would that I saw all my children every day."

"Sit, Mama. I don't want to interrupt your work." He glanced down, not really knowing why he had come by. To hide his embarrassment, he asked after his brothers and sisters.

His mother patted the seat beside her. "They are all fine, knock on wood. Tirzah is looking lovelier each day. You know she and Solomon are already expecting a little one early in the year?" Her mother smiled in satisfaction.

He nodded. Yes, his sister seemed to be blooming more and more each day.

She shook her head. "I worry about your brother Nathan. I don't think he's happy at the bank." She fingered the edge of her embroidery hoop. "Is there nothing you can say to him? I know

David is set in his ways, a lot like your father, but he only means it for good."

Simon said nothing. How was he expected to fix his brother's life when he couldn't even manage his own? What would his mother say if she had an inkling of his affairs?

"How is everything at home? Rebecca? I was just by to see her yesterday." Mrs. Aguilar clucked her tongue, shaking her head. "So thin. Are you sure she's eating enough?"

Simon's mouth twisted in a smile. It was not worth arguing against his mother's belief that all ills could be cured if one ingested enough food.

"How is your work coming, *hijo?*" she asked, peering at him. "Your *abba* tries to explain to me the difficulties you face. Everyone arguing. Why can't they all agree on what is best for the country?"

Simon chuckled. "Then, perhaps, all those of us in Parliament would be out of work."

He crossed his legs and fingered the material of his pantaloons. "What do you think of Miss Breton, Rebecca's nurse?" he asked abruptly, then regretted the question as soon as it was out.

His mother looked at him from her deep-set black eyes. "Miss Breton? A nice enough woman. She is a godsend for Rebecca. Rebecca thinks the world of her. Why do you ask, *hijo?*"

Simon shifted. In for a penny, in for a pound. "What if your son was contemplating marriage to someone of her sort?" he ended lamely. God, what was he thinking in even voicing such a thought?

His mother's mouth dropped open and a look of fear entered her eyes. Her mouth moved silently a few times as if she were trying to speak but couldn't enunciate the words. "Simon, you're not—" she finally managed to say. "Oh, Simon, she—" His mother stared at him in anguish. "She is a good woman, a lady, I can see, but, Simon, she's a Gentile, a nurse. Her beliefs—" Her voice implored him.

Simon looked at her silently, not having expected any different reaction. Finally he said, "What if you knew absolutely—without a doubt—that her God and yours is one and the same?"

The fright in her eyes deepened, but as the two continued looking at each other, he could see hope warring with the fear. Her fingers came up to her mouth.

Finally she said, "It would give me great peace."

Midsummer came and went. The city became hot, Mayfair deserted of most families who were off to the country. Simon returned to his routine but avoided Althea as much as she him. His manner when they did meet was formal, causing Althea to long for the old mockery and impatience. He spent every hour not at Rebecca's bedside closeted in the library, and from Giles she knew he was working at a feverish pace to complete his book. Parliament had recessed, but Simon still spent the evenings out, after spending the early part with Rebecca.

He had hired a night nurse, whom his older sister, Simcha, had sent over, and told Althea in no uncertain terms that he didn't want her sitting up until all hours with Rebecca.

Rebecca's family came at intervals to sit with the child. Althea's polite greetings grew to a few pleasantries, until gradually she began to form an acquaintanceship with Simon's sisters and mother. His mother seemed to take particular pains to draw her out.

One day Mrs. Aguilar reached over and patted Althea's hand, saying, "I just want my children to be happy."

With the hiring of the night nurse, Mrs. Higgs, Althea had a little more time to resume her work with the kitchen staff. She enjoyed this work for the added benefit that it kept her below stairs, further removed from any contact with Simon. She fretted over Cook, who had had a few relapses during the time Althea had been more occupied with Rebecca. Harry and even Giles now joined the Sunday morning Bible study. She had begun to talk with those at the mission about beginning a chapel service somewhere in Simon's neighborhood.

One Sunday morning in late July, Dot did not attend the Bible study.

"Oh, she's ailing, miss," explained Martha.

"That's too bad. I shall go up and see her later. Let us lift her up in our prayers this morning."

After the study, Althea went up to the attic rooms. Dot lay sleeping, but roused at the sound of Althea.

"Don't know what's wrong with me. Sore throat and 'eadache."

Althea bent down to feel her forehead. "Oh, dear, you have a fever."

"Went to visit my mum last week and all the young 'uns was sick. Must o' caught it from them. I was holding 'em and tendin' to 'em."

Althea went to fetch her some hot tea with lemon. "Here, drink this. Let's swaddle your neck, even though I know it's beastly hot up here. I shall call the doctor later if you show no improvement. On no account are you to come downstairs. Try to sleep."

Althea didn't want to disturb Simon. The few times they had come into contact he seemed to look right through her. Instead she instructed Giles to tell the master. She sent Mrs. Coates to tend to Dot, wanting as little contact with her as possible, for fear of contracting anything that could be passed on to Rebecca.

Rebecca greeted her happily when she came to sit with her later in the afternoon.

"*Abba* brought me this new book. Aren't the pictures pretty?"

"Oh, yes, they are indeed." Althea took the book from her and leafed through it. She read her a few pages, then set it down when the tea tray was brought up. They drank their tea and chatted a while.

"You know what I wish, Althea?"

"What, dear?"

"That I could hear you playing the pianoforte again."

"Why, of course you may. I'll just get Harry to carry you down, and I'll play for you."

They arranged this, and Althea played for her until Rebecca tired.

Later that evening, Simon came up to visit with his daughter. He said a brief good evening to Althea as he usually did, although he hardly met her eyes.

"Good evening," she replied, giving no hint by her tone or demeanor that his words affected her at all. For all she demonstrated, they had never had any encounter but the briefest between employer and employee. "I shall be down in the kitchen if you require anything." She had begun sitting with the servants on Sunday evenings. They would sing some songs and read a few Scriptures, and she would tell them some of the testimonies of things she'd seen in her years of ministry. They listened wide-eyed when she spoke of the miracles of deliverance and healing she'd seen firsthand.

A few days later, she heard a knock on her bedroom door. It was still early evening. She had just put down her Bible to prepare for bed.

"Yes, who is it?"

"Simon."

She hurried to the door, wondering what was the matter. He usually only dealt with Mrs. Higgs, the night nurse, in the evenings when he came in.

She opened the door. "Is something the matter?"

"Forgive me for disturbing you. It's Rebecca. She seems feverish. Can you come for a moment?"

Her heart sinking at the news, Althea hurried after him.

"Mrs. Higgs hasn't arrived yet," he said over his shoulder. "Besides, I trust your opinion over hers." They had reached Rebecca's bedside. "What do you think? Should I call a physician?"

Althea leaned over Rebecca and felt her forehead. "Yes, she seems hot. Are you feeling poorly, darling?" she asked, smiling at the girl to hide her own fear.

"Uh-huh."

Althea asked her a few more questions as she examined her, her concern growing. "Perhaps we should call Mr. Russell," she said, mentioning the young surgeon from the mission.

"I doubt even his devotion would bring him across town at this hour," he answered shortly. "I shall send for Dr. Roseberry. He's much closer on Harley Street."

Althea looked at him sharply. It wasn't like him to behave so capriciously where his daughter was concerned, but all she said was "Very well," and she turned her attention back to Rebecca. After Simon left the room, Althea rang for Mrs. Coates.

"Yes, miss, you called for me?"

"Yes, how has Dot been?"

"She was quite poorly for a few days, but now she's on the mend. I'm afraid, though, Martha has come down with it."

"Oh, no." Althea thought a moment. "Has Martha brought up any food for Rebecca in the past few days?"

"Oh, dear, I suppose so. It's usually Daisy or Dot, but with Dot sick, Martha has been helping bring up Rebecca's tray. Is something amiss? Did one of them forget to bring something? I'm always after them for something—"

"No, no, nothing like that. It is just that Rebecca is feverish, and I was wondering, since I knew Dot had been ill...." She heard her own voice trail off, not wanting to formulate what was in her thoughts.

"Oh, no! Don't tell me. Poor mite." As she spoke, she approached Rebecca's bed and bent over her. "Oh, my, yes, she's contracted it for sure, poor thing. Now, don't you fret, Becca, we'll get you feeling better. Let me just bring you up a nice hot toddy. Your throat pains you?"

Simon came back up as Mrs. Coates was leaving. Althea went to get some lavender water. When she returned, she found Simon seated beside Rebecca, her hand in his. Althea stooped over and placed the cool compress upon Rebecca's forehead.

"They will inform Dr. Roseberry as soon as he returns," Simon told her.

"He is out?"

"Attending the Duchess of Lansdowne's ball."

Althea clamped her lips shut against the retort forming on her lips. Quietly, she told him instead about her fear that Rebecca might have contracted the infection that had gripped a couple of the servants.

His dark eyes flashed. "Why wasn't I told of this?"

"I did inform Giles as soon as Dot took ill."

Simon rubbed his face, his frustration clear. "I don't remember his saying anything. He's an old man—it could have slipped his mind."

She said nothing.

Her silence seemed only to anger him. "Perhaps he did mention it. I simply don't remember!" He swore. "I could have removed Rebecca from the household. Why didn't you come to me?" He looked at her, the anguish visible in his eyes.

She looked down at her hands. "I'm sorry, I should have come to you directly."

He didn't say anything more, and she knew they were both thinking of that night and how they had been at such pains to avoid one another since then. Would their foolishness cost Rebecca now?

When the physician didn't arrive within an hour, Simon finally called for Mr. Russell, who came in under an hour. Simon and Althea watched silently as the doctor examined her. He gave her a sleeping draft and then went out into the corridor with the two of them.

He had already questioned them about any other illness in the household. He didn't mince words now. "It's clear she's caught what the servants have. There's nothing to do now but nurse her through it, and pray to God she has the strength to live as it runs its course."

By then Mrs. Higgs had arrived and prepared to take the first watch. Althea retired to her room, planning to check in at dawn. Simon left instructions with the night nurse to call him as well at first light.

Althea walked around her room, not knowing even how to pray. She felt the weight of discouragement press down on her and didn't feel the power to fight it. She knew the words; she knew the weapons she had been given, but she didn't feel the strength to use them. She finally crumpled at her bedside and simply murmured, "Oh, God...oh, God...oh, God...help her!" Over and over she cried the words quietly, feeling like a little child crying on her parent's lap, not knowing how he would answer, only needing to feel the solid comfort of that lap, knowing it wasn't going to move.

She finally fell asleep, but awakened throughout the night to pray. At dawn she arose and peeked in on Rebecca. The child was worse, and Althea quickly washed and dressed to return to her bedside, her Bible in hand.

Simon came in shortly afterward, but the two didn't say much to each other. He sat for a while with his daughter. Althea exited the room to leave him alone with her, telling him softly to call her as soon as he needed to leave. In the meantime, she knelt in the sitting room and continued to pray. She decided to fast that day.

The day blended into night and the night into another dawn. Althea thought it was ironic how beautiful those summer days were. She would peer out the window at the street below, see the bright sunshine on the lush treetops, hear the shouts of children running and playing in the nearby square, and listen to the *clip-clop* of horses trotting briskly on the cobblestones—sounds of life, when within the confines of the mansion on Green Street were heard only dull, muffled sounds, as if everyone was afraid the least noise would somehow hasten things.

Althea continued her fast, hoping Simon would not notice, but at the fourth day he asked her sharply if she was not eating. She shook her head, hoping he would ask her no more.

"What, are you hoping to appease your God with sackcloth and ashes?"

She made no reply, feeling no desire to defend her actions. In her fast, though her body felt weak, her spirit felt strong. By the fifth day, her physical desire for food had disappeared and she had an increased hunger for God's word. When she was alone with

Rebecca, she read the Word aloud, saturating the room with it. In those moments, she felt the presence of God strongly and hope awakened in her.

Chapter Sixteen

❧

"Miss Althea?"

Althea started awake in her seat. She must have dozed off for a moment. She looked immediately toward Rebecca's bed. "Yes, dear, what is it?" she asked, leaning over her.

"Oh, Althea!" The little girl's face was radiant and she stretched out her hand, reaching for Althea's. Althea took the hot hand in hers and clasped it.

"Oh, Miss Althea, I must tell you about it."

"About what, dear?"

Rebecca turned dark, luminous eyes to her. "I just met Him!"

"Who, dear?" Althea smoothed her forehead with her other hand.

"Jesus!"

Althea's heart began to pound. "You did?" she asked in awe. "Tell me about it."

"I must have been dreaming, but I saw Him. He was right here with me. Oh, Althea, it was wonderful!"

Althea nodded. "Oh, yes, dear, it must have been. What did He say?"

Rebecca closed her eyes. "He told me so many nice things. He said I would be coming to stay with Him soon. Oh, Miss Althea!" Her expression was earnest. "I wanted to stay with Him already. He was so beautiful. I didn't want to ever leave His side.

"He gave me His hand and I didn't want to let it go! But He comforted me, saying it would be soon. There was so much light around Him. I felt as if it reached right through me, lighting me up, too. I felt so warm inside!

"He told me not to be afraid, that I would be with Him for always. There was such a glow about Him and so much love in His eyes." She peered at Althea intently as if wanting her to understand.

"Yes, I know, sweetheart," said Althea through her tears.

"You're crying. Are you sad?"

Althea shook her head. "I'm so happy you met Jesus." She cupped the girl's cheek with her hand. "I shall miss you, dear, ever so much, but I will see you again. You know that now, don't you?"

"Yes. I understand what you meant, too, when you told me God is always with us. He truly is. I can feel Him here now. Can't you?"

"Yes, oh, yes!"

Rebecca's eyes clouded for a moment. "It only made me sad about *Abba*. I asked Jesus about him. Could he not come, too? Jesus told me not to be sad about *Abba*." Rebecca's eyes smiled once again into Althea's. "He said He loved *Abba* just as much as I did, and He wouldn't leave him comfortless. Those were His words—He wouldn't leave *Abba* 'comfortless.' He gave me the warmest smile and told me that *Abba* would be all right."

Rebecca held up Althea's hand and spread it open. "Jesus held out his palm to me like this, to show me where *Abba* was, engraved right in His hand."

One of Althea's tears dropped onto her palm, and she wiped her eyes.

"Oh, Miss Althea, don't cry!" She looked into her nurse's eyes.

"I saw the scar!" Her voice was hushed in awe. "That's when I knew it was Jesus."

The two sat quietly for a few moments, drinking in the experience. After a while, Rebecca spoke again. "He told me right before I woke up that He would leave someone to take care of *Abba* for me until it was his turn to join me."

Althea took out her handkerchief and covered her eyes, knowing that something momentous had just occurred. She realized that Rebecca would not be with them much longer, but she felt, too, the deep joy of knowing where Rebecca was going.

"Rebecca." She spoke softly, wondering whether the girl had fallen asleep.

"Yes, Miss Althea?" Her dark eyes looked joyfully into Althea's.

"Would you like to be baptized, the way we've read about?"

She considered for a moment before a slow smile spread across her face. "Yes. Just like Jesus when the dove came upon Him."

"Yes."

Althea prayed before going to see Simon. She asked God for favor with her employer in the matter pertaining to his daughter's baptism. With great trepidation she knocked on the library door. When Simon bid her enter his sanctum, she felt like Esther entering the king's chamber. It had been a while since she'd crossed the threshold of that room.

"What is it?" he asked as she approached his desk. "Is it Rebecca?"

"In a manner of speaking." Seeing he was ready to rise from his chair, she stopped him with a motion of her hand. "She's sleeping. Mrs. Higgs is with her." She cleared her throat as she watched him resettle himself in his seat. "I merely wanted to ask you for something."

He said nothing, his somber eyes attentive.

"Would you consider allowing Rebecca to receive baptism?"

She could see he had not expected that. He rubbed a hand

across his jaw, his glance going back to the papers on his desk. "One more of your God's requisites before entry is granted into Paradise?"

Althea said nothing.

Silence fell. Then he looked at her and asked abruptly, "Is this your idea or Rebecca's?"

"I asked her if she would like to be baptized and she expressed her wish for it."

At his look of skepticism, she added, "You may ask her yourself. I did not influence her in her decision."

"I'm sure you didn't," he replied dryly. The silence drew out so long, Althea thought he wasn't going to reply, when he sighed deeply. "Very well."

As Althea breathed a prayer of thanksgiving, Simon asked, "What must I do to have it arranged?"

"It's all right. I can see to it."

"How will it be done? A baptismal font?"

Althea hesitated. "I was thinking...perhaps we could use the tub where she is bathed. I know she is weak, but if the room and water are well heated, I don't think it will cause her any harm." She waited, praying silently.

"You mean immerse her fully in water?" His dark eyes expressed their shock.

"But only for an instant. We'd have her right out and into dry things immediately and into her warm bed."

His look was hostile. "I think it's madness."

She bit her lip. How could she tell him the physical aspects at this point didn't much matter, that only the spiritual concerns had any import now?

"Don't expect me to attend," he said abruptly.

She blinked at him. Was that a consent?

Swallowing her disappointment at his lack of interest in witnessing the event, grateful only that he wouldn't oppose it, she said, "You needn't if you don't wish it."

"I don't." He took up his pen in dismissal.

* * *

Althea asked the man who served as pastor at a chapel near the mission to come and administer the baptism. He came a few afternoons after her conversation with Simon. Giles and Harry had moved the tub up to Rebecca's room and the maids had filled it with warm water. All the servants were present.

Just as the pastor was ready to begin, the door opened quietly and Simon stepped in. He stood by the door, and everyone seemed instinctively to sense that he didn't want his presence to be noted.

Althea nodded to the pastor to begin.

Knowing Rebecca's weak condition, he kept things brief. He sat by her bed and took one of her hands in his. "Hello, my dear. I'm here to baptize you. Would you like that?" His voice was kindly.

"Yes, I should like that."

"You just need to repent of your sins, Rebecca, and when you go under the water, you're showing obedience in following Jesus in His death, being buried with Him, and when you come up out of the water, you're believing you are raised to new life in Him. Do you think you're ready to do that?"

"Oh, yes!"

The pastor led her in a short prayer, and then gave a nod to Harry, who approached the bed and bent down to pick up Rebecca. At that, Simon moved forward and touched his sleeve. "I'll see to my daughter."

Harry stepped aside and allowed Simon to pick her up. At the pastor's direction, Simon carried his nightgown-clad daughter over to the tub. Everyone drew near.

The pastor began to read from the Bible. "'Who is he that overcometh the world, but he that believeth that Jesus is the Son of God? This is he that came by water and blood, even Jesus Christ; not by water only, but by water and blood. And it is the Spirit that beareth witness, because the Spirit is truth. For there are three that bear record in heaven, the Father, the Word, and the Holy Ghost: and these three are one. And there are three that bear witness in earth, the spirit, and the water, and the blood: and these three agree in one.'

"Today, Rebecca, you are bearing witness of the truth by following Jesus in baptism by water. Jesus declared before He departed this earth that 'he that believeth and is baptized shall be saved; but he that believeth not shall be damned.'

"Therefore, we now baptize you, Rebecca Aguilar, in the name of the Father, the Son, and the Holy Ghost." With those words, the pastor leaned forward and helped Simon submerge his daughter into the water.

Althea felt the lump in her throat at the reading of the words and the sight of Rebecca being baptized, the meaning of the act hitting her afresh although she had witnessed countless baptisms. As soon as Rebecca came up, smiling, Althea and Dot hurried forward with warm towels and wrapped Rebecca in them. Simon carried her back over to the bed, where the two women quickly changed her wet garment for a dry one and tucked her back in.

Simon left as soon as it was over, as quietly as he had come.

Two weeks later, Rebecca passed away quietly in her sleep. Althea and Simon were both sitting by the bed. He felt her pulse then turned to Althea, his gaze unreadable. She felt for herself. Gently she laid Rebecca's arm across her chest, knowing the little girl was no longer there with them. She slipped out of the room, leaving Simon alone with his daughter's body. She didn't know whether Rebecca had had a chance to say goodbye to her father or to tell him about her experience. She had been unconscious more than conscious in those days following her baptism.

Althea sent for Dr. Roseberry, and after she accompanied him up to Rebecca's room, she left him with Simon and went to inform the servants.

By nightfall, Simon's family had descended upon the house. She had no idea where Simon was, but assumed he was behind his closed library door. She helped prepare rooms for the family members that would be staying. She learned from his sister that the funeral would be the next day and that the family would spend a week at the house, sitting *shiv'ah,* observing the mourning period, during which time they would not leave the house and would spend the mornings and evenings reciting the mourning prayers.

Simon's mother and the eldest of the two sisters came at once and readied the house. They covered all the mirrors and brought low wooden stools on which the mourners would sit in the coming days.

A special group of people took charge of Rebecca's body for the ritual bathing and dressing in a shroud before it was laid in the plain wooden casket, which contained no metal fastenings of any sort. A special watch was kept over the casket until the time of interment.

Althea sent word to her brother and his wife about the funeral. She discovered that regardless of Simon's religious beliefs, or lack of them, his family had determined that his daughter would have a full Jewish funeral with all the rites observed.

Seeing she had little to do, Althea cleared out her things from her bedroom and made it available to Simon's mother and father. She spent the night upstairs in the servants' quarters in order to accompany them to the funeral the following day.

The next day dawned clear and warm. Althea could see it would be another hot August day. Later that morning she stood with her brother and sister-in-law at the rear of the Jewish cemetery at Miles' End. Many people had come to the burial. Althea spied Colonel Ballyworth amid the mourners.

She watched as the simple wooden casket was lowered into the earth. Each of the family members covered it with a handful of earth. Then they tore at an article of their clothing. Most were wearing a black ribbon on their lapel especially made for the occasion.

As they left the cemetery, they washed their hands in a ritual cleansing ceremony. She noticed Simon did not participate in any of the rites. Althea had not spoken to him at all since Rebecca's death. He looked like a man turned to stone. All she could do was to hold on to that conversation she had had with Rebecca and the promise that the Lord would not leave her father comfort-less.

That night after the funeral the Lord gave her a Scripture: "A bruised reed shall he not break, and the smoking flax shall he not quench...." She could only trust that the Lord would not break that fragile reed that was Simon's hurting soul, nor put out the smoldering spark left in the man she loved.

She grieved for him, but could not help him. He was unreach-able to any in those days, even to his own family. He didn't leave the library, and Althea felt powerless to do any more in his house-hold. She stayed one more day, in order to be sure she was not needed in any way. That evening she bid each one of the servants downstairs goodbye. They cried and hugged her, and she prom-ised to be by to see them at a later date.

She quietly packed her few dresses, the puppets she and Re-becca had made together, and a few other mementos, such as drawings, childish attempts at sewing, and a note Rebecca had written to Althea one day. As Althea wrapped them in a parcel she let the tears fall.

"Yes, I shall miss you, my sweetheart," she whispered, looking at Rebecca's things.

Before leaving she did one last thing. Knowing she could not go into his library, and not knowing whom else to entrust her gift with, she finally went to Giles.

She handed him a Bible. "I would like you to give this to the master when you have an opportunity. I don't want to disturb him at present."

Giles nodded, taking the book from her. As he did so, a folded paper fell out. Althea bent to retrieve it.

"It's for him," she explained, placing the paper between the pages.

He looked at her with kindly eyes, and she couldn't help re-membering how indifferently he had eyed her when she'd first ar-rived.

"Very good, miss."

"Thank you, Giles." Not knowing how else to express what she felt, she held out her hand. "Goodbye, then."

He enveloped her hand in his large, gnarled one. "We'll miss you."

"And I you." She hesitated. "Take care of Mr. Aguilar."

He nodded with understanding. "I shall do my best, miss."

As she left Green Street for the last time, she turned back for a final look at the house. If she viewed it from the world's eyes, she would call her sojourn there a total loss. Her patient had not recovered, and her employer was as far away from his Savior as he'd ever been. The death of his daughter had undoubtedly sealed his heart against God.

In her mind and body, Althea felt like a complete and utter failure. All she could do was trust that her labor had not been in vain. She recalled the Scripture about a servant's acts of righteousness remaining forever. She had to believe that her obedience in fulfilling what the Lord had called her to do in Simon's household would remain forever. She knew it was so. Although her heart mourned Rebecca, it also knew there was great rejoicing in Heaven.

She went to her brother's town house and spent an evening with them, but would not let them persuade her to stay longer. She knew where her place was, and she had been away too long already. She returned to the mission early the next day, closing the preceding chapter of her life.

Simon wandered the dark halls of his house, listening to the silence. Even though the mourning period would go on for some time, with Kaddish prayers being said in the synagogue, the portion under his roof was over. After a week, his family had walked around the block, signaling the end of *shiv'ah.* Then they had departed, each to resume a normal life.

He had barely spoken to them while they had been at his house. He hadn't interfered with their rituals but neither had he permitted them to draw him in to their prescribed form of mourning.

He walked the hallway one more time in his dressing gown and slippers. He thought about Job. That poor fellow had lost everything because of some game God had been playing with Satan. Is that what had happened to him? First his wife and now Rebecca. Had they been the innocent pawns caught in the middle? Had they been the expendable elements in Simon's life when God had looked down on him and decided to allow Satan to amuse himself with his life?

Was Simon going to be allowed to succeed in the political arena but not in the domestic? Was God saying, in effect, "I shall let you rise in Parliament, but you shall never know happiness in hearth and home?" What if God changed His mind and said to Satan, "You can have it all. Take whatever Simon has—only keep him alive, we want him to feel his losses."

Well, Simon wasn't going to be caught in the middle anymore. They'd taken the best from him; he wasn't going to participate in their game anymore. He'd fold his hand and withdraw from the play. It was too deep for him.

Simon ended his midnight perambulation in Rebecca's bedroom. The bed was made, everything put in order. It was almost as if his daughter were just away at her grandparents' for a few days. Tomorrow she would be returning, her eyes sparkling, her words tumbling out, wanting to tell him all at once about everything she'd done. Simon walked past her row of dolls— What had she called them? He couldn't for the life of him remember and he felt a stab of pain at the lapse. Sarah? Angel? Anna? Rebecca— yes, one was named after herself—and Althea. Althea. He picked up a porcelain one, remembering the countless tea parties he'd had with this one. Rebecca seated at her little table on her good days, propped up in bed on her bad ones, her dolls at her sides.

"*Abba,* Miss Althea wants to know how you like your tea? Miss Althea is going to the ball next week. There's a prince there she is going to be introduced to...."

Where was Althea, anyway? Simon half turned, his eyes going to the door to the sitting room. He hadn't seen her in how many days? He tried to recollect. He'd lost track of the days since the funeral. It seemed as if he'd been walking around in a fog since that day he'd beheld Rebecca's warm features grow into a marble-like mask.

He'd left the remains of his little girl to his family and sought refuge in the library, no longer aware of days or nights as he sat huddled in his chair, staring at his papers. Ivan, his valet, had come to see that he was dressed and ready for the funeral. His father had tried to comfort him. Simon had sat mute, not hearing the words, seeing only the man who could buy and sell others, as the Mother Goose rhyme went through his head, "All the king's horses and all the king's men couldn't put Humpty Dumpty together again."

Simon stared at the chairs where he and Althea had shared so many evening conversations. What would she say about the situation now? She had been fond of Rebecca. Had she been able to accept her charge's death so gracefully?

All of a sudden Simon felt a desperate longing to talk to her as he used to, to unburden himself to someone who wouldn't be ruffled by anything he said or offer platitudes to his pain. Even when she'd angered him, there was a comfort in her certainty.

He tried to pinpoint when he'd seen her last. He was certain she had been at the funeral. With no clear idea of what he intended, nor of any thought to the time, he entered her sitting room. Here, too, all was neat and silent. The moonlight illuminated the outline of the furniture, touching her chair by the fireplace where she'd sat reading that Bible every night.

After some hesitation he knocked on her bedroom door, his need more pressing than any considerations of propriety. There was no answer. Of course not, he thought, thinking of the hour. He shouldn't wake her. But his yearning at that moment for the human contact he'd been shunning since Rebecca's death overwhelmed him.

He knocked harder this time, calling out, "Miss Breton!"

It was funny, she used to be up in seconds when Rebecca cried out in the night. But now only silence greeted him. He knocked and called again. Finally, hesitantly, he turned the knob and entered. It took only a second to discern through the moonlight that the bed was vacant. He walked over and stood by it for a moment. Then he walked around the rest of the room and found it empty of all personal belongings. There was not a trace of Miss Breton to be found.

Had she, too, been a ripple in his existence? Gone now, every last trace? Like a dream, completely evanescing upon waking. Would the memory of her disappear as quickly? Had she even been real?

Then he understood. She was gone. Of course she was gone. He didn't need her anymore. Her patient had succumbed to her illness, so Miss Breton's services were no longer required. When had she left? Directly after the funeral? Again he struggled to remember when he had last seen her. But the preceding days were indistinct, like a heavy opiate veil. The only clear memory was of shutting himself in his library, away from prying, sympathetic eyes. He had either sat in his chair or slept fitfully on his couch, the only sounds intruding being the soft footfalls of his valet or butler entering to leave him a tray of food and tea, along with a strong libation in the evenings.

So, Miss Breton had vanished without a trace. Simon hadn't even paid her her last quarter wages.

He turned on his heel, leaving the empty room, ignoring the call of his heart.

Chapter Seventeen

❧

The next morning Simon got up and shaved. He gazed at his reflection in the mirror, feeling the smoothness of his jaw. Unwittingly, he had observed that part of the Jewish ritual, remaining unshaven during the period of *shiv'ah*. He descended to the library, where he was able to sit down at his desk and do some work for the first time. He had decided last night to draw a definite line between his present and his past.

In the early afternoon, Giles announced that Lady Stanton-Lewis had come to see him.

"Show her into the sitting room. And bring some tea."

Giles bowed his head silently.

Eugenia sat in the settee, a perfect picture of health and beauty. She was a welcome sight to his weary eyes.

"I haven't seen you since the funeral, so I thought I'd better come and see what hole you were digging yourself into."

"Good afternoon, Eugenia." He bent over her hand, its skin white and soft. "How have you been? And Lord Stanton-Lewis?"

"I'm fine, he's fine. Sends you his condolences. You looked

awfully peaked at the funeral and you don't look much better now."

"Thank you," he answered wryly, seating himself on a chair beside her.

"Don't wallow in self-pity. We all know what you've been through. The thing is to get through it. That's what your friends are here for."

Harry brought in the tea. After he'd left, Eugenia poured and handed Simon his cup.

"What are your plans, Simon?" she asked when they'd each taken a sip.

He gave her a sidelong glance. "Plans? I haven't the foggiest."

"Why don't you get away for a while?"

The idea had an immediate appeal. If he spent another night wandering the empty corridors and rooms of his house, there was no telling what he would do next. "What did you have in mind?"

She gave a rich, throaty laugh. "Scotland." At his look of interest, she continued. "Griff and I have a place on the moors. We always go there for the grouse shooting. The season is just commencing. Why don't you come along with us now? There will be only a small group on our estate, a very select few. You can see them or not, as you choose. It's quite isolated. You may mourn your daughter in peace. It's the ideal place for long walks and contemplation. It will do you a world of good." Her eyes brightened. "You may also work on your book. You'll find yourself much more productive up there, I'll warrant."

He pondered it, looking at the clear cinnamon hue of his tea. The more he thought about it, the better the prospect tempted him.

When he didn't speak right away, Eugenia put down her cup and saucer and leaned toward him. She laid a hand on his arm. "Simon, you and I are two lost souls."

He met her clear-eyed gaze. God, but she was beautiful: wide, pale green eyes, flawless ivory complexion with just a hint of rose in each cheek, pale blond hair curled about her head. Her words drew him.

"Lost souls?"

"You know what I mean. We know the hopelessness of the situation. That's all the more reason to grasp all we can today." Her eyes widened, imploring him. "Come away with me and let us be damned together."

He would go. After all, wasn't he damned already?

The next day as he was leaving the house, he spotted Althea walking towards it. He stopped short, wondering for a moment if he had conjured her up from his thoughts the other night. He quickly recovered, however, when he noticed she didn't even see him, but turned toward the service entrance, her steps never hesitating.

Abruptly he hailed her. She started, and then stood as if unsure what to do.

He approached her, feeling annoyed with himself. He looked at her with no smile of greeting. She looked so dowdy, like someone's charwoman reporting for duty. "You disappeared," he accused.

She reddened and looked down. She was wearing an ugly-looking bonnet and drab brown gown. He couldn't help contrasting her looks to Eugenia's fashion-plate appearance.

"I was no longer needed," she answered simply.

It angered him even further that she didn't even apologize for not saying goodbye. "Where are you headed?"

"I— Just to see Mrs. Bentwood and Mrs. Coates. I had promised them to stop and visit them."

To visit the servants, and not him? He felt as if she had slapped him in the face. And to think he'd been yearning for those evening conversations with her. What would he have done? Poured out his heart to her?

He only nodded. "Well, I still owe you your wages." He felt contempt for his weakness even as he found himself saying the words. "Can you spare a few minutes and step into the library?"

"I— That's all right. You don't have to pay me."

That angered him even further. Was she refusing his money?

"You disdain to accept your wages?" He kept his voice deliberately cool. "You mean you cannot even use them at the mission—or have your patrons grown so rich, you can refuse a small donation?"

She reddened even more. "Of course not. I thank you. Very well, I can accompany you to the library, unless you are on the point of going out?"

"It can wait. Come."

He held the front door open for her. The two were silent until they reached the library, where he beckoned her to a seat. He shoved aside a stack of papers.

"How is—is your book coming?" came the timid question as she removed her bonnet and pushed aside her windblown hair. Her cheeks were flushed.

He swallowed, realizing how wrong he'd been. She was beautiful.

"I'm sorry," she was saying, "I suppose you haven't been able to work on it lately."

He looked at her from under his brows as he unlocked a side drawer of his desk. "You are correct. I haven't made much headway on it lately."

"I'm sorry," she repeated quietly, her hands holding her bonnet and reticule in her lap.

He counted out the coins, aware of her sitting there, as serene as always. It annoyed him. Didn't she care?

He pushed the coins to the edge of the desk and sat back, watching as she opened her brown reticule and dropped them in without counting them.

When he said nothing more, she hesitated, then stood. Suddenly Simon panicked. Was she leaving already? She'd walk out that door and he'd never see her again. How could she turn her back on him and his household so easily?

Pride kept him from saying anything as she thanked him for the money.

"Don't thank me. They're your wages," he answered shortly.

She licked her lips. "Well, thank you...I'm much obliged to you. I...I can make my way downstairs," she said quietly.

As she turned, remorse filled him. God, what had gotten into him? None of this was her fault. She was probably just as much a pawn as the rest of them. She'd only tried her best to help. And what a help she'd been to Rebecca all those months.

She was halfway out of the library when he called out, "Please, Miss Breton, can you stay a moment? I— I have something I'd like to say to you."

She stopped and looked at him. He walked to her and motioned to the chairs in front of the fireplace. When they were both seated, he didn't know exactly where to begin. He sat with his hands on his knees and cleared his throat. "Miss Breton, I'd like to thank you for all you did for Rebecca. I don't know what we would have done without you."

When she tried to interrupt, he stopped her. "Please, let me finish. You were always there for her. I didn't really appreciate it at the time. I'd like to apologize if I neglected you during the funeral and those days following—I wasn't quite myself."

"Oh, Mr. Aguilar, please don't trouble yourself. I didn't expect you to act in any other way. I mean, I understood your grief—"

His lips twisted. "No, I don't think you quite did, but that is not the point. I merely wanted to apologize for any unkind words or treatment while you were in my employ."

He stood, too restless to sit, wishing now, as the other night, that he could really say what was in his heart, but not knowing where to begin. She seemed to sense he hadn't finished, because she remained seated, for which he was grateful. He didn't know what he would do if she scurried off, as she had seemed to want to do earlier. He leaned his arm against the mantelpiece, staring down at the empty grate.

"I have grown so tired of being surrounded by death—it seems to have stalked me of late. I sometimes wonder whether I even hastened Rebecca's death with my attitude. I sometimes just wanted it to bring down its scaffold and be done—then I'd be horrified with myself. But it seems it's been there, looming over my entire adult life."

When she didn't say anything, he turned to her testily. "Why don't you ever say anything? You just look at me with those soulful eyes as if you had the answers but are not sharing them."

To his surprise, she answered right away, "I suppose it makes all the difference when you think in terms of eternity. Jesus said, 'He that believeth in me, though he were dead, yet shall he live.'"

Simon made an impatient gesture with his hand. "Words! All words! Eternity. What is that? Does it make up for the hell on earth we are required to partake of in our short sojourn here? Does it justify being cut down in one's infancy or youth in the here and now? Why are we given someone to love in the flesh if they are only to be torn from us and we are expected to be satisfied with the poor consolation of the promise of some hereafter in some shadowy spirit realm?"

"It is not like that—"

But he was too wound up to let her speak. He began to pace in front of her, the thoughts he'd agonized over finally spilling out. "Am I to be content watching first my wife, and now my daughter, being buried in some pit, to know the worms will be eating up their bodies, and that mine will end up the same? That they are waiting in some eternal 'rest'? Or worse, but much more likely, that they have ceased to exist altogether?

"And that pit— What did Rebecca do to deserve that? Why couldn't she live a normal life span?" He continued railing at her God, her beliefs, his father's, the bitterness he'd kept in check finally pouring out.

Althea watched, knowing she could offer no solace but to listen. *Oh, Lord,* she prayed, *give him the answers he needs.* He finally came and sank down on one of the chairs, his head in his hands, his voice breaking.

"Oh, Simon, I'm so sorry," she whispered, moving toward him immediately and crouching beside him. She reached out her hand and touched his head. He seemed completely unaware of her in his grief. As his angry tears fell, his body shook. All she could do was offer him the comfort he had once given her when she had broken down. She patted his shaking back, wondering all the while whether this was the time to tell him about Rebecca's vision. Would it comfort him or would it be like pouring salt on his wounds?

Finally, as he calmed and silence once more reigned in the room, she began to speak. She spoke in a near whisper, her hand smoothing the unruly curls on his bent head. She spoke as she would to a child who had skinned its knee. She told him all that Rebecca had related to her, only refraining from mentioning the part about the Lord leaving someone to look after him. She wasn't even sure if he heard her. She kept up the steady motion of her hands as she spoke softly to him.

"Oh, Simon, if you had seen her joy, her radiance when she woke up, you wouldn't look at that pit as her resting place. You would understand the angel's words when he stood at the tomb of Jesus, telling Mary and the disciples, 'He is not here...he is risen!'"

His hair was so soft and springy under her hand; it reminded her sharply of all the times she had brushed Rebecca's, and she wished she could tell him how much she missed his little girl, too. Finally, Althea stood. When he made no movement, she removed her hand. Slowly, hesitantly, she bent down and planted a kiss on the crown of his head.

She straightened before moving away, quietly letting herself out of the library, afraid that when he returned to himself, he would be ashamed of his display of grief to her. She feared it would be as the last time when he had expressed himself to her. She couldn't bear to experience his cold formality once again, especially as this time it would concern the Lord. He could reject her as a woman, but she didn't want to endure his rejection of the Lord.

A month later she heard from her brother that Simon had gone away to Scotland at the invitation of Lord and Lady Stanton-Lewis. Althea hid her grief from her brother, and threw herself more deeply into her work at the mission.

* * *

Simon tramped over the fields of autumn heather, too tired to keep up the pace, but knowing he must if he wanted to return. These daily walks over the moors were always a chore; he did them only to weary his body physically, but they did not offer solace to his mind.

Sleep eluded him. It seemed as if his thoughts, which were in a near-somnolent state throughout the day, chose the night hours to awaken. His mind became a busy beehive, then. During the daylight hours, he found it a difficult task to focus on what people were saying, much less form a coherent reply, but as soon as he got into bed, his mind became razor sharp.

He had tried to use those hours after midnight, when everyone else had finally gone to bed, to work on his book, but his body was too tired to allow him to concentrate on labor laws, tariffs and universal suffrage. As soon as he blew out his candle, however, and rested his head on the pillows, the thoughts would begin and he found himself wide-eyed in the darkness.

He tried to marshal the thoughts and use them constructively, thinking over all that had been said that day, going over the outline for his book, preparing for the next day's direction, but his thoughts refused to obey him, going off in too many directions, but always returning to Rebecca.

Where was she? Where was his darling baby? The tiny bundle he had held in his arms? The little toddler who had stumbled over to grasp his legs? The clever little girl who'd been so quick to learn her alphabet? The laughing girl who'd wanted to know everything he was doing, everywhere he was going, and had managed to guess even when he didn't tell her?

Was she in some resting place awaiting the resurrection, as his people believed? Was she at Abraham's bosom? He couldn't escape the image of her in some bottomless pit without a glimmer of light or hope. Or worse, was she burning in the flames? He knew from his study of the Scriptures that God's wrath was expressed in flames. He knew his people's tradition taught a way to

Heaven by good deeds. A person could help his departed loved one into Heaven by saying the correct prayers over them.

He had spurned participating in all those traditions, considering them superstitions, but now the doubts assailed him. Was his daughter now paying for his negligence? Was her grandmother's piety enough to ensure Rebecca's entry into Heaven? Or would her father's sins be visited on her? What about her grandfather's sin? After all, the God they served said the sins of the fathers would be visited on the children to the third and fourth generation.

Simon's father had lived a life of ignoring the religious precepts that were inconvenient to him, and making up for breaking the Law by giving more generously to the synagogue. With every new mill opened, he would give enough to erect a hospital ward or establish an orphanage. When the rabbi had objected to his having Simon baptized in the Church of England, Leon Aguilar had donated enough to build a new synagogue and found himself a rabbi who would turn a blind eye to his business dealings.

Would the good outweigh the bad in the Aguilars' balance sheet? During the day, Simon's rational mind took over and he managed to dismiss these fearful thoughts, but in the wee hours of the morning, they came alive in all their gruesome possibilities. Was the God of Abraham, Isaac and Jacob, that fearsome God that demanded an eye for an eye, a tooth for a tooth, now extracting His payment from the Aguilar family? Was that righteous, Holy God, which had sent a plague upon the children of Israel when they had built themselves a golden calf, now laying His curse upon Simon's offspring?

When Simon would finally drift off into a light sleep, he'd awake with a start in a cold sweat, seeming to hear his daughter's cries from the burning pit. He covered his ears, thinking he'd go mad.

He tried putting off the moment of retiring to his bedchamber until everyone else had gone to bed. He'd sit for hours over the coffee and brandy with the poets and philosophers Eugenia had permitted around her table. They would get deeper and deeper into their cups, but Simon refused that escape. They even offered him opium, encouraging him to find relief from pain in the mind-dulling smoke. They would sit in their numb state and spout the greatest inanities as if they were revealing to him the secrets of the universe.

He refused these aids, having an even deeper dread of losing all control and seeing what he had only dimly imagined, in all its horrifying clarity. If he was under the influence of a drug he might not be able to return from that deep, bottomless pit. If his natural imagination could vividly present him with a taste of hell and damnation, what would the enhanced image of a mind inflamed by alcohol and opium be like? So, he drank sparingly and remained with them only because he didn't want to face the solitude of his bedchamber.

In the mornings, he rarely rose from bed before mid-morning, more often than not lying there till noon. No one else bestirred himself before that hour.

Eugenia was as good as her promise; she left him to his own devices during most of the day, but always made her presence and availability known to him in various subtle ways. Her unspoken message to him was crystal clear. Whenever he wanted her, she would give herself to him.

So, why didn't he seek that solace? At least it would mean not having to sleep alone at night, he thought cynically to himself.

Lady Eugenia Stanton-Lewis was beautiful, intelligent, charming and accomplished in every way. Though past the first flush of youth, she was nevertheless still in her prime, perhaps even more beautiful because of her sophistication.

Why wasn't he tempted, then?

Was it her lack of virtue? A woman who would pick and choose her lovers as deliberately as a chess player, with the tacit approval of her husband, somehow left him cold. Yet, what kind of a hypocrite was he to judge her? Hadn't he treated people the same way—weighing, analyzing, judging how best they could serve him in his present and future plans?

He must be mad, indeed, not to accept what she offered him. He continued to examine his behavior as he lay in bed, preferring to think about anything but what lurked in the shadows of his mind.

Perhaps it was also his grief, as Eugenia tactfully implied, that kept him from satisfying himself with her. Wouldn't it be the most natural thing to assuage his grief in the arms of a woman?

None of these reasons satisfied him completely.

What kept him from experiencing the bliss—however fleeting—of an illicit relationship?

Was it the memory of someone else? Was it the picture of a fresh-faced woman who knew nothing of the art of cosmetics, but whose inner beauty gave her a radiance no rouge or powder could ever duplicate?

Was it the memory of that loving, gentle hand stroking his head as she had Rebecca's so many times in the past? The memory of those soothing words she'd whispered, and which he scarcely let himself believe even now, and of that soft kiss—had he imagined it?—that she'd planted on his head?

Simon reentered the castle after his walk. The baron's Scottish retreat had proved to be a mammoth stone fortress. No one was about as Simon walked down the flagstone entry beneath a variety of trophy heads jutting out from the oak-paneled walls, staring ahead with their glass eyes like mute sentinels.

He wandered toward the library, thinking of time in terms of so many hours to kill. He had just poured himself a shot of scotch whiskey from a decanter left out for the guests, when Eugenia entered the room.

"There you are. How was your walk?"

"Fine," he said, regarding her over the rim of his glass, beginning to be annoyed with her ability to appear silently at his side the moment he entered a room. In his present state, it made him think of a wraith.

She certainly didn't look like a wraith. As usual she was exquisite. Simon wondered whether she ever looked rumpled. Her attire today consisted of a lovely royal-blue gown trimmed with a blue and green tartan. The color only accentuated the pale satin of her skin and deepened the green of her eyes.

"You look beautiful," he commented, thinking such beauty shouldn't be wasted. It seemed a pity she had so few guests here. In London, at least, she graced a salon where dozens of men flocked to pay her court.

"Thank you." She gave him a soft smile, then reached for his glass. She took a sip, her gaze holding his. She handed the glass back to him, her fingers making contact with his.

"I worry about you." As she spoke, she touched the curls over his forehead. "All this walking, and yet you are looking paler than ever. Are you sleeping?"

"Not well."

She tsk-tsked, moving her head slightly from side to side. "I could help you, you know."

"Could you?"

She removed her hand from his face. "You know I could. You've been awfully coy with me."

"Have I?" He wasn't sure if he wanted this conversation to lead where he suspected it would, but felt powerless to stop it.

"Yes, Simon," she replied patiently. "It's time you stopped playing the innocent. You are a big boy, and if you ever hope to succeed in the world, you have to begin playing by its rules." She turned away as she spoke and walked to a vase of flowers a few steps away.

Her words reminded Simon of his father, and he had to make a conscious effort to dispel the distasteful image of a cunning manipulator who played by the rules that he himself created. Was Eugenia cut from the same cloth? Surely not the beautiful vision of female frailty who now took out a yellow chrysanthemum and twirled it around, watching it. "Rule number one—don't keep a lady dangling indefinitely."

Simon looked down at his drink. "You are absolutely right. I have been an awful bore, haven't I." He drained the glass in one swallow, realizing he might as well be hanged for a sinner as for a saint.

"You can be quite tedious at times with your *mal humeur* and injured looks," she went on, her back still to him.

"Undoubtedly," he agreed as he set his glass down on the silver salver beside the vase, its *thump* signaling his resolution to play the game to its conclusion.

"It's understandable, but really Simon, we have all been through what you have been through." Now that he'd finally decided to be amenable, she seemed to want to punish him. "You lost a daughter. Who hasn't lost someone?"

"I understand that," he said evenly, hurt despite himself by her callousness.

She turned to him, putting the flower up to his cheek and twirling it against his skin. "I am not a woman used to being ignored."

He eyed her lazily. "I have just been telling myself that your beauty is being wasted here."

She smiled at the comment, mollified to a degree. "It needn't be, if the right man were to notice it."

"Am I the right man?" He covered the hand that held the flower to his face.

She moved her hand away from his and brought the flower up to her exquisitely formed nostrils, as if to remind him she was the one establishing the rules. "Are you? That is the question, is it not?"

He was in no mood to be toyed with. Why couldn't they just get on with it? "I realize the honor you are bestowing on me."

"I feel I have been extremely patient. You have been here over a month, and yet you've ignored me the entire time." Her well-modulated voice took on a petulant tone.

"I must apologize once again," he said. "If I've been removed, it has only been because of my grief. You invited me here to get away from people. I'm deeply grateful for that. It is not your fault if I can't seem to shake my gloom."

"I *invited* you here so we could be *alone*." Her voice lost its huskiness and became hard.

"With your husband?" he asked.

"Griffith and I understand each other. Besides, he is no longer here."

"So I see." Simon picked up a snuffbox from the table. "His presence does seem to pervade the place, don't you find?"

"Oh, Simon, your scruples are a tad middle-class, are they not?"

He smiled at her, though he didn't find the situation amusing in the least. "That is, after all, my background."

She yawned. "I try to overlook it, but you do make it rather apparent at times."

"Forgive me." He bowed ironically.

"Oh, come on, Simon, let us get past this charade. I didn't invite you up here to have you traipsing through the moor all day and sit with those old cronies all night. I invited you here because I find you attractive. I expected we could have a mutually satisfying seduction. How much more clearly must I spell it out for you? It is not every man I favor, Simon." She tapped him with the chrysanthemum, her voice resuming its coy tone. "Do you know what my favor implies?"

Simon liked the turn of the conversation even less. "I believe I do."

"I can make or break a gentleman's public career, do you understand that?" She no longer looked like a woman to him. She reminded him more strongly of his father and his ilk, laying their plans, dealing with people's lives with no consideration to right and wrong, concerned merely with the profit line.

"You think much of yourself," he said lightly. "Are you indeed so powerful?"

Her laugh was deep and rich. "Do you want to try me?" She tossed the flower aside and ran her fingernail up his chest. "Liverpool is considering you for junior lord, is he not?"

He kept his expression neutral, not wanting her to see how much her knowledge surprised him. "And if he is?"

"Do you want it sealed and delivered by the time you return to London?"

"I shall have it, one way or another," he replied evenly.

She smiled. "I wouldn't be so sure. It has been some months, hasn't it?"

He looked at her, distaste beginning to cool any ardor he could have worked up. "I have made it to where I am without a lady's favor."

Her voice softened as she took a step closer and regarded him. She was so close that Simon could detect the powdery surface of her skin.

"You have done well with your family's wealth. But there is always that taint of— How shall I put it?" She pursed her beautiful lips. "The Levant?"

At her words, Simon flinched as if she'd slapped him. Very deliberately he removed her hand from his chest and took a step back. "Forgive me," he said quietly, suddenly realizing the awful mistake he'd made in coming here.

He went up to his room and told Ivan to begin packing. Then he went down to the stables and informed his groom and coachman that they would be leaving the following morning at first light.

When Lady Stanton-Lewis came down at noon the next day, she asked a servant for Simon's whereabouts. She was informed he had left a little after dawn. "I see," she said calmly, her voice revealing nothing of the sudden, violent rage she felt within her.

A few days later she was back in London. The next evening she knocked on her husband's door as he was preparing to go out for the evening.

"How was Scotland after I left?" he asked dutifully as his valet put the finishing touches to his cravat.

"Loathsome." She watched as the valet helped him into his coat and then stood back to inspect the result. She waited, knowing her husband would dismiss the man shortly. Griffith knew she never came to see him unless she had something specific she wanted to discuss.

Sure enough, a few moments later they were alone. Her husband gave himself a final inspection in his mirror as he asked her, "Yes, my dear, you wanted to see me about something?"

"Yes. I've been thinking I really need to disassociate myself from that tiresome little Jew. He has become a bit of a nuisance. Any suggestions?"

Her husband smiled at her from the mirror. "I have just the thing. I've been watching him for a while now."

Chapter Eighteen

Simon returned to London and sat down to his writing. This time he found himself making some progress. Although Parliament was not in session, he went around and visited those members who were not away hunting. He knew his only salvation now was his work, and he needed to connect himself once again with the people in power. He'd lost too much time.

A fortnight after he'd arrived and was well into a schedule of work, he had a visit from Althea's brother.

The two shook hands, and Tertius looked at him earnestly. "I'm so sorry I wasn't able to speak to you as I wished at the funeral and offer our condolences," he began.

"No, no, that's quite all right. It was I who was in no shape to hear anything anyone said to me. How is your wife, the baby?"

"Fine, everyone is fine." He paused awkwardly, as if ashamed of their good health in light of Simon's situation. He cleared his throat, looking away. "This is only the second time they're in town, actually. Gillian has been eager to do some shopping and visit with friends and acquaintances while she's here. We'd like to have you over for dinner some night."

"Certainly," Simon replied, though he knew he would find some excuse to refuse the invitation when it arrived.

"Listen, Simon," said Tertius when they were both seated. "The reason I have come by today, is...." He hesitated.

Simon wondered what was wrong. It wasn't like his friend to draw back from telling him something. Was it...could it be about Althea?

"Have you seen this?" Silently he handed Simon a folded-up copy of *The Royalist,* a Sunday paper known for its gossip.

"No." He hadn't read the society news since he left London. It no longer interested him.

"Look at the page it's opened to."

Simon dutifully unfolded the paper and scanned the headlines. "Young M.P. Serving King and Country under False Pretenses?" immediately caught his eyes. He read the small column, which described a young member of the Tory party, who, although baptized and swearing allegiance to the Church of England, was in fact a dyed-in-the-wool Jew, still participating in their ancient rites. The article ended with the question, Was he a member of the Tory party or of the party of the circumcision?

"Have you made any enemies recently?" was Tertius's only question.

In the following days, the two-penny papers took up the story, adding lurid details. They insinuated at Simon's involvement with a certain society lady without naming her name, called his father a moneylender, and referred to him as the "Ephraimite." Grotesque caricatures pictured rituals he and his family practiced in secret.

Finally, Simon had had enough. He went to Eugenia's residence one evening, in the hopes of getting to the bottom of the scandal. He could scarcely believe she would lower herself to such a thing for spite, but perhaps her husband had suddenly suffered a fit of jealousy.

Instead of immediate entry into her salon, he was made to cool his heels in a small antechamber. After a while he believed he wouldn't see anyone but a servant, but finally Eugenia showed herself.

She greeted him indifferently.

"Good evening, Eugenia," he said. He came straight to the point, throwing a newspaper on a chair. "Are you or the baron, or perhaps someone who attends your salon, behind these stories?"

She shrugged. "I know nothing of them."

"Do you have someone else do your dirty work for you?"

"I told you in Scotland you were becoming a bore. Don't become a nuisance as well."

"For my part, I didn't think you would prove so petty."

"Tell me, Simon, can you refute these stories?" She eyed him sardonically. "Because if you can, the scandal will die down on its own." She shrugged. "And if you can't, well, I pity you."

He clenched his fists, wishing for a second he could throttle that long, pale throat. He didn't doubt she had made good her threats in Scotland. His rage left him as quickly as it had come. Did he really deserve anything better than this?

"Why, Eugenia?" he asked wearily.

She took a step closer to him and looked him straight in the eye. Gone was any tenderness he had seen on earlier occasions. "You know, Simon, I can't believe I once found you amusing." She gave an abrupt laugh. "Did you really think I would condescend to sleep with a conniving Jew?" She turned and left him then, the sparkling train of her evening dress swishing behind her as she exited the room.

For the first time in his life, he felt truly dirty.

Simon tried to ignore the attacks, but the stories became more and more lurid, insinuating the most awful customs practiced by his family members. His father tried to investigate the source, and suspected a connection to the man who had put Simon up for Parliament from his borough, but he couldn't prove anything.

Finally, the chief whip called Simon in. The gist of the talk was that the prime minister himself felt the only honorable course left to Simon was to resign.

Simon left, feeling dazed and disoriented, like a boxer who has received one too many punches to the head. He began walking along the Thames, not seeing anything or anyone. He finally stopped when he reached London Bridge, exhausted. He stood there for a long time, looking out over the forest of masts down-river—a jumble of moored ships and small craft moving hither and thither. Everyone with a purpose, something to accomplish—everyone but him.

Finally he hailed a hack to take him back home.

A few days later he tendered his resignation.

Simon fought the yearning he'd had in him since he'd returned to London, but finally he could fight it no more. One afternoon he called for his carriage. He had hardly shown his face outside his house since his resignation, so the coachman's alacrity in obeying him was almost comical. Simon instructed him to go across town. The address caused his coachman to cough and hesitate, but Simon told him it was all right.

Simon had never been to that section of London, although he knew one of the oldest synagogues in the city was located near it. His ancestors who had immigrated to England had probably helped found it and worshiped there.

Simon disembarked from the coach in Whitechapel. The first thing that assailed him was the smell. Garbage and filth was piled in the gutters to the sides of the muddy road. He brought a hand-kerchief up to his nostrils as he looked around. The dilapidated state of the structures shocked him despite what he had prepared him-self for. He needn't have worried about finding the mission. The neatly kept building stood out among the boarded-up and crum-bling structures around him, like a cultivated flower among weeds.

Two painted window boxes were filled with evergreen boughs and sprays of holly berries. The door was neatly painted, too, the stone steps washed clean of the smelly garbage that littered the rest of the area. Simon picked his way through it, aware of the eyes of the loiterers upon him.

He was getting ready to lift the knocker, when the door opened and two lads rushed out. He looked down the hallway and, seeing several people standing or sitting about, he entered. The place smelled of soap and cabbage.

He hesitated a moment in the long corridor. From the comings and goings, he deducted the right-hand side held an infirmary. He walked down a ways, and heard the sound of children in the rooms on the left-hand side. He finally retraced his steps and knocked at the first door on the left, labeled Office.

"Come in." He recognized Althea's voice with relief.

He opened the door and immediately regretted having come. Four pairs of eyes turned in his direction. He recognized the young surgeon immediately. He was leaning over the desk where Althea sat. Another young man, dressed in a clergyman's cassock, sat in a hard-backed chair before the desk. Another, older, woman sat in another chair. They all stared at Simon, as he stood with his hat in his hand in the doorway.

Althea was the first to recover. "Mr. Aguilar! Please come in." She rose from the desk and came around to greet him.

"Hello, Miss Breton," he said, entering the room fully and closing the door behind him. She held out her hand and he took it. She gave him a welcoming smile and firm handshake.

She turned to the others in the room and made the introductions, which Simon didn't really heed, too intent was he on looking at Althea, whom he hadn't seen in some months. She was explaining to the others that he was her former employer. Mr. Russell greeted him quietly.

Simon was aware they were all looking at him curiously, but he didn't care. One by one the others excused themselves, finally leaving him alone with Althea.

The last time they had been together was that day in his library. Her color was high, as if the unexpected sight of him had flustered her. Had she never expected to see him again? He remembered the words she had once spoken to him—about going anywhere with him. Had she ever meant them, or had they been merely sentiments spoken in the heat of the moment?

"You're back," she said quietly.

"Yes, a few weeks ago."

"How was Scotland?"

"As can be expected." He didn't want to talk about Scotland.

"Please, have a seat." She motioned to a chair. "Can I get you something? A cup of tea?"

Just then, there was a knock on the door and it opened before she had a chance to answer. "'Scuse me, Miss Thea, but where do you want the crates they've just delivered?"

"Oh— Have them put in the first classroom." The door banged shut. "I'm sorry. Where— Oh, yes, can I get you some tea?"

"No, thank you." He took the seat she had indicated. "So, this is the mission," he said to fill the silence. He took a look around the spartan office, but didn't really notice anything. His gaze soon came back to her. He realized he should not have barged in unannounced.

"Yes." Her small hands knotted together in her lap. She had on the ugliest brown dress, and yet he had never seen anyone more beautiful.

He looked down at his hat, not even sure now why he had come. "The reason I stopped by—"

They were interrupted by a boy poking his head in the door. "Miss Thea, Mrs. Burrows says to please come to the kitchens at your first convenience."

"Yes, tell her I'll be there shortly." She turned back to him. "I'm sorry, you were saying?"

"I just wanted to thank—"

This time there was a light tap on the open door.

Althea answered with a frustrated "Yes?"

The older woman opened the door a fraction more. Althea gave Simon an apologetic look and stood. "Excuse me a moment, will you?"

"Certainly."

She went to the woman, and the two held a short conference in the doorway. She closed the door and returned to her seat. "I asked her whether she might be able to forestall any further interruptions. I don't know how much good that will do, but please continue."

Simon shifted in his chair. "You seem rather busy here."

"Oh, it's always like this. We are perpetually shorthanded. 'The harvest is plentiful but the laborers are few....'" she quoted with a smile.

"I shouldn't have just dropped in."

"Oh, no!" She looked crestfallen. She gazed down at her hands and said more quietly, "I'm glad you did."

"I suppose I just wanted to thank you for all you did for Rebecca." He looked down at his hat, turning the brim in his hands. "I don't think I ever really did it properly. I also wanted to apologize for my behavior the last time we met. I wasn't myself and—"

"There is no need to apologize—" she cut in quickly. "You had just lost your daughter, a dear little girl, whom we both loved very much."

He nodded slowly, realizing it for the first time. She had loved Rebecca, too. He sighed. What a stupid fool he'd been. But it was too late for that. "It doesn't excuse my treatment of you. I never meant to blame you in any way. You were the best thing that happened to Rebecca during those last few months. The closest she could have to...a mother—" He swallowed and looked away.

After a minute she said softly, "I miss Rebecca, too."

The two looked at each other, understanding in their eyes.

"You seem to have many children here," he remarked with an effort at normalcy. He smiled, the first genuine smile he'd managed in a very long time.

She smiled back. "Rebecca knew them all." At the question in his eyes, she said, "I used to tell her about them."

Suddenly the door was thrown open. It hit the wall behind it.

A big burly man marched in, red in the face, sweating and cursing.

"So, there you are!" He came at Althea, looking as if he meant to take her in his big, hairy hands and crush her. "Sittin' pretty there, no thought to the likes o' us out on the streets!" He vilified her with every epithet he could think of.

Both Simon and Althea stood as soon as he entered. Simon could see the man was clearly under the influence, incoherent from both the alcohol and his rage. He looked like a common laborer. Simon caught the sour smell of an unwashed body when the man neared. His clothes were stained and looked as if they'd been slept in for several days. More alarming was the fury in his face. Simon was afraid he'd have a fit of apoplexy.

"You lyin' cheat—takin' a man's 'ard-earned coin, leadin' 'im on with those promises. You Christians is all alike. Nothin' but money, money, money!"

Althea stood her ground, not showing by a flicker of expression an ounce of fear. "Mr. Smith, what are you talking about? What has happened?"

"Wot 'as 'appened, she asks?" he mimicked her. "Easy fer you to say—livin' in yer lap o' luxury 'ere. Wot do ye know of goin' 'ungry, o' being thrown onto the streets? Eh? Answer me that, will ye?"

"You are not going to be thrown onto the streets. Now, if you will just calm down, take a seat and explain to me just what has happened...."

"I paid me tithes just like ye told me to, and this is wot I get. Lost me job this afternoon." His forefinger jabbed inches from Althea's face.

Simon had had enough. He grabbed the man's arm and jerked him around to face him. The man towered over him. "Now, look here. Miss Breton does not deserve to be treated—"

The man was so surprised that he stopped and stared at Simon. "'Oo the 'ell are you?" For a second the man looked at Simon as if he were some strange critter, the like of which he'd never seen before. But then his eyes squinted as he took in Simon's appearance. "Oh, I knows yer type." He rocked back on his heels. "We got ourselves a nob 'ere. What does yer 'ighness know of 'ard work? You sit in yer clubs all day, while the likes o' honest folks and their children go 'ungry.

"Wot do ya know of losin' yer position, yer livelihood, o' 'avin' to see yer wife and kids wi' not a morsel o' food for their mouths? Wot do you know? Eh?" With each question he jabbed Simon harder in the chest, forcing him backward. "Wot do you know of bein' kicked out into the streets, wi' nothin' to eat?"

"But enough to drink, eh?" Simon asked ironically.

That infuriated the man. His face turned purple, his eyes bulged out at Simon.

Just then, Althea grabbed the man's two hands and shoved herself between him and Simon. "Where is your faith?" she rebuked him. "I never told you it would be easy, but I promised you that if you began trusting God for the welfare of your family and begin following His laws, He will bless you. You will never lack any good thing. Now the devil wants to make you doubt. It is he who comes to steal and kill and destroy. We are going to pray, and you are going to repent of this unseemly behavior. You are going to begin believing God for this situation." Without waiting for his acceptance or rejection of her demands, she closed her eyes, bowed her head, never letting go of his two big, hairy paws, and began praying in a voice that brooked no interruptions.

"Heavenly Father, we stand before You this day, pleading the case of Arnold. You know he has stepped out in faith, bringing You his tithe and offering. Now the enemy wants to make him believe he has been deceived. But we know better. We know You have already defeated the enemy; every principality and power of darkness has been utterly defeated by Your Son, Jesus. Your Word says to prove You, and see if You will not open up the windows of Heaven and pour down on us a blessing we cannot contain when we bring You our tithes and offerings. Your Word says You have never seen the righteous forsaken, nor his seed begging bread. We stand on Your promises for Arnold, asking You to protect his family, asking You for shelter for them, food on their table and a livelihood for him. We ask these things in perfect confidence, knowing You already have provision for him, You already know his every need..."

Simon stood in amazement, watching the blustering Arnold turn as tame as a lamb, submitting to Althea's prayer. He watched the man's hands shake as Althea shook her own in emphasis at the words she prayed. Simon crossed his arms, enjoying the scene. It was like watching an exhibition of bear baiting, with one little dog bringing down a giant, hairy bear.

By the time Arnold left, he was apologizing to Althea. Then she demanded he apologize to Simon.

Arnold shuffled, shamefaced toward Simon. "Sorry, guv'nor. Don't know what got into me."

"No need to apologize," Simon told him quietly, half amused, half ashamed for the poor fellow.

Althea led him to the door, telling him she would be by to see his family as soon as possible and to bring them to the mission if they found themselves out on the street before then.

She leaned against the door after she had closed it behind Arnold, and let out a deep breath. She and Simon stood looking at each other.

Simon finally said, "That was a remarkable prayer."

"I felt a little like Peter must have when he saw the cripple sitting outside the temple, and told him, 'Silver and gold have I none, but such as I have I give thee: In the name of Jesus Christ of Nazareth, rise up and walk!' If I'd had the money to pay his rent I would have, but I don't, so I must give him my faith." She smiled sadly. "It's unfortunate, isn't it, that so often we don't rely on our faith until we are forced to? How much we must miss out on."

He didn't really understand what she was talking about so he said instead, "I feared for you."

Her smile widened. "And I for you. I thought he might kill you."

"You know it's been proven it's very hard to eradicate my race."

She laughed. "Thank heaven."

"I think you took a few years off my life with the scare you gave me when you intervened between the two of us."

"I didn't know what to do, so I did the only thing I know how to do. I started praying."

"Poor fellow seems to have lost his job."

She nodded. "Yes, he's one of so many. And he wasn't exaggerating when he said he and his family would be thrown into the streets. The landlords haven't but to hear a rumor of unemployment when they immediately start threatening eviction."

Simon looked down. "It's ironic, you know, that he accused me of not knowing what it's like to lose one's position, one's livelihood." He looked at her to see if she had heard anything of the scandal.

One look told him she had. "I— That is, my brother told me. I don't read too many newspapers, but he did show me an article in the *Times*. I've— I mean, we have been praying for you."

"Thank you."

"I'm so terribly sorry."

"It's no more than I deserve, I suppose. You once warned me about the dangers of society."

"But I never imagined anything as awful as this...." Her voice trailed off.

Seeing there was nothing else to say, he collected his hat and gloves. "Well, I didn't mean to interrupt you. I didn't realize quite how busy you would be here. Otherwise, I shouldn't have called unannounced."

"Oh, no, please. You had no need to be announced. Won't you stay for a cup of tea?"

He smiled slightly. "No, that's quite all right. I really must be going."

"How is Mrs. Coates? Mr. Giles? I haven't been able to get away in a while to visit them."

"They're fine."

She seemed on the verge of saying something more, but once

again there was a knock on the door. She seemed torn between answering the door and speaking to him, but finally she turned and opened it to deal with another request.

When she gave him her attention once again, he hesitated. "Miss Breton—"

"Yes?"

"That story you told me about Rebecca—the last time I saw you. Was there any truth to it? Or were you merely trying to comfort a grieving father?"

She moved toward him. "Oh, no! It was no story. Of course I wanted to comfort you, but I wouldn't invent such a story just for that. I told it to you just as Rebecca related it to me. Oh, Mr. Aguilar," she breathed, "if only you could have heard Rebecca, could have seen her face. She was so happy, so full of joy."

"Perhaps it was the delirium of a fever. Or the fancy of a child?" he asked, wanting to believe her, yet unable to do so fully.

Her shoulders slumped. She took a step back, and he felt as if her very spirit had withdrawn from him. It made him feel unutterably lonely—for a few moments he had been able to bask in the sunlight, and now he was left in the shadow once again.

She looked at him steadily. "If that is what you wish to believe."

This time when they were interrupted, she said a quick, apologetic goodbye to him and gave her attention fully to the person who was seeking her aid.

When Simon descended the steps back out into the street, he looked at the various people sitting or standing around. He turned to an urchin hanging around the doorway. "Did you see that big fellow leave here a few minutes ago?"

The lad shrugged. "Maybe I did, maybe I didn't."

Simon took a half-crown from his pocket and flipped it into the air, catching it in his hand. "Did you or didn't you?"

The boy approached him, watching the coin in fascination as it twirled through the air again. "Guess maybe I did. Big fellow, warn't he?"

"Yes, I'd say so. Looked sort of like a great shaggy bear."

The boy laughed, his face soot-stained. "Yeah, that's just wot 'e looked like. Wot ya want know about 'im?"

"To begin with, where he lives."

"Aw, that's easy. Everyone knows where Arnold lives."

"Perhaps you could take me to him."

The boy rubbed his dirty coat sleeve against his runny nose, leaving a streak of pale skin showing through the soot. "Sure I could."

"Is it far from here?"

"Naw, just up a couple o' streets." He pointed down a narrow alley.

"All right. Let me inform my driver where I'm going." When he told his coachman, the man leaned toward him.

"Oh, Mr. Aguilar, do you think you should? No telling where the lad'll lead you."

"It's all right. If I'm not back within half an hour, you can go inside and inform Miss Breton that I went to see Arnold."

The man still looked concerned but said nothing more.

"Let's go," Simon told the boy.

The boy hurried off, but slowed at the next corner, giving Simon a chance to catch up. After a few more turns down narrow streets and alleys, Simon was hopelessly lost, but the boy was as good as his word, stopping finally before a run-down building. He gave a loud knock. A severe-looking woman opened.

"Yeah. What d'ya want?"

The boy jerked a finger toward Simon. "Gent 'ere's lookin' fer Arnold."

"Yeah?" She regarded him suspiciously. "What're ye, the law?"

"No, madam. I am merely a prospective employer. May I come in?"

She opened the door wider and let them pass through. "One flight up. Second door on the right."

They ascended the steep, dark stairs, which smelled of urine and cigar smoke and other, less identifiable smells. At the door, the boy knocked with enthusiasm. The door opened a crack to show the slice of a woman's face peering out at them fearfully.

"Good day, madam," Simon said gently. "I am looking for Mr. Arnold Smith." Before the woman could become alarmed, he added, "I may be able to help him."

"Who's at the door?" Arnold's bellowing voice reached them.

The woman closed the door. Simon assumed she had gone to consult her husband. A few seconds later, the door burst open.

Upon recognizing him, Arnold lifted up his chin. "What d'ye want? Come here to cause me trouble?"

"No, sir." Simon reached inside his coat and drew out his pocketbook. "I came to offer you your month's rent."

The man's mouth fell open at the sight of the pound notes.

"May I come in?"

Arnold opened the door to let him pass through. He took him to a rough table in front of the fireplace. Simon saw the rude implements laid on it. There was no fire in the grate and the room was cold. A baby lay swaddled in a cradle and three other children of varying ages clutched their mother's skirts, peering out from behind them at Simon, two of them sucking their thumbs.

Simon smiled tentatively at them, thinking of Rebecca and how she would have enjoyed listening to his tale of how he spent his afternoon. He would have to tell her all the details of the room and its occupants.

Arnold pulled out a wooden chair for him and took the remaining one himself. His wife sat on a rickety wooden stool by the fender.

"You have no fire?"

Arnold sniffed and rubbed his nose. "Got to conserve the little coal we 'ave left."

"What was your job?"

"Operated a loom."

Simon took out a calling card and scrawled something on the back of it. "If you report to the Guildford Mill in Islington tomorrow and present this card, I think they can find you a place." He counted out some coins and placed them in a stack in the middle of the table. "That should suffice for your rent. Here is some additional with which to purchase coal and victuals."

The man could only stare at the neat stacks on his table.

Simon rose. "Well, I must be going."

The man stood up hastily. "Uh...could I offer you a drop?"

"No, thank you. Another time, perhaps," he added. "Mind you don't spend your money on the bottle." He indicated the children behind him. "You have a lovely family. Take care of them."

"Oh, yes, sir," he said quickly.

Simon walked toward the door. Arnold was there before him, holding it open for him.

Arnold sniffed again. "Thank y', sir."

"Don't mention it." Simon turned back for an instant. "If you would be so good, I would prefer you didn't mention my visit to anyone at the mission, least of all to Miss Breton. Is that understood?"

"Oh, no, sir. Mum's the word. My lip's buttoned tight," he said, indicating it with a gesture.

"Very good. Well, so long. I wish you the best. I'll check on you in a month to see how you made out."

When he returned to the street, the urchin was waiting for him.

He smiled at the boy, feeling suddenly very good inside. "Ready to show me the way back?"

The boy saluted. "Right 'way, guv'nor."

The two sauntered back. "What's your name?"

"Tim."

"Timothy."

"That's what my mum named me."

"Where's your mum now?"

"Oh, she died a while back."

"I see." Simon looked down at the boy, who seemed about Rebecca's age. The boy didn't seem affected by his loss. It must have been some time ago.

"What have you been doing since then?"

The boy shrugged, his hands shoved into the pockets of his corduroy trousers. "Oh, this 'n' that. Worked for the rat catcher for a while, but he beat me too bad every time he was drunk. So I decided to go off on me own. I was a crossing sweeper for a time. That was a good occupation, 'specially when I stationed myself down at Aldgate. Lots o' people crossin' there. But then I 'ad an accident and couldn't do that no more."

"What kind of an accident?"

He shrugged again. "Barrel fell off a dray and got me 'ere." He pointed to his shoulder and ribs. "Couple o' broken bones." He smiled up at Simon confidentially. "Would'a died right there in the street, but that's where Miss Thea found me."

"She found you?"

"Yes, sir. She picked me right up. 'Ailed an 'ack and brought me right 'ere. Doc mended me right up. They would 'ave me live there with them all the time, but I prefer the independent life." He gave Simon another sly smile.

"So, where do you live?"

"Oh, around. But you can usually find me at the mission. Things are always goin' on there."

"Yes, I begin to see that."

Chapter Nineteen

✣

Althea didn't get a chance to visit Arnold and his family because two days later he came himself. The transformation in him was astonishing.

"Miss Breton, forgive me for ever doubtin' your word. You was right. It was Satan tryin' to steal from me, not God. God 'eard your prayer."

"Oh, thank the Lord," she said, clapping her hands together. "Tell me what happened."

"Well, I got a new job."

She smiled in delight. "God be praised."

"Not only that, but I got better pay. Everything's better at this factory. And I got a little—" he hesitated as if searching for the right word "—a little advance, you might say—enough to buy coal, pay the rent, get us some vittles, and still have some coin left over."

Althea sighed in delight. "Oh, praise our wonderful God!"

"Mary 'n' me'll be in chapel come Sunday, you can be sure o' that."

"Why don't you come Friday night, instead of going to the alehouse?"

He looked at her as if considering. Then he slowly nodded. "Well, per'aps we will at that."

It was another two days before Althea could find a moment to go by and visit them. She wanted to hear more about Arnold's blessing. He was at work, but his wife was there with the children. She insisted on preparing Althea a cup of tea.

"Been so long since we 'ad any tea," she said with a smile.

Althea drank from the chipped cup. "It's looking quite cozy in here," she commented with a glance around. Things looked cleaner and neater, and the glowing coals in the grate filled the room with warmth.

"Miss, Arnold promised not to say a thing, but bein' as I didn't promise, I think I can safely tell you."

"Tell me what?" Althea frowned, wondering whether Arnold had involved himself in something illegal to suddenly better his fortune.

"Well, 'is new job and all the rent money...it all come from that gent."

"Gentleman? Which gentleman?"

"The one what knows you. From the mission. Arnold told me 'e was there that day. 'E was visitin' you, then 'e came by 'ere and gave Arnold all the money to pay the rent, buy us some coal, and 'e told my Arnold where to go to get that job."

Althea's thoughts were in a tumult. Gentleman? That day? Simon! Of course! Her mind went back to the day he'd visited and replayed all that happened when Arnold had burst in on them.

She questioned Arnold's wife further, but could discover little else. But when she returned to the mission she ran into Tim, who seemed inclined to linger with her. She noticed he had seemed mighty pleased with himself for the past few days.

"Did you happen to notice that gentleman who was here the other day?"

He began whistling nonchalantly, and she was certain he knew something. After a bit of cajoling, she finally got the story out of him. He bragged how he and the fine gent were swell friends now. He showed her the half-crown he'd received from him. "I ain't gonna spend this. This is my lucky coin," he said, spitting on it and polishing it with the corner of his jacket before putting it away in a secret pocket.

"But don't tell 'im I told you anything. I promised I wouldn't. It was between us men, 'e told me. 'E'd be awfully disappointed if 'e knew I'd gone and spilled the beans to some female."

She smiled and tousled his hair. "Don't worry. If it comes up at all, I shall tell him I got it out of you. You weren't to blame."

Later that afternoon, she put on her bonnet and warmest cloak. She walked a few blocks to a busy intersection where she could hail a hackney.

She arrived at Green Street with great anticipation, only to find Simon out. She had to hide her disappointment from Giles and Harry, who greeted her warmly and wanted to know how she was getting on.

After chatting with them, she asked permission to pass into the library to leave Simon a note, and promised to go down to the kitchen afterward to greet the other servants.

The library was dim and quiet. Althea walked to Simon's desk. She breathed in the scent of the room and a wave of nostalgia washed over her. She thought she had successfully left that world behind, but it all came back to her in a rush. She sat on the edge of Simon's chair and grasped the leather-bound arms. Earlier when she had discovered Simon's role in Arnold's situation, Althea had wanted nothing more than to find Simon and hug him.

Now, in the stillness of Simon's abode, she felt a longing to gaze once again into those deep brown eyes which could look so mocking one moment and so tender the next. She brought her fist up to her mouth, fighting the sudden urge to cry. When he had appeared so suddenly the other day at the mission, it had been as if she were seeing someone who had died, so completely had she convinced herself she would never see him again.

Her gaze roamed over the usual stacks of books and papers across the surface of the desk. "Oh, Simon, Simon," she whispered, her eyes blurring as her fingers riffled through a stack of papers with his writing, "why do I love you so?"

She brought her lips together, knowing she must leave. It would do her no good to pine over something she couldn't have. She wiped her eyes and looked around until she found a sheet of notepaper. Dipping Simon's quill into the ink, she composed her thoughts.

Since it was clear he had wanted to keep his generosity a secret, it was also clear he probably would not be back to the mission. A simple, straightforward thank-you. Nothing to embarrass him, but she had to let him know how happy he had made her, and what a good deed he had done.

Dear Simon,

Oh, dear, what was she doing, addressing him like that? She hurriedly crumpled up the paper and tossed it into the wastebasket and took another.

Dear Mr. Aguilar,

She rubbed the feather against her chin, mentally composing the note. I am deeply grateful? Thank you so much? God will bless you?

When she brought the pen back down to the paper she wrote none of these things. Instead she found herself writing:

I join my brother Tertius and his wife in wishing to invite you to Pembroke Park for the Christmas holidays. I shall be leaving for Bishop's Green, Hertfordshire, at the end of next week. We would all very much like to have you in our midst during this time.

Your servant,
Althea Breton

On a sudden inspiration, she added, "P.S. Bring your Hanukkah candelabra," unable to remember what Rebecca had called the branch of candles used in the Jewish holiday.

There. She had written something she had had no notion of a few minutes earlier. Her brother didn't even know it, although she knew he would immediately second the invitation when she told him.

Father, help me. Let Pembroke Park be a place of solace for Simon. I ask nothing for myself. Only let him find You. Oh, he needs You so much now.

She knew he must be suffering terribly. First, Rebecca and now his seat in Parliament. He had looked awfully thin and tired when he'd come to the mission. What he must be going through! All that he'd worked for all these years. The shame, as well, of how he'd been made to resign. Would this cause him to scorn Christians more than ever?

"'A bruised reed shall he not break, and the smoking flax shall he not quench...'" she repeated to herself for the countless time. The Lord would not break this tender, bruised reed, nor quench that tiny ember deep inside Simon's soul.

Althea had been at Pembroke Park three days, and each day she'd been keyed up, listening for the sound of coach wheels on gravel. She'd heard nothing from Simon when she'd left London. Tertius had heartily approved her invitation and followed up with one of his own, but neither had he heard anything from him.

Althea tried to hide her disappointment, telling herself to let God's will be done. She busied herself helping Gillian decorate the house with holly boughs and tried not to jump at the sound of anyone at the door. But there were lots of people coming and going at this time of year in preparation for the holidays.

It was half-past seven when Althea was sitting in the drawing room with her brother and Gillian, waiting for dinner to be announced, when they heard the sound of a carriage drive up. Althea kept herself from jumping to the window, but Tertius had heard the sound as well.

"Perhaps Simon has decided to accept our invitation and is arriving at last," he said as he rose and went toward the hallway.

Althea waited, her ears straining to hear the sounds from the entryway.

"Oh, I do hope it is Simon. I have heard so much about him by now, that I am finding myself anxious to meet him," Gillian said, putting down the book she'd been reading.

They didn't have to wait long. Tertius was soon back, bringing Simon with him.

Althea's gaze went to Simon. She kept her seat, afraid suddenly of her eagerness. He looked so good, his dark hair windblown, his color high from the cold night air. Her heart beat faster and she prayed silently that God would help her to do His will.

Tertius was already introducing Gillian to Simon. Gillian was making a remark and laughing. Simon bowed over her extended hand. Then they came to Althea.

"I am so glad my sister convinced you to join us for the holidays. I hope you can stay a good fortnight at least. It's a miracle we managed to drag Althea away from the mission."

"Hello, Miss Breton." Simon's dark gaze penetrated hers for an instant, then he too was bending over her hand. His hand and lips felt cold against her skin.

"Hello, Mr. Aguilar. I am pleased you could join us." She longed to tell him so much. Her heart felt as if it would burst with gratitude.

He rubbed his face. "I wanted to thank you for your kind invitation."

She could feel her face warming.

"I didn't want to intrude on your family festivities."

"Nonsense," put in Tertius immediately. "Thank heaven my sister had the sense to invite you. I've been a laggard with all my holiday preparations." Her brother slapped Simon on the back. "It is good to see you. I hope you haven't eaten yet. We were just going in to dinner, but we have time, if you'd like to freshen up."

Tertius escorted him back out of the room, talking with him the whole way.

"You must have come to know Mr. Aguilar quite well when you were nurse to his daughter," Gillian commented.

Althea met her gaze, hoping she didn't reveal too much. "Somewhat. He was busy with his work much of the time, but he would spend some part of each day with his daughter."

"Tertius thinks the world of him."

"Yes, it was he who wanted me to nurse Rebecca."

"Does he know the Savior?" asked Gillian.

Althea swallowed. "I don't believe so."

"Let's hope we can show him the light of Christ during his stay here."

Althea smiled. "Yes, that is my prayer."

The four of them had a lively meal. Althea was so thankful to her brother and sister-in-law for their good humor and warmth. They kept the conversation going, not dwelling on the terrible things that had happened to Simon over the past year. Instead, they talked of things in the country, of the work at the mission, and Tertius spoke of many things he remembered from their schooldays.

"You were close at Eton?" Gillian asked.

Tertius gave a wry smile. "Not at first."

"That is an understatement if I ever heard one," said Simon.

Tertius chuckled. "What Simon means is that I despised him in my naturally arrogant fashion, as I despised most of my classmates back then. But then his sharp wit and keen intellect caught my attention."

"When did that happen?"

"Some of the boys from the upper form were teasing him. I think I must have been particularly bored that day to stop and see what they were about. Certainly they had tormented him unmercifully since the beginning of term—burning up his assignments, stealing his books, blaming him for things that went on in the classroom. I don't think there was a boy flogged more than he in all the time I was there—oh, and much worse, things unfit for a lady's ears."

Althea listened, horrified. She had a vague conception of the things that went on in public school but had never heard firsthand, since a boy was expected to take such things like a man and keep silent.

Tertius continued his story. "For some reason I decided to come to Simon's rescue that day. I think it was his wit that caught my attention most. There he was, outnumbered and outflanked by a group of boys older and bigger than himself, but his tongue was sharper than the whole group's put together."

"What did you do?" Gillian asked eagerly.

"Oh, I outranked his tormentors on several counts, not least of which was my own inflated opinion of myself. So, I very deliberately began exposing each one's weaknesses—they all had their secrets—until before I had reached them all, they had skulked away."

Althea smiled. "Like the accusers of the woman taken in adultery?"

"Except I was no Savior, nor was Simon a grateful penitent. There he stood, battered but not cowed."

"Is that when you became friends?"

He smiled. "Not right away. I still considered him beneath my notice. He was in the lower form, and I in the upper, for one thing. But then I reconsidered. I thought he'd make a useful fag. Oh, I don't mean in the usual way—having a boy to black one's boots and toast one's bread. No, he would be much more useful for his brain." Tertius shook his head in recollection of the past. "Many an assignment did you complete for me, Simon. Before you look so disapproving, Gillian, he was just as calculating as I."

Simon shrugged, taking up the tale. "The prestige of being admitted into your husband's circle. No one dared touch me there. We eventually did become close friends, despite our self-serving beginning. I don't know exactly why."

"Oh, I know why, on my part. I appreciated your brilliance. I don't know what you were able to see beyond my egotism."

Simon smiled, and Althea could see the genuine affection he had for her brother.

"Oh, I don't know, there were one or two qualities to admire in you, I suppose," he said.

"Well, when you remember them, please let me in on them," put in Gillian, straight-faced.

Simon chuckled. "Certainly. It may take a while, though, I warn you."

"Althea, you must help me here. I am being besieged."

Althea wiped her mouth with her napkin. "I don't know, Tertius, you always were well able to stand on your own."

They laughed and had a merry evening.

The next afternoon, Simon found Althea in the library. He looked at what she was reading. "*A Practical Treatise upon Christian Perfection*. Perfection. Can such a thing be achieved?"

She looked at his face, but detecting no mockery in his tone, only simple curiosity in his dark eyes, she answered, "It is that which every Christian strives for, but which can only be achieved in Christ."

"In Christ. Which means?"

"It means when I accepted Jesus as my Savior, I became crucified with Him, so that my old nature could die. Only then could I share in His resurrection, which means a new life in Him with His spirit living on the inside of me."

His eyelids drooped over his eyes. "You are a funny creature. Talking in such riddles."

He continued analyzing her through his half-closed eyes. "I almost didn't come."

She swallowed and looked down at her book. "I was afraid you might not."

"You know me so well."

"I only know you a little," she answered honestly, still not able to meet his gaze. "But as your friend, I thought perhaps you would enjoy a brief respite from London." Oh, no, she thought, wasn't that what Lady Stanton-Lewis had already offered him in

Scotland? She reddened. She looked down at her fingers, gripping the edges of the opened book. "Perhaps you already had enough of that in Scotland."

He snorted and took a step away from her, going to stand by the deep embrasure of the window. "Scotland was like a short preview of hell."

She gasped, her eyes flying upward. "What do you mean?"

"I mean," he answered, continuing to gaze out at the stark gray landscape, "I feel as if my adult life has been a series of short previews of hell. Nothing as yet unbearable—though close to it—but enough for one to know what awaits one in the afterlife, if one chooses to believe in hell."

They remained silent for a few seconds. Then, without looking at her, Simon said, "I want you to know I never—how shall I put this?—behaved dishonorably with Lady Stanton-Lewis. Unless you call my enjoying her hospitality for what seemed an inordinately long period, without putting forth any effort on my part to be agreeable, dishonorable. But let us say, I did nothing for which the baron would have been justified in calling me out."

Althea could only look at his profile. Was he telling her that there had been nothing between him and Lady Stanton-Lewis? Why was he confiding it to her? As if reading her mind, he turned to her suddenly.

"I don't know why I'm telling you this. I...I just want you to know it."

"I see."

He gave a hint of a smile. "Your prayers must have been heard."

"I dearly hope so."

"You know why I decided to accept your kind invitation to come here?"

She shook her head.

"I read your note, and my first impulse was to refuse."

She sat silently, waiting.

"I couldn't quite get myself into the spirit of the season."

"That is understandable."

"Then I happened to glance down at my wastebasket and saw a crumpled piece of paper."

She swallowed, remembering her first attempt at a note.

"It intrigued me, because I knew that wastebasket had been empty earlier in the day. You know how I knew that?"

"No," she whispered.

"Because although I had spent the morning sitting at my desk, I had done no work." He glanced at her. "You don't understand? It means, although I spend my days in the library, I produce nothing."

"I see." How she wanted to go to him and comfort him. Instead she looked down at the book, curling the corner of the page with her fingertips.

"My curiosity piqued, I bent down to retrieve the crumpled paper—"

He paused, and Althea could feel his gaze upon her.

"You had begun another note, hadn't you?"

She nodded, not daring to look at him.

"'Dear Simon' was all that was written on it. But it was enough."

Again her gaze flew to his.

"'Dear Simon,' I read and then decided to come."

She bit her underlip, mangling the pages under her fingers.

"The other note was so formal and correct. 'Dear Mr. Aguilar.' It made it very easy for me to refuse. But 'Dear Simon'—it was like a hand held out in friendship."

He looked back out the window. "Do you know, friendship has become a scarce commodity these past few months?" His lips twisted. "Do you remember the hordes at the funeral?"

"Yes."

"I have seen none but my family since then."

She gazed at him, her heart breaking at those lightly uttered words. He spoke as if he was commenting on the scene out the window.

He turned back to her. "Do you think, here in the company of your brother and sister, you could continue addressing me as Simon?"

She felt her cheeks heat but held his gaze. After a few seconds she gave a slight nod, telling herself she was silly to continue calling him Mr. Aguilar after what they had been through, when Tertius and even Gillian were on a first-name basis with him. It meant nothing more than the friendship Simon had alluded to.

"That's a very pretty gown you are wearing. You are finally sporting a becoming shade."

She looked down at the blue woolen dress. "Gillian insists on disposing of her wardrobe on me, and if I don't wear some of the things, she accuses me of not liking them—"

"I must thank your sister-in-law, then." He sat on the edge of the embrasure. "Whatever the reason, I think the results are to be commended. You look quite fetching."

She wasn't sure where to look, knowing only that her face was growing warmer once again. "Thank you," she whispered.

He chuckled. "The other day when I saw you, I thought you had on just about the ugliest dress imaginable, and yet I had never seen anyone looking prettier."

She knew her face was scarlet by then.

Before she could formulate an offhand reply, he said, "Tell me something. Why can't you wear such becoming colors at the mission? I would think the children at least would enjoy something bright in their lives. Doesn't your God approve? Didn't He, after all, create beautiful things?"

"If the Lord's glory shines through us," she replied, glad to be on surer ground, "our outward adornment is no longer important."

"Why can't you have both?"

She didn't know how to answer. He wouldn't understand how overwhelmingly superior the Lord's glory was.

After a bit, he came closer and crouched at the side of her chair. "Are you afraid of being attractive to the male eye? Did your experience with that lecherous scoundrel leave you so scarred that you are afraid of attracting an honorable man's admiration?"

She dared not look at him, feeling as if he were probing too deeply. But his voice was gentle, not scornful.

"Althea, you are so fond of telling me that your Jesus doesn't want you to live in fear, that fear is merely another form of bondage. Are you absolutely certain you have been freed from your fear of men?"

She said nothing, but once again began to worry the corner of her book.

After a few moments she heard him stand.

"Forgive me for my impertinence, Althea. I only meant to thank you for your kind note. This visit has been just the tonic I needed at this particular time."

"It's quite all right," she whispered, still not looking up. She felt so ashamed, even though she knew in her head that she had nothing to be ashamed about. She heard him leave the library softly.

That evening, he came down with the nine-branched candelabra he told them was called the Chanukiah.

Althea, who had recovered from their earlier conversation by then, clapped her hands. "You brought it! I remarked on it one day in the salon, and Rebecca explained to me about its use during this holiday—Hanukkah, you call it? That's why I asked you to bring one here."

Gillian went over to examine the brass candelabra. Simon explained how it had to be set in a window to be seen from the outside. "This is to publicize the miracle of light."

They observed him light the center candle and use it to light the first candle. He sang a traditional hymn in Hebrew as they watched the candle burn. Althea sneaked a look at Simon as the candlelight reflected off his face. Although he might profess skepticism, at that moment he looked so solemn, Althea could well imagine the myriad of Jews who had performed the same ritual for centuries, dispersed to different lands around the world but still united by their heritage.

Afterward, he told them the origins of the festival, how a Jew, Judah, called Maccabee, and his followers had defeated overwhelming Gentile forces under Lysias, to recover their temple and city of Jerusalem in the second century B.C.

"It was then they purified the temple of all the desecration committed by the Gentiles—they even rebuilt the altar. Then they rededicated the temple. Afterwards, they proclaimed that an eight-day festival be celebrated every year, starting on that same day, the twenty-fifth day of the month of *Kislev.*

"It normally corresponds with your month of December. Legend has it that the oil used to light the lamps in the lamp stand was only enough to last one day, but that miraculously it lasted eight days, sufficient time to obtain new, pure oil," he added.

Simon stayed a fortnight at Pembroke Park. It was an interlude of peace and quiet from the hectic pace of Althea's life in Whitechapel. Although they didn't speak of Rebecca, being once again with Simon caused Althea to miss the little girl afresh. It felt as if someone were missing from the gathering. She had been so accustomed to being with Rebecca whenever she saw Simon, and now it was only Simon.

After his very personal words to her in the library, Simon did not seek her out privately. He treated her with a brotherly courtesy, the way she had seen him treat his two sisters, and she told herself she was glad. It put her mind at rest that her gesture in inviting him for the holidays had not been self-serving.

To her gratification, her father took an immediate liking to Simon. And although Althea knew Gillian and Tertius were very hospitable, especially during the Christmas season, she saw that they had deliberately cloistered themselves during this holiday to allow Simon to escape the scrutiny of outsiders.

Althea's father and Tertius took them out on long walks, roaming over the vast property. Afterwards they would return to the warm, intimate family circle. Baby Judith was no longer a swaddled infant but a chubby little baby who would grasp anything in her effort to stand. Neither Gillian nor Tertius had their firstborn baby banished to the nursery, but kept her in the midst of them during many of their afternoon gatherings.

The evenings were often spent with music. Althea and Tertius both played and sang. Usually Althea's father engaged Simon in a game of whist or chess.

One afternoon Althea came back from a solitary walk. They had had their first snowfall the day before, and she couldn't wait to go out when the weather had cleared, to enjoy the pristine white landscape. When she was approaching a pond a short distance from the house, she spotted Simon. He sat on a tree stump at its edge, under the denuded willows and elms, contemplating the scene before him. Althea read defeat in his slumped back. For a moment, she felt an acute disappointment that neither she nor her family had really been able to reach him in his loneliness and pain. It was he who had had to make the effort to join in their amusements, putting on a front of normalcy in order not to spoil their holiday cheer.

Suddenly Althea reached down and grabbed a fistful of snow. It was ideal for what had just come into her mind: wet and just sticky enough to hold together. She patted some more snow between her mittens. When it was the size of a good-sized apple, she heaved it. She watched in delight as it sailed through the air, exactly where she had intended it should go, and landed with a *splat* on Simon's back.

He jumped up with a shout. "Hey!" His indignation turned to a shout of laughter when he spotted her.

"Why, you!" He stooped down, and she gave a little yelp as she anticipated his revenge. Sure enough, a wet ball of snow hit her hard on her cloak. She quickly bent to form another, just as one of his landed on her shoulder.

"Take that!" she shouted, pelting him on the crown of his hat as he bent down. It knocked his hat off and she laughed out loud.

They continued back and forth, as many missing as striking their target. Soon their outer garments were covered in white, but neither would give up. Althea scrambled around looking for a better supply of snow at her feet. She bent sideways, and just as she turned back to face Simon, a snowball hit her square in the face, catching her full on one cheek.

"Ouch!" she cried, laughing and indignant at the same time.

"Oh, I beg your pardon!" he cried immediately. "Are you hurt?" he shouted out, running awkwardly through the snow to reach her.

She shook her head vigorously, holding her cheek with her mittened hand. Suddenly, the absurdity hit her and she just started laughing. Two adults, who could no longer claim youthful high spirits, tossing snowballs!

When Simon reached her, she was laughing so hard she couldn't speak. She just pointed at him, and he realized how covered with snow he was. He looked down at his greatcoat and started brushing off the worst of the snow, which only made her laugh harder. She looked so joyful, her cheeks reddened by the snow and her laughter, her bonnet askew, that he began to chuckle.

She made several attempts to tell him how funny he looked, but she couldn't get the words out. Each time she thought her laughter had subsided, she began afresh. She finally could not sustain herself any longer, but sat back in the snow. "Y-you sh-should have seen y-yourself! Y-you didn't know wh-what hit you! And your glasses! They're all covered with snow. Y-you look like a s-snow monster!" She put a hand to her mouth to try to stop laughing, but to little avail.

He smiled down at her, enjoying her laughter as he removed his glasses and wiped them off with his muffler. She looked like a young girl. He wished he could join her down there, take her in his arms and roll in the snow. He clenched his gloved hands, knowing that was not possible. Not now. She must never know how he felt about her.

When she finally lay relaxed, he said, "Come, now you've had your laugh at my expense, I'll help you up."

She narrowed laughing eyes at him. "Can I trust you?"

He raised his eyebrows at her. "You have little choice, do you not?"

"I trust you," she said, extending a gloved hand. He pulled her up easily.

"Now," he said, eyeing her, "if you think I look as if I've just come from the worse end of a snowball fight, I think you should see yourself." He brought up his hand to her cheek. "Did I hurt you with that last one?" He removed his glove, wishing he had a handkerchief, but it was inside his coat pocket, beneath the greatcoat. With his bare hand he attempted to wipe the snow off her face. Her skin felt cold.

She shook her head. Her lips looked so red and inviting that he had to concentrate all his attention on his task. If at one time he might have considered putting aside all the reasons why he could never consider marrying her, now it was certainly out of the question. He could never offer himself to any woman now—a man who had lost all reputation, all honor.

He began brushing the snow off her cloak.

"Oh, don't bother." She giggled again, pointing at him. "It's obvious who got the beating today."

"I think we need an impartial judge to decide the outcome. I see less of your cloak than mine beneath the snow."

"Are you going to be a poor loser?" she asked, an innocent gleam in her eyes. Today they looked gray against the gray of her cloak.

"Funny, I never took you for a cheat and liar, Althea Breton, amidst all those stellar qualities."

She laughed.

He finished cleaning off his greatcoat. "I can't think when I last threw snowballs. Possibly once or twice at Cambridge." He stopped just in time, before adding that it had usually been after a night of carousing in a tavern when they were returning to their rooms in the wee hours.

"I must confess it hasn't been so long for me. When there is a snowfall in London, before it becomes all dirty and sooty, we usually have one good snowball fight with the children."

After their hilarity, the silence between them felt awkward and self-conscious. She began to say something at the same time as he.

He gestured for her to continue. "No, it was nothing," she said with a shake of her head. When he insisted, she smiled sheepishly. "I was just going to say something trite about how lovely a first snowfall is."

The two looked ruefully at each other, acknowledging the embarrassment between them. Abruptly he said, "You implied once that I would make you forsake your God. Do you really believe that of me?"

She had removed her bonnet and was shaking the snow off. At his question, she stopped, surprise and wariness in her gray eyes. Did she think he'd forgotten the circumstances?

He watched her place the bonnet back on her head and tie its ribbons. She seemed to be taking her time to answer his question.

Finally she said, "You would not do it deliberately." She gave a final tug on the bow and looked at him. "But slowly you'd chisel away at my devotion. You perhaps might not even realize you were doing so. But with your expert use of mockery and whatever other weapon the enemy gave you, you would try to weaken my dedication and service to the Lord. You would come to use anything to undermine my faith in the Lord in order to mask your fear of confronting Him for yourself."

She smiled sadly. "I know of what I speak. I lived with unbelievers for a time, people who loved me in their own way but made life impossible by their remarks, their criticisms, their unbelief. I went to a church where I was accused of idolatry because I was reading the Bible. The vicar held me up as an example in his sermons, as he considered reading the Word excessively a form of overzealousness."

She sighed, gazing down at her mittens. "Finally you would force me to choose between my Lord and you, without ever understanding that without loving Him, I can never truly love anyone else. Love comes from Jesus. He *is* love."

She looked at him earnestly. "You can't love, Simon, really love, until you understand how much He loves you!"

"I see," he said, glancing away. He should be relieved; she had made things easier for him. "I cannot say I understand fully what you are saying, but I want you to relieve your mind of all concern on that score." He resolved on the spot to put an end to any other feelings he might have for her. "I have grown to love you as a sister—despite your assertion that I can have no concept of love. But you have become as dear to me as Tirzah or Simcha.

"Please forgive me for any liberties I ever took with you, or for anything I have ever said to offend you." He met her gaze and knew they were both thinking of that night. She had made it plain then and she was making it plain now that she would never accept a man who did not accept her Lord Jesus as his Savior.

"You have no need to reproach yourself for anything," she said softly.

He couldn't know what she was thinking. But he knew with his words, he was putting to death hope of anything more between the two of them. Already, he had lost all honor in the eyes of the world. He wouldn't have it on his conscience that he had weakened her faith in any way.

He held out his hand to her. "Sister?"

She took his hand in agreement, though neither smiled as they accepted their new relationship.

By end of their holiday together, Althea had convinced herself that all the Lord intended between her and Simon was brotherly love and fellowship. She was thankful he had spoken the way he had, although it had initially reawakened all the longing in her.

Her sister-in-law brought up her friendship with Simon one afternoon shortly before the end of the holiday. "I can see Simon is very fond of you," she remarked, her eyes intent on the frock she was embroidering for Judith.

"Yes, he cares for me as for one of his sisters."

Gillian smiled around the thread she had between her teeth. "He told you that?"

Althea quickly looked at Gillian. "Yes."

"Be that as it may, the look I catch in his eyes is far more than brotherly." She laughed a deep, rich laugh.

Althea turned away, her heart beginning to beat faster. "Please, do not speak of it."

Gillian was immediately contrite. "I'm sorry." She held out the embroidery hoop and observed it for a moment before turning her attention to the skeins of thread. Carefully she chose another color and separated a thread. "He has gone through much of late, has he not?"

"Yes."

"He doesn't talk of it, not even to Tertius, for he would have told me of it." Gillian threaded her needle and knotted it. "But he did say one thing to him." She paused as she began her first stitches. "Simon told him that there had been nothing between him and Lady Stanton-Lewis. He believes it is precisely because he refused any sort of liaison with her that he made an enemy of her."

Althea sucked in her breath. "You mean—"

Gillian nodded. "The lady and her husband are very powerful. They could do much damage to a person's reputation if they had a mind to do so."

"How terrible," she whispered, thinking of all the ugly things Simon had been accused of over the past months. "Tertius had told me how quickly Simon's career was taking off. He predicted great things for him in Parliament."

"Yes, Tertius told me Simon was on the verge of being nominated for junior lord of the treasury."

"Oh," she breathed. "Then, it was doubly harmful for him to have been forced to resign his seat at this time."

"Yes. It certainly seems like a conspiracy against him."

"I've prayed so much for him," Althea said. "Since meeting him, really. He seems so far from the truth."

"I don't know," Gillian remarked, looking at her stitches. "No one could have been more rebellious than I, and yet I was very close indeed to knowing my Savior. But no one, except He, could have supposed it, least of all myself!" Gillian put down her embroidery and came over to where Althea sat.

"You must continue praying for Simon," she told her, taking both Althea's hands in hers. "And I shall join you in this plea."

Althea smiled into her sister-in-law's warm eyes, feeling immeasurably reassured. "Thank you," she whispered.

"You know what the Word says. 'How should one chase a thousand and two put ten thousand to flight...?' We shall prevail, sister."

Chapter Twenty

❧

Simon had been back in London for a few weeks. It was now the new year, that grim month of January when he knew winter was just finding its stride.

He had returned to his house just before Christmas, not finding it in himself to celebrate the birth of a child, savior or otherwise, just then. He knew, as well, that Althea's family would only stay at Pembroke Park until Christmas Eve, then head for London on Christmas Day to be involved in the festivities and charitable work they had planned at the mission for that day.

Simon had been touched by their celebration of Hanukkah, and had joined in, explaining to them the significance of things. But deep down, the nightly ceremony had only augmented his alienation, showing him how far he was from his own family, and causing him to fight down the memories of the holiday celebrated for the sake of Rebecca's childish wonder. He wasn't yet ready to relive those times.

In London, he shut himself up again in his library, pretending to be immersed in his book, but in reality spending long hours staring off into space. Whenever Giles knocked discreetly on the door and Simon bade him enter, Simon would bury himself among his papers, picking up his pen and answering only in monosyllables.

Other times, he would turn his chair around and sit staring out at the dead garden, thinking of Althea. What had he missed there? Had he done the right thing? Of course he had. She had her destiny, he his. She was light, he darkness. Didn't the Bible say something about that? What has light to do with darkness, or something to that effect? Indeed, what could one so immersed in death have to do with one so unaffected by it? For Althea and her kind, death was merely a change of garments.

Simon's nights were spent once again roaming the passages of his house. One night, thinking he was surely and irreversibly sinking into a pit, he put on his things and went outside, not bothering to call for his coach. It was bitterly cold and he picked up his pace, muffling his face as he turned into the wind and walked toward Piccadilly, in search of life. He knew people were still going about: Wednesdays to Almack's, Thursdays generally to someone's ball, tonight perhaps the opera or theater. His own stack of invitations had dwindled down to nil. The silver salver had lain empty since the eruption of the scandal.

What would Althea's set be doing on a Friday evening? he wondered idly. He headed toward a hack stand and gave instructions for Tower Hill. That would bring him close enough to the East End. The man demanded a hefty fee for going all the way there at that time of the evening. Simon agreed with a curt nod.

When he disembarked, Simon walked the few blocks to the mission, where all looked quiet and dark. Still, he couldn't prevent himself from knocking on the door. To his surprise, someone answered almost immediately. A night watchman, he presumed, taking in the stoop-shouldered man.

"Yes, who are you seeking?"

"Miss Althea Breton, is she here?"

"No, they've all gone preaching down at the Docks this evening, I believe."

Simon swallowed his disappointment, telling himself it was best that way; he had been possessed of some momentary madness to be seeking Althea out again.

He turned away from the door. "Well, yes, thank you. Good evening."

He was halfway down the block when the man called out to him. "If you're interested in going there, I could send a boy to show you the way."

Simon half turned back, waging a battle with himself. Before he could say anything, the man was shouting down the corridor, "Jake! Hey, Jake!"

A boy came running up. "You know where Brother Alston is preaching tonight?"

He nodded vigorously. "Down by the Dock House."

"Take this gentleman there, will you?"

The boy looked at Simon and quickly assented. "Let me get my jacket."

Simon remained where he was, awaiting his return. The boy didn't take long, and Simon looked at him a moment. "You don't have much on for a walk in this weather." The boy huddled in a short jacket and long muffler.

He shrugged, his shoulders hunched against the cold. "That's all right, sir. I'll stand by the fire, once we get there."

He gave Simon no time to argue, but took off in rapid strides down the street. Just as he had the last time, Simon found himself at the mercy of a street urchin, this time in the darkened streets of the East End. For better or worse, he was committed to this undertaking.

After walking for about a mile, they arrived at the waterfront. Tall warehouses loomed over them on one side and towering masts hedged them in on the other as they walked along the dark waterfront. The evening was in full swing in this neighborhood, the harbor taverns offering their welcome light to the passersby.

Every once in a while a door would open, and they would hear the noise and smell the smoke within. They had to skirt a few areas where a brawl had broken out in the street. Finally they arrived at a wide-open square. A small crowd had gathered and was singing lustily in the icy night air. A bonfire had been kindled toward the front. Simon remained in the back, although Jake left him immediately and headed for the warmth of the fire.

Simon searched the crowd until he spotted Althea. She was standing with another woman, dishing out soup from a big cauldron. A queue of people stood to receive the food from the two women. The older woman Simon had seen at the mission was leading the singing. She stood on a box for a platform and waved her arms in time to the music. The songs were hymns like the one he had heard Althea play on the pianoforte at home. A small group close to the front was singing along with her, but much of the crowd stood silent. Along the fringes, others jeered. Many were sailors or prostitutes who called out obscene things to the singers. The singers ignored them and continued singing with all their hearts. Simon watched their red faces and swollen cheeks, heard the dull clapping of mitten-covered hands.

It was a curious sort of service, like nothing he had ever seen before. He had been to several chapel services in school and to a few as a young man. But those services had no singing. Worship meant the dignified chanting of psalms.

Simon turned his attention back to Althea. He frowned when he recognized the young surgeon who approached her. The two began talking, their expressions serious. Russell seemed to be insisting on something and Althea holding back. Finally, he saw her wipe her hands on her apron and remove it. He watched as she and Russell switched places and the surgeon began to ladle out soup.

Simon watched curiously to see what it was the doctor had convinced Althea to do. He didn't have long to wait. As Althea went to retrieve her Bible, the woman on the makeshift platform ended the last song and began to speak.

"Brother Alston has had a mishap on his way here tonight."
At the reaction from the audience, she quickly held up her hands.
"The coach overturned on the Great North Road, but, God be
praised, his life was spared. We shall lift him up before the Lord
so that he may soon rejoin us."

She led them in a fervent prayer that reminded Simon of the
one Althea had prayed with that giant of a man at the mission
who had threatened her.

"Amen!" rang out across the front part of the crowd. Those
on the fringes surrounding Simon raised a chorus of jeers. He surveyed them—rough-looking men, their faces unshaven, their
bodies tough as oak trees. He judged them to be the men who
loaded and unloaded the cargo from the hundreds of ships that
made their way up and down the Thames from every corner of
the world. The women were just as tough looking, their faces
painted, their hair and garments dirty.

"Although Brother Alston will not be with us this evening to
share the Word of God with us, we are not without a preacher.
Although you've never heard her preach before, many of you
know our own dear sister Breton. You know she is a true servant
of the Lord."

Simon turned his attention immediately back to the platform,
sure he had not heard aright. He couldn't imagine anyone preaching to these individuals, whose loud taunts embodied irreverence, much less the soft-spoken Althea.

At the sounds of dismay from the audience, the lady raised her
hands and voice again. "I know you are not accustomed to a lady
preacher, but God is no respecter of persons. To Him 'there is neither Jew nor Greek, there is neither bond nor free, there is neither male nor female—for ye are all one in Christ Jesus'!" Her
last words were said in a shout, bringing an answering clamor
from the standing crowd. Simon heard the words in bemusement; did the Bible really say that about Greek and Jew?

His glance went quickly to Althea. She stood at the edge of the
crowd, her eyes closed. At the last words of the woman on the

platform, Althea opened her eyes, gave her characteristic straightening of the shoulders and began to walk toward the platform.

The other woman ceded her the box. While a few of the faithful gave her amens or words of encouragement, he could see their dismay as well. The majority of the crowd called out insults. Simon noticed the painted prostitutes along the sidelines, mimicking the faithful: "Preach it, sister! Give it to us good tonight!"

Simon shoved his gloved hands under his armpits, prepared to hold out against the cold, curious to see what the quiet Althea he knew would do.

She started softly; her voice was almost inaudible to those in the rear, and what Simon did catch sounded wobbly and unsure. For a second it seemed as if she had seen him, her eyes intent on him, but that was impossible, hidden as he was by the crowd and the dark.

She opened her Bible, her fingers nervously riffling the pages. Simon felt anguish for her, knowing how shaky he had been the first time he had given a speech in Parliament. A few seconds in, an object landed at her feet. Simon straightened, shocked at the rotten fruit that had been aimed at her. She paid it no heed, finally having found her place. She began reading then, looking up after every few words, her voice growing stronger with each verse. By the time she finished, it seemed as if she had grown in stature.

Althea braved the scornful crowd and continued speaking in an apologetic tone. Inwardly she was quaking with fear, unsure if she was doing the right thing. Had she just allowed Brother Russell to persuade her to do something, merely because there was no one else at present to fill the preacher's shoes?

Suddenly she saw Simon's face at the rear of the crowd. He did not even form part of the gathering, but stood behind them. She strained her eyes, thinking she was seeing things. But no, it was him. He was looking at her attentively, and suddenly she knew why she had been called to preach tonight. She had resisted, thinking it wasn't right. A woman didn't preach.

Just as swiftly the message she was to preach came to her. It was a message she had been harboring in her heart, letting it brew and form and coalesce for many months. The sight of Simon's pale bespectacled face confirmed it. She opened her Bible, instructing the others to open to the Book of John. Her heart was pounding; her gloved hands only got in the way of the thin pages. But finally she arrived at the Scripture she sought.

Her voice grew firm as she read: "'The thief cometh not, but for to steal, and to kill, and to destroy: I am come that they might have life, and that they might have it more abundantly....'"

She continued reading, ending with "'I lay down my life, that I might take it again.'"

By the time she finished the passage, all fear and uncertainty had left her. Her voice was not her own, it rang sure and true. She knew the anointing of God was upon her, and she knew God had meant her to preach this evening. The burning, yearning desire she had felt for so many years to preach the Word would be fulfilled.

She looked out at the crowd, which had fallen quiet, and asked them boldly, "Do you know who the thief is? The hired servants? Are they the ones who have led you astray? Have they seduced you into thinking you needn't serve God? Have you been enslaved by their promises?"

Althea looked at them intently, seeing the uncertainty in their eyes as they began to question themselves. "I shall tell you clearly who the thief is—Satan. And those hired servants who run away when you need them—they are his hirelings, those demons, which entice you to do whatever your flesh craves, but which you know is not right. And when you've fulfilled every craving, pursued every passion, what are you left with? Have you found that abundant life? Or are you broken and bitter? Is the same emptiness still in your soul?

"Let me ask you this—when you are broken and empty, is the thief there to put you back together? Are the hirelings—those companions you allowed to lead you—are they there when you're drowning? After they've enticed you and led you to make a mess of your life, will they rescue you?"

The words flowed from her; she didn't even have to think about what she was going to say next. The catcalls stopped as the Spirit of God brought conviction upon the crowd. She hit them hard, and then preached the message of hope. She knew she was preaching to Simon, even though she hardly looked at him throughout the message. She preached all the things she had longed to say to him but hadn't had the boldness to, in the time she lived under his roof.

Simon did not approach Althea that evening. He didn't even wait for Jake to escort him back. As soon as the preaching was over, and Althea began calling forward those who wanted to repent of their sins and receive Jesus as their Savior, Simon fled. He just walked until he came back to the Tower of London, where he secured a hack to return to Mayfair.

But the next night he was back.

Althea preached every night following Brother Alston's accident. After their initial suspicion the first night, the crowds began to increase. They usually began by jeering and taunting her, but ended convicted of their sin, kneeling at the makeshift altar in tears.

Some of the preaching began to penetrate as Simon listened night after night. One night, Althea seemed to be talking directly to him when she read a passage about the "other sheep." "Do you know who Jesus was preaching to at this time? He was preaching to the Jew—one of His own, and He was telling them there would be other sheep. Those are we the Gentiles—the pagans of that time. He promised us that there will be one fold—made up of Jew and Gentile alike—and one shepherd." Her gaze cut through the crowd, piercing the darkness that separated him from her.

He surveyed the people around him, how they braved the icy cold each night. He knew the hot soup was there only to draw them in, and he looked at them in scorn to see them succumb so easily to the lure. They started out with their raucous insults and ended up trembling at the altar. Weak, contemptible fools, turning around so easily. But gradually he came to see their condition—the poor, the derelict, the delinquent—and he realized how desperate they were for a message of hope. He looked at himself and realized, despite his outer garb, he was not so different from any of them. They were considered the dregs of society: the tars, the coal whippers, the drunks, the prostitutes and the children like the boy he had met at the mission, plying their own various professions on the fringes of society—mudlarks, sweeps, match girls.

He realized he who had been championing the rights of the poor in Parliament knew very little about them. Althea had been living among them most of her adult life. Did she never tire of serving them? He wondered how much of her work would be appreciated by those coming to eat of the "loaves and the fish." He doubted the veracity of most of the conversions he witnessed nightly, knowing human nature as he did. He'd now been privileged to see a good spectrum of mankind, from his boyhood school days to his brief venture into high society. Since he had tendered his resignation to Parliament, not one member of his party had paid him a call. For all they knew, he had ceased to exist.

So, there he stood with the rest of the human refuse. And yet, despite his skepticism, he couldn't help seeing there was a power in the words he heard preached. For the first time he heard the message of a Savior. For all the catechism classes he'd been forced to take, he'd never heard about a personal Savior.

Why did he keep coming? Why subject himself to that call, night after night, to deliver his soul over to this Savior? He struggled with himself, trying to keep away, but he found the only way he could stave off the dark sea of despair engulfing him was to leave his house and come across town to these nightly meetings. He fought against coming, and yet when the sun set and the darkness began to close in around him, he began making his preparations to go out.

He also began seeing Althea in her true calling. He had had glimpses of her as a woman, nursemaid, potential wife, lady in society, but now he was seeing her as a fiery, impassioned preacher. He had suspected the passion dormant in her, but now he was seeing it unleashed from the crude platform. Once she stood on it and opened her mouth to speak, gone was the shy, retiring spinster. In her place was a skilled orator, who could rival many of the best speakers in the House.

Sometimes the messages filled him with anger; other times he flatly refused to accept them. He looked with skepticism at the antics of the crowds. Their emotions seemed faked, as when some went screaming or crying to the altar in a show of repentance.

But the words resounded in his consciousness even after he had left the meetings.

So many of the Scriptures she read had to do with the Jew and Gentile, reconciled by Christ into one new man.

"...who hath made us both one, and hath broken down the middle wall of partition between us...to make in Himself of twain one new man...that he might reconcile both unto God in one body by the cross, having slain the enmity thereby...through him we both have access by one Spirit unto the Father...ye are no more strangers and foreigners, but fellow-citizens with the saints...built upon the foundation of the apostles and prophets, Jesus Christ himself being the chief cornerstone...unto an holy temple in the Lord...."

She seemed to understand thoroughly his Jewish tradition. She read Scriptures from the New Testament and Old, which referred to sacrifice and always pointed them back to Christ as the sacrificial lamb without blemish, insisting again and again that Jesus was the hope of the Jews, the Messiah foretold to them through the prophets.

At home, Simon dug up the Bible Giles had given him one day not long after Rebecca's death. Althea's parting gift to him. He had been too bitter over things, including her abrupt departure, to do more than stick it on a shelf. Now he took it down and brushed the dust from its cover. When he opened the book, he spotted the paper inside it. He read it with curiosity, but it contained nothing personal, only a list of suggested readings in Althea's script.

He put it aside for a later time. He was more interested in looking up the Scriptures she had preached on, convinced some of the things she cited could not be found in the *Tanakh,* what the Christians called the Old Testament, but which in fact was his people's book, the book of the law and the prophets.

"Who hath ascended up into heaven, or descended? Who hath gathered the wind in his fists? Who hath bound the waters in a garment? Who hath established all the ends of the earth? What is his name, and what is his Son's name...?"

His Son... Could God—Yhvh—the God of Abraham, Isaac and Jacob have actually sent His Son? *"Hear, Oh Israel, the Lord your God, the Lord is one."* The words he'd been taught throughout his childhood reverberated in his mind, and it rebelled against the thought of God and a Son. He couldn't reconcile that ancient prayer, given by God Himself, with the verse he was reading.

In her sermons Althea demonstrated the parallel between the Old Testament and New, revealing the thread of salvation that bound the one inextricably to the other. Simon was compelled to delve into that latter section of the Bible to read for himself and discovered it had been written by Jews using Jewish allusions.

"...the precious blood of Christ, as of a lamb without blemish and without spot: Who verily was foreordained before the foundation of the world, but was manifest in these last times for you, Who by him do believe in God, that raised him up from the dead, and gave him glory; that your faith and hope might be in God."

"Jesus said unto them, Verily, verily, I say unto you, Before Abraham was, I am."

The words shook him to the core. Jesus using the very name of God, *I am.* But the words no longer sounded like blasphemy to Simon's ears.

"...Jesus said, For judgment I am come into this world, that they which see not might see; and that they which see might be made blind."

"But that no man is justified by the law in the sight of God, it is evident: for, The just shall live by faith."

"That the blessing of Abraham might come on the Gentiles through Jesus Christ."

The words hammered at him. Could his entire ancestors' religion be in vain because it had missed the fulfillment of its promise?

Hadn't he already discarded his ancestors' religion, finding in it no assurance?

Simon tried to escape the words, yet the questions kept coming back to him. During the days, he reread the Scriptures. Many times he struggled to find them if he hadn't jotted them down during the preaching. All he could do then was thumb blindly through those onionskin-thin pages.

Sometimes he never did find the passage he was looking for, but discovered another instead that only served to corroborate the preaching he'd heard. How could he have read the Bible in Hebrew school and catechism and never heard these things before? He couldn't understand it. The verses seemed to come out at him, answering his questions before they were even voiced. He'd heard passages of Scriptures read in the synagogue, in the Church of England services, in studying Greek in school, but they had never held any meaning beyond their historical value.

He remembered the night Althea had told him that he could only discern the Scriptures when the Spirit of God breathed life into them. Was that what was happening to him now?

The fear he'd felt at the beginning—fear of what he might find in the Word—transformed into thirst. Now he was like a drunken man seeking a drink; no matter how it might harm him, he must hear more of the Word.

But at the sermons, Simon refused to draw any nearer than the outer circle, which kept him out of the light of the bonfire and in the seclusion of darkness. He had even considered donning workman's gear. Although he tried to stay in the shadows, he knew he drew the curious gaze of the onlookers. Some of the prostitutes had even approached him, but after a few nights, they no longer took note of him.

He also began to develop a burning jealousy of young Mr. Russell. He seemed always to be with Althea before she approached the platform. When she didn't preach, he was there, assisting in the food line or helping to hand out tracts. Simon told himself he'd already renounced any claims he had to Althea's affections, yet he couldn't control the bitter bile that rose in his throat at the sight of the young surgeon at her side.

Chapter Twenty-One

❦

One night after Simon had returned from the open-air meeting, he sat at his desk, knowing the night was just beginning for him. He contemplated the stacks atop the desk, wondering whether he would ever finish the work. He had begun it with such enthusiasm and zeal, thinking it might make such a difference. This would be the work that would catapult him into a leading role in government. Now he saw it all as futile.

Looking at all the papers, he came across the one Althea had stuck in the Bible. Once again he unfolded it. In it she exhorted him to read the Bible, and she cited a few places where he should begin.

Among them were whole books, Isaiah and Hebrews. That seemed beyond him. Another sounded like a short passage, so he decided that night to look it up.

After a search, he finally found the book of the prophet Micah. His fingers ran down the page, searching for the chapter and verse. The verse was about his enemies not rejoicing against him when he fell. His lips twisted. How apt—most likely his enemies had forgotten him by now. The last part caught him: "...when I sit in darkness, the Lord shall be a light unto me."

He paused, the words sinking in. Would that they were true. His eyes skimmed the surrounding Scriptures and were caught by the one above it: "...I will wait for the God of my salvation: my God will hear me."

Again that word *salvation,* which the preachers were always spouting. But this appeared in the Old Testament, his people's book. Was salvation a Jewish concept?

A verse he'd heard that night kept coming back to him, something that had been said of Jesus: "Behold the Lamb of God, which taketh away the sin of the world."

Deciding he had better settle in for the night, Simon rose, the Bible in his hand, and made his way to the fireplace. He stirred up the coals and added a few more hunks. He drew an armchair closer to the fire and opened up the Bible once again. It was with much trepidation that he turned to one of the books Althea had suggested.

Like a man on the edge of some vast uncharted land, he began to read.

When he looked up and saw the clock on the mantelpiece, he realized an hour had passed. He had been reading the Book of Hebrews, and now he stared at the title across the top of the page and realized it was written to his people. It was written to *him.*

He stared at the burning coals, the ash white around them. He thought about his life up to that time. It was as if someone had jerked him to a standstill and forced him to examine it in its entirety—from his family and his ambitions to all the vain pursuits he'd chased after, trying to mold himself into a Gentile: to the finality of death.

He realized if he used his rational mind, which he'd always prided himself on, there were only two choices left to him. End his life or choose the life that this book in his lap promised him.

He still felt torn; it seemed tempting on the one hand, so easy to believe. But was it true? Or would it be another chimera, as had been all the other things he'd reached for?

Finally he stood, the Bible still in his hand, too restless any longer to sit still. He paced the library carpet, the struggle crystal clear to him for the first time. He stopped and shook the book heavenward. "You want me, then, is that it? Is that it? Is that why You've put me through hell? Am I worth so much to You?"

He swore, throwing the book across the room with all the force of his anger. It crashed against a Chinese vase, toppling it. The sound of shattering porcelain in the stillness seemed to rend the last shreds of resistance within Simon. "Then, take me!" he yelled in bitterness and distress. His cry, as if it drained his last ounce of energy, caused him to fall to his knees on the carpet, his head bowed upon it.

There! He surrendered, and he had nothing left to do.

In the stillness following, Simon knew with a certainty beyond reason, beyond logic, that he wasn't alone. He didn't know how he knew it, but he felt the tangible presence of someone in the library with him. Slowly, hesitantly, he raised his head, afraid the sense would leave him at the least movement. When he still felt it, he opened his eyes, looking around. He saw no one, but still he knew he wasn't alone. He sat back on his heels, waiting. Then he felt as if someone reached deep inside his heart and broke a band of iron that had wrapped itself around it since the moment of Rebecca's departure—in truth, it had probably been there much, much longer.

In that instant Simon felt a light so great it penetrated his soul; he felt as transparent as if the sun were filling him, flooding him, the room he was in, flooding every particle of his being, leaving nothing hidden or untouched.

He looked down in wonder at his hands, realizing for the first time in his life that he felt free of guilt. "Free of guilt." He spoke the words, relishing the experience. Free of encumbrances, doubts, fear. With a sudden clarity he understood what the blood of Jesus had done. What it was still doing so many centuries later at that very moment upon the library floor of No. 10 Green Street, Mayfair, London, in the year of his Lord 1818, in the life of a man who was unworthy, so unworthy. That blood was washing him, making him worthy. Simon instinctively raised his arms heavenward and uttered a cry.

"Oh, God!" With his whole being he magnified the Lord.

He could see! He understood it now: Jesus as the sacrificial lamb, His blood shed to reconcile Jews and Gentiles to God the Father once and for all. The law of his forefathers couldn't reconcile anyone; rather, it condemned them and drew them farther and farther from a relationship with their Creator. That was why his own religion had never filled him, nor had the dead religion of the official English Church. They were all based on performance.

In the stillness of the predawn hours, he could hear the voice of Jesus speaking directly to his heart. Scriptures were being revealed to him: "Behold my hands and my feet...."

"For thou wilt not leave my soul in hell...."

"...and they shall look upon me whom they have pierced, and they shall mourn for him, as one mourneth for his only son...."

In full clarity he saw the agony of his Messiah and His resurrection. He began to cry in sorrow for the One he had pierced. In the midst of his anguish for his Messiah's death, he felt a wonder and joy such as he had never experienced in his life.

Is this what joy was? A heart full to completeness, so full that if one more drop of emotion were added, it would not be able to hold it? More Scriptures came to him: "Arise, shine; for thy light is come, and the glory of the Lord is risen upon thee."

"The people that walked in darkness have seen a great light: they that dwell in the land of the shadow of death, upon them hath the light shined."

Is this what Rebecca experienced before she passed? He felt a deep comfort, remembering Althea's words. She'd known. Rebecca had known! He was certain of it. It brought on a new wave of gratitude toward his Savior. He began to weep, not wrenching tears of anguish as he had cried only once before in this very room with Althea present, but soft, flowing tears, tears that expressed gratitude, joy, sadness for what had passed, and peace that God had been present—had known and seen all.

He cried until no more tears came, then he lay quiet, experiencing the love of God for the first time in his life. He felt enveloped by it. It came in wave after wave. He couldn't fathom such love; he could only receive it, accept it and feel himself being made whole by it. Finally, he dozed, a sleep of perfect peace.

Simon shivered and opened his eyes, finding himself on the cold, hard floor. He remembered it all at once. He hadn't dreamed it. He jumped up, his muscles protesting against the sudden movement, but there was too much energy in him to stay still another moment. He was alive!

Suddenly he realized how cold the room had grown. He stood and went to the fireplace. He'd let the fire go out. He took up the poker and stirred the ashes. Good, a few coals at the bottom of the grate still glowed. He placed a few new ones on top of the embers. They did nothing. Clearly the embers were too few to rekindle the coals. Perhaps some paper? He went over to his desk, thinking he could cheerfully throw all the stacks into the fire.

He crumpled up a few pages and went back to the fireplace. A few seconds later they caught and flared upward, and Simon sat back on his heels in satisfaction. But after the initial flame, they were consumed, leaving only a black shadow of their former shape. He frowned, what now? He thought how all of his life he'd had all his material needs taken care of; his parents had seen to it, and now as an adult, his money saw to it. But neither his parents nor his money could have guaranteed his spiritual security.

He stirred the embers once more, looking for a glow of red. Yes, fewer now, but some glowing red still buried beneath the gray ash. They reminded him of his heart, that little glowing coal. God had given it a reason to keep on living, striving, wanting.

He sat back again, resting the poker on the fender. Well, he was no god in the face of these coals. He would need someone's expertise. He rose and left the library. No one was about, as far as he could hear. He finally wandered down to the kitchen. He heard a noise from the butler's quarters just off the kitchen. Simon knocked. Giles answered the door, still in his dressing gown.

Simon explained the problem, and Giles followed him up to the library, bringing with him a basket of kindling. Simon watched the butler's expert moves before the fireplace, and asked him to explain the procedure. Giles, if he thought it odd to teach his master how to light a fire, did not express it, but patiently explained each step.

"Funny, I wager Miss Breton would have been able to start up this fire without calling for help." Simon voiced this thought aloud.

Giles chuckled. "That she would, that she would. More'n once she started her own fire. We looked down on her at first for that, but then we understood. Aye, she was a rare 'un."

"Yes, she was a rare one," Simon echoed.

"You know, I'm ashamed to admit it now, but we were pretty hard on her those first few weeks she was here."

Simon eyed him curiously, beginning to feel the heat of the flames from the fireplace. "Is that so?"

"Well, you weren't here much, and we could pretty much do as we pleased." Giles added a few more sticks to the grate. "We were suspicious of her, for one thing. You had told us to treat her as one of the family, for she was quality. But then, what was she doing working as a nurse? We didn't know how to place her. Did she belong upstairs or down? Then, of course, there was her Methodism. We've been taught that's as good as heresy." Giles sat back on his heels, brushing off his hands. "We weren't going to have her convert us. So, we didn't hardly heed her summons— let her pretty much do things for herself, all the fetching and carrying for Rebecca."

Simon rubbed his chin, feeling the beginnings of whiskers. "I had no idea."

Giles grunted. "I'm sure we'd have all received a well-deserved reprimand if you had." He shook his head, staring at the flames. "But it didn't take her long to win our respect...and our love," he added quietly.

"How did she do that?"

Giles set some of the coal onto the fire. "See how you put the coal on once you get a good flame?" The black coal sizzled as it touched the fire. Giles took a handkerchief from his pocket and finished wiping off his hands. "Well, you remember your dinner party back last winter?"

Simon smiled. "Yes, my first and last."

"Don't be so hard on yourself. It was a successful party, if I'm any judge. And I don't imagine it'll be your last, whatever ye be feeling now. But getting back to Miss Althea. Do you know, you almost didn't have any dinner to serve that evening?"

"No? Whatever do you mean?" Simon listened in amazement as Giles told him the drama of Mrs. Bentwood's lapse.

"We knew she took a nip now 'n' again, but she'd never fallen so as to get into a total stupor. There it was, getting on to three o'clock, when Miss Breton came down to check on things and found Cook passed out at the table."

Giles chuckled. "Well, you can imagine how we felt below stairs at that moment. All was lost—we'd all be out on the streets by next morning, if not sooner. Not Miss Breton. She put on an apron, surveyed the work and started issuing orders like a commander. She soon had us each assigned some task. And she was right there in the midst, doin' more'n any of us. Standing over that hot stove, stirring pots, checking the scullery maid chopping vegetables, showing Harry how to chop ice." Giles shook his head at the memory.

"Mrs. Coates had to shoo her out o' the kitchen so she could dress and join the company for dinner."

Simon stared at Giles, remembering that evening. "You mean to tell me that when Miss Breton joined us for dinner, she had just come from cooking it herself?"

Giles chuckled. "I remember seeing her when she entered the drawing room. She was a mite late. I could see she had rushed downstairs, still flushed from the heat of the stove. There you were, fuming at her for coming late, maybe spoiling the dinner party, when she had saved it for you! Without her, you'da sat down to nothing."

Simon frowned in amazement, thinking about it. So much he hadn't known. So many mistaken assumptions he'd made.

Giles soon left him, having coaxed the new coals to a glow. Simon didn't stay long in the library, but put on his greatcoat, muffler and hat, and went out walking. He felt too alive inside to waste the dawn indoors. He walked quickly along Park Lane until he reached Piccadilly. He walked past the Green Park until he reached St. James's. By the time he reached Whitehall, his legs were beginning to tire. He glanced briefly down the street lined with the government buildings he'd haunted until recently. In the distance, the dawn sky showed the outline of the Parliament building along the Thames. Not far from it rose the towers of Westminster Abbey, that other bastion of power in England.

Simon turned his back on both buildings and kept walking until he came to the river's edge. The sky was a luminescent pink over the arches of the recently dedicated Waterloo Bridge. The air hurt his lungs it was so cold, his breath gusted out a white puff each time he released it, but never had he felt so good.

He stood a while looking out over the water, watching the sky lighten and the small craft begin to leave their moorings. Behind him he could hear the sounds of the awakening city. When the cold began to seep through his clothes, he began walking again, not sure where to go. Passing by a hack stand, he decided, on the spur of the moment, to go to the one place that drew him.

Simon paid for the coach a few blocks from the mission, preferring to finish his journey on foot.

All was still quiet in that part of town—the majority of people still sleeping off a night of drinking, he imagined. He stood across the street from the mission, deciding not to disturb Althea at that hour. He was content to stand looking at the building where she lived and worked.

But suddenly she appeared in a fourth-story window and spotted him. She pushed up the sash and poked her head out the dormer window. "Simon?" she called down.

He held up a hand in acknowledgment, there being no point in hiding himself.

She leaned out the window, her braids dangling beneath her cap. "Simon, is that you? What are you doing here?"

"Close that window, you'll catch your death," he answered calmly, although he didn't feel calm inside.

"But what are you doing here at this hour? Has something happened?"

"No. Yes."

"Is something wrong?"

Her dear face looked so concerned. "No, nothing is wrong. Everything is perfectly fine. More than fine, in fact." He started feeling ridiculous shouting from the street.

She leaned farther out the window, her braids swinging forward. "Simon, what's happened?"

"Careful, Althea, don't lean out so!"

"Never mind that!" But she moved back a little. "Tell me this instant what's happened!"

"I'll come by later, at a proper time, to tell you. Or better yet, come to my house." He chuckled, and then laughed out loud. It felt good to laugh. "It'll be quieter there."

"Simon Aguilar, don't you dare leave! If you don't come inside and tell me this instant what's happened, I promise I shall come straight down myself."

He laughed out loud again, a deep joyous sound.

"I'm coming down!" she yelled, and slammed down the sash. When she opened the front door, he was waiting for her on the stoop. He just smiled at her. She was in her dressing gown, a flannel nightgown visible at the neck, her two long braids hanging sedately down each side now, a white cap tied neatly under her chin.

He couldn't seem to stop grinning.

She looked at him searchingly. "Is it...have you? You have!" He nodded slowly, smiling all the while. She opened her arms and he received her into his embrace. Laughing, hugging and crying, he twirled her around on the stone step.

"He is real! Jesus is real!" he shouted.

When he put her down, he kept his arms loosely around her.

She looked deeply into his eyes. "Oh, yes, Simon, isn't He? Nothing else matters when you know that. You *know,* don't you? *Really* know, not just believe?"

He nodded. As if becoming conscious of their positions, she made a move to disengage herself. He let her go at once, remembering all the rest that still kept them separated. She shivered, crossing her arms in front of her.

"Please come in, it's freezing out here. I'll make us some tea, and you can tell me all about it."

He didn't dissuade her. He had no right to tell her anything else, but he didn't want to be apart from her, not yet.

Only a few people were about in the mission, so they had the kitchen to themselves.

"Let me start up the fire," Althea said as she went toward the stove.

"Do you know, I just learned to start a fire myself this morning?"

Althea gave him a glance before turning her attention back to her task. "Indeed? How was that?"

"Yes, Giles showed me how it's done." He recounted the story, ending with "He told me a few other things, as well."

"Oh, yes? Such as?"

"Such as how miserably all the servants treated you when you first arrived and how you won them over the night of the dinner party."

She brushed her hands off and surveyed the fire for a few seconds before turning to him. She didn't say anything, although he could see the color rise in her cheeks.

"You never said a word to me. I was even displeased that evening with you, coming down late, making us wait for our dinner," he said with a smile.

"How could I tell you? I didn't want you to dismiss Mrs. Bentwood. Poor woman."

"You saved us all that night," he said.

She smiled at him. "And I know a certain family you saved from eviction and starvation." She laughed when she saw his embarrassment.

"He promised not to say anything!"

"But not his wife," she added.

He shook his head. "Women! Why is it they can never keep a secret?"

She came toward him. "Oh, Simon, I wanted to thank you. You don't know what it meant to me—to them. When I found out what you'd done for Arnold and his family I went to your house, but you weren't in. I was so disappointed that I couldn't thank you in person. That's when I decided to invite you to Pembroke Park for the holidays. I hadn't planned on it when I went there."

He took her two hands in his. "You saved me again with your kind invitation. I don't know what would have happened to me if I'd stayed shut up by myself during that time." He ran a hand through his hair, turning away for a moment. "You don't know how close I came to ending my life."

"Oh, no, Simon," she breathed.

He turned back to her with a smile. "That's all over now. I have found Him!"

The two looked at each other in joy for a moment, until Althea once again gently drew her hands away, as if conscious of their nearness to one another. Simon let her go, although he longed to take her in his arms.

She turned away from him quickly, going to pour water into the teakettle. He watched her as she bustled about, content to sit and drink in her presence, and to feel another presence as well. He knew he would never again feel alone. He knew God was with him.

Over tea, he began telling her of the past couple of weeks.

"You were there every night," she commented softly.

"Yes, I couldn't keep away, for some reason. I hated your words some nights, but something always drew me back."

"But you never came forward, you never acknowledged me."

He shook his head. "I couldn't. Not yet. Not until last night." He began describing what had just happened to him. She listened to his every word. By the time he told her how he'd felt the Lord's presence, he could see the tears glistening in her eyes.

Afterward they sat in silence a while, the sounds of the water simmering in the kettle behind them.

"I know what joy means now," he said quietly, looking down at the teacup in his hands.

"Oh, yes."

"Rebecca knew, too, didn't she?" He needed to be reassured again.

Althea smiled. "Oh, Simon, if you'd seen her that day. She was radiant. She knew the Savior's love."

He swallowed. "That's the only thing that was really unbearable. Not knowing where she'd gone."

"But now you do, don't you?"

He nodded. After a few seconds they again became conscious of looking at one another, and both looked away at the same time.

He fingered the whiskers along his jaw. "I really should go. I just rushed out this morning without changing my clothes or shaving." But he didn't move.

She fingered the buttons at the neck of her nightgown, as if drawn to an awareness of her own appearance.

After a moment, Simon cleared his throat. "Your brother told me before I left Pembroke Park that there was a chance for another seat in Commons. It's in his district. He offered it to me."

"Oh, Simon, that's wonderful!" Her eyes glowed in encouragement. "When can you stand for election?"

He set his cup on the saucer beside him and shrugged. "I haven't decided whether or not to accept it."

"Why ever not? Isn't...isn't that what you want?" she asked slowly.

He gave a slight smile. "You of all people should understand how things have changed."

She nodded. "Because of last night? Are you questioning if this is what the Lord has in store for you? Do you think perhaps He has something else?"

He searched for how to explain the results of the past few weeks. "It's funny, I spent several years after university toiling away in different ministries, a lowly clerk under a lot of incompetent fools who had received their appointments through a sinecure, with no effort, much less talent, of their own, merely because they were related to someone who was owed a favor. I felt I was getting nowhere, with no chance of getting into Parliament, when less clever men than I were getting in.

"Then my father got a lord in his pocket, because the man was up to his ears in debt. In exchange for standing me up in his district, the man's debts would be forgiven." Simon snapped his fingers. "Like that. I didn't have to appear in the county, or make any speeches. The only price was to uphold this man's interests as well as my father's.

"And then, just like that—" again he snapped his fingers "—I was back out again, made to resign because I was a Jew. I know that was merely a stratagem to get me ousted because I began voting according to my conscience and not according to the interests of the landed class."

He looked at her, not sure if she understood what he was saying, not even sure if he understood himself. Everything was so new still.

"It's ironic isn't it, that I was accused of professing the Christian faith but practicing the Jewish in secret? I was branded a hypocrite. And now that I am a...Christian—" it felt odd to say the word "—no one would believe it to be true."

Althea smiled in answer. "You know you won't be the first."

"No, I suppose not." He looked at her closely. "You have endured your share of criticism."

"The Bible calls it persecution. You had an ancestor named Paul, who got into lots of trouble because of people accusing him of all sorts of things. Do you know what he said?"

"Tell me."

"He said that if he were still trying to please men, he should not be the servant of Christ. The Lord gave me that verse early on, when I first started out. It was a good one to have."

They looked at each other, and Simon understood the difficulties she must have encountered. But she spoke of it lightly now.

She continued quietly. "All I can tell you is that you must search your own heart and seek the Lord's counsel. Only He can tell you if what my brother is offering you now is for you. Don't be afraid of it. If that's where the Lord leads you, it means He has a purpose for you to fulfill there. All those things you were fighting for in Parliament—they were not wrong. But only the Lord can continue guiding you in this."

Simon looked down at his hands and rubbed his thumb against his knuckles. Suddenly he had a strong urge to say more. He hadn't planned to say anything; he knew he shouldn't, that he had no right. But he found himself unable to stop. "So you have no feelings about it either way?" he asked in an offhand tone, continuing to study his knuckles. "Would it make any difference to you whether or not I'm an 'honorable' or a 'mister'?"

"Oh, Simon," she answered, "you know the answer to that. I made it very clear to you."

He dared to look at her then. There was no subterfuge in her eyes, only light and warmth. It emboldened him to continue. "You said once that you would follow me anywhere, face anything with me—whether a life of poverty or as a prime minister's wife." He swallowed, suddenly needing to know. "Were those merely words said in an emotional moment?"

"How can you even ask that?"

"Does...does that mean your feelings haven't changed?"

He felt the charged atmosphere between the two of them. He looked down at his hands again, gripping them together. It was too soon. He shouldn't. But he found himself speaking. "I would never presume to— That is, if before I had no right, I certainly haven't any now—" His eyes pleaded with her to understand.

"No right to what?" she asked him softly, her eyes welcoming.

"It wouldn't be easy. I could certainly not offer you the life of a prime minister's wife now," he said in an attempt at a jest. "I've lost whatever good name I once possessed, my honor—" He rubbed his jaw. "If it hadn't been for last night...I would never even presume to ask you to sacrifice...."

In reply she held out both her hands to him. He clasped them in his as if clinging to a lifeline.

"What I'm trying to say, my dear, sweet Miss Breton—Althea—and botching it up dreadfully, is, would you do me the very great honor of becoming my wife?"

She smiled into his eyes, all the love she felt for him expressed in them. "Yes, Simon, the honor would be mine."

He lifted their joined hands to his lips.

Then he drew her forward until she was sitting on his lap. His lips found hers as her arms went around his neck. "Oh, Althea—" he breathed against her. "How I've missed you...."

"And I you," she whispered back before their emotion for each other overwhelmed their ability to speak.

They heard the door swinging open. Althea jumped, but Simon was reluctant to let her go very far. He held her imprisoned in his arms.

An older woman gaped at them. "Oh, sister, I didn't know anyone was in here!"

Althea tried to stand. Simon smiled at her embarrassment. "That's quite all right, Sister Kate. We were— We were—just leaving—" Althea answered hurriedly as she pushed against Simon. Finally he let her go.

"This is Mr. Simon Aguilar," she said, smoothing down her dressing gown and attempting to straighten her cap, which hung askew. She finally gave up, untying it and removing it completely. "He just stopped in unexpectedly." She gave a nervous pat to her head. "Mr. Aguilar—" she blushed as she looked back at him "—may I present Mrs. Burrows, the woman who does much of the cooking for us here at the mission?"

Simon stood with a smile and approached the older lady, his

hand held out. The cook approached hesitantly and took his hand. "Pleased to meet you, Mrs. Burrows."

"Likewise, I'm sure," she said with a nod, her voice sounding doubtful.

Simon took pity on her. "I will take my leave, then, and leave you to your kitchen. Miss Breton, will you show me out?" He winked at her, wanting to shout to the world that this woman standing so primly before him in her nightgown and dressing gown had agreed to be his wife.

"Yes, of course," she answered quietly.

Silently the two entered the hallway. A few steps down the corridor, they both glanced at each other and suddenly started laughing. Althea tried to stifle her giggles, but Simon let his deep laugh ring through the hallway.

"Shh!" She gestured futilely at him before they both erupted in laughter again.

She looked at him in indignation. "This must stop!" When he only laughed some more, she began walking ahead of him. He caught up with her. As they mounted the stairs to the ground floor, he suddenly halted, sobering.

"What is it?" she asked immediately, touching him on the arm.

He looked at her small hand, moved by the gesture and warmed by the realization that he had a companion who could sense what he was feeling before he said anything.

He covered her hand with his. "With you a Dissenter and I a Jew, the church won't even acknowledge our vows as legal."

"But God will."

"It won't be easy. Not even those who call themselves Christians will accept me."

She nodded, her brow clouded. "I know. Not everyone will accept *us*. But we have One who will never leave us nor forsake us, haven't we."

He nodded, finally allowing himself to accept the love he read in her face. She was all light, that light that had drawn him from the first time they met.

* * *

As the bustle in the mission grew, Simon reluctantly left, telling Althea he would come for her that afternoon to take her to her brother and his wife, who were still in London, to announce their engagement. In the meantime, he would contact her father, who was in town as well.

When Simon returned to his house, he bathed and shaved, then went down to the servants and told them. They all burst into spontaneous applause.

Giles looked at him and said quietly, "Well done, sir."

Simon impatiently counted the hours until he could direct his carriage once more to the mission. When he arrived, Althea was waiting for him, dressed becomingly in a dark green pelisse and cream-colored skirt. When she seemed reluctant to meet his eye, he took her chin in his fingers. "You look very pretty, although I must say your cap and dressing gown were most becoming as well this morning."

He could see the color rising in her cheeks and he chuckled, bringing her hand to his lips.

"Shall we go?" she asked him.

He escorted her to the carriage. During the carriage ride, he sat across from her, content to regard her. But it didn't take him long to sense her unease. She kept her gaze locked on the passing scene. When the carriage slowed through the traffic on Fleet Street, he came to sit beside her.

"Is something wrong?" she asked quickly, startled from her reverie.

He smiled at her. "Only one thing."

"What is it?" she asked in concern.

"Merely this." He touched her cheek with his fingertip, bending toward her until his lips found hers. He lingered there, cupping her cheek with his hand, tasting an oasis after years of abstinence. His passion intensified, hers mirroring his, until he pulled back, saying breathlessly, "I can scarcely imagine being able to do that whenever I wish." He was surprised when she didn't answer his smile, but looked back out the window.

"What is it?" he asked immediately, feeling bereft.

Althea kept her eyes fixed out the window. How could she tell him what worried her? She could feel Simon's gentle touch on her arm. She swallowed, knowing there could be no secrets between them.

"Is it...wanton of me to kiss you like that?" The words came out in a hesitant whisper.

Simon forced her to look around to him. He kept her chin anchored in his fingers as his brown eyes regarded her with tenderness. "Are you thinking about your mother?"

She nodded.

His forefinger rubbed her jaw softly. "What we feel for each other is God-given. Read the Song of Solomon. Read how Esther prepared for her king. Read about why God created Eve for Adam. God has given us to each other, to enjoy each other, to pleasure each other. Don't ever be ashamed of what you feel in my arms, Althea."

He gave her a rueful grin as his fingers traveled upward, stroking her cheek.

"I fear we mustn't spend too much time alone, however, from now until our wedding day."

She blushed under the direct look he was giving her.

"I will not dishonor you, Althea, nor my God, who has granted me this second chance, by taking what He has sanctified through the marriage vows, until that day." He paused. "I don't want you to be frightened. I promise you it won't be as that last time. Can you trust me?"

Slowly, she nodded, seeing the love in his eyes. Tentatively she reached for him this time. "I love you, Simon, and I trust you with my heart...with my body...."

His lips felt warm and soft. They nuzzled hers, not pushing, but teasing, until hers parted of their own volition. As they explored each other, her body began to react, not in terror and dread, but in a gradual awareness, as if something long dormant were being called to awaken. Her body felt drawn to his, and she rejoiced knowing she wanted with all her soul to be joined to this man fully in the way God had given. The Lord had truly set her free of her past.

When at last they drew apart, Simon sighed. "I only hope it won't be a long engagement. You are too beautiful and too tempting for my weak nature." As her color deepened, he chuckled. "Yes, you are wanton, but I want you wanton for me. When we are married, I want you to show me just how wanton you are," he said, covering her lips with his once more. He was still kissing her when the carriage arrived in Mayfair at the home of Althea's brother.

When the two stood hand in hand before Tertius and Gillian, Gillian smiled broadly. "Does this mean what I think it means?" she asked, her face alight.

Simon looked at Althea's brother. "Tertius, I think I have lived a lifetime in the past twenty-four hours. I received your Jesus, and He showed me the truth—" Suddenly his voice broke, and he looked down.

Tertius walked quickly over to Simon and extended his hand. The two looked deeply into one another's eyes.

Gillian embraced Althea and they all began talking and laughing together.

"Nothing could make us happier than to see the two of you wed," Tertius told them both as he held Althea's hand, his arm around his wife.

Gillian added, "We knew it could be no other way, when we saw you together. We are so happy for you."

This time, rather than just take his hand, Tertius embraced Simon. "Welcome to the family, brother."

Epilogue

❧

East End, London, 1823

Arnold Smith stood on the platform introducing Simon amidst great applause. He lauded Simon for all the good work he had done in their neighborhood over the past five years. He began with his own personal testimony—how Simon had rescued him when he had lost his job and been threatened with eviction.

From the shouts of the crowd, it was evident how much they thought of their new member of Parliament. Then Simon stepped up to the platform and began his acceptance speech.

Althea sat on a little bench they had set up for her to the side. It was getting hard to stand too long in her condition. Standing next to her, his little hand on her knee, was three-year-old Simon, Junior. She felt the new child move about in her belly and automatically put her hand up to it. Three more months to go.

She was thinking how uncomfortable Simon would be with so much praise. Her husband had become very modest over the past five years. She thought back over that time. Simon had eventually turned down her brother's offer of a seat in Parliament, telling them that if the Lord ever gave him another chance at office, it would have to be on his own merits, from a constituency that knew him and voted for him because he came from them and truly represented them.

Shortly afterward, Simon had purchased a property next to the mission. Together he and Althea had refurbished it, with help from Arnold and many others at the mission. Two months later, when they were married, they had moved in. Their son had been born there, while Althea had continued her work at the mission. Simon had worked alongside her when he wasn't managing a factory for his father—fighting tooth and nail with him for every improvement. When the factory had begun to show both profit and higher productivity and no strikes in that awful year of upheaval, 1819, a year of executions and transportations, his father had begun to be convinced of his son's arguments.

Now, Althea was preparing for another move, this time back to Simon's home in Mayfair. A maiden aunt of Simon's had lived in it, in the interim, and she would continue to live with them now that they were returning.

Althea thought of the passage from Proverbs that had been given to Simon at their marriage: "Seest thou a man diligent in business? He shall stand before kings, he shall not stand before mean men."

She had no doubt those words would be fulfilled in the coming years. Simon would be reentering the political realm, and Althea's life would once again involve what she had avoided for so long—society. But she was no longer afraid of society, nor of her position in it. She didn't have to face it alone, for one thing. She had two allies with her: her Lord and Savior, and the man He had given her, Simon. The Lord had never let her forget His burden for those women He'd had her pray for that evening at Simon's dinner party. Now she would be going into their midst once again. She would not be abandoning her work at the mission, but a new door was opening.

Simon had finished his speech and was now holding out his

hand to her. She rose, with little Simon at her side, and went up to the platform.

Simon pulled her up to stand beside him. "I could have done none of this without the dear woman the Lord gave me five years ago. I would like you to welcome and applaud her as you have me, for without her, this journey would never have begun."

He looked deep into her eyes at these last words, his dark eyes shining with light, as he spoke for her ears alone. "I love you so very much. Thank you, dear Althea."

They both turned and looked at the crowd then, seeing the harvest field the Lord had given them.